BACK IN THE TEXAN'S BED

NAIMA SIMONE

THE HEIR

JOANNE ROCK

MILLS & BOON

First Published in Great Britain 2021
by Mills & Boon, an imprint of HarperCollinsPublishers,
1 London Bridge Street, London, SE1 9GF

Back in the Texan's Bed © 2021 Harlequin Books S.A.
The Heir © 2021 Joanne Rock

Special thanks and acknowledgement are given to Naima Simone for her contribution to the *Texas Cattleman's Club: Heir Apparent* series.

ISBN: 978-0-263-28280-1

0121

MIX
Paper from
responsible sources
FSC® C007454

This book is produced from independently certified FSC™ paper to ensure responsible forest management.

For more information visit: www.harpercollins.co.uk/green

Printed and bound in Spain
by CPI, Barcelona

BACK IN THE TEXAN'S BED

NAIMA SIMONE

To Gary. 143.

Prologue

Love.

Russell "Ross" Edmond Jr. sipped his scotch, relishing the smoky flavor with hints of caramel, fruit and a bite of salt, while staring out the window of the Texas Cattleman's Club meeting room at the beautiful couple currently wrapped around each other in a passionate embrace.

Ezekiel Holloway and Reagan Sinclair—Reagan Holloway now—had caused quite a scandal in Royal, Texas, some months ago when they'd eloped to Vegas against her family's wishes. Especially since Zeke's own family had been embroiled in a dirty criminal investigation that involved embezzlement and drug smuggling. But that had all been cleared up, their reputation restored, and now the newlyweds were living out their happily-ever-after.

Ross barely contained a derisive snort. Sure, the two appeared enamored and, yes, happy. The married couple kissed as if Ezekiel was heading off to sea for a months-long absence. Ross would say they were in love. Or, at least, they believed they were.

Unfortunately—or fortunately, in his opinion—he wasn't a devout disciple at the altar of the emotion that seemed like a convenient excuse for people to lose control, validate idiotic behavior or justify satisfying any impulsive desire.

What *did* he believe in?

Raising his glass to his mouth again, he turned from the view of the couple and surveyed the elegantly appointed room. Due to recent renovations at the Club, the design was less dark wood and stone, and now boasted brighter colors, larger windows and higher ceilings. Yes, the hunting trophies and historical artifacts still adorned the walls, and the stables remained, as did the pool and tennis courts. Yet, now the Club had a day care and sported painted murals, as well. The whole effect exuded a warmth that had been missing before.

But it all still conveyed wealth. Influence. Exclusivity.

And those ideals he trusted.

Money and power. They could be counted, measured, handled, manipulated, if need be, and were unfailingly consistent.

They'd never let him down.

Unlike people. Unlike *love*.

Hell, he couldn't even keep the sneer out of his inner voice.

"Ross, get over here," Russell Edmond Sr. boomed as if Ross stood farther out in the club's entryway instead of just several feet away from him. "Do that brooding shit on your own time. We have business to attend to."

Rusty. Oil mogul. Texas Cattleman's Club member. Tycoon. All things people called Russell Edmond Sr. Whereas Ross considered him *brilliant, ruthless, domineering*. And, on occasion, *manipulative bastard*.

They all fit.

With his tall, wide-shouldered and athletic build that had only gone a little soft around the middle, dark hair dusted with silver at the temples and intelligent, scalpel-sharp gray eyes, Rusty still possessed a powerful physique and commanded respect. Ross strode over to the long, cedar conference table, his gaze fixed not on his father but on the thin stack of documents in the middle of the table. His heart thumped against his sternum in anticipation. To others, those ordinary sheets of paper might seem innocuous. But to him?

Independence. Autonomy.

Identity.

Yes, this deal included the financial and marketing backing of The Edmond Organization, but this project—the luxury food, art and wine festival called Soiree on the Bay, which was to be held on a small, private island—was his baby. Well, more aptly, it was a baby that belonged to him, his siblings, Gina and Asher, and his best friend, Billy Holmes. But for the first time, he wasn't a figurehead wearing the Edmond name and the ineffectual title of executive. Wasn't a puppet tasked with carrying out Rusty-given orders. Wasn't just the useless playboy son riding the coattails of his daddy's success and reputation.

With this project, this event, he would finally step out from under his father's shadow and show everyone he hadn't just inherited the Edmond name—he'd *earned* it. Ross would play an integral role in raising the bar, in solidifying and expanding their legacy as he elevated The Edmond Organization from the national stage to the international one. Something even Rusty hadn't managed to do in the company's history.

But Ross would.

And in the process, maybe earn that thing that had eluded him the entire twenty-eight years he'd been Rusty's son—approval.

Again, not love. Men like his father believed in that emotion even less than Ross did. Just ask Rusty's four ex-wives.

Just ask his children.

"So this is it? The final contract?" Ross set his tumbler

down on the table, trying not to stare down at the documents as if they were the Holy Grail and he a Texas version of Indiana Jones.

"This is it," Billy Holmes, his college friend and future business partner, said, grinning. "The last step before Soiree on the Bay moves from dreams to reality."

"Dreams," Rusty scoffed. "Dreams are for men who don't have the balls to get out there and pursue what they want."

Ross glanced at his sister, Gina, across the table, arching an eyebrow in her direction. She rolled her eyes, but he noted the ever-present frustration there. Even this throwaway comment reflected Rusty's dismissal of women, especially in regard to business and autonomy. All because they'd had the misfortune of being born with a uterus instead of a penis. Though Gina had become as adept as Ross at masking her emotions, he caught the aggravation in her eyes. The hurt.

"Fortunately, everyone in this room is well equipped with their balls," Billy drawled, slanting a grin at Ross's baby sister. "Except for you, Gina. And thank God for it." His gentle teasing garnered the desired effect, and the shadows in her eyes dimmed, lightening with humor and gratitude. "And once we all sign, no one will ever question the influence and reach of The Edmond Organization."

Rusty grunted and slid the contract over the table toward him. As he scanned through, Billy glanced at Ross and winked. Ross smothered a snort, shaking his head. His pal had been a charmer in college, and since he arrived in Royal two years ago, he hadn't changed a bit. With his impeccable appearance and manners, generosity with his time, acumen and money, Billy had everyone from business associates to the often clique-ish members of Royal society wrapped around his finger.

Including Rusty, which was a feat unto itself.

The older man had even vouched for Billy with the Texas Cattleman's Club, and Ross's friend had scored a much-coveted membership. Billy shared a camaraderie and closeness with Rusty Edmond that even his kids couldn't claim.

But that was Billy. The Billionaire Whisperer, they jokingly called him.

All right, maybe not so jokingly.

"This looks good," Rusty announced, reaching inside his suit coat to remove a thick gold pen. With flourish, he signed his name on the designated line. "You did good, son," he praised Billy.

Picking up his drink, Ross sipped, waiting for the dark slick of jealousy to slide down his throat to his chest along with the liquor. After all, his father had just called another man *son*, and Ross was human. So yes, pinpricks of jealousy did sting him. But relief reigned as the most prevalent emotion.

And if that wasn't a fucked-up indictment on the Edmond family dynamic, he didn't know what was.

But one quick glance at Gina and at Asher, his stepbrother whom Rusty had adopted after marrying Asher's mother—wife number two—verified he wasn't alone in this sentiment. That same relief shone his siblings' gazes, as well. Anytime Rusty leashed in that infamous mercurial temper was a reason to breathe deep and bask in the peaceful, and probably brief, moment.

A knock on the door reverberated in the room, and Billy waved toward the contract. "That's my surprise. I'll get that while you finish up here."

Ross moved forward first, adding his signature to the contract, followed swiftly by Gina and Asher. By the time they all finished, Billy returned, bearing a silver tray laden with a bottle of champagne and five glass flutes. In moments, Billy had the sparkling wine poured and they'd all lifted their glasses to meet high over the table.

"A toast." Billy paused, blue eyes gleaming. "To The Edmond Organization stamping its indelible brand on not just the US, but the world. I think we've all waited for this day to arrive. So, to achieving long-awaited goals. And finally, to all of you, the Edmond family. May you all get what you so richly deserve." He smiled. "Emphasis on the rich."

They clinked glasses and sipped the champagne, celebrating this deal that they'd all put so much time into bringing to fruition.

"Vendors have already been contacting me about the festival, just from rumors alone. They want in. I predict tickets will sell out within hours of going on sale," Asher said. "Soiree on the Bay is going to be wildly successful. For all of us."

"It needs to be," Ross added gruffly. "This is the inaugural launch. The potential to make this a coveted, exclusive and profitable annual event is huge. So the first one needs to go off without a hitch. Besides, vendors and investors are pouring money in with ours, and the charities that will benefit from this are counting on it. On *us*."

"We'll do it," Gina swore, her tone firm. "I have zero doubts about that."

"With the Edmond reputation and money on the line, hell yes, you'll make this a success. You have no choice. I want people talking about this festival for months before and after."

"Oh, they will. Rest assured, Rusty, they will," Billy murmured, a corner of his mouth lifting in a half smile. "I promise you. This will be an event that no one will ever forget."

Once more, excitement stirred in Ross's gut. In just months, vendors, investors, the press and ticketholders would flock to *their* festival. He sipped from the bubbly wine, savoring the light flavor with a smile. It would be business for him, but not *all* business. People from all over the world would be visiting the private island where the event would be held. Which meant hordes of beautiful women. Most specifically, women who wouldn't expect more from him than the temporary, mutually agreed upon use of each other's bodies for the hottest, dirtiest pleasure.

He knew the reputation he'd earned—they called him a playboy. And admittedly, it was a moniker he deserved. Flings, one-night stands—the filthy hot fun without the messy emotional attachments that could wrap around a man, trap him, strangle him until he couldn't think, couldn't function, couldn't fucking *breathe*.

His chest tightened, a vise slowly turning until he could practically hear his ribs creak in protest. A face, faded and nebulous, wavered across his mind's eye like a mirage a dying man glimpsed seconds before his heart and body surrendered. Ross's grip tautened around the glass, his jaw clenching. He wasn't a dying man, but he'd beat the shit out of himself if he ever allowed himself to be that humiliatingly *weak* again. To allow himself to believe fucking was more than that—two people satisfying an itch before going their separate ways. It didn't have anything to do with emotion…with love.

God, why in the hell did that word keep rebounding in his head today?

He mentally shook his head, dislodging the wayward thoughts—and that damn face—from his head. Focus. He needed to focus.

He and his siblings hovered on the precipice of obtaining their individual and collective purposes. Of achieving those *goals* that Billy had toasted about mere moments ago.

And nothing would stand in their way.

One

"Charlotte, can I borrow you for a moment?"

Charlotte Jarrett looked up from plating and double-checking the dishes before sending them out for customers to dine on. This was her kitchen, her baby. And her recipes were her soul. If the food wasn't flawless, she sent it back for another plate to be prepared. Nothing less than perfection went out of here.

"Sure thing," she said to Faith Grisham, the manager of Sheen, the restaurant where Charlotte had been working as head chef for two weeks now. "Give me just a couple of minutes to finish up here and get these out and served."

Faith, a beautiful, no-nonsense woman who could've passed for actress Zoe Saldana's younger sister, nodded with a flick of her fingers. "Of course." Number one rule in this kitchen: the food came first, because the customer did. And though Sheen enjoyed popularity and success, they couldn't afford to become lax. One negative review, one bad write-up, and their status as Royal's newest favorite could quickly spin the other way. Nobody wanted that.

Least of all Charlotte.

Not when she'd sacrificed everything to return to the hometown she'd had no intention of ever stepping foot in again.

Not when she had so much riding on this.

Like expanding her clientele to include more exclusive and influential connections. A possible owning partnership in Sheen. Growing her reputation, to take one more step toward becoming a world-renowned chef. Earning her Michelin stars.

And most important, providing a stable, financially secure future for herself and Ben.

Even as she executed the finishing touches on her signature dish of braised beef over Thai noodles with seared tomatoes and asparagus, that warm rush of joy that only thoughts of her beautiful little boy could conjure slid through her like melted sunshine. He'd saved her, blessed her with a reason to keep pushing forward, instead of lying down and fading away. He was her *everything*, so it seemed only fair that she would be more than willing to give up everything to ensure he had a well-rounded, happy and full life.

Even if it meant swallowing her pride and being the one to try to bridge the divide that had estranged her from her parents after she'd left Royal.

Even if it meant facing the memories—and demons—that continued to plague her three years later.

Smothering a sigh, she refocused on the task at hand. Satisfied that the meals were ready, she quickly cleaned the edge of the plates with a paper towel soaked with white vinegar, then set them on the custom-built warming shelves for servers to come pick up.

"Rachel," Charlotte called to her sous-chef, "fire those plantain burgers. They're up next."

"Yes, Chef, on three," the older woman immediately replied, informing Charlotte that the Kobe beef burger, set between two slices of fried plantain, would be ready for her to plate with her made-from-scratch avocado ranch dressing in three minutes' time.

Wiping her hands on a towel, Charlotte turned to Faith, smiling as the manager typed out a message so fast on her ever-present phone that her thumbs blurred.

"What'd you need?" Charlotte asked.

"You, your effervescent personality and beautiful face."

"Do you want me to clue you in on how pimp-ish that sounds, or are we just going to ignore it?" Charlotte drawled, quirking an eyebrow.

"Ignore it."

Charlotte snickered, then grinned. As she had been headhunted from the California restaurant where she'd been working, so had Faith, from her native San Antonio, to run Sheen.

Faith had created a name for herself as a Jon Taffer in heels. Not that Sheen had been failing and needed rescuing when Faith had been brought on several weeks ago and prior to Charlotte's hiring, but the owners had wanted to make sure their venture hit the ground running from the beginning.

"Okay, give. I have nearly a full restaurant of hungry customers to feed," Charlotte said, crossing her arms. "What's up?"

"What's up is I just heard from a source who shall remain nameless that the food critic from the *New York Voice* magazine will be dropping by Sheen next Tuesday."

Astonishment vibrated through Charlotte, and she rocked back on her nonskid sugar skulls clogs. "What?" she whispered excitedly. "You're *kidding* me!"

The *New York Voice*. Holy… The alternative e-zine had only been around for the last five years, but it had immediately become popular not just within New York, but nationally and internationally, too. With its hard-hitting investigative journalism stories on societal issues, along with its focus on the cultural community of art, music, literature and food, it had already won the National Press Foundation Award as well as the George Polk Award. For Sheen to receive a positive review in their food column would be amazing publicity not only for the restaurant, but also for Charlotte's career.

"Nope, all true. Which means we need to be at our very best next Tuesday. I'll handle the front of the house and make sure it's super clean, all the servers are on point. And you're responsible for the back. I don't think I need to explain what a rave review could do for us."

"You don't." Charlotte shook her head, grinning. "And believe me, we will be better than perfect."

"I know it," Faith said, and for several moments they stood there, grinning at each other like two giddy fools. "We got this," she whispered.

"Oh, we *so* got this," Charlotte whispered back, the excitement still humming inside her joined by a steely resolve.

Yes, a glowing write-up and recommendation would mean great things for Sheen, but it went deeper than that. This restaurant was managed by a black woman. The kitchen was run by a black woman. The staff were women of various ethnicities—but they were all women. When the owner had come up with the concept, maybe it'd been a gimmick to differentiate Sheen from the other new restaurants popping up. But both Charlotte and Faith had vowed that they wouldn't let it remain some publicity ploy. Their restaurant would be one of the most successful establishments known for its sublime service and outstanding food. And so far, they were succeeding at this aim.

"Chef, your presence has been requested at one of the tables. They asked to meet you," Carlie, one of their servers, interrupted.

"Thanks, Carlie." Charlotte nodded at the younger woman. "I'd better get out there," she said to Faith, trying to conceal a grimace.

But apparently, she hadn't been quick or stealthy enough. A smirk curled the other woman's mouth.

"Part of the job, Charlotte," she reminded her.

"I know, I know," Charlotte muttered, unsnapping her baggy white executive chef coat and shrugging out of it, revealing the large T-shirt underneath. She strode over to the hooks near the door that led out of the glass-enclosed kitchen and removed her more formal and fitted turquoise chef coat with three-quarter-length sleeves, black piping and fabric-covered buttons. "It's not that I don't like going tableside," she grumbled, slipping into the coat and quickly fastening it over her chest. "I'd just much rather be cooking. I always feel like I'm on display."

"Well, get used to it. You're not naive enough to not know these days it's as much about the chef as the food. That face and pinup body is an asset along with your truffle mac 'n' cheese." Faith's matter-of-fact tone stole a bit of the wind out of Charlotte's imminent tirade about the unfairness of her appearance being a factor at all. Mostly because, as unreasonable as it might be, Faith was correct.

It still annoyed her, though.

"Thank you for those words, oh, wise one," Charlotte drawled. Then, turning to Carlie, she smiled. "Lead the way."

As they exited the kitchen, Charlotte couldn't help surveying the restaurant, where she spent nearly as much time at as the home she rented for her and Ben. A sister site to The Bellamy's Glass House restaurant, Sheen was made entirely out of glass. This evening, the low lighting complemented rather than competed with the setting sun's rays that poured through the ceiling-to-floor windows, bathing the tables and patrons in its orange-and-red glow.

Beautiful.

And one day, hopefully, hers. Well, partly.

Carlie led her through the restaurant toward the far corner that boasted one of the best tables because of its gorgeous view of Royal. The table, which sat on a small dais, overlooked the entire restaurant. Which meant one thing—VIP guest.

Charlotte fixed a polite smile to her face as she neared the table. Five minutes, max, then she had to return to—

Oh, God.

Frigid fingers of shock crackled through her veins, and her feet stuttered to a stop. Startled stares swept over her like ants marching over a picnic blanket, prickling her skin. But she couldn't move. Couldn't jerk her gaze away from a pair of icy blue eyes.

Her heart attempted to drill a hole through her rib cage, each beat pumping pain and fear to every artery and organ. Pain, fear and something so much more complicated.

Pain, because for the first time in three years she stared into the beautiful, cold face of the man she'd once loved. A man who had been willing to take her body but not her heart.

The convoluted emotion was a noxious mixture of anger, resentment and—Jesus, she hated herself for this—a residue of the delight that just a glimpse of him used to stir within her.

And fear… Damn, the *fear*, because she wasn't just coming face-to-face with Russell Edmond Jr., the man who'd broken her heart.

She was coming face-to-face with her son's father.

A son he had no idea existed.

Two

*F*_{uck no}.

Ross stared at a ghost from his past.

A ghost that, as much as he'd tried to banish with time, work and other women—sometimes alcohol—he'd failed to exorcise.

Charlotte Jarrett.

Former head chef at his family's ranch. Ex-lover. The woman who'd walked away uncaring of the damage she'd left behind.

Another woman who'd abandoned him without a backward glance.

Ice coated his skin, sinking deeper, seeming to freeze the very marrow of his bones.

He hated seeing her again. Hated that she hadn't changed. Hated that her tall, graceful frame still boasted the same gorgeous, deadly curves that his hands could trace from muscle memory. That she remained as beautiful as ever—silken, hickory-brown skin, oval-shaped eyes framed by a thick fringe of dark lashes, regal cheekbones with slightly hollowed cheeks, an elegantly sloped nose and…

He transferred his hands to his thighs so the white table-cloth hid his clenched fists.

And a mouth that should be slapped with an indecency

citation. Those plush lips were so flagrantly sensual he dared any man to glance at them and not imagine them dragging him willingly to the edge of ecstasy. An edge he'd hovered and plummeted over many times with her...

He hated that his cock had hardened the instant his eyes clashed with that startled, wide, espresso gaze. Most of all, he despised the heavy, primal thud of his heart that echoed in his stiffening flesh.

What the hell was Charlotte doing back in Royal?

She'd left him. Discarded him like trash. As if she'd never taken him inside her. Or moaned his name in that sexy whimper he'd become addicted to eliciting from her. As if they'd never curled their sweat-dampened bodies around each other, wrapped in their own private cocoon where the outside world couldn't intrude.

Charlotte Jarrett had completed the lesson Ross's mother had started; he'd earned a well-learned and hard-won degree in the field of emotional desertion. *Be foolish enough to become attached, and they don't stay.* Maybe it was something in him that made it so easy for them to walk away from—his father's four marriages were exhibits A through D. Rusty went through women as often as the change of guard took place at Buckingham Palace. Like father, like son. At least Ross didn't marry them.

No, he'd finally learned, courtesy of Charlotte. Fuck and move on to the next one. No promises. No strings. No entanglements. No feelings. As long as he adhered to those rules, no one would ever play him for a fool again.

Never hurt me. Never leave me.

With a sharp mental slash, Ross incised those ridiculous and too weak words from his head. He hadn't been hurt when Charlotte had up and left Royal. Left *him*. He'd been mad as hell. And that anger continued to simmer inside his chest, kindling lower in his stomach as she neared the table where he and Billy dined.

If he'd known that when his friend requested to meet Sheen's chef he would be confronting Charlotte again, Ross would've stalked right out of this place.

Hell, he still might.

"Good evening," Charlotte greeted, her gaze fixed on Billy. Out of habit, Ross rose from his seat, manners drilled into him from birth. Even as he stood, with his pal following suit, that soft, low voice slipped underneath Ross's suit jacket and his shirt, stroking over his skin. Even before they'd become lovers, that husky tone had reminded him of tangled sheets, throats sore and chafed from pleasure-soaked screams. "I'm Head Chef Charlotte Jarrett here at Sheen. I hope the meal is to your liking and you're enjoying your experience with us tonight." Then, just when Ross believed she wouldn't acknowledge him at all, she peered at him and dipped her chin. "Hello, Ross. It's good to see you again."

Lie.

The word scalded his tongue, roared in his head. She was as happy to see him sitting in her restaurant as he was to be here.

"You two know each other?" Billy asked as they lowered back into their chairs, saving Ross from having to reply to that fake smile and sentiment. His friend glanced back and forth between the two of them, a small frown creasing his brow even as curiosity lit his blue eyes.

"Yes," Ross ground out, then inhaled, deliberately releasing a breath and relaxing his clenched jaw. "Charlotte worked as the head chef at Elegance Ranch several years ago," he said, referring to the Edmond family ranch. Then added, "Before she moved to California for another job."

Damn, why had he added that? Yes, she'd moved; it was in the past, and he no longer gave a damn. But still… What the hell was she doing back in Royal?

"What a small world." Billy did the tennis match back-

and-forth once more. "California?" His buddy arched a dark eyebrow. "What part, if you don't mind me asking?"

"Santa Monica," she replied evenly, still wearing that damn polite smile he detested. He recognized it; her mask, he'd called it. She'd always given it to his father, but never Ross.

Until now.

"I love Santa Monica. It's a wonderful city. Not that Royal isn't just as beautiful. But California's loss is our gain." Billy smiled warmly and rose once more, extending his hand toward Charlotte. "Well, since you and Ross don't need to introduce yourselves, allow me. Billy Holmes, and it's a pleasure to meet such a lovely and talented chef."

"Thank you." Charlotte took his hand into hers, and even though it was just a simple press of palms, Ross had to fight back an inane urge to lurch to his feet and step in between them, to prevent his college friend—whom he trusted as much as his brother and sister—from touching her. But she'd revoked that privilege three years ago, and he didn't want to request it again. "Are you enjoying your meals?"

"Yes," Billy praised. "We had your braised beef signature dish, and it's delicious. I can't say I've tasted better."

"Thank you," she repeated, real warmth entering her smile. "Then I'd suggest trying our signature dessert, as well. A peach meringue torte with chocolate crumbles and a dollop of Chantilly cream."

"We'll take it. How can we say no to that?" Billy chuckled, reclaiming his seat. But clearly, he wasn't ready to let Charlotte go, much to Ross's aggravation.

Shit. How much longer did he have to sit here and pretend as if he couldn't catch her sweet yet sharp scent of sugar and figs. If he'd been blindfolded and set in a room full of people, he could still detect her delectable essence. Still locate *her*.

"I'll place your dessert order myself," she said. "Thank

you both—" for only the second time since she arrived at their table, she quickly glanced at him, then away "—for joining us at Sheen tonight. If you'll excuse me—"

"Wait, Chef, one more moment of your time, please," Billy called out, and Ross narrowed his eyes on him. Jesus, what now? He needed Charlotte away from him before he did something stupid. Like escort her out of this restaurant and demand answers. Or commit the cardinal sin of digging his fingers underneath that neat bun at the back of her head and loosening it, freeing her dark brown hair to see if it still contained that same coarse silk texture. Discover if it still swept her shoulder blades or if she'd cut it. Find out whether she'd emit that same low gasp if he fisted the thick strands and tugged, whether her eyes would darken with desire...

Yeah, she had to go.

"Sure," Charlotte said, her tone even, and if Ross hadn't been studying her so closely, he would've missed the flicker of impatience in her eyes. That, too, he easily remembered about her. Cooking, *creating* had been her number one passion, and she had to be chafing at this dog and pony show when she could be back in her precious kitchen. "What can I do for you?"

"Well, we're—" Billy waved a hand toward Ross and then back at himself "—working on a luxury food, art and wine festival called Soiree on the Bay, to be held late July on Appaloosa Island. Are you familiar with it?"

"Yes." She nodded, her focus fully trained on Billy... and only the rapid beat of her pulse at the base of her neck betrayed her agitation. Right now, she probably wished the collar of her chef's jacket fully covered her neck. Because if it did, he wouldn't guess that she was most likely recalling the time he'd secretly taken her to the small, private island in Trinity Bay that his family owned. He'd escorted her there in her first helicopter ride, though it was also accessible by private ferry and airplane. They'd spent a lazy day and sizzling night at the boutique resort on the pristine beaches that occupied the western side of the island along with several large vacation homes.

Man, the things they'd done to each other in their room…

He shifted in his chair, unbidden lust burning an incendiary path through him at the sultry, hot memories of slick skin sliding against slick skin. Of groans punctuated by greedy whimpers and blissful laughter. Of moonlight streaming across sheets wrapped around tangled limbs.

Her gaze slid toward him, and for a long moment, their eyes clashed. Was she as steeped in the illicit past as he was? Did that sweet, tight flesh, which even now he could feel wrapped around his cock, pulse and dampen with liquid heat from those recollections? His own body throbbed so hard he feared one abrupt move could crack him down the middle.

He glanced away first.

"We're already in plans to develop the eastern side of the island," Billy said. "The festival is going to be huge, and we already have vendors lined up, with tickets projected to sell out within hours. Would you consider hosting a tent for the event? For Sheen?"

Ross jerked in surprise. The hell? They hadn't discussed this. He stared at his friend, but Billy continued aiming the full force of his charm on Charlotte. No. Just…no. Spend more time around his ex-lover? Have her involved in this event that could change the trajectory of his career. His *life*? He couldn't have a split focus; he couldn't afford it. And then… She didn't deserve to be involved in this project that meant so much to him. *She'd* walked away. *She'd* left him. So she didn't get to benefit from what was *his*.

And yes, he acknowledged how fucking petty that made him sound. But he didn't give a damn.

"I—" She frowned, shaking her head. "I'm flattered that

you're asking, but I can't give you an answer without conferring with the owner and the management team."

"Please, do that and let us know your answer. With the thousands of people—both potential customers and clients—attending the festival, it could be advantageous for us and for Sheen. Not to mention you, personally, Chef. You're the magic behind the food, and as beautiful as the design and decor are and professional the service, it's the food that makes or breaks a restaurant. I believe this could be a huge opportunity for you."

Billy paused and tilted his head to the side. "In the meantime, while you're thinking the invitation over, would you also consider something else?" He chuckled, the sound self-deprecating. "I know we just met, and I'm already throwing a lot at you. But we're compiling an advisory board for the festival, and we're seeking the best creative minds in Texas. I've heard you're one of them, and it'd be an honor and asset to have you take part in it."

He'd heard she was creative—where? *When?* Ross had been under the impression that the other man hadn't known of Charlotte until five minutes before he'd asked to meet the chef after raving over their meal. Which, Ross grudgingly had to admit, had been exquisite. But then again, he expected nothing less from a woman who placed her career over everything else. She hadn't even cared that she'd left her parents behind.

Or me.

He locked that irritating and insidious thought down. Because that was in the past. His pride had been hurt. But as his reputation had proven, he was over it—over *her*.

Besides, he'd never give one woman that much sway over him again.

For the first time, unease crept across Charlotte's features, and he damn near felt the tension emanating off her. *Say no*, he silently ordered her.

"I don't—"

"Excuse me, I'm so sorry for interrupting." The server who'd escorted Charlotte to their table appeared, shooting an apologetic glance at Ross and Billy before addressing Charlotte. "Chef, your babysitter called. There's an emergency with Ben. He's running a fever, and she needs to know if she should take him to urgent care. Also—" her voice dropped but not low enough that Ross couldn't catch her next words "—she said he's crying for you."

Charlotte recoiled as if the words had been physical blows, her shoulders actually curling in before she jerked them back. Maybe remembering she had an audience. Because when she turned back to him and Billy, she'd carefully composed her features into a smooth mask.

If only he had the same superpower.

A baby? Charlotte had *a baby*? Shock, bone-deep, chilling and sickening, swam through him, burrowing to the dark soul that he'd believed too jaded to be stunned by anything.

"I'm sorry," she said in a calm tone that belied the worry gleaming in her coffee-colored eyes. Worry and…something else. And that something else had the hair on the nape of his neck prickling, standing at soldier-straight attention. If it had been anyone else, he'd have called that quicksilver emotion in her gaze fear. But he had to be mistaken. Sure, there wasn't any love lost between them, but why in the hell would she be afraid of him? His stomach twisted, clenched. "I need to go, but I'll place your dessert order. I hope the rest of your evening here at Sheen is—"

"You have a son?" he rasped, only the second time he'd spoken to her since she'd arrived at the table.

Again, that flash of something-that-couldn't-be-fear glinted in her eyes. And he wanted to erupt from his seat and demand she either stop looking at him like that or, better yet, explain why just glancing at him caused that reaction.

"Yes," she abruptly answered. Then, nodding, she edged back a step. "Again, thank you for dining with us."

With that, she whirled on her heel and quickly wound a path through the tables toward the rear of the restaurant. Ross stared after her retreating figure, frowning.

Don't even think about going after her. Keep your ass in this chair.

He growled that at his conscience, at the muscles in his thighs that already bunched in preparation of launching him from his seat. This restaurant—and her son—were her business. Not his. She was no longer his concern and hadn't been for three years.

"Did I overstep there?" Billy murmured, picking up his fork and flipping it between his fingers. It had been a nervous gesture of his since college—a small tell in an otherwise confident and self-possessed demeanor. "I should've checked with you first to ensure you were okay with me asking her to be a vendor and a member of the advisory board."

"It's fine," Ross said, waving off his friend's concern.

It wasn't, though. But damn if he would explain to Billy why.

No one knew of his and Charlotte's affair from years ago. They'd kept it secret for the obvious reason—him having sex with his employee had been inappropriate, at best. At worst, it was a power imbalance that he'd been too entitled, too damn infatuated and desperate for her to acknowledge. He'd justified it by convincing himself he'd never be the kind of asshole that would fire her if—no, *when*—their affair ended.

His father was that kind of asshole, though. His son involved with a staff member? Hell no. Rusty Edmond possessed enough good ol' boy in him to rate that sin just under murder but above stealing.

That had been cause enough to keep their...relationship quiet. But he'd harbored another, more private one.

Charlotte had been his. His choice. His beauty. His secret haven from a world where he was judged by his name, his reputation. His entire life, his father had determined his schools, career, even the women he'd dated. But Charlotte? She'd been the one person—the one decision—that had been strictly his own.

She'd been special.

But he couldn't tell Billy that—couldn't tell anyone. And even if he'd been free to, he still wouldn't. Because in some ways, Charlotte still remained the only autonomous decision in his life. And despite everything, he treasured that.

"Are you sure? I—" Billy frowned, his lips snapping closed as he studied Ross.

"What?" he asked, just shy of a snap. He wanted to be done with this conversation, hell, this restaurant that seemed to bear the stamp of Charlotte in its walls, in the decor, even in the scent of its food. Now that he knew she was the chef here—that she was back in Royal—she permeated everything.

"Fine. I'm just going to say it," Billy said, setting the fork down and leaning back in his chair. "I might be out of line here, but there seemed to be...tension between you two. Am I wrong?"

"Yes," Ross clipped out, but then inhaled, forcibly relaxing his jaw. "Yes," he repeated, this time more evenly. "Charlotte was our head chef for a while before she left for another job opportunity. We were amicable, but that's it. Nothing more, nothing less."

"Okay, if you say so. I believe you." But that steady, unwavering stare didn't shift from Ross's face, and he smothered the urge to snap at his friend again. Finally, Billy shrugged a shoulder and picked up his wine. "She's a beautiful woman," he observed before sipping from his glass. "And obviously talented and successful. So you wouldn't have a problem with me asking her out? There wouldn't be an issue because she used to be your employee?"

"Of course not," Ross growled. Yes, honest-to-God *growled*. Because just the thought of Billy's fingers spanning that slender waist or cupping that dramatic flare of hips had him clenching his own wineglass so hard he feared it might shatter under the pressure. "I don't have any claim on her. She was just our chef, for God's sake. Do what you want."

The words, the tone sounded angry to his own ears, so when the other man said nothing but pinned him with a speculative look, Ross didn't challenge him on it. Didn't snarl out another protest. Why bother? He didn't believe his own damn self.

"I'm just going to say this, then leave it alone," Billy murmured. "From one friend to another, whatever is eating at you? Deal with it before it deals with you. Now—" he took another sip of wine and set his glass on the table "—as for the advisory board, I was also thinking about approaching Lila Jones from the Royal Chamber of Commerce…"

Ross went along with the subject change, nodding and replying when appropriate. But his mind had drifted back to the past. To that day when she'd ended their affair. When she'd announced that she was moving to California. He'd been angry. Hurtful. Harsh. Not because he'd been in love—he hadn't believed in that emotion then any more than he did today. Yet, it had shown him that wanting something for himself—believing someone could want him just for him—was a dream better left behind for the boy who'd once believed in superheroes, purple, singing dinosaurs and mothers who stayed.

And he'd stopped dreaming long ago.

Three

There were worse things in life than listening to your mother complain and nag. For instance, volcanoes exploding and drowning whole cities under their molten flow of lava. Wars that left countries devastated and torn. Pandemic viruses infecting the population and turning them into hordes of flesh-eating zombies.

Firefly being canceled.

Yes, so many worse things than having to sit quietly while your mother criticized your parenting.

But right now, Charlotte wouldn't mind a zombie bursting into her house and chasing her around her kitchen. It would definitely be a good excuse to end this phone call.

Smothering a sigh, she pinched the bridge of her nose and prayed for patience. "Mom, I'm sorry I didn't tell you myself about Ben, and that you had to hear about it when you called the restaurant," she apologized. *Again.* "As soon as I got home, I rushed him to the emergency room. But I promise I would've called you this morning."

"It was just so humiliating and hurtful to find out from an employee, instead of my daughter, that my grandson was sick," Cherise Jarrett harped. Only the genuine hurt in her mother's voice kept Charlotte from snapping back in irritation. "I know we've…had our differences in the past few years, Charlotte, but we love Ben, and when we couldn't reach you…"

Had our differences. What a nice way of saying "estranged because you got knocked up and had a kid out of wedlock."

But she clenched her teeth, locking the sarcastic words down. Wasn't this part of the reason she'd returned to Royal? To try to heal the fractured relationship between her and her parents? She'd disappointed them three years ago when she'd called with the news that she was pregnant, but they'd also disappointed her with their reaction.

Brian and Cherise Jarrett had always been strict, conservative but loving parents. Charlotte had expected them to be worried and upset by her news, but not to practically disown her. Nor for them to be relieved that she moved to California so they could avoid gossip about their daughter having an illegitimate child. If not for her sister, brother-in-law and niece in California, Charlotte would've been all alone in the world. Her parents' rejection and disapproval had been like a dagger to the chest, and for months she'd felt adrift, no longer anchored by their love and friendship.

But Charlotte had to give her parents credit. Once Ben was born, their cold demeanor had thawed. Her son and their love for him had helped bridge the divide that had sprung up between them seven months prior. Even if they allowed people to assume that she'd married and divorced while in California, and Ben was the child of that union. Yeah, that continued to sting. Still, now that she'd moved back to Royal with Ben so they could be closer to her parents, she hoped that distance, and the hurt, would disappear altogether.

Then there were days like today…

"They made me shut off my cell phone at the hospital, and it was after 2:00 a.m. when we arrived home. I didn't want to wake you and Dad. Especially when Ben was fine.

If it'd been more serious, I would've found a way to contact you guys. But his fever broke while we were there, and the doctor said it's likely nothing more than a twenty-four-hour bug. So please don't worry."

"Still—"

"What was so important you had to call me at the restaurant?" Charlotte interrupted, hopefully diverting the subject. She had to try before she opened the cabinet where she hid the emergency bourbon and poured it into her coffee.

"Well, it doesn't seem such an emergency now, but…" Her mom paused, and Charlotte's stomach clamped down tight on the unease twisting through her. Silly to feel this way. And at one time in their relationship, she wouldn't have. Instead, she would've teased her mother about being dramatic. But that wasn't their relationship anymore. Now Charlotte tensed, unsure what to expect, bracing herself against what was possibly to come. "But the caterer for the church's Women's Day celebration backed out at the last minute. The event is in two weeks, and I wanted to see if you could step in with small appetizers and finger foods. Nothing too fancy, since I know this is short notice…"

"Sure, Mom," Charlotte murmured, even as *Are you out of your mind?* rang in her head. She already had so much on her plate, yet she didn't rescind her agreement. Her parents had always supported her dream of being a chef even though they'd envisioned her following in the footsteps of her father and sister as an attorney.

And when was the last time her mother had asked anything from her?

No, that part of her that still longed to please her parents, and hungered for their smiles of approval and love, couldn't turn her mom down. "Send me a list of the food you were thinking of, the place and time of the event, and when you need me there to set up."

"Thank you, Charlotte," her mother breathed, relief

flooding through their connection. "You have no idea how much I appreciate your help and jumping in at the last minute."

"You're welcome." And for the first time since she answered the phone, she smiled, a warm glow pulsing in her chest. "I'll get—" She broke off as the doorbell echoed through the house. "I'm sorry, Mom, that's the door. I need to go. But I'll check back in with you later about Ben. Don't forget to send me the information."

"I won't. And give that beautiful boy a huge hug and kiss from his grandma."

"I will," she promised. "Talk to you later."

Ending the call, Charlotte strode from the kitchen down the short hall toward the front door. She glanced down at her smartwatch, noting the time with a frown. Nine twenty. Who would show up at her house so early on a Friday morning? Even Faith didn't call her until after twelve because Charlotte had made it known that her mornings belonged to Ben. And she'd already called and left a message with both Faith and Jeremy Randall, the owner, to inform them she wouldn't be in today because her son was still under the weather.

Her thoughts drifted to Ben as she pushed aside the curtain over the window bracketing the front door. He had still been napping when her mother called, but she needed to check on him—

Jesus.

Her arm dropped like a leaden weight to her side, the curtain drifting back into place as she helplessly stared at the window.

No. It couldn't be. God wasn't that unkind.

But she doubted God had anything to do with who stood on her porch. All that credit belonged to the guy a lot farther south.

She squeezed her eyes shut, and as if of its own volition,

her hand rose to her neck, fingers lightly stroking the necklace underneath her long-sleeved shirt. As soon as she realized what her wayward fingers were doing, she jerked her arm back down. *Dammit.* As much as she fervently wished otherwise, nothing could change the fact that he stood on the other side of her door.

The thunderous pounding of her heart and the rush of her pulse in her head only validated it.

She could pretend not to be home. Avoid him. After all, he'd shown up at her house unannounced and definitely uninvited. This wasn't Sheen, and she didn't have to speak to him. Or look at him. Drown in those eyes that both threatened frostbite and to consign her to flames. Inhale his masculine, earthy, *raw* scent that carried notes of sandalwood, man and sex. Burn in the contempt that leaped from him in rolling waves of heat.

She owed it to herself, and especially to Ben, to protect her son at all costs. Because the alternative was…unthinkable.

Fear fissured through her, its impact stealing her breath. Ross believed she'd "gotten rid of him," as he and Rusty had ordered her to, three years ago. What would he do if he found out she hadn't obeyed his command…

The doorbell pealed again.

Dammit. Her fingers curled into her palms, the short fingernails digging into her flesh.

She wasn't a coward. Ross Edmond no longer wielded any power over her. He was a nonfactor, and to not answer that door and hide would mean he affected her emotions, her life. And she refused to grant that to him.

Before she could talk herself out of it, she twisted the lock and doorknob, flinging the door open.

Maybe she should've taken a few extra minutes…

Yes, she'd just seen Ross last night, but those hours hadn't inoculated her against the force of his presence.

Three years and over a thousand miles' distance should've been enough. But that had been wishful thinking on her part.

Silently, she shuffled backward, and his ice-blue gaze didn't shift from her face as he stepped inside her home. Which was fair, she supposed, since she couldn't remove hers from his.

It wasn't fair.

Someone who led the dissolute lifestyle of a playboy should wear the corruption of it on his skin, his body. Like a masochist, she'd occasionally done a Google search of Ross's name over the years. And every time, an image of him with a different woman as they emerged from this party or that club had popped into the feed.

But no. His golden skin remained as unblemished and smooth as ever. His lean, broad-shouldered body stood as straight and powerful as before. The wide, carnal curves of his mouth still promised sex and sin. Those penetrating, bright blue eyes were as clear and incisive as she remembered.

Not that she could ever forget the arrogant slashes of his cheekbones or the patrician slope of his nose or the strong, bold facial structure. Every day she looked into her son's features, she saw Ross. Was reminded of the man who'd fathered her beautiful little boy and rejected them both.

She couldn't escape him.

Couldn't forgive him.

The reminder of his unpardonable offense—not wanting her or the baby they'd created together—wrenched her from the dazzling tapestry he'd always been capable of weaving around her. He might have the appearance of an archangel, but he possessed the morals and heart of one of the fallen brethren.

"Ross," she greeted flatly, closing the door with a soft, definitive click. "This is a surprise." *What are you doing here? How did you know where I lived? When are you leaving?* She slid a surreptitious glance down the hall toward Ben's room. He needed to go before her son woke from his nap. "What can I do for you?"

He didn't immediately answer but surveyed the postage-stamp-sized foyer with its generic paintings and cherry wood mantel that had come with the home. The living room opened up off to the left, with the large bay windows, small gas fireplace, overstuffed couch and love seat, and the glass coffee table visible. From his vantage point, he couldn't glimpse the connecting dining room with its long, cedar table and chairs that seated eight people, or the pretty chandelier that hung from the tall ceiling.

Her home couldn't compare to the palatial Elegance Ranch where his family lived and where she'd once ruled the dream of a kitchen that could compete with any restaurant's commercial space. But this single-level, two-bedroom, two-bath house was comfortable, cozy and more than enough for her and Ben.

"You have a nice place," he finally said, his glacial gaze resting on her once more.

"Thank you," she replied, refusing to shiver under that stare. "That's not why you're here, though, is it?"

A corner of his mouth lifted in a just-short-of-humorous half smile. "Still direct, I see," he murmured.

No, she'd never been that direct with him. Not that honest, either.

If she had been honest—if she'd trusted him enough to be—she would've confessed how she hadn't felt safe at Elegance Ranch in those last couple of months she worked there. How his father had been steadily hitting on her. Rusty Edmond hadn't touched her, but the flirting, the sly compliments and innuendos…those, in a way, had been more insidious. Because if she confided in others, they could wave it off as harmless, warning her she didn't have concrete evidence to complain. And complain to whom? Her boss? The very man who made her feel uncomfortable and threatened?

Threatened, because if she dared called Rusty on his actions, he would've fired her. And he probably wouldn't have just stopped here. With his power and privilege, he could've destroyed her career as easily as he ordered a rare T-bone steak for dinner. She'd felt trapped, cornered. Defenseless. And the only way out that she'd seen was leaving.

She'd could've told Ross about the situation with his father; she'd been tempted to confess all. But every time she gathered the courage, something held her back. No, not something. *Fear*.

Fear that he wouldn't believe her.

Fear that he would believe her and still side with his father over her.

He was an Edmond first. And his family took precedence over everything—and everyone.

"I have things to take care of before I leave for the restaurant, so…" She trailed off, letting her not-so-subtle hint to get on with it linger in the air between them. The most important subject she hadn't been direct or honest with him about lay sleeping down the hall. She needed Ross out of the house. Five minutes ago.

He nodded, sliding his hands into the front pockets of his pants, the motion opening his suit jacket. And she tried to convince herself that she didn't remember how wide and strong his chest had been. How that divot in the middle of his pecs had been perfect for resting her cheek. How hard and muscled that delicious ladder of abs had been between her thighs when she straddled him.

Tried and failed.

"Two reasons. First, I wanted to check on your baby. How is he feeling this morning?" he murmured.

"He's fine. Better," she amended, hesitant.

Why would he care? No hint of anger threaded through his voice… Oh, God, wait. He'd said *baby*. How old did he think Ben was? Did he assume she'd had a child with another man? Relief trickled through her. But underneath, winding through like a silver thread, lurked an irrational fury. He hadn't wanted their baby, so how dare he show concern over another man's.

Fucking great. Now she was getting all fired up over an imaginary partner who'd supposedly fathered her child.

This was what being around Ross Edmond for five minutes did to her.

"The father," he hedged, his voice slightly deepening even as his words confirmed her suspicion. "Where is he?" Once more he scanned her home. "Did he move back with you?"

She barely smothered her snort. "His father isn't in the picture." Not a lie. "It's just us," she added, skirting him and heading into the living room.

Not because she relished the idea of him having more access to her house, her private sanctuary. She would be a fool not to guard her life, her secret against him. But she also needed to be free of that tiny space where his scent filled her nostrils, sat on her tongue, clung to her clothes, her skin. She just craved a breath that didn't carry *him*.

Ross stared at her, his crystalline gaze unreadable before he glanced away, a muscle ticking along his jaw. "Charlotte, I—" he ground out, thrusting a hand through the longer strands of dirty blond hair that waved away from his face.

"What else, Ross?" she interrupted him, not bothering to prevent the edge from creeping into her voice. She tried not to glance down at her watch, but the minutes steadily ticking by before Ben woke drummed against her skin like impatient fingertips. "You said there were two reasons you stopped by."

For a moment he studied her, flint in his eyes and the

sculpted length of his jaw still tight. "Last night, Billy asked you about joining the advisory board for the festival. It was awkward as hell for him to put you on the spot like that, and I understand if you decide against it. But I wanted to see if you'd made a decision."

"You couldn't have called and asked me this?"

"I don't have your number."

"No," she shot back. "But somehow you found out where I lived, so unearthing my phone number probably wouldn't have been that much of a leap."

"Touché," he murmured, his lips quirking in that maddening—and damn sexy—half smile that had never failed to tempt her into stroking her fingers across his mouth. Three years ago, she could, and did, submit to that urge. Now she curled her fingers into her palms, convincing herself that the itch tingling in her fingertips and palms had zero to do with that old impulse. "You've been away from Royal three years, but surely you haven't forgotten how not much remains secret around here. It didn't take but asking the right question of the right person to find out where you'd moved to. Just making that clear so you don't think I took up a second career as a stalker in your absence."

She snorted, crossing her arms over her chest. He spoke the truth. And she hadn't missed the "everybody knows your name and your business" mentality of this small Texas town.

Of course, she and Ross had achieved the miraculous. Their affair had been one of the best-kept secrets in Royal.

Until she'd outed them to Rusty, that is.

"Right. About that." She shook her head, loosening her arms to hold her palms up. "I'm sure your friend meant well, but given our…past, it's probably not a good idea for me to be on your advisory board."

"Last night, I agreed with you. But I've been thinking…"

His gaze narrowed on her, and she resisted falling into that storm of ice and heat.

"Thinking what?" she prodded.

"That the success of this festival, Soiree on the Bay, is important to a lot of people. With that in mind, I'm willing to put aside our *past*—" his lips twisted as he mimicked her word "—to achieve that goal. And this advisory board is part of that. We need the best creative and forward-thinking minds in this group. And whatever happened between us, I remember you were a brilliant, innovative chef. You can bring that originality, imagination as well as your business sense to the board. It can only benefit all of us."

What had that silent but deafening pause been about? What was he *not* saying? She gave her head a hard, mental shake. None of her business. She couldn't afford to get bogged down in anything Ross. In anything Edmond.

Been there, done that. Had the stretch marks to prove it.

"I'll consider what you're saying, Ross." She absolutely would *not*. "But I can't make any pro—"

"Mama."

A light patter of rapid footsteps followed the plaintive, soft and utterly sweet voice calling out to her. Chubby arms wrapped around her lower calf, and in spite of the dread pumping through her veins like a freight train and flooding her mouth with the metallic taste of fear, she knelt to the floor and pulled her son into her arms. His arms wound around her neck, and he burrowed close. Her heart hammered against her ribs, threatening to break each of them, but she still placed a gentle kiss on top of Ben's thick, light brown curls, breathing in his precious scent. She squeezed her eyes against the sting of tears that suddenly pricked her eyes. Not just because one day he would lose that sweet baby smell.

The abrupt rush of overwhelming sadness and dismay was due to the silent man who loomed several feet away from them. The man whose gaze seared her like a flaming hot brand.

The Sword of Damocles that had hung over her life—over Ben's life—had suddenly fallen.

And there was nothing she could do to sweep them out from under its crashing, lethal weight.

"How're you feeling, baby boy?" she asked, pressing the back of her hand to his forehead and then to his cheek. Relief was a soothing balm inside her at the coolness of his skin. No fever. Thank God. No mother ever felt as helpless as when her child was sick.

"Good," he mumbled, crowding closer to her, his arms tightening as he notched his head under her chin and tried to crawl up her torso. In spite of the bile churning in her belly and burning an acidic path toward her throat, she smiled. Ben was a friendly, bubbly child with seemingly endless energy—except when he fell ill. Then he clung to her, not wanting to let her out of his sight. Not that she minded. Holding him, having his small, sturdy body pressed close, and listening to him breathe were just small things to reassure her that her baby was okay. "Eat," he demanded. "Hungry." Even though the order sounded more like "hungwy," she fully understood it.

"You want banana pancakes?" she asked, suggesting his favorite breakfast. Okay, so sue her. She was spoiling him this morning.

He nodded, his tawny curls brushing her chin. "'Nana 'cakes. Juice."

"You got it." She pressed another kiss to the top of his head. "Can you go play with your trucks for a minute while I finish talking to this nice man?" She fought to maintain her soft, even tone, but with her heart lodged in her throat, it was becoming more of a struggle.

For the first time, Ben turned his head and looked at Ross. Shy with strangers, he didn't say anything, but the

panic crackling inside her, dancing over her skin like a
live wire, ratcheted to a higher, dissonant level. Her son
stared at his father for the first time, although he didn't
know it. It was a surreal moment. Father and son studying
one another... Especially Ross, with that narrowed, enig-
matic scrutiny...

Part of her wanted to thrust Ben behind her, shield him
from Ross. Protect him and yell that she wouldn't allow
him to hurt her son.

But the other half... That proud, almost smug half
yearned to stand Ben before him, let Ross get a good, long
look and brag that this was the precious, brilliant and perfect boy that he'd wanted her to get rid of. That he'd wanted
nothing to do with.

That vindictive, ugly part of her wanted him to soak,
fucking *drown* in regret.

Did that make her a bitch? Probably. Still, the primal
need to protect Ben superseded any petty desires.

"You play for a few, then we'll eat banana pancakes."
She stood and, taking his tiny hand in hers, led him to
the corner of the living room with a trunk full of his toys.
After removing a couple of trucks and making sure he was
entertained, she inhaled a deep breath that did absolutely
nothing for her nerves and turned to face Ross. Jerking her
head toward the foyer, she said, "Over here."

She didn't wait for him to agree but strode out of the
living room and returned to the small entryway. There
would be questions; one glance in his glacial gaze and she
could practically see the suspicion crowded there. But she
wouldn't have this conversation within earshot of her son.

"I thought he was a baby," Ross murmured, but she
didn't mistake that low tone for calm. Not when she noted
the thunder rumbling underneath. "And you let me think
that."

She didn't wilt under the dark accusation in his voice.

Didn't flinch from it. It wasn't *her* fault that he'd assumed she had an infant instead of a toddler.

Ross shifted his stare away from her and back to the living room. Silence descended between them, and in the cramped foyer, the weight of it threatened to crush her. Again, she fought the urge to jump in between them, guard her son from that razor-sharp speculation, that ice-cold face. She silently ordered her arms to remain by her sides instead of wrapping around her torso in a telltale, too vulnerable gesture of self-preservation.

"How old is he?" he snapped, the frost melting under the steam of the heat throbbing in that deep, raw timbre.

"Ben is two," she replied, reaching for and clinging to a calm that was as fake as the flowers in the vase behind her.

"Two," Ross rasped, still not removing his eyes from the little boy who crashed trucks together, complete with sound effects. Blissfully ignorant to the jarring tension that hissed and popped just feet away from him. "The eyes," he continued in that same hoarse voice that almost hurt her ears. "They're you. The hair, the skin, they're…" *They're both of us,* she silently finished for him. Skin just a shade darker than his light brown curls—curls that were softer than hers but a little coarser than Ross's hair. Ben was a beautiful melding of his genetics and hers. "But his face, his features… It's like looking at a picture of me as a kid."

She still didn't say anything as he sussed out who Ben was to him. Instead, she stood silent as he swung his attention back to her, stoically witnessing the succession of emotions that marched through his expression. Shock. Disbelief. Rage. And something not as simple, but just as dark and powerful. But then the rage returned, capsizing everything else until lightning flashed in the sky blue of his eyes. The fury tautened the skin over his cheekbones, his jaw, until the bones seemed ready to slice through. His sensual mouth flattened, tightened until only a cruel slant remained.

"Is he my son?" he growled. "And think carefully before you answer me, Charlotte. Especially since the evidence is staring me in the face. Don't lie to me."

"Why would I need to lie to you?" She notched up her chin, defiant, but unable to quell the shiver jetting down her spine, vibrating through her. "Ben is yours."

If possible, his eyes brightened, so hot with fury that her skin bore the brunt of that heat.

"You didn't think I had a right to know? If I hadn't shown up here today, would you even have deigned to inform me that the son *I didn't know existed* lived in the same goddamn town as me?"

"Lower your voice and watch your mouth," she snapped, and even though every self-protective instinct in her roared a warning to keep her distance, she shifted closer to avoid even the chance of Ben overhearing them. "And the answer is no, I wouldn't have told you. Don't try to turn this around on me," she hissed, her own hurt and anger burning through the coolness of her tone to leave it trembling. God, she hated that it trembled. She hated any sign of weakness in front of this man. The last time she'd betrayed her vulnerability with him, he'd shut her down. *Rejected* her. He would never get the chance again. "You decided you didn't want him, didn't want to upset your life with the inconvenience of a baby. So I don't owe you a damn thing, nor do we need anything from you. I made the decision to become both mother and father to him, so you don't get to act the victim now."

"What the hell are you talking about? You never—" He shook his head, his hand slashing between them. "Not here. And not now. I don't give a fuck what you believe your reasons were to lie and keep my son away from me. Just so it's clear, there *isn't* a good enough reason," he snarled.

"To protect my son from being hurt is a damn excellent reason. The best," she hurled back.

"Protect him from his father?" A quicksilver emotion flashed in his eyes, and if she'd believed Ross capable of feeling anything beyond lust, pride and self-gratification, she might've called it pain. His face hardened further, and he shifted backward. As if being in such close contact with her disgusted him.

Screw. Him.

And screw herself for that thin sliver of pain that slid between her ribs and buried right in her heart.

"I want a DNA test done."

She tilted her head to the side, arching an eyebrow. "I thought he was the image of you as a child. Now you're questioning his paternity. That turnaround was quick," she drawled, offended that he would dare doubt Ben.

Dare doubt me.

The shifty, taunting whisper brushed across her mind before she could smother it. No, she didn't care if he doubted her. She didn't care how he thought about her at all, because he didn't matter.

Only Ben did.

His lip curled into a derisive sneer. "I don't question whether he's mine. It's you and your motives that I have zero trust in. So before I can make my next move, I need concrete, *legal* proof that he's mine so you can't deny me access to him."

Her breath stalled in her throat, and she stumbled back. On a low curse, Ross moved, reaching for her, but she batted away his hands, forcing her knees to strengthen, willing every ounce of the meager strength she retained to her legs.

Though so much fear poured through her that she ached with it, she managed to speak the dreaded words. "What is that supposed to mean?" she pressed. "Before you make your next move?"

His gaze crystallized, and his big, lean body straightened so he seemed to loom larger. More intimidating. "I'll be in touch, Charlotte. Word of advice—don't even consider pulling another vanishing act like you did three years ago. This time I will follow."

With those ominous words echoing in the foyer and ringing in her ears, he crossed the short space to the door, jerked it open and exited through it.

She didn't move—couldn't, even though Ben waited on her. Ross's statement rooted her to the floor.

His next move.

What was he planning? Custody? Taking Ben from her? With the full weight of the Edmond name and the power of their money and connections behind him, he could. He might—

No.

The objection slammed into her head, and she fisted her fingers. No, she wouldn't allow him to rip her baby from her arms. Not when Ross had been the first one to walk away, to abandon them both.

She shoved away from the wall, resolve gelling inside her, fortifying her.

She was no longer that lonely, needy girl who'd left Royal and nearly begged him not to turn his back on her and their baby. Motherhood had made her a warrior.

If Ross wanted a battle, then a battle was what he would get.

Four

He had a son.

Ross stared at the paternity report that had been emailed to him a couple of hours earlier. For what could've been the hundredth time, he scanned it, his gaze settling on the line at the bottom that changed his life forever.

"The alleged father is not excluded as the biological father of the tested child. The probability of paternity is 99.9998 percent."

His pulse roared in his head, the thunderous crash of sound a sonorous backdrop for the seething cauldron of emotion boiling over in his chest. Shock. Fear. Pain. Joy.

God, so much joy.

Until the moment three days ago when he'd stared down into a tiny face that could've been a replica of his twenty-five years ago... Until he'd met familiar brown eyes brimming with curiosity and shyness... Until then, children had been a "someday" notion that bore no place in his hedonistic life. But the moment Ross met his son, someday had become now, in an instant.

He'd wanted those brown eyes to reflect delight and love when they looked at him. Wanted those arms to lift to him in a show of faith and confidence.

Ross just longed to call that beautiful boy son. To claim him as his own. And to be claimed as father in return.

The intensity of that need burned so fiercely that his skin and bones almost couldn't contain the strength and power of that yearning.

His gaze scanned the report once more, passing over the name at the top. Benjamin Jarrett. *Ben*.

For some reason, he hadn't been able to say his son's name aloud at Charlotte's home. As if it were some kind of talisman that would make this too real. Real, only to be stolen from him with greedy, vicious hands.

But not now. Not with these paternity test results.

"Ben," he whispered, finally giving his newest but deepest hope voice, a name.

Even as a now recognizable and intimate anger stirred within him like a flickering, dancing flame. He'd been denied the first two years of his son's life, and Charlotte had denied their son his last name. She hadn't even given Ben that—given Ross that.

Did she really hate him that much? His fingers curled into a fist on top of his desk, the skin over his knuckles blanching before he deliberately relaxed his hand, extending each finger one by one. He inhaled, held the air in his lungs, then slowly released it, attempting to blow a cooling breath over his rage.

It didn't matter if she hated him or not. Or what her trumped-up reasons were. *She* had chosen to leave Royal. *She* had chosen not to tell him she was pregnant. *She* had chosen to rob him of his son. Every step of the way, Charlotte had made the decisions for all three of them, uncaring of the repercussions. Ben deserved both of them—a mother *and* a father.

And Ross was through letting her have all the power in their lives.

His desk phone intercom buzzed, interrupting his

thoughts. "Ross." His assistant's voice echoed through the console speaker. "There's a Charlotte Jarrett here to see you."

Pressing the button, he ordered, "Send her in, please."

Rising from his office chair, he rounded the desk. Grim satisfaction thrummed within him. As soon as he received the paternity report, he'd texted Charlotte and asked her to come by his office so they could speak.

Those dots had bubbled for a while before she actually replied. But she'd agreed, and now that she stood on the other side of his office door, the anticipation of getting answers, of demanding his rights as a father to their baby coiled inside him like an agitated rattlesnake ready to strike.

The knock came a second before the door opened, revealing his assistant and Charlotte. But all he saw was *her*. It was that goddamn superpower of hers, that ability to dominate a man's attention so all else faded to blurred nothingness. Today she wore a short black leather jacket in deference to the February morning. A simple but formfitting white shirt emphasized the full curves of her breasts, and dark blue skinny jeans clung to her sensual, rounded hips and thick thighs. Camel-colored ankle boots elongated legs that already seemed to stretch for eternity.

She might as well have been wearing a couture ball gown with miles of skin revealed by strategic cutouts. Or nothing at all. She commanded every bit of his full, undivided attention. And even unwillingly, he complied.

With her, he'd never been able to do anything but be attuned to her.

To *want* her.

She'd left him, lied to him, kept his son from him. And yet, his dick didn't give a damn.

Yeah, if only it were that simple.

His cock had gotten hard for plenty of women over the years. But none had elicited this visceral, nearly primal hunger like Charlotte Jarrett had from the very first time he'd seen her in his father's study when Rusty had hired her.

If he could, he'd claw that traitorous part of him out of his body, his soul, wherever it hid inside him.

He tore his gaze away from Charlotte to nod at his assistant. "Thank you, Sandra. No interruptions for the next hour, please."

She nodded and left the office, closing the door behind her.

"Do you want to put your things down?" He gestured toward the large purse slung over her shoulder that was more akin to a messenger bag. "Can I take your coat?"

"No, thanks. I have to be at the restaurant soon, so can we get this over with?" she asked. The belligerent words belied the calm tone. The same calm tone she'd employed at her home before her temper had flared and she'd lit into him. "I assume you received the DNA results."

"I did," he said and waved a hand toward the couch and chairs in the sitting area. "Please sit."

"Really, Ross." Her lips twisted into what could've been called—incorrectly—a smile. "Pleasantries? We're past that, aren't we?" She shook her head and crossed her arms over her chest. Then, as if thinking better of the gesture, slowly lowered her arms to her sides. "I'd rather stand. And get to the point of this."

"The *point*, Charlotte? Okay, we'll do this your way. For the last time," he murmured, moving toward her.

He halted when several inches separated them. Far enough away that he couldn't accidentally touch her, but close enough that he could read the flash of apprehension in her eyes.

Did it make him an asshole that a dark gratification filled him at the sight of it?

Probably.

Fuck it. He owned it.

"The report confirmed that I'm Ben's father," he said, uttering those words aloud for the first time. Absorbing that punch of joy, shock and fear again.

"So now you know for certain." She notched her chin up, and in spite of the anger swirling through him like combustible fuel, he had to battle the need to grip that stubborn chin and cup the vulnerable nape of her neck and drag her closer. Had to smother the urge to slam his mouth to hers until she melted under him, until her lips parted for him... until all those soft, dangerous curves pressed to his frame, surrendering. He wanted to fuck the insolence out of her. Clenching his jaw, he resisted the lust, the grinding lure to conquer, to dominate. "What now?" she continued. "Because we both also know you have no interest in being a father—you didn't three years ago, and you didn't right up until you found out about Ben."

"You have no idea what I want. You've never *asked* me what I want," he snapped, bitterness coating his voice. "Every decision has been yours without thought or care to the consequences or who you were hurting."

"Because I've had to," she shouted back at him, the words bouncing off the walls, echoing in the room. A breath shuddered out from between her lips and, visibly shaken, she swept a hand over her thick brown hair. Straightening her shoulders, she sucked in a breath and glanced away from him.

Several seconds passed before she faced him again, and a mask had dropped over her features. Composed, she said, "You can't revise history to suit your narration, Ross. I did what I had to in order to care for my son. I've provided for him, and I'll continue to do so. I don't need or want your money, but this isn't about me. Child support is about Ben. So if you want to contribute, I'll set up an account for him, and the money can go toward his college education or whatever he decides to do with it when he's of age."

"How magnanimous of you to allow me to provide for *our* son," Ross drawled. "I hate to break it to you, Charlotte, but you can't keep me out of his life any longer. And if you would for just a second put your love for him ahead of your hate for me, you would see that he needs me, *his father*, in his."

"How fucking dare you?" she whispered, her eyes narrowing, but it was the telltale glistening in those brown depths that relayed the level of her anger. Charlotte only cried when her rage reached a level that it was either explode or crumble.

And Charlotte Jarrett never crumbled. She might cut bait and run, but collapse?

Not possible.

"All I've ever done from the moment I found out I was pregnant with Ben was put him first. I almost lost my relationship with my parents. I left my old life. I started over in a new city. I worked long hours. I put my goals on the back burner. *For. Him.* Always for him. And I don't regret a single one of those choices. So, hell no. You don't get to sit in judgment of me with your righteous indignation. Where were you, Ross? Playing the international playboy hopping from party to party, woman to woman, while I sacrificed and cared for Ben. *Loved* him."

"You didn't give me that choice, Charlotte. Didn't even grant me the damn option of deciding if I wanted to put aside that lifestyle and be in his life. So now you don't get to be a martyr and cast me in the role of devil because you made decisions all on your own without anyone else's input," he snarled.

"Please." She slashed a hand through the air. "You believe donating your DNA grants you some rights to him? You're wrong. An absentee father is better than one who will play with him like a shiny new toy, then abandon him as soon as something important like a social event, gala or business prospect pops up. Or better yet, a father who didn't want him in the first place."

"What the hell are you talking about…that I didn't want him in the first place?" he growled, latching on to the last accusation because trying to unpack the others lanced him to the core. Was that how she really saw him? A self-indulgent player who didn't give a damn about anything but the next good time and his dick? Was that the real reason she'd kept Ben from him? The pain bloomed in his chest, radiating outward in a toxic, blazing red mushroom. "You said that before, and I call bullshit. Because it implies that you gave me a choice. When you didn't, Charlotte. You stole two years of my son's life from me that I can never get back," he finished, voice hoarse with fury, hurt…grief.

He'd missed his son's first smile. His first word. His first step. Ross knew nothing about Ben. Not his favorite food or toy. Not how cranky he could be when he was tired. Not his laugh.

The hole that yawned wide inside him spread big enough for him to plummet into and never hit the bottom.

"Are you serious, Ross?" She speared him with a look of such disgust it rolled over his skin, polluting him. "Is this the game you're going to play? You don't remember telling me to get rid of our son?" She snorted. "Plausible deniability doesn't become you. Neither does playing dumb."

He almost lashed out with a reply designed to strike and hurt. But then her words penetrated his skull. *You don't remember telling me to get rid of our son?* The question ricocheted inside his head, and he almost stumbled back from the vileness of it. The acidic horror that crowded into his throat and spilled onto his tongue.

"Charlotte, please," he rasped. When she parted her lips, no doubt to blast him with more contempt, he held up a hand, palm out. "Just…pretend I don't know, and tell me. What do you mean I told you to get rid of Ben?"

She glared at him, her chest rising and falling on loud, staccato bursts of breath. For a moment he didn't believe she would grant him that. But then she shook her head, huffing out a hard chuckle. "This is crazy," she muttered but then waved a hand. "Fine. Where should I start this trip down memory lane?"

"The beginning. And leave nothing out."

"Right." Another abbreviated laugh that wasn't a laugh, and she said, "A few weeks after I left Royal, I realized I was late. I called you. Do you remember that?"

"Yes," he ground out. How could he forget? For four weeks, his pulse had leaped every time his phone rang. Only for his stomach to drop and his anger to rise when it turned out not to be her. So when her name had appeared on his screen, and her voice had caressed his ear, taunting him with its sultriness and sweetness that he could no longer have, he hadn't been welcoming. Hadn't been kind. "You mentioned nothing about being pregnant."

"No, but I tried. You didn't give me a chance to, because you had to go. A date that you couldn't be late for," she reminded him.

He'd lied; his ass had been planted on the couch in his sitting room at the ranch while he treated himself to his father's eighteen-year-old scotch. But his pride hadn't allowed him to admit that to her. He'd made up the date so she didn't know he hadn't been with a woman since she'd left him.

"Here's how you should've gone about that, Charlotte. 'Before you go, Ross, I'm pregnant.' Which, I repeat, you *didn't* do."

"No, I didn't," she replied, an edge honing her tone until it could slice clean through his sarcasm. "But I did try again. And when the call went straight to voice mail, I tried the ranch. The housekeeper told me you weren't home, but before I could hang up, she transferred me to Rusty. He demanded to know why I was attempting to contact you when

I'd quit. I think…" She faltered, and this time, she did wrap her arms around herself and her gaze slid over his shoulder to the large window behind him. "I was so stunned that I just blurted out the truth about the pregnancy. He ordered me to get rid of the baby. That his son, an *Edmond*, would not end up raising a child with 'the help.'" Her lips twisted into a grim caricature of a smile, and his fingertips itched to rub those lips, smudge that ill-fitting smile from her mouth like faded lipstick. "He also told me he knew about our… relationship. Courtesy of you. And you'd assured him that you were done with me."

"That's a lie," he snarled, and her gaze jerked back to him. "I've never said anything to my father about us. I've never told anyone."

"Of course you haven't," she murmured, and those four words sent a slick, sour glide into his stomach.

"Dammit, Charlotte," he said, thrusting a hand through his dark blond hair, gripping the strands tight. "That's not how I meant it. I—"

"It was a long time ago, Ross," she interrupted, then flicked a hand. "And whether or not he lied about that, he didn't about you moving on, did he?" She didn't wait for his answer but continued, "Anyway, he promised to have you contact me, but not before warning me that if I didn't go through with the termination of the pregnancy and breathed a word of it to anyone, he'd ruin me. And he wouldn't stop with just me, but he'd harm my parents, as well. I believed him."

"I can't believe…" But yeah…he did. His father would've been—was still—capable of doing all she'd relayed. He wouldn't have been above threatening an ex-employee to protect the precious Edmond name.

"Don't bother, Ross," she murmured, that bitter note making a reappearance. "You might be able to deny knowing about the phone call with Rusty, but you can't ignore the letter."

The letter. What letter?

Maybe she glimpsed the confusion in his eyes, because she scoffed, tipping her head back and muttering something toward the ceiling. Then she tugged her bag open and rummaged inside. Seconds later, she emerged with a worn, brown leather wallet. Opening it, she removed a folded piece of paper from the billfold and, crossing the short distance between them, slammed it onto his chest.

On reflex, he lifted his hand, covered hers. And that small contact—the first time he touched her in three years—nearly knocked him on his ass. Pleasure crashed into him, an anvil that had his fingers clasping hers, as if she were the one thing anchoring him to this world. His fingers flexed, starting to tighten around hers, needing to trap the burn from her palm that seemed to sear straight through to his skin.

But she snatched her hand back, retreating a step, leaving him clutching the paper. She cupped her palm, rubbing a thumb over it. Then, noticing that he caught the betraying action, she dropped her arms to her side.

"Do you want to read that aloud, Ross?" she asked, the rough silk of her voice a stroke over his chest, abdomen… lower. "Maybe it will jog your faulty memory."

He studied her closed-off expression but couldn't forget that telling gesture of hers…as if she were trying to erase the imprint of his touch. Not until the pointy edges of the paper bit into his fist did he glance down and slowly unfold it.

"Charlotte, you were intended to be a fling, not the mother of my child. Get rid of it. Use the enclosed check to pay for the procedure and your trouble. Then move on with your life, because I've moved on with mine. Russell Edmond Jr.," she recited the letter as he read it. "Russell

Edmond Jr.," she repeated on a chuckle. "Like I no longer had the right to call you Ross. Nice touch."

Shock blasted him in an icy deluge. He damn near shattered with it.

"No," he breathed, rereading the paper for a second time. A third. Though typed, it was his signature. What *looked* like his signature. Because he damn sure hadn't written this, signed it or mailed it. "How…"

He knew the how. His father. Rusty had never mentioned a call with Charlotte, and he'd sent the letter, forged it.

Charlotte hadn't robbed him of the first two years of his son's life. Rusty had. Fury raged through him, an uncontrollable inferno desperate to destroy, to consume. And if his father had been in the building instead of attending an out-of-town meeting, Ross would've stormed down to his office and unleashed hell on him.

What a goddamn joke. He'd accused Charlotte of placing her needs above her son. Ross should've known better. After all, his father had been a prime example of a parent doing just that for years.

"You have no reason to believe me, Charlotte, but—" He cleared his throat of the thick snarl of emotion—the anger, the betrayal, the sadness—that lodged in his throat, and tried again. "But I didn't write this. I didn't even know where you lived in California to send it."

"It was mailed to my parents, who forwarded it to my sister, where I was staying. I kept the check, by the way," she supplied, her scrutiny like a magnifying glass determined to analyze every detail and nuance of his expression.

And he held nothing back—not the devastation over his father's lies. Not the grief over what they'd cost him. Not the pain of knowing she'd believed the worst of him. Yes, he might be guilty of being a man-whore, but not a deadbeat father. Not a poor excuse for a man, who would walk away from his responsibilities and ignore the existence of his child.

"I don't give a fuck about a check," he ground out, mind whirling a thousand miles a minute. "Why did you keep the letter?" he asked, holding it out to her, studying its perfectly folded edges that seemed permanently creased into the paper—as if it'd been opened and reread dozens of times. "Why are you carrying it around with you in your wallet?"

"As a reminder." She tugged the paper from his fingers and carefully refolded it, stowing it away in her purse before lifting her head and meeting his eyes. Resolved hardened her gaze. "Whenever I start to doubt myself, or am so tired I don't think I can go on, I pull this out and reread it. Remind myself that I did it once before, and I can do it again. Also, to remember that the only person I can truly count on is myself. Others might have failed me, but I refuse to do the same to myself."

"I didn't know, Charlotte," he murmured, that quiet but fierce statement a brutal blow to his chest. "I didn't know you were pregnant, and I never wrote you a letter telling you to get rid of my baby. I wouldn't…" He scrubbed a rough hand down his face. *I wouldn't abandon you, or my child.* Not after he'd been on the receiving end of that by his own mother. He understood the pain, the confusion, the sense of unworthiness. No, he wouldn't ever inflict that on another child, much less his own. "Give me a chance to prove to you that I can be a good father to Ben. A co-parent with you. I understand you don't owe me or my family anything, but I need you to give me a chance. Please, Charlotte."

She shook her head, and for the first time, indecision flickered across her face. "I—"

The door to his office swung open, and his sister strode in, frowning down at the tablet she held in her hand. "Ross, Valencia Donovan with Donovan Horse Rescue called.

We need to send over—" She finally lifted her head, and spotting Charlotte first, jerked to a stop. "I didn't…" Gina glanced at Ross, then back at their ex-employee. "I'm sorry, Ross. Your assistant wasn't at her desk, so I just…" Her voice trailed off again, but with a small shake of her head, she gathered the poise and manners that had been instilled in her from the cradle. "Charlotte Jarrett. It's been a while," she greeted, walking toward Charlotte with her hand extended. "It's wonderful to see you again."

"Thank you," Charlotte enfolded Gina's hand in hers for a quick shake, before dropping it. The smile she summoned for his sister was small, weak. "It's good to be back home."

"Not to be nosy…" Gina grinned, shrugging a shoulder. "Forget that, I'm *definitely* being nosy. What're you doing here? Is your family okay?"

"Billy and I ran into her at Sheen a few nights ago. Charlotte's the new head chef there. I asked her to stop by and talk about hosting a tent at Soiree on the Bay, and possibly serving on the advisory board."

Gina smiled, nodding. "Wonderful. I've heard so many great things about Sheen and its new chef. I can't believe I didn't know it was you, Charlotte." She glanced down at her tablet again. "This can wait a little while, then. Could you find me after your meeting, Ross?"

"I can. Give me a few more minutes, and I'll come to your office."

"No need," Charlotte interrupted, and the desperation in her voice might not have been clear to his sister, but Ross caught it. "I need to get going anyway."

He almost objected; they weren't finished with their conversation, not by a long shot. But at the last moment, he swallowed the vehement protest, unwilling to draw undue attention to them. He wasn't ashamed of Ben—even now, he wanted to rent a billboard, post it on top of the Texas Cattleman's Club and declare to the world that he had a son.

But this decision wouldn't affect just him, but also Charlotte and especially Ben. Until they hashed out details and he digested these new, earth-shattering revelations of the past, the information had to remain private.

"Oh, no. You don't have to leave on my account," Gina said, frowning.

"I'm not," Charlotte countered, though clearly she lied. Someone who'd just been pulled into a lifeboat off the sinking *Titanic* wouldn't have appeared more relieved than her. "It was nice seeing you again."

Gina crossed the short space separating them to grasp her elbow and give it a warm squeeze. "Same. And I'm so glad you're going to join us at Soiree on the Bay. You were a brilliant chef, and we'll be lucky to have you there. Welcome home, Charlotte."

"Thank you," she murmured. Barely sparing Ross a glance, she lifted a hand in a wave as she turned toward the office door. Her escape hatch. "Ross, I'll let you know about the advisory board position."

"I'll call you," he vowed, and they both knew he wasn't referring to the advisory board or the festival. He didn't care if it sounded ominous. If she tried to hide from him, or attempted to keep Ben from him, there were no lengths he wouldn't go to, to be in his son's life.

She nodded, then exited his office, pulling the door closed behind her.

"Are you sure I wasn't interrupting something more… personal?" Gina asked, her dark eyebrow arched high. Only his father failed to see and appreciate his sister's insightfulness and intelligence. Rarely did anything skate by her. Including the undercurrents of tension that fairly vibrated between him and Charlotte.

"No," he said, voice flat, inviting no further discussion on the topic. "Now what's going on with Valencia Donovan?"

Gina treated him to one last narrow-eyed scrutiny before diving into the reason behind her impromptu visit.

And Ross offered up a silent promise.

Charlotte might have escaped him for now.

But unlike three years ago, wherever she decided to go, he would damn well follow.

Five

"Well, the Hudsons can't stop raving about your food," Faith praised, strolling into Sheen's private dining room, from where Candice Hudson, her mother, aunt and several of their friends had just left, taking their excited chatter and laughter with them.

A glow of pleasure and satisfaction bloomed in Charlotte's chest as the restaurant manager sprawled in one of the chairs that Candice, the happy bride-to-be, and her party had just abandoned. Hearing that her food had been enjoyed never got old. Gathering up the last of the cards where the guests had scored the selection of food, she shot Faith a narrowed glance.

"Why are you so tired? I'm the one who did all the cooking, and the staff did the serving," she drawled.

The other woman waved a hand, flicking away her tart words. "I had to talk. Do you know how exhausting it is to entertain and be *on*?" She sighed. "It's not a job for the weak."

Charlotte snorted, slipping the cards in the pocket of her chef's coat. "You poor, fragile thing."

"I know, right? But one must do what one must." Snickering, Faith jabbed a finger in Charlotte's direction. "But enough about me. The Hudsons just laid down a five-thousand-dollar catering deposit, and all because of your food. Not that I had any doubts that they wouldn't love your menu. Who could possibly resist grilled oysters with sweet basil, pesto and Parmesan? I swear, I just orgasmed saying that…"

"Oh, God, you're awful." Charlotte laughed, heading out of the private room and making a beeline for the kitchen. Faith followed, hot on her heels.

"What? They're aphrodisiacs. You're doing both the bride and groom a service for their wedding night."

"Stop it," Charlotte chided, even though she swallowed another burst of laughter. The first time Faith's naughty sense of humor had made an appearance, Charlotte had been in the middle of sampling a Parmesan lobster bisque. It hadn't been pretty. "I'm just glad they enjoyed what I put together."

The menu included additional food items for those guests who didn't like oysters or the balsamic and rosemary steak options. Coordinating the menu for the high-society wedding that would include nearly five hundred guests had been a challenge requiring hours of work. But the clients' obvious pleasure had been well worth the effort.

"*Loved* it," Faith corrected, trailing behind Charlotte into the bustling kitchen. "And the proud mother of the bride mentioned recommending us to all of her wealthy, connected friends for their wedding receptions and events. Now I have to speak with Jeremy about possibly printing out new brochures that focus on weddings and receptions. If the Hudsons are open to it, we could possibly hire a photographer to take some shots of their wedding and reception to spotlight in the pamphlets," she mumbled to herself, tapping away on her phone.

Switching her formal chef coat out for her work one, she washed her hands and left Faith to her notes and emails. Just as she moved to the stove to begin preparing the creamy wine sauce for her signature dish, the kitchen door opened and Jeremy Randall poked his head inside.

"Charlotte," he called, a tiny frown etching his brow. "Can I speak to you out here for a moment?"

"Sure." Inwardly sighing, she tossed a pining look at the stove and her ingredients. Faith hadn't been wrong. Entertaining people was exhausting, and after presenting each dish to the Hudsons and their guests, and explaining the ingredients in each one, all she longed for was to return to the kitchen and get lost in cooking. It was her happy place. But when the owner of the restaurant requested her presence, she couldn't refuse.

Seconds later, after instructions to her sous-chef to take over in her absence, she pushed through the kitchen door. It swung closed behind her and she joined Jeremy in the hall between the main dining area, the kitchen and prep area. "What can I do for you, Jeremy?"

The handsome older man ran a hand over his salt-and-pepper hair. With his smooth, unlined brown skin and tall, fit frame, Sheen's owner could've been anywhere between forty and sixty. The gray hair only lent a distinguished, composed air to his appearance. But right now, with his frown and the anxious gesture, he appeared more agitated than composed.

"Ah, Ross Edmond is here to see you."

Damn.

She should be surprised...but she wasn't. Ever since she'd left—okay, *bolted* out of—his office yesterday, she'd been expecting him to call her or turn up at her house as he'd done before. But not here at Sheen. She wasn't ready to field curious questions as to why the eldest son and heir to the Edmond Organization had an interest in her.

Out of habit, she reached for the necklace beneath her chef coat. She'd sent up so many prayers since her first and last encounter with Ross that he hadn't noticed its presence.

How did she explain to him that she didn't want anything to do with him, wanted to erase him from her life, but she still wore the one gift from him that she'd allowed herself to keep? She'd thought she'd left it behind along with the other bracelets, earrings and clothes he'd purchased for her during their affair. And when she'd discovered it among her things in California, she'd almost thrown it out. But... she couldn't. Not when memories were attached to the gold chain and diamond-encrusted heart pendant like ghosts connected to an old house.

"I showed him into my office to give you a little privacy. But uh—" he cocked his head to the side, that dreaded curiosity glinting in his hazel gaze "—is there something I should know? Do you need me to stay with you?"

She shook her head, appreciative of his willingness to be her protective shield. But this battle was between her and Ross. "Not necessary. It's probably just about the tent for the Soiree on the Bay festival that I was telling you about," she said. "Nothing to worry about. But I shouldn't keep him waiting."

Although she wanted nothing more than to do just that.

"Okay, if you're sure," he said with a note of hesitation. "I'll be at the bar if you need me."

She nodded, and moments later, she twisted the knob to Jeremy's office and pushed it open. Ross's back faced the door, but as soon as she entered the room, he turned around, his startlingly blue gaze falling on her.

For a second, she froze. Because his crystal eyes, which were usually shuttered and guarded, were awash with anger and pain. God help her, but in that instant, she believed him about not writing the letter. And if she accepted that truth, then she also had to admit that he hadn't known about Ben, either. Those eyes...they didn't lie.

Where did that leave her? Well, she'd been trying to figure that out for the past twenty-four hours. Because three years of hurt and betrayal didn't just disappear overnight. She still didn't trust him—didn't trust that he would put Ben first over his family, put aside his lifestyle and make Ben a priority or take care not to trifle with her son's feelings.

Or her own.

She shut that thought down with a hard, open-handed slap. This wasn't about her; she had no claim on Ross other than him being Ben's father. Nor did she want one. Because he had shown her long ago that settling down with one woman wasn't what he desired. Especially not with her, a woman his father would never approve of. She wasn't rich enough. Her parents weren't connected enough. Her pedigree didn't reach far back enough.

And she'd rebuffed Rusty's advances.

No, she was through hoping for the impossible with Ross. She was done three years ago, when he hadn't fought for her before she left Royal. It'd been her fault that she'd fallen in love with him knowing he could never offer that love in return.

She wouldn't be guilty of such blind devotion again.

"Ross," she said, shutting the door behind her. "What are you doing here at my job?"

"Tomorrow morning, I'm headed to Dallas for the next few days for meetings," he replied, his scrutiny flicking over her body before returning to her face. She convinced herself that her breasts didn't feel heavier, her belly didn't tighten and her sex didn't pulse from that cursory glance. She didn't feel *anything.* "I needed to settle things between us before I left. Charlotte—" the full, sensual curves of his mouth flattened before he continued, voice deepening "—I don't want any more time than necessary to pass by without me being in Ben's life or getting to know him. I've already lost so much of it."

"I—" She sighed, briefly closing her eyes. "I don't want you to, either, Ross."

"Then you believe me?" he pressed, shifting forward, his intense gaze hot on her face. "You believe that I didn't know about the phone call, the letter. About *Ben*."

"Yes," she murmured. "I do. But it doesn't change the fact that he doesn't know you. All he's ever known is me. We have to introduce you to him with care. I'm not going to disrupt his life or upset him."

Ross nodded. "I agree… Which is why I want him to live with me."

Horror and shock punched the breath from her lungs, and she could only stare at him. He intended to sue her for custody? Anger surged through her, a backdraft of emotion. And not just at him for planning to take her baby away from her. But at herself for actually believing he'd changed, that he wasn't selfish and self-absorbed any longer.

"I'm leaving," she said, turning away. There was nothing else for them to discuss—

"Dammit, wait," Ross growled, long fingers wrapping around her upper arm, drawing her to a halt. She tensed under his hand, hating the heat that radiated out from that firm grip. Hating that it seemed to brand every part of her. "I'm sorry. That came out wrong. Shit, Charlotte. I'm so far out of my depth here. Just… Just give me a minute."

Ross. *Apologizing?* She froze for an entirely different reason now. It was the apology and that frustrated, helpless note in his voice. Two things she'd never heard before from this confident, arrogant, charismatic man. It astonished her enough that she slowly pivoted, facing him again.

He released her, but her skin under her chef coat continued to throb as if his hand still clasped her.

"I don't want just Ben to live with me, Charlotte. I want you to move in with me, too."

Jesus, would he stop throwing verbal punches today?

Just when she recovered from one, he opened his mouth and another plowed into her, pilfering her equilibrium.

"That's your idea of easing into this change?" she rasped, incredulous.

"Yes," he said. "Live together platonically as co-parents. So Ben can have you and me under one roof, raising him together."

"So, basically shacking up," she scoffed, shaking her head. "No, thank you."

"Charlotte—"

"No," she interrupted him. "Do you know what finding out I was pregnant and unmarried did to my relationship with my parents? Almost wrecked it. Healing that rift is part of the reason I returned to Royal. Now you want me to just obliterate all the progress we made by telling them I'm moving in with a man—with *you*? I won't do it."

Informing them that the heir to the Edmond Organization was the father of their grandson already promised to be one hell of an uncomfortable conversation.

"So we're supposed to live according to other people's views or opinions?" he challenged. "This is our son, not theirs."

"That's easy for you to say," she slung back. "You're Ross Edmond, Rusty's son. Heir to a fortune. No one would dare criticize or ostracize you. I can't live for myself, Ross. I have other people I'm responsible for, indebted to. And yes, I care about my parents' opinion. I'm not willing to lose them again."

"Fuck," he growled, thrusting a hand through his hair, tousling the ruthlessly styled strands. He paced away from her, halting in front of the far wall and staring at it for several long moments before whirling back around. "Charlotte, I feel like I'm clutching a handful of sand and it's steadily slipping through my fingers, no matter how tightly I hold on to it." He stretched his arm out, thrusting his fist forward, then peeling his fingers open, spreading them wide. "That's the years I've missed. The milestones I've lost. I can't get those back, and I'm trying so hard to grab on to the ones ahead of me. Every day that passes without me there is another day, another minute where something else could happen that I'll miss."

She blinked, taken aback by the vehemence, the *passion* in that plea. This man wanted his son. Wanted to be a part of his life. As a mother, as a woman with a heart, she couldn't deny him. Couldn't deny Ben, either. Because the truth was, although single mothers raised children all the time and did a damn fine job of it, there were things she couldn't teach Ben about manhood. There were things only his father or a male role model could. And while she loved having her father and brother-in-law in his life, they couldn't replace Ben's father.

She owed it to her baby boy to give Ross a chance to be a real father.

But move in with him?

She couldn't.

"I don't want to take that away from you, Ross," she murmured. "You should have every one of those moments, but…"

I can't compromise one more standard for you.

At one time in her life, she'd dreamed of living with Ross as his wife. Even when she'd called him three years ago, she'd still naively clung to that hope of being a family. Now what he offered was practically a marriage of convenience—without the benefit of marriage. She was a single mother, and proud of it. But in the eyes of society, she would be the "baby mama" whom Ross screwed and knocked up. She refused to be the live-in woman who accepted his handout of a home but wasn't good enough to be "blessed" with his last name.

She had a line and couldn't cross it. Even though a part

of her—that woman from three years ago who still clung to daydreams and impossible hope—yearned to not just cross it but leap over it.

"Don't say no just yet," Ross urged, erasing the distance between them with his sensual prowl. "Think about it for the couple of days I'm gone, and we can discuss it again."

She hesitated, then shrugged. "Okay, fine. I'll do that." Not that a couple of days would change her mind.

"Thank you."

He moved even closer, his arm lifting, that big hand hovering between them. Her breath snagged in her throat, and she stared at that so-damn-familiar hand with its short, buffed nails, long, elegant fingers and incongruously calloused palm. Ross might be a businessman and have possessed no interest in cattle ranching, but he'd loved horses. Sometimes it had seemed like he'd enjoyed their company more than people. That abraded palm appeared to testify that he still did. She also recalled how that skin used to feel against hers, that sensual contrast of rough and gentle, coarse and soft. A molten, sinuous warmth coiled around a jagged-edged lust, settling low in her belly. That was also how it had been between them.

Tender with teeth.

Just when she thought he would touch her, bring past and present colliding together, he lowered his arm back to his side. Then slid that hand into his pants pocket as if he didn't trust it to behave if not landlocked.

"I'll call you tomorrow morning, if that's okay. Check in on Ben, at least say hi to him so he can start to become familiar with my voice."

She nodded. "That's fine."

Silence settled between them, as fragile and volatile as an undetonated bomb.

This is about Ben. This is about Ben.

The mantra marched through her mind, and she clung to

it. Even as his sandalwood-and-earth scent embraced her, teasing her with the temptation of his big, powerful, sensually charged body. There'd been a time when she would've surrendered to that lure, cuddled against that tall frame and just inhaled his fragrance straight from the source of his sun-warmed skin. Let him cup her hip and the nape of her neck, press himself against her. Felt his cock nudge her stomach, promising her exquisite pleasure unlike anything she'd ever known.

Stifling a full-body shiver, she shifted backward, injecting desperately needed space between them. Space that didn't contain the memory of sex. Amazing, bone-melting, screaming-until-your-throat-was-raw sex.

"Talk to you soon," he said in that deep rumble of his that added more sensation to her imminent sensory overload.

She moved back and away, granting him room to exit the office. And only once the door closed did she exhale hard and loud.

Ross Edmond was trouble for her.

Some things never changed.

Six

Ross pulled his Aston Martin DBS to a stop in front of Elegance Ranch's scrolled, black iron gate. Pressing the automatic opener on his dashboard, he waited for it to part before driving through to the circular drive. He paused, his nearly soundless engine idling while he stole a moment to stare beyond the palatial Palladian-style villa to the setting sun. Beams of gold, deep orange and brilliant red streamed across the rich ranchland and rolling fields, transforming the estate into a beautiful world that appeared to be on fire.

This was his favorite time of day. For some, it was morning when the day loomed rich with possibilities. But for him, it was evening. It meant a day of hard work, accomplishments and completed goals. It meant a sense of satisfaction that he'd pulled his weight, been a man, not just an Edmond. And the beauty of the sunset congratulated him.

Sighing, he slowly drove into the air-conditioned multicar garage, and after switching the ignition off, just sat there inside the car's plush interior. A quiet peace filled him at being back home after three days in Dallas. Meetings and dinners had filled those hours, for both the Edmond Organization and the festival business. Everything had gone well, and pride filtered through him. Even his father couldn't complain about the connections and headway he'd made. Well, Rusty Edmond actually could find something to criticize, because that was what he did.

Speaking of Rusty...

Clenching his jaw, Ross shoved the car door open. For days he'd put off this conversation with his father because it wasn't one he'd wanted to have over the phone. He needed to look into Rusty's eyes, see each nuance and tick of his expression as Ross confronted his father about lying to him for three years about Charlotte.

Rage that had simmered at times, but never fully extinguished, flared to a flash fire as he exited the garage. Each step through the sprawling and luxurious home stoked those flames. This time of evening, his father would be in one place—his study. Sipping on a tumbler of whiskey before settling in to continue the work he hadn't finished at the office.

For as long as Ross remembered, work had been his father's obsession. Well, work and women. A man couldn't marry four times and not make room for play. But each marriage had ended because he treated his wives the same way he did his children. Like employees. There for his instruction, censure and disposal. And very rarely his praise.

When any of those wives dared complain, he'd sweep an arm out as if inviting them to look around them. Telling them that the work they nagged about had bought the estate, with its many rooms for entertaining, bedrooms and private baths, resort-style pool, stables, several guesthouses and miles and miles of ranchland. Moreover, his many hours at the office paid for the designer clothes, purses and jewelry in their walk-in closets and the extravagant parties they threw on the entertainment pavilion.

Yes, Rusty Edmond could be an arrogant, sarcastic dick.

Which, again, explained the four ex-wives.

On his way to Rusty's study, Ross passed the state-of-the-art kitchen with its separate service kitchen, butler's pantry and wine cellar. It didn't require exerting too much imagination to remember Charlotte rushing around in there, owning the area like the pro she was. That was how she'd first nabbed his attention. That confidence. That cool poise in the midst of controlled chaos. That wild beauty.

And those quick, clever hands.

Shit, did it make him a pervert that those hands so easily and assuredly chopping vegetables, stirring sauces, flipping meat or skillfully plating exquisite dishes had hardened his cock so it resembled the marble floor in the entryway? So delicate, so fine-boned, but strong and capable. He couldn't watch her sauté food and not visualize those fingers wrapped with the same dexterity and talent around his dick.

It hadn't just been her flagrant curves and gorgeous face that had drawn him to her like a moth to a flame. He'd been surrounded by beautiful women since before his balls dropped. But Charlotte had possessed...something more. To this day, he couldn't put his finger on it. But whatever that "something" was, it'd captured him...hell, *enraptured* him. Whereas other women had been transient, he returned time and again to her. Unable to stay away. Unable to satisfy that hungry hole that only being with her had seemed to fill.

Then she'd left.

But it had been his father who'd kept her out of his life.

His father who had prevented him from knowing his son.

His father who *owed* him.

Ross didn't knock on the closed door of Rusty's study but twisted the knob and entered. His father, still in a light gray dress shirt, barely glanced up from his desk, sparing Ross a narrowed look before returning his focus to the computer.

"You're back," he said in that booming, deep voice that could issue curt orders and deliver charming compliments whenever the occasion warranted. "Sometime between when you left and now, did you leave your manners in Dallas? A closed door usually means you knock and wait to be admitted."

"Sorry," Ross said, without the faintest hint of sincerity. Which his father must've noted, because he shifted his wintry gaze away from the monitor to settle on him. "I need to talk to you."

"I'm in the middle of something. It'll have to wait."

"No. Now."

His father's big frame stiffened, and for several seconds they stared at one another, adversaries engaged in a visual battle. Usually, Ross would be the first to look away, to end the pissing contest that always struck him as macho bullshit.

But not today.

Maybe his father sensed this, because the corner of his mouth lifted in a smirk as he leaned back in his massive black leather chair that more resembled a throne than office furniture.

"Well, if you insist, son," Rusty drawled, arching an eyebrow and sweeping a hand toward the visitor chairs in front of his desk. "Sit."

Like a dog.

But with fury rumbling and festering inside him like an angry, infected wound that needed to be lanced, he wasn't in the mood to heel.

He strode closer to his father, ignoring the chairs and coming to a halt directly in front of the massive glass desk. "Have you been to Sheen yet?"

"The restaurant?" He frowned. "No. What's this shit? You have your balls in a sling over food?"

That was his father. All class.

"Then you don't know who the owner hired as executive chef?" Ross pressed, ignoring the vulgar question.

"No, Ross, I don't know," his father growled. "Since it's

not putting money in my pocket, I don't really give a damn who the cook is."

"Chef," Ross corrected. "And it's Charlotte Jarrett, Dad. Charlotte is the new chef."

An emotion too quick to identify flickered in his father's gaze before it shuttered. Rusty had created and patented the poker face. He only displayed what he desired anyone to see. And right now his expression was as shut tight as one of the infamous NDA clauses he demanded of his lovers.

"Charlotte Jarrett," he repeated, voice cold and flat. "I had no idea she'd returned to town."

"Yes, she has."

"So? What does that have to do with either of us? She was an employee years ago. Staff has come and gone from this place before, and I never made it my business to keep track of them. Why should it interest me?"

"Is this the game you want to play?" Ross murmured, not surprised in the least. He hadn't expected his father to admit what he'd done. Rusty considered himself a master chess player, and not just on the board, but in life. He would allow his opponent to make their move so he could counter, evade or trap. "Okay, fine. Have it your way." He cleared his throat, then prepared for battle. "Well, three years ago, after Charlotte quit, she called here looking for me but got you instead."

Rusty didn't respond, just continued to stare at him with that unwavering gray stare. Silently daring him to proceed.

Ross shoved down the rage, covering it with a sheet of ice. He refused to hand his father ammunition to use against him, to turn around and accuse him of being irrational. "She told you about her relationship with me."

"You mean, she told me you two were fucking."

Those red-and-orange-tinged flames licked at his gut. Enticing him to let this consuming anger loose. *It's what he wants. I'm not giving him what he wants.*

"But that wasn't the only thing, was it?"

Again, no answer from Rusty. But the slight flare of his nostrils, the even slighter thinning of his mouth telegraphed his annoyance.

"She was pregnant. And you told her to get rid of it. Get rid of my baby," Ross ground out.

"So?"

You can't hit your father. You can't hit your father.

The mantra spilled through his head, and Ross silently repeated it several more times before he was fully convinced that he couldn't take that course of action.

"So," he echoed coldly. "You told her to get rid of *my* baby. *Not yours.* You had no right."

Rusty snorted. "The hell I didn't. You're my son, and I wasn't allowing some random girl to trap you."

"And that baby is *my son*," Ross threw back. "You didn't even tell me about him, didn't give me the opportunity to make a choice that was mine, not yours."

"What the fuck do you mean—*is my son*?" Rusty asked, voice soft, dangerous, eyes narrowing.

"Yeah, Dad." Ross nodded, scalding satisfaction flooding him. "*Is.* As in Charlotte didn't do what you ordered her to do in that phone call or that phony-ass letter you sent with my forged signature." Disgust churned inside him. "Despite all your manipulations, she had my baby. My son."

"How do you know, Ross?" Rusty demanded, slowly rising from his chair. He planted his fists on his desk, leaning forward.

"Because I've seen him. Met him."

"You're fucking lying," his father snarled, pounding a fist on the glass desktop. "She didn't have that baby."

"Yes, she did." Ross smiled, and not with a small amount of pride. Charlotte had done what he, himself, had found difficult to do. Stood up to and defied the great and mighty

Russell Edmond Sr. "For once, someone didn't obey your edicts. And he's absolutely mine."

"Why? Because some loose-legged girl who you fucked says so? If she opened her legs so easily for you, Ross, who else did she give it up for? Use your head, not your dick."

"Watch yourself," Ross growled. "You don't get to talk about her like that."

"What? She's your supposed 'baby mama' and now you're her champion?" Rusty chuckled, the sound mean, dirty. Because his father didn't know how to fight any other way but down in the mud. "She was the *help*, son. And if you think she didn't see you as a ripe opportunity to climb into a world she has no business in, then you're a goddamn idiot. She was a user then, and she's one now if she's showing up out of the blue with a kid and trying to pawn it off on you. Do you really believe you were the first one she tried to get under? I promise, you weren't."

"Last time, Dad," he warned, steel threading his voice. "Keep your mouth shut about her. And Ben is mine. I had a DNA test done. And despite your best intentions, I'm claiming my son and intend to get to know him."

"The hell you are," Rusty snarled. "I refuse to allow you to tarnish this family's name by having anything to do with this woman and her baby."

"Get used to it." Ross mimicked his father's pose, flattening his hands on the desk and leaning forward so only inches separated them. "Because I've asked Charlotte to move into the ranch with me. Her and Ben. I'm going to be a father to my son whether you like it or not."

"I forbid it, Ross. This is what she wants, what she wanted when she called up here looking for you years ago. Don't you see that? You're upset about the letter I sent her? Well, did she happen to mention the check I included? Ten thousand dollars, son. And she cashed the check. Wake up, Ross, she's just a gold digger."

Ross barked out a harsh crack of laughter. "Is that supposed to mean something? Am I supposed to look down on her for that? She was a soon-to-be single mother who'd left everything behind—her family, her home, her job. You really believe I begrudge her using that check for whatever she needed to care for herself and our son?" He shook his head. "And gold digger? That name doesn't exactly apply since she hasn't asked me for a damn cent in three years."

She's not my mother, hovered on the tip of his tongue. She hadn't abandoned her child, taken the money and ghosted out of his life. Charlotte might have walked away from Ross, but not their son. He granted her major points for that. "It's happening, Dad. She hasn't agreed yet, but it's only a matter of time."

"Not under my roof. And let's not pretend that this house, this land, this company, hell, your *life*, aren't mine. I own all of it. The lifestyle of cavorting off to different cities around the world to do whatever the hell you want without a care? That's courtesy of me. The expensive suits and watches you like to flash? Me. All me. And if you go through with this...idiocy of claiming this woman's son, of trying to move her in here, there will be repercussions. Repercussions you literally can't afford to deal with. Don't force my hand on this, Ross. Cut ties with her and this boy. And cut ties *now*."

"Two years," Ross whispered, deliberately straightening, his gaze never leaving his father's.

"What?" Rusty snapped.

"Two years. That's how old my son is. Two years of not knowing he existed. Two years of firsts. Two years of his life that you stole from me. From us. Do your worst, Dad. Issue your threats. But you don't get another day, another hour."

"Goddammit, Ross—"

"Hey, fellas." Ross turned around in time to see Billy

shut the study door behind him and walk farther into the room frowning. "I could hear you two all the way down the hall. And so can the staff. What's going on?" He cast a look from Ross to Rusty, then back to Ross, concern darkening his eyes. "Is everything okay?"

"Hell no, everything isn't okay," Rusty growled. "Talk to your friend, Billy. See if you can pound some sense into him, because I can't seem to. But somebody better," he threatened.

"Ross—" Billy said.

"Later," he threw at his friend before tossing a look at his father over his shoulder. "We'll finish this later."

"No, we won't. Don't push this, Ross."

"No, don't push *me*, Dad."

Stalking across the study, he jerked the door open and left, the anger, disappointment and, yes, sadness, propelling him down the hall toward the steps that led to the second level and his wing of the house. He'd expected his father's reaction. But he hadn't been prepared for Rusty to deny a child—to urge Rusty to desert a child—that was their blood. All Ross's life, Rusty had preached about teaching his son to "be a man." But a man took care of his responsibilities, provided for his children. A man protected the vulnerable.

Though Ross and his father had their differences, he'd always seen his father as a man upholding those values.

Now the sadness inside him threatened to capsize the anger. The sadness for who he'd believed his father to be. For the death of that belief.

"Ross, what the hell?" A hard grip surrounded his upper arm, drawing him to an abrupt halt. Billy appeared in front of him, blocking his path to the staircase. "What's going on?" Before Ross could answer, his friend guided him through the formal living room on their left and out the glass French doors that led to one of the terraces facing the stables. Once they were several feet away from the house and on the lighted, pebbled path, he stopped, thrusting his hands over his black hair. "Talk to me. What the hell happened in there with Rusty?"

Initially, Ross hadn't any intention of talking about Charlotte and Ben with anyone. At least not until his temper cooled. But the story burst out of him on a ragged, streaming torrent. When he finished, his chest rose and fell on his harsh breaths and the maelstrom of emotions that continued to roil through him.

"Well, damn," Billy murmured. "I wasn't expecting all that."

For the first time since entering his father's study, Ross snorted with true humor. "Yeah, when it comes to drama, I'm all go big or go home." But in the next instant, he sobered. "Just tell me what you're thinking, Billy."

His friend sighed. "I don't agree with how your father handled the situation those years ago. Lies always end up hurting everyone in the end. But trying to see it from his point of view, I can understand his motives—"

"Are you *serious*?" Ross barked. "He kept this—"

"Hold up." Billy thrust up a hand. "I said I could understand his motives, not that I agree with them. Ben is your son, and no man should ever walk away from his child. I like your father, respect him, but I can't back him on this. You're my friend, and whatever you need, I got you."

Love and gratitude for this man, who was as close to him as his brother, Asher, filled Ross, soothing the jagged edges left behind by the argument with his father.

"I appreciate it, Billy," he said, then exhaled roughly. "I'm going to need all the moral support I can get. Especially when this comes out. Because I refuse to hide Ben or Charlotte."

"You mean you're going to need all the support because of Rusty."

"Yes," Ross murmured. "Why does it feel like I'm about to go to war with my father?"

"He'll calm down," Billy assured him, clapping a hand to his shoulder. "Right now he's upset, but once he calms down, he'll see reason."

Ross chuckled sadly. "You don't know Rusty Edmond at all, do you?"

Because *he* did. Rusty didn't forgive or forget. And Ross had openly defied him, when in the past all he'd had was his son's obedience.

No, this wouldn't blow over. Not when neither of them were ready to back down.

But this was one battle Ross couldn't afford to lose.

Seven

This time as Ross approached the small house in the older but cozy section of Royal, he was expected. He'd called Charlotte as soon as he'd hit the city limits last evening to let her know he was back in town. And asked if he could drop by the following morning to see Ben.

Over the three days that he'd been in Dallas, he'd called and talked to her, and had even video-chatted with Ben over his phone. Not that a two-year-old could chat. But he had been able to coax a *hi* out of him. Those moments had carried him through the long, interminable three days. And one day, hopefully sooner rather than later, his son would smile when he saw Ross's face and heard his voice. Would run to Ross when he saw him.

God, he lived for that day.

Butterflies. He'd never experienced butterflies in his stomach before. The closest had been the tightening and twisting of his gut when he'd known he would be with Charlotte. But that had been about anticipation, desire. Not nerves. No, these were honest-to-God nerves. And not over a woman, but for a boy. A toddler who had the power to squeeze his heart so hard that the ache throbbed in his chest.

Climbing the shallow steps to the front door, he dragged in a breath, then knocked. Within seconds, the door opened as if the person on the other side had just been waiting on him.

Charlotte stood in the entryway, her dark hair hanging in a long braid over her shoulder. A long-sleeved, emerald dress clung to her full breasts before the soft material fell to the floor. She looked casual, even comfortable. But there was nothing comfortable about how his cock thumped against his zipper, stretching, hardening. Dammit. The woman could make a nun's habit sexy as fuck.

"Hi, Ross," she greeted, stepping back, granting him room to enter. "Come on in."

"Thanks." Instead of studying the elegant slant of her cheekbone or the sensual curve of her mouth or—hell—the lush rise of her breasts, he surveyed her home. As if it were his first time there. As if he hadn't memorized every square footage of the place that he'd seen. Anything was better than staring at her like a starved animal.

Hell, he shouldn't find her sexy. Shouldn't want her. Shouldn't fucking *feel* around her.

He accepted she hadn't lied to him or kept his son away from him out of spite or malice, but he still didn't trust her. Didn't trust her not to disappear—she'd done it once before. He also didn't trust her not to renege on allowing him access to Ben.

But while he might be angry—an *understatement*—with his father, Rusty Edmond had still raised him. And one thing he'd taught Ross was to understand what your opponent needed and find a way to supply it. It might seem inherently wrong that he viewed Charlotte as his adversary, but right now he wanted her and Ben to live with him, and she was opposed to the idea. So he'd found her weakness and was prepared to lean on it until she surrendered. She'd shown him that he wasn't enough for her to stick around for. Maybe his incentive *would* be.

Fighting fair? No. Was he being his father's son at the moment? Probably.

Did he care? Not even a little bit.

"Where's Ben?" he asked, glancing toward the living room.

"My parents have him. I usually run later than usual on Friday nights, and they offered to keep him until this morning. They're bringing him home shortly."

Disappointment coalesced inside his chest, tight and hot.

"I texted you last night to let you know, just in case you wanted to drop by later this morning," she said, her tone apologetic.

"Yeah, I didn't see it." In his haste to confront his father as soon as he got back, he'd forgotten his phone in the car, and hadn't checked it for messages yet when he'd retrieved it today. "Maybe this works out better. We can talk over some things before he gets here."

She stared at him, then slowly dipped her head. "Fine." Without waiting for him, she strode toward the living room, and he followed. She didn't sit on the couch or love seat but turned and faced him. The resolute jut of her chin and the thrust of her hip relayed that he didn't have an easy battle ahead of him.

He hadn't expected it to be.

"I spoke with Billy while I was in Dallas," he said, starting with a more innocuous subject. "He told me you agreed to serve on the festival advisory board."

"Yes. I brought it to Jeremy, Sheen's owner, and Faith Grisham, the manager, and they both agreed it would be in the restaurant's best interest to host a tent and for the head chef to be on the board. Billy assured me the meetings wouldn't interfere with my work schedule. And as long as they don't take up too much of my time with Ben, I'm willing to do it."

"We appreciate it. Whatever input and ideas you can add will be valuable. Thank you for doing this, Charlotte."

She shrugged a shoulder and unfolded her arms. Skimming a hand over her braid, she huffed out a breath. "We'll see how it works out," she said, and then added, "Rip the Band-Aid off, Ross. You want my answer about moving in with you, and it's still the same as it was before. No, I can't."

"Hear me out first, Charlotte," he requested, shifting closer to her, and after a second, slid his hands in his suit pockets. That was becoming a habit when around her. Occupying or trapping his hands so they didn't rebel and do something heinous like run the backs of his fingers over the delicate but stubborn line of her jaw. Trail his fingertips over the lush curve of her bottom lip. Grab that braid, fist it and tug her head back...

Fuck.

Refocusing, he gazed into her brown eyes and proposed the arrangement that he'd been formulating over the last three days.

"I understand your reservations about moving in with me. Especially given our...past. But I have a counteroffer." The rough thudding of his heart belied the calm of his voice. He *needed* her to agree. But pride kept him from letting her know that. In his experience, voicing what you wanted, *begging for it*, had zero effect. The one time he had, his mother had walked away and left him and Gina anyway. It'd been the best and the cruelest lesson he'd learned. "Commit to one year of you and Ben living with me. Just one so I can get to know my son, and we can work out how to co-parent. Then if, at the end of the year, you decide it's not working, you can leave."

When she didn't say anything, he risked moving closer, and that sharp and sweet scent teased him with a heavier, spicier fragrance. One that had to do less with figs and sugar and was more raw, pure woman.

Fuck if he didn't hunger to lap it off her smooth hickory skin.

"Also, at the end of the year," he continued, centering his attention once more on the conversation and not how delicious she used to taste, "I'll gift you with five hundred thousand dollars to go toward anything you desire—like maybe opening your own restaurant. I remember that was your dream."

He'd anticipated surprise or even a token resistance before quick capitulation. But he hadn't predicted the indignation simmering in her dark eyes.

"A bribe?" she bit out. "That's your counteroffer? Your solution to the problem I represent? Throw money at me?"

"It's not a bribe—"

"Right," she drawled, her tone so sharp it sliced through the thick tension crowding the room. "It's a *gift*. Like the ones you used to leave in the guesthouse for me to find. Or the ones you undoubtedly give all the other women you sleep with and don't bother to call. Same sentiment, different dollar amount. No, thanks. I don't need your guilt gifts."

Anger surged inside him, joined by a scalding hot retort to her unfair accusation. Hell, he'd been trying to give her what she wanted, and she was…damn, she was *right*. Realization doused the flames. He blinked at her, and for the first time, he glimpsed himself in her eyes.

It was true. While they were together, he'd think nothing of having his secretary purchase the latest, most expensive purse or shoes. Or have his jeweler send over a glittering pair of earrings, ring or bracelet. The gifts had been an afterthought, nothing to him. And after her, he'd done the same with the parade of women who'd graced his arm, his bed. None of them had ever complained when he sent jewelry and a note of thanks for a wonderful night.

It wasn't meant as a demeaning or dismissive gesture; it was…what he knew. He'd witnessed his father do it time and time again with his wives and girlfriends, and it'd appeased them, momentarily healing the rift between them and Rusty.

Even his mother had taken a hefty divorce settlement and left, happy to go about her way without her family in her daily life.

Yet the explanation lodged in his throat. At one time in their relationship, he might have been able to share this with Charlotte. Like after the scent of sex perfumed the air of her bedroom, the sheets tangled around their sweat-dampened bodies as she lay sprawled over him, her breath tickling his chest. Back then, in those quiet soul-baring moments when they'd shared their hopes and dreams, disillusionments and disappointments, he could've admitted this revelation of how he used money as emotional currency.

But not now.

"I'm sorry," he said, his mind whirring to find the words to convey his sincerity while struggling to convince her not to abandon this plan. "I didn't mean to offend you, Charlotte. I was only thinking that other than your job at Sheen, you would be rearranging your life for an entire year for me, the least I could do was help you achieve what you've always wanted. It's only a gift. Whether you stay or you leave, the money is yours."

She didn't immediately reply but simply stared at him. Finally, she glanced away, murmuring something he couldn't catch under her breath.

"And after a year, Ross?" she asked quietly, returning her scrutiny to him. "What then? Do we just walk away from the little experiment as if it didn't happen? Do we pretend we haven't let Ben become accustomed to a certain living arrangement where he has both parents every day in his life to separate houses again with biweekly visits?" She sighed, shaking her head, her gaze sad. "What about you? After being a father every day, how do you handle going to only seeing him a few times a week? Have you thought about how that will affect you?"

Again, she stunned him.

By broaching another aspect he hadn't considered, but also because she was concerned…about him.

"I hadn't thought about that," he admitted gruffly. Narrowing his gaze on the neat stack of toys across the room, he swallowed past his suddenly constricted throat. "For me, I'd rather have that year where I wake up to Ben and have the privilege of putting him to bed. Where I can feed him breakfast, can experience his good and bad moods, his smiles and frowns…hear him call me Daddy. I'd rather have twelve months of that even knowing there's a possibility that I might not have it in exactly that way afterward."

She glanced away from him, and her slender throat worked before she returned her attention back to him. "And what about Ben?" she whispered.

Ross studied her for a long moment. "You're a wonderful mother—I can tell that from being with him those ten minutes. Hopefully, you can teach me to be an equally great father. And between the two of us, I know we can help him navigate and adapt to any change. He needs to know me, Charlotte," he said, voice lower, rawer, exposing the depths of his emotion. "And I need to know him."

He didn't voice it, but he assumed that at the end of the twelve months, she would want to leave. But what if she *didn't*? What if she discovered she enjoyed a more luxurious life at the ranch where she didn't have to worry about bills, expenses or day care? They could go on indefinitely with the living arrangement. Hell, even a…marriage, maybe. Bottom line? They could essentially live separate lives but still be a family for Ben.

But he needed her to say yes first before bringing that option to the table.

"Jesus, I can't believe I'm actually considering this,"

she muttered, and the low grumble most likely not meant for his ears had a cautious joy and sweet satisfaction pulsing through his veins. "*If* I agree to this, I have a couple of conditions."

He risked a nod.

"One, I'm not moving to your family's estate." When he frowned, she shook her head. Hard. "No. I'm not compromising on that. I won't be under your father's roof. I've worked too hard to be independent, and I won't give that up to be reliant on you or Rusty."

"Where would we stay then?" he asked, glancing around her living room. What he'd seen of her home was nice, but the house was small. "How many bedrooms do you have?"

"Two."

He shook his head. "I'm not saying no to this condition. But would you concede to us looking for another place together? I don't want to confiscate Ben's room, and then he'll have to move into your room. That's not fair to either of you."

She studied him for a moment, then finally, she nodded. "Okay, I can concede to that."

"And you're renting, right?" When she dipped her head again, he said, "I'll cover the rest of the rent that's left on your lease. No, Charlotte, I'm *insisting* on that," he growled as her lips parted, undoubtedly to object. "It's because of me and what I'm asking you to do that you're moving in the first place. It's the least I could do."

She sighed and grudgingly muttered, "Fine."

"What's your second condition?" he asked, anxious to get all her concerns out there so he could tackle them one by one.

"I'm not accepting your money or *gift*," she added.

"No." This time he shook his head, vehemently. "For two years, you've provided for Ben on your own without any financial help from me. If I'd known about him, I would've gladly paid child support. Consider this a lump sum of back payments. The money is yours and Ben's, Charlotte. I'm not negotiating on this."

Again she hesitated, but eventually nodded. "Okay. That's fair."

"Good. Now *I* have one last condition." He paused. "I want Ben to have my last name."

He braced himself for her argument, had his reasons ready—he was, after all, Ben's father; if he'd been at the birth, he would've signed the birth certificate; and he wanted to claim his son.

But shock erupted inside him, stealing those words and his breath when she whispered, "Okay."

"Thank you," he said softly.

They stared at one another, and the tension vibrating between them thickened, tightened to the point of bursting. As if of its own volition, his gaze dropped to her mouth, and he could practically feel the softness of it. The tender give of it. The gut-twisting greediness of it.

Fuck, he wanted it. Wanted it all. That uninhibited response to him that held no artifice. That needy moan he remembered so well he could hear a faint echo of it now. That sultry, addictive taste that'd had him counting down the hours until he could see her again. Indulge in her again. *Devour* her again.

He'd never been one to deny himself. And he didn't now.

Lust throbbing in his veins, he edged closer, eliminating the space between them. Immediately, the heat from her body and the rich, heady perfume from her skin inundated him, and he inhaled. It was visceral. Intoxicating. Borderline…sexual. Taking a part of her into him, just as he'd once slid so hard and deep inside her.

He granted her time to move, to avoid him—at least he convinced himself he did. And when she didn't, just stared up at him with those lovely, bottomless eyes, he surrendered to the urge that had been riding him since the moment he'd seen her cross that restaurant floor, her sexy, confident stride carrying her to his table.

Need was a growling, straining animal inside him, but he didn't pounce on her like that beast demanded. Not when it had been three years of deprivation, of starving for the touch that taunted him in his most secret, dirtiest dreams.

Because it had been that long, he intended to *savor*.

Dragging his fingertips up the elegant column of her neck, he relished the softness of her skin before tunneling his fingers under her braid and over her scalp. Her low, soft gasp bathed his lips as he lowered his head, and when he took her mouth, he took that small, hungry sound, as well.

He groaned as his lips closed over hers, unable to restrain it. Not when her lips parted for him so sweetly, as if she didn't resent every breath he drew. As if this need wasn't one-sided. As if she'd been dying for a taste of him, too.

He slid his tongue over that overripe bottom lip, sucking on it for good measure before slipping between. Slipping into heaven. Into *her*. With another moan, he pressed closer, aligning his larger frame against her curvier one. God, she was made for him. Even as the thought prowled through his head, he hated it, shoved it aside so hard it ricocheted off his skull. Sentimental drivel had no place here. Not when her tongue greeted his, lapped at his, tangled with his.

This. He lifted his other hand, cupping her cheek, holding her for a deeper, harder possession. *This* was what he'd been searching for the last three years with the nameless, faceless parade of women. This hit, like an unhealthy combination of dopamine and alcohol, arrowed straight to his system. That lethal mix pumped through his arteries, aided by his wildly hammering heart, and pounded in the erect thickness of his cock.

One kiss. She had him on the verge of coming with *one* kiss.

He angled her head, positioning her so he could take more. No, to hell with that. *Conquer* more. He wanted to brand her with his kiss so she would remember clearly how he made her body convulse with pleasure, made her throat raw by eliciting scream after scream.

He could do that for her now. Fuck, he *needed* to do that for her now. For him, too.

She released a whimper then leaned her head back, turning to the side. "Ross," she rasped.

He trailed his damp lips over her cheek to her ear. There, he pressed a kiss to the tip and murmured, "Come away with me this weekend."

The invitation tumbled from his lips before the idea had fully formed. A warning alarm blared in his head, loud and screaming, What the fuck? But he didn't rescind the offer. Though she stiffened against him, he didn't release her, just shifted his hand from her face to her hip, steadying her.

"I have a cabin in Colorado. You, Ben, me—we can fly there tonight after you're finished at the restaurant, spend tomorrow there, and I'll have you back Monday in time for work. We can talk over the details of the move and how we're going to proceed with our families. I want to spend time getting to know my son with his mother. Take a risk and a day off work, Charlotte."

"I don't have to take a day off," she murmured, almost absently. "One of my conditions when I accepted the job at Sheen was that I have Sundays off to be with Ben."

Whether she realized it or not, she was halfway to agreeing to go with him. He pushed his advantage, because the invite might've been spontaneous, but he wanted this. Wanted her and Ben alone.

"Say yes, Charlotte," he said, finally stepping back even

though his body screamed in rebellion and promised swift retribution. Even though his palms tingled with the need to cup that rounded, firm hip again. To squeeze it. Mark it. "This is about Ben. What happens afterward—*if* something happens—is up to you."

Her eyes darkened, and the thick fringe of her lashes lowered. But not before he caught the gleam of arousal in her eyes. The uncertainty, too. Yes, she'd understood his meaning. He hadn't been referring to their co-parenting plan or how they intended to break the news to her parents that he was Ben's father.

He'd meant that kiss.

And the hot, raw sex that followed.

When he'd proposed their…cohabitation, he'd stipulated it would be platonic. And that had been his plan. Up until she'd moaned into his mouth.

Now he was leaving it up to her; the ball was in her court. And if she wanted to play, he was all in. A year with free access to her body, to her pleasure?

He wanted it. He wanted *her*.

Trust her? No. Dying to be buried inside her? Hell. Yes.

"Come away with me." The offer, roughened by the lust tearing at him, still hung between them.

Her lips parted, moved, but nothing emerged. She bowed her head, pinching the bridge of her nose. Anticipation and the need to press for an answer whipped inside him like a gathering summer storm, but he held back. Granting her space and time to come to her decision. Because it had to be hers, freely given.

Finally, she lifted her head, met his gaze. Desire still simmered in her eyes as did the doubt. But so did resolve. He had his answer even before she murmured, "Yes."

He exhaled. "Good," he said. "Call me when you're about to leave work. I'll come by to pick up you and Ben tonight."

"Okay." She sighed. Then whispered, "I hope we're not making a mistake, Ross."

The assurance that they were doing the right thing hovered on his tongue, but he couldn't utter it. Because it would be a lie.

He didn't know.

And right now, he didn't care.

Eight

A cabin, he said.

Charlotte shook her head, smiling wryly down into the steaming cup of coffee she cradled between her palms.

Only Ross Edmond would call this luxurious four-story chalet in exclusive Telluride, Colorado, a cabin. She scoffed. *Right*. And Godzilla was a cute little lizard with anger issues.

Leaning on the wood railing, she studied the beauty of Mount Wilson and sipped the fragrant brew. Somehow the coffee tasted better up here in the mountains, with the crisp air biting at her cheeks. It should've been too cold to stand outside, but bundled up in her oversize sweater and a coat Ross provided from one of the cabin's fully stocked closets, and with the freestanding fireplace at her back, she was warm enough.

And even if she'd been in danger of frostbite, she still would've remained out here on this ridiculously gorgeous terrace, watching her son and his father play together.

Ben had gone a little crazy at the sight of snow; he'd never experienced it in California, and though it did fall in Texas, none had fallen since they'd returned to Royal. His excited squeal had filled her chest with joy, and even if she was questioning her wisdom in agreeing to this impromptu trip, that delighted and wondrous sound had silenced every misgiving.

Ross had always appeared to her as self-confident. Arrogant. So sure of himself. But from the moment he had picked them up from her house, through the drive to the airport and the trip here in the Edmonds' private jet, he'd been different. Uncertain. Even a little bit…nervous. And she knew the reason why.

Ben.

The small, three-foot-tall boy had humbled Ross Edmond.

He was in awe of Ben, and the fascination seemed mutual. Between the phone calls over the days Ross had been in Dallas and the trip here, Ben had lost most of his shyness, and had been stuck like glue to Ross. Falling asleep in his arms on the flight here. Climbing on his lap and contentedly eating with his father. And now building a really abysmal-looking snow fort in the huge yard behind the chalet.

They had a real bromance going on.

One of Ross's reasons for this trip had been to bond with his son. Well, she snorted, that could be checked off the list. The other reason—hammering out the details of their arrangement—had yet to be accomplished.

God, she still couldn't believe she'd agreed to moving in with him. Before he'd arrived at her house, she'd been firmly entrenched on #TeamSeparateHouseholds. But Ross always had possessed a silver tongue—and a gifted one. No, dammit. Don't think of *that*.

But once that floodgate was opened, the waters rushed in, tugging her under.

That kiss. His mouth had brushed hers, and she'd gone up in lust-driven-pride-abandoning flames. Had he guessed from her reaction that she hadn't been with another man since him? That would be utterly humiliating. Especially as he'd been with countless women if the gossip magazines and sites were to be believed.

It hadn't been for lack of opportunity, but her priorities had been Ben and working. They'd left no time for dating or even casual hookups. Besides, the last time she'd trusted a man with her body, he'd let her down in the most spectacular of ways.

Obviously, her libido couldn't give a damn about that. Even now heat pooled and thickened, beading her nipples under her multiple layers and swelling the flesh between her legs. She shifted, her thighs sliding against each other, doing nothing to assuage the ache deep inside her. The man had always been able to turn her inside out with need. With him, she threw away every rule and expectation, stripped off every inhibition and became...his. His to use, to corrupt, to imprison in a world of pleasure that she never wanted to be free of.

His to cast aside when he was finished.

She sucked in a breath, the truth of that slamming into her like a solid punch.

Because he would do it. Just as he hadn't asked her to stay three years ago or come after her. Just as his arrangement already wore a predetermined expiration date.

Ross Edmond might be able to make her burn hotter than the sun, but he wasn't dependable. He wasn't a man for the long haul.

He wasn't *her* man.

"Mama!"

Her son's cry yanked her from her sobering thoughts, and when she lowered the cup to the railing and smiled, the warmth in the gesture was real despite the heaviness of her reality. Ben perched on Ross's shoulders, his chubby, short legs wrapped around his father's neck, his hands spread like little starfish on Ross's cheeks.

"Me!" Ben shouted, which she interpreted as "Look at me!" He patted Ross's face, ordering, "Daddy, go!"

Ross smiled, and cupping Ben's arms, he started slowly spinning around. The way their son screamed in glee, he might as well as have been on a roller coaster. Charlotte laughed at Ben's antics, but the warm joy lighting Ross's face? She pressed her hands to her chest and exhaled a long, shaky breath. Telling Ben that Ross was his "daddy" had been a spontaneous decision for her this morning. And in the face of Ross's happiness at being claimed—and ordered around—by his son, she could set any doubts aside that she'd made the right decision.

On that, at least.

"Are you hungry?" Ross called up to her.

When Ben yelled, "Eat!" in reply, his grin widened and softened at once.

"Ben cast his vote. How about you?"

"I could eat." She picked up her cup and jerked a thumb over her shoulder. "Let me go see what's in the refrigerator, and I can cook us something."

"No need." Ross tumbled Ben down into his arms, earning another delighted squeal of approval from their son. "This is supposed to be a rest for you, too. I already had dishes prepared. I got it."

And he certainly did.

A half hour later, she sat at the huge marble island in the middle of a kitchen that made her chef's soul weep with its top-of-the-line appliances. But could she expect less from a place with five bedrooms and bathrooms, a media room, a library, enough windows that a person could enjoy stellar views from each room and an elevator? An *elevator*, for God's sake. She shook her head.

"What?" Ross glanced at her over his shoulder, a glass baking dish in one hand and the other curled around the open stove door. "I think I can handle warming up a pre-cooked meal," he drawled, eyebrow arched high.

She held up her hands, palms out. "I didn't say a word about your culinary skills," she swore. "Actually, I was thinking, how many TVs are needed in a place like this? I get having the theater-sized one in the living room and in the bedrooms. But there's one out by the hot tub *and* in each bathroom. The. Bathroom."

He snorted. "That you even have to ask that question has me questioning your reasoning. Seriously, Charlotte. What happens when nature calls and the Rangers are playing the Mariners? Am I supposed to just miss out on an important play? I think not."

"No." She smirked. "You just pause the game on one of your fifty DVRs and go like a big boy."

Ross chuckled. "Touché." He slid the dish in the oven and closed the door. "Ben is having a good time," he murmured, his gaze shifting to the toddler, who sat in front of the huge, dark brown sectional couch. Ben babbled to himself as he happily played with the mountain of toys that'd been waiting for him when they arrived at the cabin.

"How could he not?" she drawled. "It's like Christmas came early."

A corner of Ross's mouth kicked up as he shrugged a shoulder. "I might've gone a little overboard." At her snort, he held up his hands. "Fine. A *lot* overboard. But I have birthdays, Christmases and all the other gift-giving holidays to make up for." He paused and cocked his head to the side, studying her. "Do your parents know that you two are here with me?"

She shook her head. "I told them I was going on a business trip and that my manager's husband was coming along to watch Ben and their kids."

He nodded but his face had settled into an inscrutable

mask that betrayed none of his thoughts. "When do you plan on telling them the truth about me?"

"Soon." She laughed softly, but nothing about this situation was remotely humorous. "Especially since we're apparently moving in together. My parents and I... As I mentioned before, we're in the process of rebuilding our relationship. And I'm more than a little worried about how this news is going to affect it."

"Yes, you told me a little bit about what happened with them," Ross said, leaning a hip against the counter behind him, crossing his arms over his chest. She tried—and failed—not to notice how the muscles flexed underneath his long-sleeved white Henley. The man could make arm porn a multi-million-dollar industry. "From what I remember, you and your parents used to be close."

"That was before I embarrassed them by getting pregnant out of wedlock. They were incredibly disappointed and disagreed with me raising the baby as a single mother. And they were very vocal about it."

Vestiges of the hurt echoed in her chest even though she'd forgiven her parents long ago.

"Needless to say, our relationship was strained for a while. It started to heal when Ben was born. They fell in love with him at first sight." She glanced over at her son, love swelling so hard it brushed away those whispers from the past like a broom sweeping out dirt from dark corners. "But I still never told them who his father was—and they never asked." She huffed, shaking her head. "They're going to have some explaining to do with their friends, though. People assumed I got married and divorced while I was in California, and they didn't disabuse anyone of that assumption. When it becomes known that you're Ben's father and that we've never been married, they're going to be scrambling."

"Are you angry with them?"

She didn't immediately answer. *What are you doing?* a small inner voice yelled at her. The last time she'd allowed herself to confide in this man, to trust in him, she'd set herself up for a heartbreak that had nearly broken her. Letting him in again would be a foolish mistake, and she'd promised herself long ago that she'd never be a fool for any man again. Particularly *this* man.

Yet... In a short time, they would be living together again. Co-parenting. They needed to have some sort of cordial relationship—some level of trust—to ensure Ben flourished in a healthy, calm environment. And that required her opening the door to Ross, even if only a little.

Sighing, she dipped her chin. "I was. They emotionally abandoned me just because I did something they didn't approve of. And I can't lie, there are moments when I still have a hard time wrapping my brain around the fact that I've forgiven them. But for the most part, I've let the anger go."

"For Ben's sake, are you going to be able to do the same with me?"

Her breath caught in her lungs, and she stared at him. At the electrifying blue eyes that smoldered with an intensity that simultaneously stirred the embers of desire inside her and set her veins racing with an inexplicable fear.

Discovering he hadn't known about her pregnancy and hadn't callously tossed her aside had gone a long way toward soothing her anger and resentment toward him. But a part of her clutched at the slick shards of bitterness that were embedded in her soul. Because that part hadn't forgiven him for not loving her, not needing her, for letting her go when all she'd wanted was to be his.

Before she could answer, Ben raced from the living room and up to her. He wrapped his arms around her legs and tipped his head back. "Mama, potty!" he announced.

Relief poured through her. Lord, she'd never been so

happy to potty train her son. "Let's go," she said, grasping his chubby little hand in hers.

Ross's gaze seared her as she escaped his question and presence. A temporary reprieve. But one she was grateful for.

She needed the time to shore up her defenses against the force that was Ross Edmond.

"Is he finally down?" Charlotte glanced up from her glass of wine to smirk at Ross. He'd left the living room earlier to put Ben to bed.

A half hour ago.

"Yes." He sprawled at the end of the couch she sat curled up on, his long, muscled legs spread out before her. "Just out of curiosity—" he rolled his head toward her, eyes narrowed "—do you usually read three books to him before he goes to sleep?"

She snickered into her wine. "Not. Even. Close."

A grin flirted with his mouth. "I had a feeling I was being suckered. That kid's lucky he's so adorable."

"Here." She leaned forward and picked up the second wineglass on the coffee table in front of her. Offering it to Ross, she chuckled. "I thought you might need this when you eventually came out."

"I appreciate it." He accepted the glass, sipping the Moscato.

Her belly dipped at the sight of those firm but soft lips pressed to the rim and the up-and-down glide of the Adam's apple in his strong throat. Damn. She couldn't even look at Ross drink without getting hot. She needed an intervention. And more wine. Grabbing the bottle off the table, she topped off her drink.

"Maybe we should talk over how we're going to make the living arrangements work," she suggested, desperate to concentrate on anything other than Ross, his lush mouth and his sexy throat muscles.

"Right," he agreed, taking another sip. "When we return, we can start looking for a house. But until we find one—" he set the wineglass on an end table "—staying at the ranch makes the most sense."

"I said no," Charlotte said, her answer automatic and adamant. "I'm not staying there, Ross. I thought we were through discussing that."

"I'm trying to understand why you're so against it. Is it because you used to work there, and that makes you uncomfortable? Or is it because it's where you and I—"

"No," she interrupted, not wanting him to finish that sentence. Not wanting to hear him describe what they used to do. Meet up? Fuck? Make love? "Like I said before, I've been independent for a long time. And you know how your father operates, Ross. He will try to run our lives if we're under his roof."

It was as close to the truth as she could come.

How could she explain to him that she dreaded being back under Rusty's thumb? Because if Rusty chose to pick up where he'd left off flirting with her, hitting on her, then he wouldn't find the same vulnerable girl; she wouldn't run scared. He would force her hand in telling Ross the real reason she'd been so eager to leave his father's employ. That Rusty couldn't keep his inappropriate comments to himself, and she feared that one day he wouldn't let it go at just talk. From the few times Ross had confided in her—and from her own two eyes—she could tell father and son didn't share a close, affectionate relationship. But Ross wanted more from his father…yearned for more. She refused to be responsible for torpedoing whatever chances they had of achieving that.

But deep inside her resided another reason. A reason that walked hand-in-hand with her insecurities. Just as she

hadn't trusted Ross three years ago to have her back with
his father, to stand up to him, she couldn't say with certainty that he would today, if he had to choose between
Rusty and her and Ben. Rusty was a powerful, charismatic
and domineering force. And for a son who looked up to his
father, hungered for his acceptance and love... Ross might
want to have her and Ben in his life, but if it came down to
it, would he fight for them?

She didn't know.

And didn't want to find out.

Therefore, living at Elegance Ranch remained out of
the question.

"I need you to just accept my decision."

Ross studied her, and she silently ordered herself not
to flinch, not to betray any reaction to that blue, piercing
stare. "Fine," he murmured. "But I am asking one thing."

She dipped her chin, indicating for him to continue.

"When we return back to Royal, come with me to introduce Ben to my family. We don't have to stay at the ranch,
but I would like you there."

Though a barb-tipped unease clung to her ribs like burrs,
she nodded again. "Okay," she conceded. "I can do that."

Even if she'd rather eat a plate of boiled okra first. With
hot sauce.

But if he met her halfway with not forcing the issue of
the ranch, then she could do this. As long as she didn't have
to spend too much time in Rusty's company.

"What is your work schedule like?" he asked, picking
up his glass again.

"Monday through Saturday. I go in at about twelve thirty
to help with food prep and then I don't leave until after closing. It's long hours, but it's also why I insisted on Sundays
off so I could spend a whole day with Ben. I was taking a
chance including that demand in my contract, since most
chefs work seven days a week, including holidays. But Jer-

emy agreed, and I have a wonderful sous-chef as well as an excellent staff to cover me."

"Those are long hours," he murmured. "How did you juggle the job and a new baby in California?"

"Let's just say I haven't slept a full night for over two years," she replied dryly. "But I leaned a lot from my sister and her family. They were invaluable. Now I have a babysitter for Ben, and my parents take him often, as well."

"I have another proposition for you to consider. Let me take Ben while you're at work." He shifted toward her, forestalling her instinctive objection. "My schedule is more flexible than yours. When you leave for work, you can drop him off to me. The office has a day care for all of our employees. So I can visit him throughout the day. And after I leave, we can come over to the restaurant and have dinner with you on your break."

She blinked, stunned into silence.

How many times had she wished that her parents would offer to bring Ben by her job so she could see him? Being a single mother with a very demanding job, she constantly battled the guilt of not being there enough for her son. Of missing out on so many little things—like his giggle at a TV show or cuddling with him at bedtime. Building her career wasn't just for her success or fame; it was for Ben, too. She not only desired to provide for him, but to show him that no dream, no goal was too far or big for him to achieve. Even more than being a master chef, she hoped to be her child's inspiration.

But being his inspiration sometimes cost her time with him. *Precious* time.

"I—" She cleared her throat. "If you're sure it wouldn't be an inconvenience…"

"My son could never be an inconvenience."

His son. Not her.

Good. She was glad he said that. It served as a reminder that their sole connection was the child they had together.

"Thank you, then." She wrapped both hands around the bowl of her wineglass. "We can do that." Lowering her gaze, she studied the ruby depths as if it were a scrying glass. "I'm afraid to trust in this," she whispered, the confession slipping from her without her conscious permission.

"In this...or in me?"

She jerked her gaze up, meeting his shuttered scrutiny. *Retreat*, a voice hissed. *Retreat into casual chitchat and surface topics.* Because those subjects didn't tread on ground she'd burned long ago.

"Both." *Dammit.*

"I asked you before, but you didn't answer." He swirled the wine in his glass, but his unwavering stare remained on her. "You let your anger go with your parents, for Ben's sake. Have you done the same with me?"

"Have *you*?" she shot back, yes, avoiding that question. It was too loaded...too dangerous. Pitted with minefields she dreaded maneuvering.

Several seconds ticked by where only the crackle of logs burning in the cavernous fireplace filled the space. She waited with bated breath, every part of her clamoring for his reply.

"Yes," he said. "Knowing the circumstances and knowing you didn't intentionally keep me from Ben, I'm not angry anymore."

"Liar." Good Lord, her mouth had launched a rebellion, and she couldn't bring it back under control.

Ross arched an eyebrow. Didn't speak. But his eyes... No longer shadowed, they gleamed with—what? Surprise? Anger? Something darker...hunger?

"A part of you will always blame me for missing the first couple of years with Ben. But that's not even what you're lying about."

"Really? Enlighten me then, Charlotte."

"You still haven't forgiven me for leaving in the first place," she said brazenly. "Before you knew about Ben, you seethed with that anger, Ross. And it didn't just disappear."

Deliberately, Ross set the glass down on the end table. He stretched an arm out along the back of the couch, and the other settled on his thick thigh, long fingers splayed wide. But he didn't look at her, his attention seemingly transfixed on the fireplace's dancing orange-and-red flames.

"You think you know me? That's presumptuous of you, isn't it?" he murmured, no rancor in his low voice, but she caught the edge. Sharp enough to leave stinging cuts.

"I knew you better than most," she said, and at her words his head turned toward her, and the icy shock of his wintry blue gaze slicked over her skin like sleet.

"We fucked, Charlotte," he stated bluntly.

Though he spoke the truth, it still drove a fist into her stomach, leaving her winded and hurting. Because he said what she'd always known but had mourned. For him, it had been just sex with the family chef. For her, it had been so much more. And that was her fault, not his. But wisdom didn't mean shit when the heart became involved. Lucky for her, she'd stopped being that foolish, naive girl three years earlier.

"And yet, you still resent me. Come on, Ross, get it off your chest now that you have the chance. Want to tell me why?" She taunted him, and fire leaped in his eyes as if she'd poked those flames.

Did she want to be burned?

Yes.

The word vaulted, unbidden, to her mind. And she wanted to deny that need, but her actions belied it.

"What are you doing?" His hooded scrutiny dipped to her mouth, then lower. Over her suddenly sensitive breasts, down to her thighs...to the aching space between them.

When his gaze met hers again, the heat from it licked at her skin.

God, she wanted to lean into it. Bask in its warmth. Let it consume her.

Even though every self-preserving instinct screamed at her to protect herself.

"I don't know what you mean," she said, the rasp of the tone making a mockery of the statement.

His sensual lips curved at one corner, lending it a carnal, almost cruel cast. "Don't you? Do you want a fight, baby? Is that it?" he murmured. "Or do you just want to use it as an excuse to get your mouth on me?" He cocked his head, and his teeth briefly sank into his bottom lip as if he were nipping her mouth instead of his own. "You don't need that charade, Charlotte. If you want to taste me without having to feel guilty afterward, it can be our little secret."

Little secret. The words clanged in her head, a warning bell.

That's all you are to him. All you've ever been.

Truth. She *knew this.* Yet…lust pumped through her like an engine with greased, faulty brakes—fast, screaming, out of control.

Maybe he was right; she did want his anger to take the decision out of her hands so she could give in. So she could blame emotion instead of accepting that she wanted his mouth again. Craved his tongue licking at her, sucking on her.

A kiss. That was all she'd allow herself. Another kiss. Then she could sate this need that had been teasing and taunting her since yesterday. For three years, she'd been sacrificing—for her career, for her son.

Tonight, she could take for herself. Just once.

One little taste. Who could it hurt?

You.

Bullshit. Because she wouldn't let it.

"That's nothing new for us, is it?" she whispered. Rising from the couch, she slowly moved across the short distance separating them. "Secrets. We're made of them. So what's one more, right?" She pressed a knee into the cushion along his outer thigh. "Except this time, you're mine. I'm not yours."

"Charlotte." A faint frown marred his brow as she lifted her other leg, straddling him, caging him between her thighs. His hands shot up to cradle her hips. "What're you—"

"Taking."

Without breaking his gaze, she lifted her glass, sipped. Then, turning it around so his lips would close over the same spot, offered it to him. He accepted the drink, and the intimacy of the gesture had her sex clenching, an empty ache pulsing deep inside her.

The moment he lifted his head, she dipped a fingertip in the wine, swirling it. Setting the glass on the end table next to his, she turned back to him and slowly, sensually painted first his top and then the fuller bottom one with the wine. She stared at his stained mouth, her breath a ragged, heated thing in her chest.

Lowering her head, she hovered above him, halfway expecting him to tilt his head back and confiscate this kiss. But with his blue eyes like crystal flames in a face of harsh, almost severe angles, he didn't move. Just watched her. Waited. And for a man accustomed to control in the bedroom and out, this show of temporary submission was unusual…and hot as hell.

A moan caressed her throat, but she trapped it, not willing to betray the erotic storm that whipped and howled through her body. And she hadn't even kissed him yet. But she'd rectify that.

Now.

Curling her fingers around the back of the couch, she

closed the scant distance between them. Swept her tongue over his plush bottom lip. Tasted Moscato and him. Again, she locked down that telltale moan. She repeated the stroke over his top lip, drawing the flesh between her teeth, sucking every bit of the wine from him.

His grip on her hips tightened, his fingers digging into her skin. What did it say about her that she secretly hoped he would mark her, leave a souvenir from this taboo and unwise pocket of time? Either that she was desperate or sad, or a total sucker for this man's possession.

Probably all three.

Shoving the distressing thought aside, she sank into the kiss, stroking her tongue between his lips, tangling with him, sliding against him, licking at him. That raw sandalwood, rain and Texas wind scent that clung to his skin was stronger here inside his mouth. Richer. Even more delicious. She could drown in his taste. Drown in this almost overwhelming sensation of heat, liquid lust and pleasure.

The moan she'd been so determined to rein in broke free, and she released the sound into his mouth. His tongue curled around it, claimed it as his own, and with a tilt of his head and a hard thrust, demanded another. And God help her, but she gave it to him. Surrendered it, along with the control she'd wielded but now wanted him to seize.

As if sensing the shift, he grabbed her ponytail, tugged hard on it, jerking her head back. Smoking lightning bolts of need struck her, and the whimper that escaped her would probably bring the sting of humiliation later, but not right now. Now she closed her eyes, relishing the sting across her scalp, dwelling in the sense of vulnerability from her exposed throat.

"If you're going to be sorry for this later," Ross murmured against her skin, his breath a hot, damp caress, "then I'm going to give you something to really regret."

Then he dragged his teeth down her neck, the slight burn

vibrating through her so it reverberated in her nipples, down her spine, in her sex. And when he clamped a firm, possessive bite on the crook where her neck and shoulder met...

"Ross," she groaned, loosening her clutch on the couch to burrow her fingers through his thick, dark blond hair, fisting it. Holding him to her.

"Missed that," he growled, rubbing his lips over the spot that had just received his teeth. "Missed the sound of my name when I'm about to give you what you need. And you need this, don't you, baby?"

She shuddered, her grasp on him tightening. The scraps of reason that still remained forbade her to answer, to give him this ammunition against her. But those remnants didn't stand a chance against the lust coursing swollen and unchecked through her body.

"Yes," she gasped. "Give it to me."

His dark chuckle tickled her skin, a faintly menacing warning wrapped in seductive, rough silk. "Ask for it. Nicely."

For real? She ground her teeth together, trapping the order to "get on with it." Because past experience had taught her that when he was in this kind of mood, a taunting mood where anger roiled just below the hunger, he could—would—drag out this pleasurable torture until she begged for what only he could deliver. An ecstasy that would break her.

"Ross, I need—" The word *you* lodged in her throat. But she didn't need *him*; she needed what he did to her body. Two different things as he'd so expertly shown her. "I need you to make me come."

"Damn right you do," he rasped, and hauling her head down, he crushed his mouth to hers.

This kiss was fire and ice. Gasoline and cooling water.

A reunion and searing loss.

He ate at her lips, and she tilted her head, serving herself

up. Leaving her mouth tender and wet, he dragged stinging kisses down her chin, lower to her neck and lower still
to her collarbone. He paused, sucking the thin skin there
between his lips, marking her. And she loved it. Silently
urged him to suck harder, *longer.*

Impatient fingers gripped the bottom of her sweater and
yanked it up and over her head. For a moment, panic flared
bright inside her, and she almost lifted her hand to her
neck. But then, she barely managed not going limp in relief. She'd removed the necklace and pendant before leaving the house. *Thank God.* What would his reaction be if
he saw she'd kept it? She shook her head as if that could
erase even the possibility.

"What's wrong? Where'd you go?" he murmured, tossing her top to the couch, leaving her clad in only a thin
tank top and a black, scalloped lace bra. Being a chef who
worked long hours, most of the time her body only knew
chef coats, T-shirts and black pants. As a concession to the
woman who loved fashion, she had an addiction for pretty
underwear. And the desire flaring in those light eyes telegraphed his approval.

"Nothing," she replied, skimming her fingers over his
shoulders and avoiding his gaze. "Nowhere."

He didn't call her on her bullshit; instead he slowly slid
a hand up her side, rucking the tank top so the fire-warmed
air brushed her exposed skin. She held her breath, her chest
lifting and falling on her deep, labored breaths. Oh, God.
It'd been so long. And she ached so much. *Touch me.* The
words screamed in her head like a pissed-off banshee. *I
need. I need. I need.*

The chant exploded in her head like pop rockets, quick,
loud and bright.

His lips closed over her nipple. And she cried out. Jerked
in his hold. Melted against him.

"Shh," he soothed, sweeping his lips over the tip through her thin top and bra.

They proved to be an insubstantial barrier to his tongue, his teeth, his passion. He drew on her, alternating with a quick lash and a lush lick. Big, capable hands cupped her, molded her, lifted her to his lips and plucked at the peak that hadn't received his mouth yet.

She sank onto his lap, her sex grinding against the steely length of his cock. With a ragged groan, she tipped her head back on her shoulders, clinging to his head and working his erection. Lust had a way of burning away good sense, shame and inhibition. And as she rode him, circling her hips, bucking against him, racing toward an ending that she would gladly fly into, she shed all of them.

With an impatient growl, Ross tugged down the top of her tank and her bra cup. That needy sound roughened as he bared her to his gaze and his mouth. He switched to her neglected breast, drawing it deep to grant it the same erotic attention, and she trembled, unable to tear her enraptured gaze from the sight of him loving her body. His hand slipped down her belly, not stopping at the waistband of her black leggings, but sliding underneath. Drifting lower... Until he stroked a caress over wet, aching flesh.

"Ross," she breathed, stiffening as pleasure arced through her, momentarily stunning her. His attention on her breasts—God, yes, it was good. But this? This light but firm strumming of the taut nerves cresting her sex? The delicious stroke between her swollen folds? This defied "good" and rammed straight into "exquisite."

"I need it," she pleaded, hips jerking and rolling in an uncontrolled rhythm. "I need it so badly. Please."

Hunger reduced pride to smoldering cinders. Desperation razed caution to the ground. She wanted this man with a desire that should've scared her. Maybe later, when lust didn't cloud her mind, it would. But not at this mo-

ment, with those elegant fingers swirling a diabolical caress around that sensitive nub. Not when she hovered on
the verge of coming apart with him for the first time in
three long years.

He hushed her, freeing her breast with a soft pop then
reclaiming her mouth again. The indulgent thrust of his
tongue, the luxurious tangle reflected his touch down
below. He glided through her sex, fingers flirting with her
entrance before slowly, deliberately pumping into her.

She cried into his mouth, and he greedily took it. On a
rumble of pleasure, of approval, he withdrew, then stroked
back into her, burying one then two fingers inside her
grasping core. Pleasure spun, a crazy, blinding storm that
built and built, threatening to sweep her away and never
return her to who she'd been before she made the impulsive decision to start this.

Her fingers scrabbled at his shoulders, clutching at his
head, as she held on for the inevitable climax. Yet, even
as her hips bucked and ground against his hand, her body
demanding more, she fought that ending. She feared never
feeling this again, never *having* this again.

Pushing the thought aside, she buried her face in his
throat and chanted soundless words against his skin. But
maybe he heard them, because he thrust harder. Curled his
fingertips against that high, soft-and-hard place so deep
inside her.

And she surrendered.

To the pleasure. To the power. To the lust.

She shattered, and as his low, insistent and ragged voice
urged her to fuck his fingers, to take everything, she threw
herself into the fire, knowing she would emerge scarred,
marked...

Changed.

And not for the better.

Nine

"Thank you for leaving work early to do this with me." Ross glanced across the middle console of his Aston Martin toward the silent woman perched on the passenger seat.

Charlotte stared out the window, her hands folded on top of her thighs, her spine poker straight. His gaze trailed over the tight bun of her hair, the almost fragile beauty of her profile and the sensual pout of her mouth. Clenching his jaw, he dragged his perusal back to the road where it belonged. Where it was safer for a number of reasons.

Aside from the obvious, with his attention focused squarely on driving, he couldn't stare at her and reminisce on how good that mouth had softened against his. How the flavor of her still lingered nearly two days later. How he could still feel the tight grip and flutter of her silken, hot sex on his fingers.

Jesus, she'd nearly burned him alive. The memories of how they'd been together hadn't compared to the reality of Charlotte in his arms, twisting on his lap, screaming in release. A shiver rippled through him, and he shifted on his seat, his body stirring, hardening. This was what she did to him. And it scared him what he'd do—what he'd give up—just for another chance to have her over him. Under him.

To be inside her.

"I agreed to go to the ranch with you and introduce Ben to your family," she murmured, yanking him from his thoughts. Thankful for the distraction, Ross checked the rearview mirror to see their son asleep in his car seat.

It was nine o'clock at night, which was past his bedtime. But when they returned from Telluride the day before, Rusty hadn't been in town. He'd just arrived this afternoon, and Ross didn't want to put this introduction off any longer. His father, Gina and Asher needed to meet his son, so they could all start on this road to being family. He didn't worry about his sister and brother as much as Rusty. But Ross clung to the hope that once his father laid eyes on this beautiful little boy, he would set aside his stubbornness and anger and embrace him as his grandson. Embrace Ben's mother, as well.

"Does Rusty know that we're coming?" she asked in that same even, flat tone that contained no emotion.

He tossed another glance in her direction. That note in her voice. It rubbed him the wrong way. As did her reluctance to even *visit* the ranch. He accepted her reasons for not wanting to live at his home, even if he still didn't agree with them. But something small, almost undecipherable continued to needle him like an irritating bee sting. Like there was more to her objection than she was telling him...

"Ross?"

He gave his head an abrupt shake. "Yes," he replied, his fingers curling around the steering wheel in a tighter grip. "I spoke with him earlier and told him we were coming over. And why."

"I hope this turns out the way you want," she said. "For your sake, I really do."

He didn't reply because the turnoff to Elegance Ranch appeared before him. Yet, it didn't prevent an ominous trickle from tripping down his spine. Shaking it off, he slowly drove to the big gate with its elegant scrolls of *E* and

R worked into the black iron, and lowered his visor. He and Rusty had experienced their difficulties and disagreements, but when it came down to it, family and the Edmond name meant more to his father than anything else. Rusty might threaten, but he'd never abandoned him like Ross's mother had. Grim assurance rolled through him as he pressed the button on the automatic gate opener. No, Rusty was guilty of a lot of things but he wouldn't—

"Son of a bitch," he growled. He jabbed the button again. But the gate remained shut. "He did it," he whispered, shock crackling through him on an electrified, discordant wave. "The bastard really did it."

Grief and anger crashed fast on the heels of the astonishment. Hadn't he just thought his father, who claimed family to be more important than everything, wouldn't cut him loose? Had Gina and Asher known what he'd planned? Would they abandon him, too?

A yawning vacuum opened inside his chest. *Alone.* He was alone, and the emptiness threatened to swallow him whole. In an instant of time, he was swept back to that ten year-old boy who watched his mother walk out of their house. This void had swamped him then, too, and he'd tried to fill it with the stingy love and approval of the only consistent parent he'd had left. And now he didn't even have that.

He'd been rejected, discarded.

Again.

"Ross, what's wrong?" A hand settled on his taut forearm, and only then did he realize that he had such a stranglehold on the steering wheel that his knuckles had blanched white. Peeling his hand free, he flexed the fingers, the blood rushing back into them with a tingle. He turned to Charlotte, who studied him in the deepening darkness, with a slight frown.

"I can't open the gate," he murmured, still staring at it as if at any moment it would belatedly swing open. He laughed, and the bitterness of it filled the interior. "He essentially changed the locks on me so I can't enter the property. My father kicked me out." Out of the house. Out of the family.

"Damn," she whispered. Her fingers curled around his arm, squeezing gently. "I'm sorry, Ross. I'm—"

"Doesn't matter," he cut her off, shifting the gear into Reverse and then hooking his arm over the back of her seat so he could turn the car around. At the same time, shaking off her touch. He couldn't handle her sympathy—her pity—right now.

Not when the betrayal, the fucking hurt, of the person who was supposed to love him, support him, *accept* him, tore at him with greedy, poisonous claws. The temptation to pull over, call Rusty and try to convince him to reconsider tugged at Ross. Hard. But Rusty had not only passed down his name to him. He'd bequeathed to Ross his stubbornness, as well. And Ross refused to beg his father for anything. Especially to let him come home.

He hadn't run after his mother.

He hadn't run after Charlotte.

Damned if he would with his father, either.

"Ross," Charlotte said, and her soft voice with its hint of worry scraped over his senses, leaving emotional welts.

"Sorry about needlessly taking you away from work. I'll drop you two back off at your house," he interrupted her again.

"Where will you go?"

He shrugged a shoulder, the gesture deliberately nonchalant. "I'll grab a hotel room for now. Doesn't matter." Goddamn, he was getting tired of saying those two words. Of *needing* to say them. "We planned on looking for a house together anyway."

Silence hummed in the car for several moments, and he could feel the weight of her speculation.

"We're going with you."

He whipped his head to the side, spearing her with a quick glance before returning his attention to the road. But that look had been enough to glimpse the resolve in her expression.

"No, that's not necessary," he said with a shake of his head.

"Maybe not, but we're still doing it."

"Charlotte—" he snapped.

"I'm not leaving you alone tonight," she murmured. "You were just cut off from your family several minutes ago. I know what that's like. To feel alone. Without the anchor you always counted on to be there." Her voice trailed off. But a second later, she cleared her throat. "So no, Ben and I are going with you. And tomorrow morning, we start the house search."

"I don't need your pity," he ground out.

Another beat of silence. "How about my friendship?"

The objection welled in his throat again and pushed onto his tongue. But that part of him...the part of him that constantly surrounded himself with people, parties, with *noise* because he hated the deafening and crushing silence of loneliness, smothered the prideful rejection.

"Okay."

Ross paced the sunken living room of the luxurious hotel suite, his fingers clasping the tumbler of scotch ferociously tight. Either as a desperate lifeline or a potential weapon, he couldn't decide at the moment. Maybe after several more sips, he could weigh in more decisively.

Thrusting his other hand through his hair, he stalked to the floor-to-ceiling glass wall and stared out over the lavish gardens that The Bellamy, Royal's five-star resort, boasted. Usually, when he had occasion to visit The Silver Saddle bar or enjoy fine farm-to-table dining at The Glass

House, both housed within the luxury hotel, he paused
to appreciate its beauty. Inspired by George Vanderbilt's
iconic French Renaissance chateau in North Carolina, Dea-
con Price and Shane Delgado had built its newer, hipper
cousin. With over fifty acres of gorgeous gardens, a spa,
two hundred and fifty richly appointed en suites that included the latest in technology and amenities, The Bellamy
was a crown jewel in Royal.

And for the first time since stepping foot in the resort,
his corporate credit card had been declined.

He downed another swallow of alcohol, the burn of it
mingling with the fury that still seethed in his chest. Not
only had his father banned him from the only home he'd
ever known, but he'd cut him off financially. Trying to
break him. To make him heel like a naughty puppy.

But he wasn't anyone's pet.

And he had resources and investments his father couldn't
touch. He'd use those to purchase a home for him, his son
and Charlotte.

And he also had the name Rusty had given him. Ross
had used *that* to place this stay on his own tab.

Turned out the one thing that was so important to Rusty,
he couldn't snatch away from Ross. He smirked down into
the drink. The irony didn't escape him.

"Ben is asleep." Charlotte's voice reached him, wrapping
around his chest, sinking into him. With his back to her,
he briefly closed his eyes, savoring that low, husky tone.
"Considering it's late, he didn't put up much of a fight."
A small hand settled just below his shoulder blade. "Ross,
are you okay?"

"I'm fine," he replied, not removing his stare from the
amber alcohol.

She released an impatient sound that landed somewhere between a scoff and a tsk. "You're *not* fine. How
could you be?" She moved in front of him, and he lifted

his head, meeting the concern in her brown eyes. "Listen, I know we're feeling our way through being co-parents and possibly friends, but you can talk to me. Like you used to."

"That's when we were naked and sex had loosened my mouth," he drawled. Yes, he was being an asshole. But agreeing to her staying with him had been a bad decision. He was too on edge. Too angry. Too raw. And with her scent teasing his nose, her beautiful eyes on him and that gorgeous body close, he was too reckless.

She had every right to snap at him for his crass reply. Instead, she silently studied him. And like a coward, he turned away, striding back over to the bar to refresh his drink. And avoid that piercing scrutiny.

"Now who's spoiling for a fight?" she murmured, lobbing a variation of his words from the cabin back at him. "Classic Ross Edmond move," she taunted.

Bile churned in his gut, but he shoved it back down, nursing the bitterness. Anger was better than the emasculating need to curl his arms around her and lean on her, until not every breath he took carried the ache of loneliness. "Lash out. Hurt before they can hurt you. Push away so no one can see that you actually feel. You told me it was presumptuous of me to claim I knew you. But some things haven't changed in three years."

He didn't see her approach him again, but the thick, cream carpet couldn't muffle her footsteps. And the hand that, once more, rested on his shoulder blade seemed to singe him through his shirt, branding him.

His movements turned jerky, and a little of the scotch spilled over the rim of the glass as he splashed the alcohol into the tumbler. Quickly recapping the decanter and smacking it back down on the bar, he seized the drink and downed a big swallow.

Only then did he step away from her—from her and the

hand that he didn't want on his back. No, he wanted those delicate, skillful fingers farther south. Wrapped around him. Squeezing him and trading one pain for another.

"I don't want to fight, Charlotte. But I'm beginning to suspect maybe there's another reason you're out here pushing me. Maybe there's something you want from me other than…honesty," he said, sipping slower as he faced her. Making a show of scanning her from head to toe, his eyes drifted down the blue-and-white ruffled shirt and slim navy pants she'd changed into for the meeting with his family and to the tips of her black stilettos.

On the deliberate path back up all those delicious curves and dips, he struggled not to reveal how she affected him. Had him damn near trembling inside with the flare of heat and a need that burrowed deeper than simple lust. Fuck, what was he doing? What danger was he courting? In his current state, she was kindling thrown on an already simmering fire. It wouldn't require much for the flames to rage higher, hotter and out of control.

"You used to do that, too," she said, tilting her head to the side. If his words or perusal had offended her, she did an admirable job of concealing it.

"Do what?" he asked, interjecting a boredom into his voice that he hoped covered the razor-thin shards of panic cutting into him.

"Use sex to avoid a conversation."

"Oh, baby, if I were using sex you would know it." He rubbed his thumb over his bottom lip, smothering a groan as her gaze tracked the motion with a fascination that she would undoubtedly hate him for noticing. "Did you forget so easily? Do you need a refresher course? First, there wouldn't be a need for conversation. Not with that greedy little tongue of yours seeking mine out, tangling with me. Getting wild with me. The second hint would be those pretty but inconvenient clothes sliding off, revealing that dick tease of a body. Third would be the needy sound you make at the back of your throat when I kiss the tops of your breasts, suck on those hard nipples or cup that beautiful ass. Fourth would be the shiver that never fails to telegraph how close you are to coming. All it would take is a touch, a stroke over that tight, wet—"

"Stop," she rasped.

It should've been triumph that crackled through him as his gaze dropped to the rapid rise and fall of her chest. But the dark thing with claws tearing at him wasn't victory.

It was lust.

Hunger.

His plan to shut her up, to drive her away, had backfired.

Big-time.

"That's not a word you would be uttering," he rumbled, mimicking her previous action and cocking his head. "Not unless 'don't' preceded it. Don't stop. More. Harder," he recited. "That's the only conversation we'd have."

"Ross, you think I can't see you're upset? That you're hurting?" she stubbornly continued, even though those expressive brown eyes gleamed, and the tight points of her nipples jutted against her shirt.

"I never claimed I wasn't hurting," he drawled, setting the glass on the bar. He then shifted forward so close she tipped her head back to maintain eye contact. "Let me show you where."

He grasped her wrist and drew her hand forward, slowly enough that she had more than enough time to glean his intention. And that same amount of time to yank her arm back. But she didn't stop him as he pressed her palm to his cock. Didn't hiss an objection when he instinctively ground against it.

No, it was his curse that assaulted the air, his hand that threw hers off.

He who wheeled around and stalked across the room.

"Go to bed, Charlotte," he ordered, voice shredded, control not too far behind. "It's been a long day for both of us."

He needed her gone, preferably tucked away behind a locked door. With the imprint of her palm branded on his dick, he couldn't guarantee he could keep his hands off her. And nothing good would come of that. Not with desire and anger roiling inside him, urging him to wreck the tentative truce they'd forged with hot, filthy sex. Because there would be nothing cleansing about what he'd do to her. *Take her. Conquer her. Corrupt her.* That was the kind of fucking he'd indulge in and demand from her to sublimate this rage, this pain.

"Not until you talk to me."

He snarled, sharply pivoting and charging back across the room. *Calm. Keep your distance.* The judicious warnings whispered through his mind, but they were reduced to ash underneath the burning riot of emotions. He didn't stop when he approached her. Didn't halt until her back pressed against the window and his palms slapped on either side of her head, caging her between glass and his body.

"Why are you pushing this?" he growled, lowering his head until his lips grazed the curve of her ear. "What do you want to hear from me? That my father is a bastard? That he evicted me like some random tenant? That he cut me off, and I'm angry as hell? Yes, dammit. Are you happy? I'm shocked, furious and even a little scared. All of that. But he isn't the first person to walk away from me, Charlotte. I'm a fucking pro at this. So save the sympathy, the pity. I don't need them. What I *do* need is for you to take your sweet ass into that bedroom, lie down next to our son and leave me alone. For both our sakes."

He shoved off the window, air plowing out of his lungs. Dammit. He hadn't meant to say any of that. But her nearness, this unrelenting need and his hurt had propelled the words off his tongue, and not even God could turn back time to erase the too-revealing confession. Slowly he backed away from her, his narrowed gaze fixed on her face. A face that betrayed her surprise and, heaven help him, resolve.

He walked away. Again. Hell, if she wouldn't leave, he would. His pride had disintegrated and littered the floor around his feet. What was one more retreat?

Her hand circled his wrist.

And the last, tattered scraps of his control crumbled.

Turning, he simultaneously lunged for her, cupping her face between his hands, tilting her head back. Her fingers curled into his shirt, holding on. Probably to maintain her balance, since he leaned over her so far that her back arched, her full breasts pressing to his chest.

He shuddered.

"Goddammit, Charlotte," he bit out, lips moving over hers. "Leave now or stay and let me use you to pound out this…thing inside me. I won't be gentle—I can't be. I'll take from you, and I can't promise to give anything back. I want to feast on you and not stop until we're too broken to even breathe." He crushed a hard kiss to her mouth, thrusting between her lips in a quick taste-and-tangle that did nothing to satisfy the craving for her. "This is your chance to walk away now, baby. Because I can't."

Harsh puffs of air bathed his lips as her fingers encircled his wrists. But not to haul them away from her face. This brave, beautiful and *foolish* woman rose on her toes and took the next kiss. Opened wide for him. Allowed him entrance. Invited him to devour.

And on a groan heavy with desire, with demand—with gratitude—he accepted.

From the onset, the kiss consumed. Raw. Carnal. Ravenous. He went wild at her taste, diving back for more, always for more. Each lick, each slide of tongues, each rub of lips and bite of teeth ratcheted the desire consuming him to combustible levels. What was it about her that could transform him into this insatiable animal that was ready to snarl, claw and maul to keep her for himself?

Tonight, the last shred of reason interjected. This was just about here and now. Getting through the night. The only "forever" between him and Charlotte was Ben.

On the tail end of that thought, Ross sidestepped, maneuvering her so she backpedaled toward the couch. Without breaking the mating of their mouths, he guided her down to the cushion. As soon as she sat, he pushed between her legs, cupping her knees and spreading her wider to accommodate his torso.

He broke off the kiss, leaned back and watched his hands stroke up her toned, sexy legs, his fingertips skirting the crease where her thigh and upper body met. Didn't matter that she still wore her clothes. Her warmth seeped past the material to his skin, and he swore her rich fig-and-sugar scent was deeper, denser...headier. His gaze shifted higher, focusing on the cloth-covered flesh between her legs, and he slicked the tip of his tongue over his bottom lip. The source of that scent, that flavor emanated from right there.

And he wanted to gorge on it.

"If you really care about this shirt, you need to take it off now. I won't be as careful with it," he advised, raising his gaze from her sex to her face.

Her lips, swollen and damp from his kiss, parted, and a soft gust of breath eased past them. He almost leaned forward to feel that puff of air on his mouth, but he didn't. Couldn't risk missing her unveil herself for him.

Silence pulsed in the room, a thunderous heartbeat that nearly drowned out his own as he studied those elegant fingers move to the hidden buttons behind the ruffle that stretched from her throat to her waist. Quickly, she undid her shirt and peeled the two sides apart, revealing another of those sexy-as-hell confections others would call a bra.

Pale green this time. Silk and lace molded to her luscious breasts. His mouth watered for a taste. And he didn't wait for her to shrug completely free of it before bowing over her and sucking a nipple deep into his mouth.

With a hushed curse, she battled the cuffs of her shirt, and he took advantage of her bound hands, cupping one breast, pinching the tip, rolling it while tonguing the other. Her tortured whimper mingled with his groan, and then her fingernails were scraping across his scalp, and he was popping the bra's front closure and freeing her.

Jesus. She was too fucking beautiful for words.

Switching breasts, he nuzzled the other mound, licking a path toward the peak. She arched into him, urging him on with whispered chants of his name, pressing his head to her, lowering a hand and closing it over his, so they squeezed and caressed together.

"Damn, I can't get enough of you," he muttered, brushing his lips over her wet nipple, then trailing a path punctuated by stinging kisses down her softly rounded stomach, pausing to trace the faint stretch marks over her skin. Marks that gave testimony to the precious life she'd brought into this world.

"Ross," she breathed, her fingers massaging his scalp, tugging at his hair. Trying to get him to look at her.

But he refused, couldn't. To do that, to gaze into those chocolate eyes, might trick him into believing this wasn't just a physical release. No, he wanted to get lost in her body, in the pleasure, not silly, deceptive notions of *more*. He skimmed one more caress over the light lines on her stomach, then continued lower. And when his lips bumped the waistband of her pants, he didn't hesitate to pop the closure, unzip and tug them down and off her.

For a moment, he froze. Drinking her in. All that smooth, silken almond skin clad in only green lace. And then, with one yank, not even that.

"Baby," he growled, raking his teeth across her hip. She jerked, a low cry escaping her. "Easy," he soothed, sweeping his tongue across the same path. "Hold on to me."

He issued the command, palming her inner thighs and spreading her wider. On a dark, hungry snarl, he dove into her. He barely heard her sharp scream, almost didn't feel the bite of her nails in his shoulders. Everything in him focused on her concentrated scent, the addictive taste and her slick flesh. God, he tried to slow down, to invoke the control he was known for. But that proved impossible. With each lap, suckle and swirl of his tongue and lips, he lost more of himself. And in that moment, his sole purpose became bringing her pleasure. Hearing her voice break on his name. Feeling that flutter of her muscles around the fingers he slid inside her.

Her hands grabbed his head, her hips undulating in a wild rhythm that seemed to demand and beg for the release she hovered on the verge of. With a purse of his lips over the stiff nub of flesh cresting the top of her sex and two hard thrusts into her, she toppled into that release. Trembling thighs squeezed his head. Pleasure-thick cries spilled into the room. Her flavor flowed onto his tongue.

This was heaven, his place of sanctuary.

Nothing could touch him here while he was between her legs.

Hunger surged hotter, fiercer inside him, churning in his gut, pounding in his cock. In lightning-quick movements, he stripped his clothes off, only pausing to grab his wallet and remove a condom from it.

He palmed the protection, and though his body roared for relief, to be buried deep inside the flesh his mouth and fingers had just enjoyed, he didn't rip the foil open. Lifting his gaze to hers, he cupped her cheek and rubbed his thumb over her bottom lip. God, he couldn't get enough of her mouth. To prove it, he leaned forward and, as gently as the lust raging through him would allow, kissed her.

"You can get up and leave if this isn't what you want," he offered, though if she backed out, he might just lose his mind.

"I want this," she whispered, shifting her hand to his dick. Giving him a tight, hard squeeze that propelled the breath from his lungs. He briefly closed his eyes and ground his teeth, giving himself over to the pleasure that careened through him at the long strokes of her hand. "I want you inside me."

He carefully nudged her hand aside and tore open the condom wrapper, swiftly sheathing himself. Weaving their fingers together and nabbing a pillow, he guided her off the couch to the floor. The plush carpet cushioned his knees as he crouched over her. Brown eyes steadily met his, and he didn't look away as he fisted his cock and notched himself at her entrance. He watched her, studying her features for any sign of discomfort, of pain. But she didn't flinch as he pressed deeper, surging forward. No, it was he who closed his eyes as the wet, tight heat of her parted for him, embraced him. *Broke* him.

He shuddered, fighting not to plunge inside her, to rut over her like a beast concerned with only his own gratification. Jesus, he wasn't even all the way inside her, and he shook with the need to come.

"Ross." Charlotte slid a hand over his tense shoulder, up the side of his neck and cradled his jaw. "Look at me." He lifted his lashes, and the sight of her damp lips, flushed cheeks and glazed eyes worsened the struggle for control. "I'm not fragile. Take what you need from me. I can handle it."

He blew out a hard, ragged breath, buried his face in the crook of her neck—and slammed inside her.

Twin moans filled the room, his dark rumble and her

lighter whimper. Fuck, she... A tremble worked over him. She was so damn perfect. Strong. Delicate. Wet. Hot. She was *everything*.

With a growl he couldn't contain, he drew his hips back and thrust forward, powering into her in a greedy stroke. She rose to meet him, her legs wrapping around his hips, and he burrowed impossibly deeper. Palming her ass, he lifted her into him, riding her, grinding into her, burying himself over and over because he couldn't bear not being balls deep inside the heart of her.

She chanted his name, her nails digging into his back, scratching him. *Marking* him. Yes. God, yes. He wanted that physical claim of ownership—

He shook his head, his mind rebelling at the thought even as he owned her body. Not ownership. Pleasure. He wanted the physical evidence that he could render her mindless with his touch, his cock. Nothing else mattered.

Gritting his teeth, he levered off her, sliding his arms underneath her thighs and hiking them higher, spreading her wider. He pistoned into her, the sound of damp skin slapping together, of his grunts and her moans littering the air. Electric currents sizzled and snapped up and down his spine, even the soles of his feet. But he held on, fought the surge of ecstasy that heralded an orgasm that might take him out of here. Not without her, though.

Reaching between them, he swept his thumb over the top of her sex, circling the little nub of flesh. Circling, then pressing. Hard.

Charlotte stiffened, her back arching hard, her beautiful breasts pointed toward the ceiling. Unable to resist the lure of them, he bowed over her, sucking a nipple deep, thrusting and riding out the orgasm that clutched her in its powerful grasp. A strangled cry escaped her, and she shook, her sex clamping down on him in a bruising grip.

Yes, dammit. He wanted to be bruised, to still feel that steel-and-silk clasp tomorrow.

As her tremors started to subside, he gave his own needs free rein. Releasing her breast with a soft pop, he reared back and let go. Each thrust shoved him closer to that crumbling, death-defying edge. Until he just leaped. Bone-cracking pleasure punched into him, and as the orgasm barreled over him, he didn't fight it.

Didn't fight the rapture.

Didn't fight her.

Didn't fight himself.

He surrendered, and for tonight—for this moment—it was all right.

Ten

Ross stood at the window of the Texas Cattleman's Club meeting room, and a sense of déjà vu whispered over him. Hell, had it only been a few weeks since he'd stood here with his father, siblings and Billy, signing the contract for Soiree on the Bay? So much had happened since then. He'd bumped into the woman who'd haunted him for three years, had discovered he was a father and had been disinherited. He shook his head. And to think, when he'd been finalizing those documents, all he'd seen ahead of him was money, success and partying.

Scoffing lightly, he turned and headed to the serving set the club staff had laid out on the small conference table. He poured himself a cup of coffee and sipped, glancing down at his watch. A couple of minutes before one. His stomach twisted, and he clenched his jaw. Another thing that had changed. Never had nerves attacked him at the thought of seeing his sister and brother. They were his best friends—no, more than that. When people survived wars together, that made them closer than blood because their relationship was forged in conflict, battle and grief. Rusty's marriages and divorces had been combat they'd endured, their childhood the battlefield where the three of them had bonded.

But in the week since Rusty had disinherited Ross, he

hadn't heard much from his brother and sister. Most of that distance could be placed on his own shoulders. He'd been so busy finding a home for Charlotte, Ben and himself as well as shoring up his own financial resources that he hadn't prioritized sitting down and talking with them. Also, a part of him had subconsciously put off this meeting. Because that part feared where they stood in this face-off between him and Rusty. Gina and Asher had always been his allies, but at the risk of incurring Rusty's wrath?

He didn't know. And he dreaded finding out.

The door to the room opened, and Gina and Asher walked in. Ross stood at the end of the table, tension drawing him tight, unfamiliar indecision humming through him. He studied their faces, searching for...what? Anger? Sadness? Resignation? Did they resent him for making them choose a side...

"Dammit, Ross," Gina snapped, striding forward and not stopping until she threw her arms around him and held on. Relief poured out of him like a geyser, almost sapping his strength. He wrapped his sister in an embrace that was probably too tight, but he couldn't ease up. Not when he'd never been so grateful for a hug. "Where the hell have you been?" A smile curved his mouth at her muffled scolding. "We've been worried sick about how you've been doing, and all we can get out of you is a 'fine' or an 'I'll call you back.' Which you don't do, by the way."

Gina tilted her head back, glaring at him. "Good thing you arranged this meeting because I was ready to storm The Bellamy." She lightly punched him in the arm. "And thank goodness for the Royal gossip hotline or I wouldn't even have known where you were staying."

"She was actually ready to barge in five days ago," Asher added, voice dry but holding an unmistakable affection for their sister. "I convinced her to wait since you had a lot going on—you know, new family and being disinherited—but we didn't intend on waiting too much longer."

Asher clapped Ross on the shoulder, giving it a brief squeeze. His tone might have been amused, but concern darkened his brown eyes. Ross gave him a small nod, which his brother returned before picking up a cup and pouring coffee into it.

"Gina, quit making like a clingy octopus and release Ross. Here." He passed her the cup and fixed another for himself, a brief grin flashing across his face as she switched the glare from Ross to him. "Okay, Ross. Tell us what the hell is going on. We've heard Dad's rant about your ungratefulness, stupidity, disloyalty to family and being led around by your dick." He sipped the fragrant brew. "Now, what's the truth?"

Ross arched an eyebrow, that vise around his chest loosening at his brother's sardonic words. "How do you know that's not the truth?"

Asher snorted. "When Rusty starts trying to curry favor with me instead of treating me like the unwanted, redheaded stepchild, then I know he's full of shit. And he wants something. That something being getting me on his side to pressure you into caving and falling back into line. Which, even if you weren't my brother, would've put me firmly in your camp."

"Same here. Since you've been banned from the office, he's acting like he actually cares about my input on business decisions. When we both know he doesn't respect my opinions—never has. He's in full-on bribe mode." Gina shook her head, disgust curling her mouth. "As if we're so stupid we can't see right through his manipulations."

Or desperate enough for his attention and his approval that they would turn on him. That was how Rusty Edmond operated in business and with his children.

"So give," Gina prodded. "And start from why we're just finding out we're an aunt and uncle."

Ross did as they requested. And with the two people he trusted most in the world, he confessed everything that had happened since that moment he and Billy had spotted Charlotte in Sheen. By the time he finished with discovering he'd been locked out of the ranch, his credit canceled and then being swiftly tossed out of the family business, they'd all sunk onto the couch in the meeting room's small sitting area.

"If I doubted Dad's seriousness, the package he had delivered to The Bellamy would've confirmed it. It included a letter stating I was not welcome at Elegance Ranch and fired from The Edmond Organization, along with the newest copy of his will with me cut out of it. Congratulations, by the way." He shifted his gaze from the empty coffee cup to shoot his sister a wry smile. "You're now the recipient of the majority shares of the company and his estate."

"Awesome," she drawled. But no humor lightened her troubled gaze. "A son, Ross. You have a little boy," she whispered. "How are you handling that?"

He inhaled a breath, then slowly released it, leaning back against the chair. "Gina, Ben is…" He shook his head, his first real smile of the day curving his mouth. "He's beautiful. And amazing. At two, he's so smart and funny. I didn't think I could love someone so quick and so much. But…" He swallowed. "I do. Crazy, I know."

"No, not crazy." Gina covered his hand with hers, eyes gleaming. "You just sound like a father. And I'm so happy for you."

"I am, too," Asher said, leaning forward in his chair and perching his forearms on his thighs. "And what about Charlotte? How do you feel about her?"

Ross didn't reply; instead, he stood and crossed the room back to the table and the serving set. Yes, he freely admitted to stalling a reply to his brother's question. Because while his love for his son was uncomplicated and easy, his feelings toward Charlotte weren't nearly as cut and dried. Did he love her? No, because in order to love someone, to make a commitment to them, you had to trust them. And as much as his dick hardened for her, he didn't trust her.

But the need for her, the lust that hadn't abated just because he'd been inside her again... That muddied what should've been a simple co-parenting arrangement. Instead of satisfying his craving for her, that night at The Bellamy had only intensified it. And though he could list a thousand reasons why he should maintain a platonic relationship with Charlotte, he hadn't heeded them. Neither of them had. They hadn't discussed the ramifications of continuing a co-parenting-with-benefits arrangement, but each night that he stayed at the house with her and Ben or they came to him at the resort, they gave in to the need.

If he was a better man, he wouldn't take advantage. If he was a prouder man, he would demand more of himself. But when it came to Charlotte Jarrett, he was neither.

"She's Ben's mother," he finally said, staring at the dark stream of brew as it flowed into his cup. "We've come to an arrangement that works for both of us. For the next year, we're going to give living together a try. After that, we'll see."

"Now you know that's not what he was asking." Gina snorted. "But that nonanswer was answer enough." Moments later, she appeared at his elbow, cupping it. "What about Dad? Do you plan on trying to approach him again? In case we haven't made it clear, Asher and I are on your side. Just tell us what you need from us."

Ross encircled his sister's shoulder, giving her a small hug of gratitude. "Thank you for that. Both of you," he added, glancing over his shoulder at Asher, who rose from his chair. "But I don't want you to get involved. This is between me and Dad. I don't want you to be casualties in the fallout."

"How are you doing moneywise?" Asher interjected when Gina frowned and parted her lips, prepared to object to Ross's request. He joined them at the table and shot their sister a look, gently shaking his head. "Can we help you there?"

"No, I'm good," Ross said, grateful for his brother's intervention. He meant it; he didn't want his brother and sister's lives affected by his decisions. Rusty could be vindictive, and though Asher was older than Ross, he had to protect him and Gina from their father's possible retaliation. "I have investments in several companies, stock and connections that aren't tangled up in The Edmond Organization. And I still have Soiree on the Bay. The contracts have been signed. Dad can't kick me out of that like he did from the company."

If anything, being fired had forced Ross to rely only on himself. Thank God, he'd diversified his own funds years ago, not living completely off the family business. He wasn't a pauper by any stretch of the imagination. Hell, according to his financial portfolio, he was still a millionaire in his own right. But… Unease coiled inside his chest. But he might not have enough on-hand cash to pay Charlotte the five hundred thousand he'd promised her.

"I hate that you're going through this," Gina hissed, crossing her arms over her chest. "While I'm pissed at Dad, I can't say I'm surprised. Just look how he treated Mom when she dared to defy him."

Ross stiffened, an old but very familiar anger kindling in his veins. "This situation is completely different from that."

"Not by much," his sister argued. "She asked Dad for a divorce, and he went after her with everything he had. Forget that she was the mother of his children. He kicked her out of her house, changed the locks, made it difficult for her to see her children. He took everything that was important from her."

"She chose a big settlement over her children," he snapped. "No one forced her to leave Royal, to leave us. She divorced Dad, not us. I've only had Ben in my life for a matter of weeks, but I would do anything for that little boy. Destroy anyone who tried to hurt him. You fight for those you love. *Sarabeth*," he uttered her name on a mocking sneer, because she hadn't been Mom to him a long time, "chose to walk away. To not be in our lives except for the occasional visit or phone call. If she truly wanted to be there for us, no power in this world, including the long arm of Rusty Edmond, could've kept her away. So no, it's not similar at all."

Asher edged closer to their sister, clasping her hand in his, and Ross pivoted away, suddenly feeling like an ogre. His issues with his mother were just that—his issues. He had no right to jump down Gina's throat because she chose to see the woman who'd essentially abandoned them in a kinder light.

"When was the last time you saw her, Ross? Spoke to her?" Gina asked softly.

"Years. And I'm fine with maintaining the status quo."

"You should call her. Talk to her. I think you would be surprised with the answers she could give you."

Answers? Could her *answers* turn back time and give him her much-needed presence in his life? Could they make up for her absence? For her rejection of him? For making him question his own self-worth? How could he be worthy of anything when the two people who were supposed to love him unconditionally had rejected him at every turn? His mother had chosen freedom over him, and his father—fuck, Rusty was Rusty. Everything had come before Ross, Gina and Asher. Business, women, a goddamn prize bull.

The man had missed Ross's college graduation because of a cattle sale. And now, he put his pride before his son.

No. He didn't need to ask Sarabeth anything. Her absence and Rusty's emotional deprivation had been enough of a very thorough explanation.

"I'm through talking about her," Ross said, a sudden bone-deep weariness creeping into his voice. "Do you two want to meet your nephew?"

He'd brought Ben with him to the clubhouse and left him in the day care while he met with Gina and Asher.

"Of course." Gina crossed over to him and wrapped him in a hug. "I'm sorry for bringing up Mom and pressuring you," she murmured.

"No worries." He pressed a kiss to the top of her head.

"Let's go," Asher said. "I want to officially meet my nephew. You said he's beautiful. So that means he must take after his mother."

Ross met his brother's smirk and grinned. "Asshole."

Asher laughed, pulling the meeting room door open. "Well, that's a family trait, so let's *really* hope he takes after his mother."

Gina gasped in mock outrage. "I beg your pardon," she objected as she swept past Asher into the hallway. "Speak for yourself. I merely know my own mind and am not afraid to let others know it, as well."

Asher tilted his head. "Huh. When I do that, I'm always called an asshole."

Ross chuckled, following his brother and sister—his family—toward the front of the building.

God, he loved them.

Eleven

"This is ridiculous," Charlotte grumbled, staring at herself in the closet mirror.

Hah. As if the space that was bigger than her bedroom in her former home could be called something as simple as a *closet*. She didn't even have enough clothes to fill all the drawers, racks and hangers. Not to mention the stacks of mini cases meant to store jewelry. Besides the pair of diamond studs that was a graduation gift from her parents and the necklace Ross had given her, she only owned costume jewelry that would look laughable in those boxes.

Speaking of the necklace... She grazed fingertips over the heart-shaped pendant, then removed it, laying it on the island behind her. So far, she'd done a good job of keeping it hidden from Ross even though they now lived together.

And slept together.

No, that wasn't exactly correct.

They had sex and then went their separate ways to their separate bedrooms.

Then, in the morning, they pretended they were nothing more than Ben's parents. Cordial strangers who happened to share the same space. Sometime between his meeting with his brother and sister at the TCC clubhouse and that evening when she'd returned home from work, he'd grown distant, unfailingly polite—colder. But just with her.

With Ben, he was simply wonderful. After Ben was born, and Charlotte had faced those nights of midnight feedings, crying, explosive diapers and runny noses alone, she'd wondered how different things could've been if Ross were there. If she'd had someone to share the load. And now she didn't have to imagine. As aloof as he was with her, Ross poured all of his affection into their son. Even her parents, who'd been understandably shocked and confused when she'd confessed about Ross being Ben's father, respected Ross for how he'd stepped up and taken to parenthood with an obvious enthusiasm. Though Charlotte's unease about forever being connected in some way to Rusty and her fear of his retaliation hadn't faded, she couldn't deny Ben adored his father.

She also couldn't deny her growing feelings for Ross.

Stupid. Stupid. Stupid.

She mentally slapped her palm to her forehead over and over. As if that could shake some latent sense of self-preservation loose.

What was it with her continually falling for the same unavailable and totally inappropriate man? What did that say about her? What was it about herself that made her believe she wasn't worthy of a man who would put her first, be proud to claim her as his own, be fully committed to her?

For most of her life, she'd longed for a relationship like her parents. Total devotion. Yet, the first time she'd fallen in love, it was with a man who'd been okay with keeping her a secret from his family, his friends, the world. Yes, she'd had her reasons for agreeing to the clandestine affair, too. But deep inside, where the most vulnerable desires of her heart hid, she'd longed for him to say, "fuck that," and shout his delight in being with her to anyone who would listen. Just as she'd longed for him to stop her from going to California, to ask her to stay for him. For *them*.

She'd promised herself she'd never place herself in that predicament again. But now, here she stood. In a gorgeous home she could never afford on her own, in the exclusive, gated community of Pine Valley, living with Ross Edmond as his baby's mother. Falling for the same man again.

And her love for him was still a secret.

"You look beautiful."

Her head jerked up, heart pounding a double-time cadence. Ross leaned against the doorway, a shoulder propped against the jamb, hands in the pockets of his black tuxedo pants. As if her body had a "clap on" switch, just the sight of him had her belly clenching, lust lighting up her veins like the Vegas strip, and her sex pulsing.

Dammit. She returned her gaze to her reflection in the mirror, but that didn't eradicate the image of him from her brain. Dirty blond hair tamed and waving away from his stunning face erected of strong, arrogant angles and carnal curves. Tall, big body clothed in a white shirt, bow tie and pants that showcased the lean, muscular perfection of his frame. She intimately knew the strength of that body. Knew how he could restrain and unleash its power.

A curl of heat spiraled through her, whispering over her nipples and winding down to the empty, aching flesh between her thighs. Deliberately, she reminded herself that he'd probably uttered those same words to hundreds of women.

The compliment wasn't anything special to him—and neither was she.

"Thank you," she said, giving herself a mental fist pump when her voice emerged even, unaffected. "Although that has more to do with the dress—which you would know since you had it sent over," she added dryly.

The deep purple, sequin-embellished, floor-length gown

skimmed over her curves like a lover's caress. The wide dolman-style sleeves cuffed at her wrists, and the neckline plunged to a point beneath her breasts. A skinny belt of the same material cinched her middle, emphasizing the indent of her waist.

It was the most beautiful, expensive thing she'd ever owned besides the necklace he'd given her.

He moved fully into the closet and appeared behind her in the mirror. At five foot eight, she wasn't a short woman, but he dwarfed her. And then quickly, a visual of them from the night before flashed in her head. Her, on her hands and knees. Him, behind her, covering her...

She briefly closed her eyes, but the image burned brighter, hotter. When she opened her eyes, they clashed with Ross's hooded, ice-blue gaze. No, not ice. Heat and smoke.

Tension filled the closet, winding around them, and she could feel the stroke of his perusal over the skin bared by the daring neckline. She tried to smother the shiver working its way through her body. Tried and failed.

Apprehension that was purely feminine flared inside her, and she could do nothing but watch him. Wait for his next move. Half hope, half dread he would strip her of the dress and take her down to the closet floor and ease the sensual pain spasming in her sex.

Strip her of her dignity while he was at it.

"What's ridiculous?" he asked.

She blinked. Relief and disappointment cascaded through her, and she quickly recovered, running their conversation back in her head and realizing he must've been standing in the closet doorway longer than she'd noticed.

"All of this." She waved a hand from the top of her hair, which the stylist had fashioned into an elegant yet edgy Mohawk, and down her body, encompassing the gown. "I'm a chef. Not a socialite. I should be at my restaurant, cooking on a Saturday night, not attending some party. The most talking I do is giving orders in the kitchen and meeting customers tableside. And even then, I try to keep it as short as possible. This—" she once more flicked a hand up and down her frame "—isn't me."

"How do you know?" he countered, shifting closer so his chest brushed her spine. "Maybe this is just an aspect of who you are. Your dream is to become a master chef. That could take you around the world, to television, to endorsements. And all of that requires socializing with people, selling yourself. Consider this a training ground for the future." His words painted a picture she'd dreamed of, craved. She lifted her gaze from her neckline to meet his eyes. Did he believe she could obtain that future? Did he believe in…her? A merciless hand squeezed her heart, and she silently cursed herself for even caring about his opinion—caring about his esteem. She *was* enough, dammit!

"And Jeremy obviously thinks the same, since he approved and fully supported you attending this *party*." His lips twisted into a sardonic smile around her terminology for the swank event scheduled for this evening. "He understands you are the face of Sheen and the connection with Soiree on the Bay will only increase his profile in Royal as well as nationally, perhaps internationally."

He skimmed the backs of his fingers down her cheek, dropping to caress her throat before lowering his arm back to his side. Her skin pulsed and tingled from the contact as if it'd been sunburned.

"Besides, Brett Harston, Lila Jones and Valencia Donovan will be there," he added, referring to the other members of the advisory board.

Since joining the board, Charlotte had become friends with the other members. She snorted. If anyone had told her just a month ago that she could claim a self-made millionaire, a Chamber of Commerce employee and the founder of a charity as friends, she would've escorted them to a waiting Uber with an admonition about drinking too much.

But here she was, chummy with members of Royal high society, wearing a gown that probably cost more than her car down payment, and getting ready to attend an event at the famed Texas Cattleman's Club.

She sighed, about to rub her damp palms down her thighs, but catching herself at the last minute. *This dress isn't your food-splattered chef jacket*, she silently scolded.

"Well, I'm as ready as I'll ev—"

"What's this?"

She turned at Ross's harsh bark, and her throat spasmed, trapping her breath. Seemingly of their own accord, her fingers drifted to her bare neck, where the necklace currently clenched in his fist had rested minutes earlier.

"I—" She couldn't squeeze anything else past her constricted throat.

God, she'd been so careful. Hadn't expected him to show up in her room or her closet. But none of her intentions mattered now. Not with that arctic glare pinning her to the spot and his body so taut he practically vibrated with the blast of frigid rage rolling off him.

"Why do you still have this?" he demanded in a low, dark tone that rumbled with…emotion. Not just anger. Something else—something almost raw—threaded through it. And though she couldn't identify it, she trembled underneath it. "Charlotte," Ross growled.

She jerked at the sound of her name, dragging her gaze from the dangling pendant and chain to once more meet his stare. And try not to flinch from it.

"It's mine," she said. "You gave it to me."

"I know that, dammit," he snapped. "I remember everything I ever gave you. *Everything.* And when you ran away to California, you left it all. I went into the guesthouse afterward. It was empty except for all of the earrings, bracelets, clothes I'd given you. Like they were a message you wanted to make sure I received. That they—like me—meant nothing. Just trash to throw away once you were done with them."

With me.

He didn't utter those two words, but they echoed between them as if they'd been shouted at the top of his lungs.

"That's not true," she whispered. Leaving those things behind had been a desperate act of self-protection. It had been her survival instinct kicking in. She couldn't take any reminder of him with her to California. Because they would've been torture, constant souvenirs from a time when she'd been at her happiest—when she'd been fatalistically and foolishly in love. She couldn't keep those pieces of him and make a new life for herself absent of him.

Little had she known that she'd left with the most permanent of reminders inside her.

"Then what is the truth? Did this accidentally make the journey to California?" He chuckled, the serrated edge of it pricking her skin, her heart.

"Actually, yes," she admitted. "I didn't know it was in my suitcase until I arrived there." She clearly remembered that moment when she'd found the jewelry in her carry-on. Remembered how she'd broken down, curled on the bed, clutching it to her chest. How ironic that the pendant was heart-shaped, when hers had been shattered so completely.

"And yet you kept it? Why not pawn it? Believe me, it would've brought you a pretty penny. Several hundred thousand of them," he scoffed, the corner of his mouth pulling into a cruel smile. "Why, Charlotte? For once, give me a straight answer."

"What are you angry at, Ross?" she asked, forcing herself to face that stare that both froze her blood and heated it. "Why do you care?"

"You left," he accused in a low roar.

And there it was. The crux of why he would never forgive her. Not for having a baby he'd known nothing about. Not for missing out on two years of his son's life. No, she'd had the audacity to walk away from him before he could do the honors. To take his favorite toy of the moment away from him when he hadn't been finished playing.

If her heart hadn't already been battered, scarred and calcified, it might've broken all over again.

"I'm sorry," she replied, and surprise flickered in his narrowed stare. "I apologize for not remaining in Royal as your dirty secret. Please forgive me for being exhausted with remaining here as someone you hid out of shame."

She drew her shoulders back and tilted her chin higher, desperately grasping for an aloof mask that concealed the pain throbbing inside her like an open wound.

"You want a straight answer? Okay. You're right. I could've thrown the necklace away or pawned it. God knows the money I could've gotten for it would've helped. But I didn't. I kept it because every time I saw it, touched it, I remembered that for almost a year I allowed myself to be involved in an affair that demeaned me. That I lowered my personal standards to become the plaything of a man who deemed me good enough for a fuck but not to escort past the kitchen. Every time I wear that necklace it's a reminder to myself to never repeat that mistake. A reminder that I'm worth more than being a receptacle for a rich man's lust."

The air crackled with their fury, her hurt, her pain. The bitterness of her words lay acrid on her tongue, leaving a grimy residue that no amount of mouthwash—or apologies—could rinse clean.

I didn't mean it.

The cry screamed inside her like a banshee. It wailed in her head, begging her to say it. But she couldn't. Because part of her—that lonely, pregnant woman who'd felt betrayed by the man she'd loved—had meant every festering word.

"At least we know where we stand with each other," Ross finally said into the thick, deafening silence. "Here." He dropped the necklace on the island, the pendant clacking against the marble top. "I wouldn't want you to lose it." Turning on his heel, he strode toward the closet door. And she curled her fingers into her palms, convincing herself she didn't want to stroke the rigid line of his spine. Or brush a caress over the perfectly cut hair above the collar of his shirt. "Let me know when you're ready. We can't be late," he instructed without glancing back at her.

Then he disappeared through the door, leaving her alone. Except for the echo of her cruel words.

Twelve

"How're you enjoying yourself, Charlotte?" Billy Holmes appeared at her elbow, holding two glasses of wine.

Giving Ross's friend and business partner a smile, she accepted one of the flutes and immediately sipped. Alcoholic fortification was an absolute must to get through this night.

"What's not to enjoy?" she replied, glancing around the crowded, cavernous great room.

Whoever Ross and Billy hired to decorate needed a fat tip. The designer had turned what could've been an austere room with its cross-beamed cathedral ceiling and dark wood floors into a winter wonderland. White lights and flowers with boughs of greenery wound around tall pillars and along the massive fireplace. Crystal center-pieces adorned the round tables and mini trees painted white, and entwined with more lights, added an almost fairy-tale air. And strategically placed in all that ethereal beauty were brochures, pamphlets and even samples from Soiree on the Bay's attending vendors, sponsors and the charities benefiting from the donations. Before she'd left work earlier, she'd overseen the samples from Sheen—an Alaskan king crab cake with a sweet and spicy roulade sauce and squares of ham, feta and sweet potato quiche.

Last time she'd checked, there'd only been a few dishes left of each.

As if reading her mind, Billy murmured, "Great wine. Great food." He cocked his head. "Your samples have disappeared, and dinner hasn't even been served yet. I'd claim that as a ringing endorsement of Sheen and its chef. Congratulations." He toasted her with his glass and grinned, his blue eyes gleaming. "Far be it from me to brag, but I unashamedly accept full credit for bringing you into the fold."

Charlotte chuckled. "Well, I'm so glad you're above an 'I told you so,'" she drawled. "I admit, I had my reservations about joining the festival, but they've mostly been laid to rest. This is a great move for Sheen."

"And for you, Charlotte," Billy added, briefly cupping her elbow before dropping his arm back to his side. "A restaurant is only as strong as its chef, and your reputation as an extraordinary culinary artist precedes you. So thank you for taking a leap with us."

She nodded, unsure how to respond to the outpouring of praise. Ross's words from earlier floated through her head. *Consider this a training ground for the future.* According to him, she belonged here, receiving compliments as her due.

Of course, that had been before the blowup that had decimated all the ground they'd recovered.

Billy cleared his throat, and stared down into his glass, lightly swirling the wine. "Charlotte," he murmured, lifting his head to meet her gaze. "I don't mean to pry, but Ross is my best friend. And I can't help but notice there seems to be some—" he hesitated "—*distance* between you two tonight. Is everything okay?"

The "We're fine" danced on her tongue, but it lodged in her throat, the lie refusing to be uttered. Instead, she avoided that concerned scrutiny under the pretense of surveying the room. And inevitably, her perusal landed on Ross. Surrounded by his brother, sister and a small crowd, he appeared to be the charming, charismatic playboy she'd always known. Not a care in the world. As she watched, a beautiful brunette in a slinky gold dress inched up to his side and laid a hand on his arm. He bowed his head over her, and—

Nope. She turned away, raising her glass for a healthy gulp of wine. Not even going to do it to herself.

"That's the daughter of one of our largest investors besides The Edmond Organization. Believe me, there's nothing inappropriate going on between them," Billy said, his gentle tone almost painful.

Was she that obvious?

How could Ross's friend see what she tried so hard to hide?

"Doesn't matter," she replied, and the smile she forced felt brittle to her own self. "Ross and I are just co-parents. He's free to do whatever—or whomever—he wants."

"As long as I've known Ross, things have seemed to come easy to him. Most definitely because of his last name and family. Then add in his looks, which would make a lesser man completely insecure," he said, flashing her a smile, "and a magnetism that just seems to draw people to him, and he hasn't had to struggle. Not that I'm implying he isn't a hard worker, because he is. But it hasn't been until you came back to Royal and he learned about Ben that he's been truly challenged for the first time in his life. And he's risen to it. Being a father has given him new purpose, and yet, I can't imagine how scary all of this must be for him. So please, as his friend, I'm asking you not to give up on him. You and Ben, you're good for him."

"Yes, we're so good for Ross that his father disinherited him because of us," she said, battling back the warmth that skated too close to hope. "Did you see the two of them tonight? Rusty barely spared Ross a glance."

Billy sighed, slipping a hand in his front pocket. "I admire Rusty. He's a brilliant businessman, and no one can deny that. But the personality that makes him a force to be reckoned with in the industry is also the same personality that he brings to his family. C'mon, Charlotte, you worked in that house, you've been around the family enough to know there were issues way before now. They'll get through this—they're strong, and underneath the stubbornness is an abundance of love. But I don't know if Ross will make it without you and Ben. You two were the catalyst for this change, and he needs you."

He shrugged a shoulder. "Like I said, I don't know what happened between you two before tonight, but my friend is more focused and happier than he's been in a long time. So again, please hang in there with him. Don't give up."

Billy squeezed her hand, then walked away, his plea echoing in her head.

My friend is more focused and happier than he's been in a long time... Don't give up.

There was so much between her and Ross—too much. Mistrust. Hurt. Resentment. Insecurity. As their argument earlier in the closet proved.

And yet… She glanced across the room and unerringly sought him out. Though still surrounded by people, for once, a smile didn't curve his mouth. Someone wasn't commanding his attention. He stood there, an island in a sea of admirers, hangers-on and wannabe lovers. Alone. Untouchable. Lonely. Did any of them truly see the real man behind the tuxedo, the magnetism, the playboy exterior? The man who longed for a domineering father's approval and concealed a wounded heart behind an indifferent demeanor? The man who'd unconditionally accepted a son he hadn't known about and loved him without reserve.

No, none of them saw *that* man. But she'd been gifted with glimpses of him. And those glimpses only made her crave more of him. Made her yearn for the impossible.

That he would someday give her the same uninhibited love he so freely offered Ben.

What would it be like to love him without fear of rejection, without baggage from the past, without dread that outside forces would come between them? With the security that she was enough?

It would be the kind of dream that slowly faded when morning arrived, but which she desperately tried to cling to even if only for a few sacred moments.

As if he felt her gaze on him, Ross glanced up, and their eyes met. And even though a room separated them, she reeled from the intensity of that stare. In spite of the harmful words she'd hurled at him earlier, she needed to feel connected to him. Needed to somehow work toward erasing the distance that she'd placed between them.

God, she just needed him.

Heart thumping against her sternum, she tipped her head to the side, hoping he understood her message to follow her. Not waiting lest she lose her nerve to go through with this, she turned and slipped out one of the side doors. She walked past several closed doors, and randomly choosing one that was far enough away from the great room, she twisted the knob and entered. A large and curtainless picture window dominated one wall, allowing moonlight to stream through and illuminate what appeared to be a private and informal meeting room. A stone fireplace, several big armchairs, a small couch and a couple of coffee tables filled the space.

She didn't make it past the first chair when the door opened behind her and clicked shut. Inhaling a breath, she held it for several seconds, and then slowly released it, pivoting to face Ross. In the semidark, his large frame loomed larger, and her belly fluttered. With his impassive expression, he betrayed nothing of his thoughts or emotions. But he was here. And she'd take that as a positive sign.

"Ross," she began, then stopped. Because she had no

idea what to say. *I just needed you to look* at *me and not* through *me* didn't seem like a good opener. She shook her head, tried again. "Ross, I wanted to apologize. About earlier. This night is important to you, and what happened between us threw a pall over it that doesn't belong. I'm sorry for that."

"Is that what you and Billy were talking about?"

She blinked, taken aback by the abrupt question. "No," she said. "Well, not really…"

"Which is it?" he pressed in the low, quiet tone that still set her instinctive alarm system clanging. "Because it looked like a serious conversation, given the way you two were cozied up together."

She frowned, lifting her hands. "Wait. What the hell is going on here?"

"He asked would I mind if he asked you out. Did I ever tell you that?" He stepped away from the door, stalking closer to her. "After he first met you at Sheen," he continued, not granting her the chance to reply. "He called you beautiful and wanted you."

"What did you tell him?" she breathed, still unsure of what was happening but rapidly getting tugged down by the undertow of desire swirling around them.

Ross might appear the epitome of cool composure, but his eyes… They burned bright. Anger? Lust? Didn't matter, because both caused the air to snag in her lungs, dampened her palms and beaded her nipples into tight points, setting off a pulsing throb in her sex.

Jesus, what did that say about her?

Nothing flattering.

"I told him to go for it." He moved even closer. And closer still, until the lapels of his tuxedo jacket grazed the tips of her breasts. She just managed to swallow a gasp. "I didn't know you were the mother of my son then, but the reason still stands. We're sometimes acquaintances, sometimes enemies. Co-parents who want nothing from each other but the best for our son. We're a mistake that are now connected for the next sixteen years, right?"

"Ross," she whispered, voice breaking. "I'm—"

"Sorry," he finished, flicking a hand, the gold of his watch glinting in the shadowed room. "You said that. Did Billy flirt with you? Ask you how we were doing?"

"Yes, but not how you're insinuating," she objected, frowning.

He arched an eyebrow, and the mocking gesture sparked a flame of irritation. "Really? And what am I insinuating?" he drawled.

"If I didn't know better—and believe me, I do—I'd swear you were jealous. Which is ridiculous considering you were just out there with women not just hanging from your every word, but from *you*," she snapped.

Shit.

She didn't lose her temper often, but dammit, when she did, her mouth ran like a swollen spring river—fast, babbling and all over the place.

"And if I didn't know better, I'd think that was jealousy," he taunted, cocking his head and peering down at her through a thick fringe of lashes. "Fortunately, I know better, too. But just in case you need clarification, other than how they can benefit the festival, I don't give a damn about those women. And I definitely don't want to fuck them. You're the only one I need to be inside of. The only one who can get me hard just by breathing." He tunneled his fingers through the fall of her hair and tugged, yanking her head back so his mouth hovered over hers. "And you're wrong, Charlotte." He pulled harder, and she sank her teeth into her bottom lip, trapping the groan that almost slipped free at the corresponding tingle across her scalp. "I am jealous. Two times Billy touched you. And both times

I battled back the urge to rush across the room and shove him against the wall and away from you."

Shock crackled through her, the static of it convincing her she'd misheard. She slowly shook her head. "You don't—"

"Mean it?" he interrupted her once more, completing her sentence. "Yes, I do. To you, I might be a mistake," he repeated what she'd called him again for the second time in as many minutes, and it shredded her. "But to all of them out there, including my friend, you're mine. At night, when you're under me, moaning my name, coming around my dick, you're mine. Aren't you?" He rolled his hips, his erection, thick and hard, grinding against her belly. "Aren't you, baby?"

She squeezed her eyes closed. Trembled. And rasped, "Yes."

His mouth crushed down on hers, consuming the echo of the word and robbing her breath. Hard, rough, hot. Nothing gentle about this kiss. It was pure lust and aggression. Pure need. She shoved her fingers through his hair, fisting the cool strands, her ravenous desire rising to match his.

She didn't give a damn that just down the hallway, hundreds of people congregated. Didn't care that anyone could easily open that door—just as easily as she'd done. No, she didn't spare one more thought on any of that. Everything in her focused on this man devouring her mouth like he'd been on a hunger strike, and she was his first meal.

His arm wrapped around her waist, hauling her tighter to him, and his big frame surrounded her. Protecting her. Even as she tumbled headlong into the wild sexual chaos he never failed to stir within her, she didn't fight or fear it. Not when she had utter confidence that he would be her anchor.

"Put your legs around me," he ordered seconds before hiking her into the air.

She obeyed, wrapping herself around him, trusting his

strength, his power. In several long strides, he had her back pressed to the wall. One glance over his shoulder assured her they were steeped in shadow, the pale moonbeams not reaching them in their corner. Of course, Ross would've considered their privacy and her modesty. Even if by chance someone passed by the window that looked out over the lawn and stable, they wouldn't glimpse her and Ross. The knowledge allowed her to sink further into him, under his spell.

With the wall behind her and his body aligned against her front, she was trapped. And didn't want to escape. Cupping his jaw, she settled her thumbs on his chin and tugged. Demanding he open wider for her. Triumph and satisfaction sang through her when he complied, cocking his head so she could thrust deeper, help herself to more of him.

God help her, but she would never get enough of this man. She acknowledged that fact with a fatalistic certainty. She could no more change it than she could who fathered her baby. Ross had imprinted himself on her so long ago, branding her with his special mark of passion, of possession. Maybe it hadn't been time, work and motherhood that had prevented her from becoming romantically involved again in these past three years. Maybe it had been the knowledge that no one else could make her fly and die at the same time.

"Touch me," she pleaded, unashamed in her need. Peppering fevered kisses across his cheek and jaw, she whispered, "Please, touch me."

The night at The Bellamy, it'd been she who'd sought to help him forget with passion. Now she needed him to do the same for her. Help her forget she'd hurt him with her angry words. Help her forget she'd hurt herself.

"Where?" He cupped her breast in his big hand, his thumb rubbing her nipple over her dress. She whimpered, arching into the caress. "Here?"

"No." She wrapped her fingers around his, and with the other hand, tugged the neckline to the side, exposing her bra and flesh. Still not satisfied, she yanked down the cup, freeing herself. "Here."

He bent his head over her, his growl of approval humming against her skin as he sucked her deep. Pulling on her. Licking her. Tormenting her. She rasped nonsensical words as he worked her over. They could've been praise or pleas, she didn't know. Didn't care. Just as long as he kept hauling her to the brink. Here they let down their guards, their swords, and loved.

Or at least she did.

Biting her lip, she clutched his head, lifted it and brought it to the neglected breast. Together, they bared her, and together they offered her up to his voracious mouth. She shook in his arms, undulating wildly, rubbing her sex against his dick. Yes, layers of clothing separated them, but it didn't prevent each stroke and glide from sending more and more pleasure streaking through her. She could come from just this. From just his mouth and fingers and riding his cock.

"Back pocket," he snapped, abandoning her breasts to capture her mouth again. "Get my wallet and take the condom out." Impatient fingers dropped to her thighs, gathering her dress around her hips. "Now, Charlotte."

"No," she breathed, flattening her palms against his chest and pushing. He jerked his head up, his eyes blazing down into hers. She shoved again, and he stepped back, and in spite of the disbelief flaring in his gaze, gently lowered her to the floor. "Not yet."

And she dropped to her knees.

"Fuck." His groan reverberated in the room, and he didn't stop her as she loosened the tab on his pants. Instead he slapped his hands to the wall, looming over her. She tipped her head back, meeting his narrowed stare as she lowered the zipper, dipped her hand inside his black boxer briefs and pulled him free. "Baby, you don't have to do this."

"Yes, I do," she murmured, rubbing a thumb over the swollen and already slick head. "I need this. And so do you."

Without hesitation, she took him inside her. Their twin moans filtered through the air, followed by his sharp bark of pleasure. Or was it pain?

Closing her eyes, she lost herself in the earthy taste, the soft and steely texture, the heavy density of him. How he filled her mouth to overflowing. She fisted the bottom half of his cock, pumping it in a steady rhythm, her lips bumping her fingers on the tail end of each stroke.

"So good," she whispered, dragging her tongue up his length. "I'd forgotten how good you taste."

"Are you trying to make me come right here in this pretty mouth, baby?" He cupped her cheek, the tender gesture belying the roughness of his voice. "Keep talking like that, and I will."

"I want all of you," she confessed on a low rasp before sucking him back in. He probably assumed she meant his sex, his body, the rapture they gave each other. But she didn't. She yearned for *everything*. His body. His touch. His time. His laughter.

His heart.

Even as she pleasured him, tears glinted her eyes. Because part of her knew this would probably be all they could have. Too many words, bruises and wounds stood between them. Too many secrets.

Desperation plowed into her, and to battle it, she swallowed him deeper, his tip hitting the back of her throat.

"Enough," he snarled, jerking free, and cuffing her upper arms he hauled her to her feet. "I want inside you," he muttered, hurriedly removing his wallet and a condom. In moments, he sheathed himself and lifted her back in his arms, his hands cupping her ass. "Take me inside, baby."

Breath blasting in and out of her swollen lips, she reached between them, encircled his erect flesh, pulled the wet panel of her panties aside and guided it to her entrance. Wrapping her arms around his neck, she lifted herself and sank down. Until all of him was firmly surrounded by her.

Oh, God. She buried her face against his throat. As often as they'd had sex since that first time at The Bellamy, she'd become used to him. But she'd never become used to how completely he filled her. Branded her. *Completed* her.

"Move," she ordered. Begged. "Please, move."

Pressing her harder against the wall, Ross grabbed her hair and tugged her head up. "I want to watch it," he said, his gaze roaming over her face.

She didn't need to ask the definition of "it." Because when his hips drew back, then thrust into her, and she cried out, lips parting, eyes closing, he murmured, "That's it."

He didn't grant her any mercy. Using the leverage of the wall, he slammed into her over and over again, alternating between slow, dirty grinds and hard, abrupt strokes. Each time he buried himself in the core of her, the base of his cock massaged the top of her sex, agitating the bundle of nerves there. The slap of skin punctuated the air along with his grunts and her hoarse cries. He dragged her to the edge of the abyss, and she fought it, then willingly went.

She couldn't breathe. Couldn't think. Couldn't do anything but break.

And God, did she.

She erupted, shaking and seizing in his arms, flinging herself into ecstasy with no care of how she landed. *If* she landed. Her sex clamped down on his cock, and his growl echoed in her ear as he drove past her quivering flesh, pursuing his own end. She held on, and though exhaustion pulled at her, she bucked her hips, giving him the same measure he'd gifted her.

Her name, shouted in his raw voice, rebounded off the walls of the room, and she finally wilted against him, confident he wouldn't let her fall.

At least not physically.

Because for her heart, it was too little, too late.

Thirteen

Ross sat in his car in the same parking space that had been his since he'd officially started working for The Edmond Organization six years ago. He snorted. He might've been disinherited and fired, but at least his father hadn't gotten around to reassigning his spot.

Drumming his fingers against the steering wheel, he stared at the building that had been his home away from home. And now he had neither. He sighed, scrubbing a hand down his face.

What the hell was he doing here?

What did he hope to accomplish with this visit?

Immediately, Ben's face drifted across his mind's eye. Before he'd dropped his son off at his grandparents' house for an afternoon visit, Ben had wrapped his arms around his legs, beaming up at him. No hesitation. No uncertainty. His son was so secure and confident in his father's love that he'd demanded, "Daddy, kiss bye!" without any fear of rejection. Certain he'd receive the affection that was his due.

Ross huffed out a soft chuckle, the sound somehow foreign to him in the silence of the car. As was the prickle of heat behind his rib cage. That free display of love had triggered a yearning in him—a yearning that had driven him here instead of his meeting with Billy. Ben deserved to know all of his family. Especially his grandfather. Maybe he and Rusty hadn't enjoyed a loving relationship, but that didn't mean Ross's son couldn't have that with Rusty.

Though it meant swallowing his pride, he had to try.

Not just for his son. But for himself, too.

Resolute, he climbed out the car and headed into the Edmond building. Security had every right to stop him and force him to sign in as a visitor. But the guard on duty only greeted him as Ross walked toward the elevators. Even the pass that only certain personnel possessed to access the executive floor worked. It hadn't been deactivated, as he'd expected.

Frowning, but not questioning his luck—accepting it as fate—he emerged from the elevator onto the hushed floor housing his family's offices. More than a few people did a double take as he strode toward his father's assistant's desk. But he ignored them, focusing instead on the task at hand. Because getting in to see his father without an appointment would be the hugest hurdle.

"Good afternoon, Lisa," he said, smiling at the pretty blonde. "Does Dad have a few minutes available in his schedule for me?"

"Hi, Ross." She offered him a smile in return, though curiosity gleamed in her brown eyes. No doubt wondering what business the disinherited heir could possibly have with his father. She tapped on her keyboard and glanced at her monitor. "He doesn't have a meeting until two, so there's about a half hour free, but—"

"Thanks." He strode past the desk toward the closed double doors. "I'll just go in. No need to announce me."

"But—"

Inside he cringed as he gripped the knob and pushed the door open. That had been an asshole move worthy of a spoiled child, but if he'd allowed her to give Rusty a heads-up that his son wanted to see him, Ross would've spent the rest of the afternoon sitting on one of the couches in the waiting area.

Rusty could carry petty to a whole new level.

His father glanced up at the opening of the door, then scowled. "Ross, what are you doing here?"

Shutting the door behind him, he crossed the huge office, coming to a halt in front of Rusty's desk. He didn't bother taking a seat in one of the visitors' chairs since he most likely wouldn't be here long enough to become comfortable.

"I'm here to see you, Dad. We didn't have a chance to talk Saturday night."

Rusty snorted, tossing down his pen onto his desk. "Is that right? Could be because the rest of us were working while you were up that woman's skirts." His mouth curled into a hard, mocking smile. "Think no one noticed you two disappear? Or that before then, something was off between you? Christ, son, you looked like someone had shot your goddamn dog. Whether you're fucking them or arguing with them, you shouldn't let a woman interfere with business. And you failed on both accounts Saturday."

Heat bloomed beneath his collar, and he slowly dragged in a breath. *You're here to heal the rift, not widen it. You can't tell the old bastard to go to hell.*

The reminder drifted through his head, and after several seconds he could inhale air that wasn't singed by his anger.

"I'm not here to discuss Charlotte," he said.

"What else is there to discuss?" Rusty snapped, slapping his palms to the desk and surging to his feet. "She's at the root of all of this. First, she disrespected my employment and my home by sleeping with my son. Then, she gets pregnant, no doubt on purpose, and when I tell her to get rid of it, she lied about doing that. And then, she has the gall to show up here in Royal again, looking to hook you, an Edmond, with a kid that's her responsibility, not yours, since she made the decision to keep it."

"What kind of man would it make me if I denied my child, abandoned him? That wouldn't make me any better than Sarabeth," he countered.

"Don't bring up that woman's name to me. Your mother was another one who used her children for a big payday and then disappeared. And you can damn well bet that's going to happen with Charlotte," he fumed, jabbing a finger at Ross. "You think you have this happy little family? What happens when she realizes I'm serious about not giving you one red cent, Ross? Do you really believe she's going to stick around? You're being led around by your dick, and I'm not going to stand by and watch it happen. And when she leaves with that boy, I'll be damned if you come crawling back to me."

Each insult barreled into him, delivering strikes to every insecurity and doubt that hid in his subconscious. He was far from penniless, but even with the home he provided for her and Ben, Ross worried it wouldn't be enough. Especially since last week, he'd gone over his finances with his accountant, and as he'd suspected and feared, though he possessed stocks, investments and property, he wouldn't have enough liquid wealth to give her the five-hundred-thousand-dollar payment at the end of their year together. Once he told her the truth, would she pack up Ben and leave? After all, she'd held up her end of the bargain—leaving her home, moving in with him, completing the paperwork to change their son's last name—and the one thing he'd promised her, he couldn't come through on.

I lowered my personal standards to become the plaything of a man who deemed me good enough for a fuck but not to escort past the kitchen. Every time I wear that necklace it's a reminder to myself to never repeat that mistake.

He locked his knees, steadying himself as Charlotte's words threatened to knock him back into the chair. Yes, they'd disappeared during the event and had sex. And later that night, after they returned home, he'd lost himself in her again. But he couldn't eject those words from his head. Couldn't convince himself that, although she'd apologized, she hadn't meant them.

She'd called him a mistake and it was nothing he hadn't thought before. A mistake to her, to his parents, even to the women he'd fucked and forgotten. Which made sense in a screwed-up but logical way. Because if he was truly important to them, how could they so easily walk away from him?

So while he'd had Charlotte's body, he didn't have her loyalty. Definitely not her love, not that he'd asked for that, and not since she'd made it clear he was an error she'd never repeat. The bottom line was he had no hold on her, except their son, that would compel her to stay with him. And Charlotte had proven her capability in raising Ben as a single parent.

No.

The objection blasted through his head, loud and furious. Ben was his son. And regardless of whether she left or not, he wouldn't allow her to take Ben away from him.

"Don't worry, Dad," Ross said, arching an eyebrow and forcing an indifference that was a lie. "I won't come crawling back. And I'll make sure to use you as an example. Both you and Sarabeth."

With that, he spun on his heel and left Rusty's office. His every good intention in this visit had backfired. But he'd emerged crystal clear on one thing.

He couldn't count on his father to be there.

Couldn't depend on Charlotte, either.

The only person who would never fail him was himself.

Fourteen

Charlotte sighed, sliding the key into the front door. Usually, Mondays were a slow night, but for some reason, it seemed as if every person in Royal had decided to drop by Sheen tonight. Jeremy had credited the unprecedented influx with her presence at the Soiree on the Bay fundraising event over the weekend as well as the samples of their dishes. Possibly. She'd shared his opinion with Ross when he'd brought Ben by the restaurant to see her, and he'd managed not to throw an "I told you so" at her.

She frowned, unlocking the door and twisting the knob. Actually, Ross had been distant and aloof tonight. Since Saturday, they'd formed a tenuous truce, but he'd reverted to being that cold, reserved man she'd met at Sheen weeks ago. A tight ball of dread had settled in the pit of her stomach and remained there for the rest of the evening like a pebble she couldn't shake from her shoe. It had been a relief when the night ended, because she'd come to a decision sometime between preparing the sauce for her signature dish and plating dishes for a party of twelve—she needed to be honest with Ross.

She had to tell him that as hard as she'd tried, as angry as she'd been, she'd never stopped loving him.

Fear trickled through her as she entered the house. But

intertwined with those dark tendrils was excitement, too. He'd been jealous, possessive on Saturday. And there was no denying he'd been hurt by her. That had to mean he felt *something* more for her than he would for a tolerable person to co-parent with… God, she hoped so. Because she'd been here before, three years ago. Uncertain. Scared. Hopeful.

Only to end up broken, devastated and alone.

Would she survive that kind of agony again?

Would she have to?

It was those two questions that had her wavering back and forth. She didn't know if her heart could stand losing him again…but what if she didn't lose him?

That damn hope. It was both a blessing and a curse.

Still, she couldn't just continue to exist in this torturous limbo. Tonight, she'd have her answer. Tonight, she'd—

"Dammit." She stumbled to a halt, her toe throbbing in protest at whatever she'd just stubbed it on. Frowning, she glanced down. "What the hell?" she murmured, spotting the set of black luggage in the foyer. The smallest of the two listed to the side from the kick she'd inadvertently delivered to it.

"Charlotte, I need to speak to you."

She shifted her gaze from the suitcases to Ross, who stood just inside the entryway to the living room. It was a little after twelve, and most nights when she arrived home, worn jeans or loose-fitting sleep pants adorned his tall frame. But tonight, a dark gray suit had replaced the pajamas and T-shirt.

Her frown deepened. "Hey." She set her bag and purse down on the table beside the door. "Did I forget you had a business trip or were headed out of town?"

"No," he said, both his voice and face shuttered. That knot in her stomach pulled taut, and dread crept inside her, an unwelcome intruder. "Can we talk in here?"

He turned, but she didn't move. "No," she whispered. He

halted and slowly pivoted back to face her, and she shook her head. "No," she repeated, stronger, louder. "Whatever you have to say, we can do it right here. Especially since you'll be leaving directly afterward, right?" His expression remained a mask of stone, but she caught the flicker in his eyes, and she let loose a low, jagged chuckle that abraded her throat. A heavy, suffocating weight settled on her chest, shortening her breath, causing an echo in her ears. She recognized this feeling. The forerunner of panic, of an onslaught of fear. But she shoved it back, focusing on the silent, brooding and cruelly beautiful man before her. "Let's just get this over with so you have easy access to the door."

"Fine." He nodded, sliding his hands into the front pockets of his suit. How could he be so cold? So unfeeling when she was shattering into pieces? "I haven't been honest with you. After a meeting with my financial advisor, I can't afford to pay you the half-million dollars that I promised. It wouldn't be fair of me to expect you to hold up your end of our agreement when I can't. Of course, you and Ben can continue to stay here—"

"Liar."

Ross's head jerked back as if her accusation had delivered a verbal punch.

"I never asked for that money in the first place, so don't try to place the blame for you leaving on it. You saw your father today, didn't you?"

"I don't know how you found out about it—and not that it matters—but, yes," he said, eyes narrowing on her.

"Gina called me because she was trying to get in touch with you, and you weren't answering your phone. Apparently, your father was on the warpath today because you showed up at the office. She wanted to make sure you were okay." Charlotte shook her head, a bone-deep weariness and ache invading her. "And to think I felt that this time, maybe, just maybe, things would be different."

Ross sliced a hand through the air. "I don't know what conclusions you've drawn in your head, Charlotte, but like I said, this has nothing to do with Rusty. I'm trying to do what's right here. What's fair."

"I don't know if you truly believe that or if you're really trying to convince yourself of it." She wrapped her arms around herself. "When I left for California, I so desperately wanted you to fight for me. To ask me to stay. To stand up to your father and tell him you and I were together and nothing he could do would change your mind. But you didn't. And I resented you for a long time because of it. But this time, you did exactly that. Maybe not for me, but for Ben. Still, you defied Rusty, and it made me hopeful. It made me foolish," she added with a self-deprecating chuckle. "Because all it took was one visit with Rusty and you fell right back in line. Same result, just took a bit longer."

"That's bullshit," he snapped, eyes bright with anger. "I'm not abandoning you or Ben. I still want joint custody. Or are you trying to tell me that because I don't want to live in this house, I can't continue to see my son on a regular basis? Because I won't allow you to cut me out of his life."

"Wow," she whispered. "For a moment, I could've sworn Rusty Edmond stood before me instead of Ross." He flinched, paling at her direct hit, but she didn't back down. "Contrary to whatever nonsense your father might've spouted about me only wanting you for your money and withholding Ben to get it, I would never do that to Ben. He adores you. But I'd also never do that to you."

She tunneled her fingers through her hair and briefly closed her eyes. Ordering herself not to shed one damn tear in front of him. He didn't deserve to see her pain. "You just don't get it, Ross," she rasped. "Three years ago, I fell in love with you. You. An Edmond. A man I should've run far away from. But I couldn't, because under the bravado was a unique, vulnerable, funny, sweet, *good* man who made me feel more special than I'd ever felt in my life. You weren't your father, no matter how hard Rusty tried to make you conform to be the image of him. And I loved that about you."

"You never said…" Ross stared at her, eyes dark with surprise, body unnaturally stiff. "Why didn't you…"

"Because you didn't want that from me. I knew what I was to you even if I hoped for different. Your father would never accept me, and when you surrendered to that and ended things with me because Rusty didn't see me as worthy enough, I knew it would break me. So I left before it could happen. I ran from here, but I couldn't outrun my heart. And then I found out I was pregnant. I accepted then, even after the phone call and letter, that you would always be a part of me. So when you appeared back in my life, in Ben's life, I convinced myself I could be happy with our co-parenting-with-benefits arrangement. But I lied. That's what I planned to tell you tonight. I want all of you or nothing. Seems like you'd already made that decision for both of us, though."

Not giving him a chance to reply—because really, what could he say when he literally had his bags packed?—she crossed the foyer for the staircase. But she paused at the bottom step, hand on the newel.

She didn't look at him as she offered him one last confession.

"Do you remember when you gave me the diamond heart necklace?" she murmured. "You'd taken me to the resort on Appaloosa Island, and one night after making love, you surprised me with it. You'd bought it at one of the shops because it reminded you of me. You said the heart reminded you of mine—beautiful and precious. That's why I kept the necklace, Ross. Because of all the gifts you'd given me, this one meant the most. No motive behind it. You bought it simply because you'd been thinking of me. And my heart."

She climbed the steps and didn't look back.

Fifteen

"Ross? A word."

Ross froze at his father's request. Request, hell. Rusty had issued the order and expected to be obeyed. He glanced at the door to the meeting room, debating whether he wanted to give his father the "word" he wanted. But in the end, he remained in place, curiosity momentarily overriding animosity and bitterness.

"You okay?" Asher murmured, pausing beside him. His brother, sister, Billy and Rusty had met at the clubhouse for a meeting about the festival, since Ross refused to return to the family's office building. He wasn't a fan of going where he wasn't wanted. "I can stay."

"No," Ross said, studying Rusty's face as his father tossed Asher an irritated glance. "I'm fine. I'll call you later."

His brother clapped him on the shoulder, and Gina squeezed his hand as she passed by him. Billy patted him on the back, and then moments later, the door closed, leaving him alone with his father.

"What's this about?" Ross asked, crossing his arms.

Rusty took his time answering, rounding the table and hiking a hip on the edge of it. For several long moments, he studied Ross, and he steadily met his father's stare. If

Rusty expected him to fidget like a kid called on the carpet, then he'd have a long wait.

"I heard you're no longer shacking up with that woman and her kid," his father finally said, the smug note in his voice raking over Ross's skin.

"I have to commend the Royal grapevine," Ross drawled. "It's only been three days."

Three interminable, hollow, gray days since he'd walked out of the Pine Valley home he'd bought for his family. Three days since he'd woken up to Ben's laughter and demands for banana pancakes.

Three days since he'd last seen Charlotte. Heard her voice. Inhaled her scent. Touched her body.

He clenched his jaw, fisting the hands in his pockets.

Three days since she'd lobbed her bomb about being in love with him years ago and wanting all of him now.

It was also that long since he'd been able to draw a breath that didn't have razors attached to it. God, why couldn't he carve this Charlotte-sized ache out of his chest? Evict her voice from his head? Only working on the various projects he'd thrown himself into had kept him sane. The projects and Ben.

"News like that travels fast, son," Rusty said.

"I'm *son* now?" Ross chuckled. "Since when? Let me guess. Three days ago."

"You did the right thing, Ross." Rusty nodded, mouth flattening into a grim line. "I hate that I had to take such drastic measures to make you see what a mistake you were making, but if the end result was you coming to your senses, then I'll live with my actions. You deserve someone who adds to your wealth, social standing and reputation, not some faithless, disloyal *cook*," he sneered. "Just tell me the situation has been handled and we can move on from here."

Ross stared at Rusty, shocked by the venom that seemed

directed at Charlotte. Yes, she'd been their employee, but she was also a successful, gifted chef. What the hell had she ever done to deserve Rusty's enmity?

He slashed a hand through the air. Fuck it. His father took classism and snobbery to a whole new level, but he was through allowing his father to run his life like it was one of his subsidiaries.

"Is that what you assumed? That I left Charlotte because of you disinheriting me?" He shook his head, his bark of laughter drawing a fierce frown from his father. "Sorry, Dad, but I regret to inform you that I'm still as much of a disappointment as I was when I left your office. This has nothing to do with you. It was my choice because I was trying to do what was best for her. And Charlotte and Ben aren't a *situation* to be *handled*," he snapped. "He's my son, and she's the mother of my son. She and I aren't living together—" weren't together *at all* "—but I'm not abandoning my son. So your praise might've been a tad premature."

Rusty slid off the edge of the table, standing to his full, intimidating height. Well, it used to be intimidating. Not any longer. Somewhere between watching Charlotte strip herself emotionally bare before walking away and leaving him broken, and checking into The Bellamy, his father's approval and acceptance had stopped being the driving force in his life. There were only two people whose esteem mattered. One loved him unconditionally. And the other? Well, the other, he'd hurt so badly that there was no coming back from it.

"Ross, I don't know what this is, but you need to get your shit together," Rusty thundered. "You will not have any association with that woman or child. This is nonnegotiable."

Ross studied his father as if it were the first time he was truly seeing him. "You want me to choose you over Charlotte, over my son. Which is so damn ironic because in every situation you never offered me the same courtesy.

Business first. Women first. Yourself first. But never me, my happiness, my well-being. No," he stated flatly, with a finality that resonated through him. "I won't do it. Keep your money, your inheritance, your business empire. And if you're stubborn enough to demand it, your title as my father. When my son looks at me with love and respect, knowing I'll always be there for him, that's worth more than anything you could possibly hold over my head. Goodbye, Dad."

He turned and strode toward the door, the crushing weight of guilt, sadness and anger on his chest a little bit lighter.

"Don't you walk away from me, Ross. We're not finished here," Rusty bellowed. Like a child throwing a temper tantrum.

"Yes, Dad, we are."

He opened the door, stepped through and closed it behind him.

Closing it on his past.

Ross handed his car keys to The Bellamy's valet and entered the hotel's entrance. His cell phone jangled in his pocket, and like the last three times his sister had called since he'd left his confrontation with Rusty, he ignored it. He loved Gina, but right now his emotions huddled too close to the surface. They were too raw, and he couldn't hold a conversation with her.

He strode across the lobby toward the elevators, but as he passed the sitting area, a woman rose from one of the chairs. Shock barreled into him, jerking him to a sudden halt.

No. Not today. All the anger, pain and sadness simmering inside him ratcheted to a boil and flowed over him, singing him with memories, bitterness and a little boy's betrayal and love.

"Sarabeth."

His mother's smile wavered but then rallied. Probably all that beauty pageant training. Oh, how Rusty used to go on about that. How he'd found her on the pageant circuit and lifted her out of her lower-middle-class life to rarefied Royal society. And all he'd received in return was a cold-hearted gold digger more concerned with what he could do for her, instead of the wife and mother he'd wanted.

Ross hadn't cared about any of that at the time. At ten, all he'd wanted was his mother.

He studied the tall, willowy blonde as she approached him. Though nearing fifty years old, his mother appeared ten or fifteen years younger. All that free living without the baggage of children could do that to a person, he mused.

"Ross, I'm sorry to ambush you like this," Sarabeth apologized, the blue eyes he'd inherited from her meeting his. She chuckled, and it struck him as nervous. Of course, cornering the son she hadn't seen or talked to in years had to be stressful. "God, in some ways you look exactly the same. I would've recognized you anywhere." When he didn't reply to that, she shook her head, that smile finally fading. "I understand if you'd rather not see me, but if you could give me just a few minutes, I'd really appreciate it."

He smothered his initial instinct to tell her no, and dipped his chin. Pivoting on his heel, he stalked toward The Silver Saddle, trusting her to follow. At two o'clock, most of the tables remained empty, a stark contrast to how it would be jumping with patrons in just three more hours. But for now, he snagged one in a corner that would afford them privacy.

Once they were seated and had placed their orders with their waitress—a beer for him and a white wine for her— she folded her slim hands on the table and gazed at him.

"I'm sorry for staring," she apologized after an awkward silence. "It's just that… It's been a long time. I've missed you."

"I've been in the same town, at the same address all this time," he said brusquely. "If you missed me so much, you knew where to find me."

"I deserve that," she whispered, hooking a strand of hair behind her ear. "There's so much I want to say to you…" She cleared her throat, momentarily dropping her eyes to the table before lifting them to him. "Will you hear me out? Please? And at the end if you still want to walk out of here and have nothing to do with me, then I'll understand."

"Fine." He leaned back in his chair as the waitress set their drinks on the table. Twisting the cap off his beer, he tipped it toward her. "I'm listening."

"Thank you." Her inhale of breath echoed between them, as did the long exhale. "I want to preface this by saying I'm not excusing my absence from your life. I just want to explain my side of it and hope that maybe you can forgive me."

She sipped from her wineglass. For courage? Because that was the reason he gulped down his beer. To try to bolster the bravado to sit here and listen to his mother explain why he hadn't been important enough for her to stay in his life.

"I married your father when I was young—nineteen. Like a fairy tale, he whisked me away to this beautiful home, provided a life I'd only dreamed about. I guess you could say Rusty pampered me, because he did. Beautiful children, a home, clothes, jewelry, cars, vacations abroad—everything I could ever ask for. Except for a faithful husband."

She lifted her glass for another sip, this one a little longer than her last. And when she lowered her arm, her slim fingers slightly trembled around the long stem.

"I couldn't stay in a loveless marriage any longer," she continued, her voice a shade huskier. "Not when I walked in on Rusty with another woman. Asking him for a divorce was terrifying, but at least I had you and your sister. Or at least, I naively believed. As punishment for daring to leave him, Rusty used all his power, including a judge who knew him, to ensure he got custody of you and Gina. I might have received a financial settlement, but what mattered most to me—my children—I lost."

Ross tried to steel his heart against her tale; he'd heard some of it through Rusty. But the cheating, the judge in Rusty's pocket? No, his father had left those details out. Not that either shocked him. When Rusty played to win, he refused to lose at all costs.

Still, she'd left his father. Why had she then divorced her children?

As if she read his mind, she continued, her voice low, pained, "I tried to maintain a relationship with you and Gina. God, I tried. But you two were growing older and preferred to be with your friends rather than a woman who was increasingly becoming a stranger to you. I got it. And Rusty didn't help matters, either. He didn't try to enforce our custody arrangement. Then I couldn't find work here in Royal, and everyone treated me like the scorned ex-wife. I had to leave town simply to survive."

As someone who'd recently been on the receiving end of Rusty's hardhanded tactics, an unprecedented empathy he'd never offered his mother swelled within him. He understood survival.

He understood trying to escape the steel, booby-trapped box Rusty could trap a person in.

"Now, in hindsight, I wish I'd fought harder to get you back. To try another court if one didn't listen. The Edmond name and power extends beyond Royal, and I didn't have the financial resources to fight. But if I'd known divorcing him would mean losing you and your sister, I would've stayed married to him, regardless of his mistreatment and cheating."

She stretched her arms across the table, hesitated, but

then carefully clasped his hands in hers. "Ross, I have so many regrets. And the main one is allowing fear of your rejection to keep me from reaching out to you in all this time. As your mother, it was up to me to connect with you, not place that burden on you. I just ask for your forgiveness." A tear slipped down her cheek, and she swiped at it before clasping his hand again. "Like I said, I have many regrets. But in spite of the hell I went through with your father, I'd do it again in a heartbeat, because it brought me you and Gina."

A quaking started in Ross's chest, and then a loud crack he was surprised no one could hear crashed in his head and through his heart. He was so damn tired of being bitter. It had eaten away at him for so long that sometimes he didn't recognize the man he'd become. He'd been punishing everyone because of this anger—his father, Charlotte, himself.

God, *Charlotte*.

Three years ago, he hadn't allowed himself to love her because he'd been so afraid she would leave him. And when she had, it had been a self-fulfilling prophecy. Then, after she'd come back in his life, offering him a second chance with her, a chance to have a family, he'd again fallen back on fear. Walking out on her before she could.

He was tired of being afraid. Tired of being bitter and angry.

He just wanted to be loved, to be…happy.

He blinked against the sting of tears as he stared at the woman he'd always just wanted to love him, to accept him.

To stay for him.

Maybe she hadn't then, but she was here now.

Just as Charlotte had wanted to be.

Oh, Christ, he'd screwed up so bad. So *goddamn* bad. But he could start fixing it now. And that healing had to start with Sarabeth—with his mother.

"I've blamed a lot of my actions and behavior on you and your leaving me. I've hurt the mother of my son, the woman I...love—" his throat closed around the word, at admitting it for the first time aloud "—because I couldn't grow up and accept accountability. I'm sorry for all that you went through, and that when I was old enough, I chose to wallow in resentment than ask you why. I needed you when I was younger, and you weren't there. So I can't say that I can magically let go of that hurt, but I do forgive you. Because forgiving you means forgiving myself."

"Oh, honey," Sarabeth whispered, more tears streaming down her face. She cupped his cheek, and he savored it. Cherished the affection from his mom that he'd craved for so long. "I can't make up for the past. If only I could. But if you'll let me, I'll be here for you now. And the woman you love? Don't make the same mistakes I did, Ross. Go after her. Fight for her."

I so desperately wanted you to fight for me. To ask me to stay.

Charlotte's voice echoed in his head, and he silently vowed that he wouldn't fail her now like he had in the past.

He would go to war for both her and Ben, and this was one he couldn't lose.

Because he was battling for the woman he loved and his child.

He was battling for his life.

Sixteen

"I need the braised beef," Charlotte called out from the warming shelves as she finished plating a Tomahawk steak entrée. "It's up next."

"Yes, Chef, on two," her sous-chef replied.

Satisfied, Charlotte returned to the dishes waiting for her to check and send out. Sheen had been packed since the Soiree on the Bay party, and this Friday night, they had a line out the building, of customers waiting to dine. The knowledge should've filled her with happiness at their success, but for the past week—since Ross had left—everything had been shrouded in a layer of gray, dulling her emotions. Which she appreciated. Because she feared feeling *anything*. Feared that if she allowed even a sliver to surface, then the pain, disappointment and grief would surge through that opening like scavengers, to feed on her.

No, this coat of numbness was saving her at the moment, and she clung to it.

"Chef, you have a guest who'd like to see you tableside."

Dammit.

Forcing a smile that probably resembled a grimace, Charlotte glanced over at Carlie, who stood in the kitchen doorway.

"Okay, I'll be out in just a minute."

Switching out her jackets, she hurried from the kitchen with instructions to her sous-chef to take over for her. The sooner she got this over with, the quicker she could return to the kitchen, her sanctuary. Where she could lose herself in work and think about nothing else. No *one* else.

"Right over here, Chef," Carlie said, guiding her toward the back of the restaurant.

Charlotte followed, threading through the tables, pausing to greet diners but steadily moving forward. Hopefully, this guest wasn't chatty. She couldn't abide a talker right now...

"Hello, Charlotte."

She slammed to a halt, the air pummeling from her lungs at the sight of the man who hadn't left her mind in a week. Her knees locked, preventing her from crumbling to the floor. What the hell? Why was Ross here?

She glanced at Carlie, but the server had already disappeared. There had to be some mistake...

"No mistake," Ross murmured, because she'd obviously said the thought aloud. He rose from his chair, his tall frame towering over her. Reminding her of how well his body sheltered her.

No. *Hell no.* Not going there.

"What are you doing here, Ross?" she rasped. God, the gazes on them crawled under her jacket, skating over her skin. She *hated* it. No doubt this little visit would be the new topic of gossip.

"I came to see you." As if that were enough explanation. He cocked his head, his blue eyes gleaming with...what? Nope, she didn't care. "You look beautiful."

"Seriously?" she hissed. "After walking out of our house, leaving a home you bought for a family you claimed you wanted, that's what you come to my place of business to tell me?" She glared at him. "I don't know what game you're playing, but I quit."

"No game, baby," he murmured, causing her heart to

shudder and twist at the endearment. He had *no* right to call her that. None. "I forfeited my privilege to come and go in the house, so I didn't want to ambush you there. Because that's what this is. An ambush. I freely admit that."

"What? You don't believe I'll cause a scene and kick you out of the restaurant with all these witnesses?" He was correct, damn him. But he didn't have to know that.

"I hoped you wouldn't," he said. Sighing, he threaded his fingers through his hair, disheveling the thick strands. That gesture of nerves from him, especially in front of a restaurant full of people took her aback. Again, what the hell was going on? "Two minutes, Charlotte. Can you give me two minutes?"

He lifted his arm, and it hovered between them for an instant before he gently brushed the back of his fingers down her cheek. A gasp lodged in her throat, and she stiffened, despising her body's programmed response. Lush desire flowed through her, as if only needing his touch to once again stir to life.

She stepped back.

His head dipped in a nod, his eyes dimming. "I came here to apologize, to *beg* if I have to, for your forgiveness. I don't deserve it, but it's not stopping me from asking for it. Charlotte—" he held his hands up in the age-old sign of surrender "—I walked away for one reason. I was terrified of losing you. I figured I'd do it first before you could do it to me. Because I believed you eventually would. Whether it was in a week, a month or when the year was up, you would leave. Especially after I was disinherited and didn't even have wealth or connections to offer you." His mouth twisted, but the disgust in it seemed self-directed. "I was so fucking scared to let you in that I convinced myself it was better to end things sooner before I became used to a life with you and Ben. Before I let myself believe the idea of having both of you could be forever. Before I fell in love with you. But it was too late. I'd fallen back in love with you the moment you approached this table weeks ago. I was just too much of a stubborn coward to admit it."

He balled his fingers into fists and stared down at them. "I was so determined to hold on to the past—of you leaving me years ago, of missing that time with Ben, of not believing you could possibly want me for myself—that I lost my future. And if that's true, if you can't forgive me, then that's on me, and I'll have to live with it. But I can't let another moment go by with you not knowing that I love you. I've never loved any other woman *but* you. For three years, you've haunted me, never left me. And finally, having you back, it's a miracle that I callously threw away."

"Ross," she whispered, stunned speechless. Pressing her hands to her chest, she stared at him, afraid to trust. Afraid to take that step toward him.

Afraid he would devastate her again.

"I broke us, baby," he said. Swallowing hard, he paused, then shifted forward, claiming the space she'd placed between them. "I'm begging for the chance to put us back together. Let me prove to you that I am the man you need. Let me give you and Ben my last name. Let me love you. I don't need an inheritance if I have you and Ben. You're all I need. And, baby, I do need you."

Pride could have her reject him in front of all these people. Teach him a lesson. But she didn't care about other people. Didn't care about punishing him. Punishing them.

All she cared about was *him*.

She loved him.

"I never cared about your money," she said, meeting his bright gaze. "I was in love with the man—still am in love with him. If you come to us penniless, it's okay. You and Ben... If I have you two, I have everything."

"Baby," he breathed, then lunged forward, cupping her face, tipping it back and taking her mouth in a blistering kiss that leveled her. Pulling back, he pressed his forehead to hers, swiping his thumbs over her cheeks. "There's so much I have to tell you. Will you sit with me? Have dinner with me?"

"I wish I could—"

He chuckled, brushing another kiss over her lips. "On the hope that you would give me another chance, I cleared it with Jeremy for you to take a break from the kitchen and have a romantic dinner with me."

"Well, didn't you think of everything?" She grinned, and stepping back, encircled his wrist and led him back to the table. "I would love to."

Once they were seated, Carlie appeared with a wide grin and set down two plates of her signature dish before Charlotte and Ross.

"You'll never believe what happened…"

Over dinner, Ross told her about the confrontation with his father and the surprise visit from his mother. She held his hand as he relayed how they tentatively started the process of healing their relationship, which had culminated in Sarabeth urging Ross to go after Charlotte.

"Wow. I owe your mother a debt of gratitude for her advice," she said, caressing the back of his hand. "I'm sorry I didn't have the opportunity to meet her."

"She's actually planning to move back to Royal so she can get to know her new grandson." He smiled, and joy for him burned like the sun in her heart.

"That's amazing, Ross." She straightened in her chair and exhaled a breath, keeping a hold of his hand. If they were going to start their relationship anew, then he deserved the whole truth. It was time for it. "I don't want to begin our foundation on secrets, so I have something to tell you. I haven't been completely honest about why I left three years ago." God, she didn't want to hurt him. "Rusty had started hitting on me."

Anger darkened Ross's face, his narrowed eyes flaring bright.

"Did he touch you?" he growled.

"No," she assured him, even as she almost sagged in her chair. Because he believed her. That had been one of her fears back then. But he accepted her word as truth. If possible, she loved him more. "He didn't get physical, but he was insistent, and I grew uncomfortable. Especially with us being involved and knowing the power Rusty wielded. I didn't tell you earlier because you love your father, and a relationship with him was important to you. And I didn't want to taint that in any way. But if we're starting over, we need a clean slate. No secrets. And also—" she briefly closed her eyes before meeting his unwavering gaze "—I want to apologize for putting all the blame on you for leaving back then. I had a part in it. And not just because of Rusty and his connections. I was afraid that if we went public, you would see how others looked at us together and not want me anymore. That had nothing to do with you and everything to do with my own sense of self-esteem."

"Baby, you have nothing to apologize for. Nothing at all." He stood, rounded the table and gently pulled her from her seat. Cradling her cheek, he smiled, his love for her so brilliant she would never doubt it again. "Right here, right now, is where we begin. The past is over with and you are my future. I need you, Charlotte Jarrett-soon-to-be-Edmond. I love you."

She turned into his palm, placing a tender kiss to the center. "I love you, too, Ross. You've always been my forever. You always will be."

* * * * *

THE HEIR

JOANNE ROCK

To my mom, for sharing her love of reading with me so seamlessly. She still claims I learned to read on my own before I went to school. Thank you, Mom. I know you had a lot to do with that!

Prologue

Tired from a long night of travel, Nicole Cruz was still in bed when her phone rang on a Sunday morning.

She answered before fully awake, her thoughts still half in dreamland. She'd gotten a flight into San Francisco after midnight, but hadn't fallen into bed in San Jose until long afterward. It had been the first time she'd slept in her own home for nearly two weeks and she'd crashed hard.

"Hello?" Propping herself up on her elbow, she shoved tangled auburn hair from her eyes for a better peek at her phone screen when she realized two things at once.

First, this wasn't a normal phone call. She'd swiped the connect button on a video chat.

Second, her caller was Desmond Pierce, the rich and powerful casino resort owner who'd footed the bill for the return flight from Prince Edward Island yesterday so that Nicole and her nephew, Matthew, could answer his summons to western Montana. Nicole had insisted they stop in San Jose first so she could pick up a few of their things.

In reality, it was so she could surreptitiously drop Matthew off at his boarding school this morning. She hadn't told Desmond she had no intention of bringing the boy with her to Mesa Falls Ranch, the site of their appointed meeting later today to discuss the mystery of the teen's paternity.

"Good morning, Nicole." Desmond's deep voice resonated through the phone as his image filled her screen. His dark brown hair looked freshly cut around the sides, but the top was longer and slightly unruly. The bristle along his jaw was trimmed, too, but the shadow effect gave an edge to his tailored, European-cut suit.

Gray eyes zeroed in on her with startling clarity, making her all too aware of the skimpy pink camisole she'd slept in.

"Desmond," she said on an awkward gasp, dragging an oversize pillow in front of her to hide her breasts. "I—probably shouldn't have picked up."

Her pulse stuttered at the sight of him, his broad shoulders filling out his suit in an appealing way. She'd liked the sound of his voice the first time they'd spoken on the phone earlier in the week. But seeing him now had the strangest effect on her, heightening her senses, making her very aware of him. And of herself and her lack of clothes. His gaze never left her face—at least not that she'd noticed. But she would swear there was a hint of amusement gleaming in their depths.

"Would you like to call me back when it's more convenient?" His tone remained even, as if unaware he was talking to a woman in bed. "I just wanted to give you the details for your flight today."

And you couldn't have just texted them? But she'd rather get the conversation over with now than have another talk hanging over her conscience, making her feel guilty about flying solo today.

"Now is fine," she assured him with false brightness, careful not to straighten up too much or she'd lose the pillow barrier she was banking on for coverage. "I should be up anyhow. I've got a lot to do before heading to the airfield."

"It's not too late for me to send a car for you," he offered, tapping the screen to life on a tablet as he spoke to her from behind a sleek mahogany desk. Behind him, a bank of windows overlooking the Bitterroot Mountains let her know he was already at Mesa Falls Ranch.

He hadn't been in residence during the few weeks she'd worked there. Shortly after Christmas she'd taken a job in guest services under an assumed name in the hope of learning more about the partners who ran the ranch. Before her sister's untimely death from a brain aneurysm last year, Lana had given Nicole reason to believe one of the men running Mesa Falls might be Matthew's father. But Nicole had been unceremoniously fired before she could learn the truth.

An event Desmond Pierce had since claimed hadn't been authorized by any of the partners. But at the time, her sudden termination had made her all the more wary of the men who owned Mesa Falls. She'd taken her nephew to Prince Edward Island in an effort to lie low and regroup, so it had rattled her to learn Desmond's private investigator had followed them. She'd spent days dodging the tail, finally giving in to talk to Desmond

Pierce the third time the PI asked her to contact him. They'd spoken briefly on the phone two times before now. Yet until she learned more about his motives, she was planning to keep Mattie safely ensconced at his school. Besides, as a gifted child with autism spectrum disorder, her nephew sometimes struggled with change, and he'd been through more than enough these last months after losing his mom.

"I can get to the airport on my own," Nicole assured him, refusing to take more help than necessary. Bad enough he was sending his jet to pick her up today. "Am I still heading to Reid-Hillview?" she asked, naming the private airfield closest to her house.

"Yes," Desmond confirmed, rising to his feet and buttoning his jacket with nimble fingers. Her focus lingered on his hand. "The pilot will be on-site at one o'clock to pick up you and Matthew, but he'll wait until you're ready, so don't rush."

Her stomach knotted. Guilt niggled for a moment before she shoved it aside. She refused to feel bad about doing what was best for Mattie. She would drop him off at school before heading to the airfield.

"I'll need a little longer than that." She dodged the mention of her traveling companion as she hugged the pillow to her chest and stood. "But I can probably be there by two."

"Excellent." Desmond rewarded her with a smile that had probably charmed far more worldly women than her. There was something compelling about him that went beyond good looks. "I appreciate you agreeing to see me."

He had an ease and competence that suggested he could accomplish anything. But then, wealth imbued people with that kind of confidence. He'd wanted Nicole and her nephew to come to Montana, so he'd had them followed until they caved to his terms.

Or so he thought. Nicole could at least keep him away from her nephew while Matthew was in school.

"It wasn't a decision I reached easily," she reminded him, needing this man to know she wasn't going to knuckle under to whatever demands he made once she was in Montana. "Being hounded by your detective didn't help your case if you really only wished to speak to me."

She feared that he and his friends—any one of whom might have fathered her nephew—would try to wrest guardianship of Matthew away from her. And he might as well know straight out of the gate that wasn't happening.

His jaw tightened at her rebuke, but he didn't deny it.

"Forgive me. I was unsure how else to right the wrong you were done while employed at the ranch. We'll make sure you're compensated for the abrupt termination."

She studied his features, looking for a hint as to his deeper motive, but his gray eyes revealed nothing. And while she was quickly running out of her personal reserves on her quest to find her nephew's father, she wouldn't be accepting financial gifts from a man who already wielded too much power.

"I'm not interested in that. I'm only coming to Montana to learn the truth about Mathew's connection to Mesa Falls."

Perhaps Desmond heard that it was a line in the sand for her, because he didn't argue. Then again, he didn't concede, either.

"I'm committed to helping you find the answers you're searching for." His gaze was unwavering.

Could she trust those words? Or was he more interested in making sure she didn't learn too much? It was impossible to tell. But she wouldn't let Desmond Pierce stop her in her quest.

And she damned well wouldn't allow his charismatic appeal to slip past her guard. Nothing was more important than protecting her nephew's best interests.

When she simply nodded, Desmond continued. "I look forward to seeing you when you land. There's a snowstorm rolling in later, so dress warm."

She knew it was for practical purposes that he was going to meet her personally, but a shiver still stole over her at the thought of stepping off the aircraft and coming face-to-face with this man for the first time.

Now the only man who'd seen her in bed in over a year.

Shaking off the wayward thought, Nicole wished her contact in Mesa Falls didn't have to be so damnably attractive.

"I'll see you soon. And…thank you." Disconnecting the call, Nicole made sure the screen went dark before she let go of the pillow.

She needed a shower to clear her head, and then she'd put her game face on for the day ahead. She would drop Matthew off at his school before boarding Desmond's private plane, then proceed to Montana alone to find out what the men of Mesa Falls had been hiding from her family. The next time she saw Desmond Pierce, he wasn't going to be happy with her.

One

Parking his SUV in a deserted lot behind the Ravalli County Airport in Hamilton, Montana, Desmond Pierce killed the engine. He'd tracked the flight of the light Gulfstream jet delivering his guests and timed his arrival carefully to meet Nicole Cruz and her ward for the first time.

Wind whipped off the jagged peaks of the Bitterroot range to the west, the snow-capped mountains casting long shadows on the valley as the sun dipped low in the sky. Desmond walked around to the front of the main hangar where the jet had just come to a full stop.

He, along with five friends, had purchased the plane at the same time they'd bought Mesa Falls Ranch, where they'd invested heavily in sustainable ranching practices before expanding into a luxury resort to showcase their environmental initiatives. The ranch had been their memorial to a friend who'd died fourteen years ago when they'd been in boarding school together in Southern California. Until this winter, Desmond had thought he'd put that hellish time in his life behind him. But the old ghosts were back to plague him after a scandal hit Mesa Falls three months ago.

A scandal fueled to a boiling point thanks in part to his guests—a woman full of secrets, and her thirteen-year-old nephew, Matthew Cruz, whose unknown paternity was a new question mark in a past Desmond had tried hard to forget. But since the boy was linked to the owners of Mesa Falls, Desmond had stepped up to take the lead in dealing with Nicole.

It was his turn to be the face of the group, for one thing. For another? He'd experienced an unusual...*curiosity* about her during their conversations over the past week since his private investigator had located her.

Hell if he knew why he'd given in to the urge for a video call this morning. But images of her in that pink camisole had tormented him every minute since then.

He paused to stand under a metal awning sheltering one of the entrances into the hangar, waiting as the cabin door opened, a member of the ground crew securing the stairs. Tapping the snow off the toes of his boots, Desmond reviewed what he knew about Nicole from the detective's report. She'd taken a job at the ranch under an assumed name, using her time there to research the six partners who owned Mesa Falls. She believed one of them might be her nephew's father after the boy's mother died suddenly of an aneurysm. Before her death, Nicole's sister indicated that someone close to the ranch's owners had been financing Matthew's education. Nicole wanted to know why.

But Nicole had been fired by her supervisor, who

quit immediately afterward. Nicole promptly grabbed Matthew from school and vanished, resulting in deeper mistrust between her and the men of Mesa Falls.

But Desmond needed her cooperation if they were going to figure out the boy's paternity. When he'd suggested she fly to Montana with her nephew for a meeting, she only agreed on the condition that he and his partners submit DNA samples for paternity tests—tests that had just come back negative for any matches. Results he had yet to share with Nicole, and which were going to give rise to a whole lot of new questions. He'd been afraid to give her too much of a heads-up on the news for fear she'd change her mind about returning to Montana.

Now shadows stirred near the cabin door, making Desmond straighten where he stood. He'd seen photos of the boy, so he knew generally what to expect. Matthew—with his sandy hair, lean frame and dark brown eyes—bore little resemblance to anyone Desmond knew.

Nicole had thick auburn waves and eyes the same deep brown as her nephew's, with features Desmond had memorized even before their video call. The detective had given him a still photo pulled from the ranch's security footage during the weeks she'd been an employee. At that time, Weston Rivera had been in charge of Mesa Falls while Desmond had been embroiled in running his casino resort on the northern shore of Lake Tahoe, so his path had never crossed Nicole's.

A missed opportunity? Or was it just as well considering the interest she stirred in him that didn't have anything to do with her connection to Mesa Falls? He didn't know what spurred the reaction. She was lovely, certainly. But that alone had never been enough to spark the kind of awareness he had for this woman. The casino he ran attracted wealth and beauty in direct proportion to one another. Nicole had something different. Warmth. Fire. He'd heard it in her voice when they spoke on the phone. Seen it in her eyes in that video call.

He'd been hungry to meet her from their first conversation, eager to see if that would ease the craving he had for more of her. Maybe that had been part of the reason he'd video-called this morning. Perhaps he hoped the fascination with her might ease once he saw her, but if anything, he was even more preoccupied with thoughts of her.

Now, the shadows around the cabin door shifted and she stood just thirty yards from him, poised at the top of the stairs. Dressed in a fawn-colored coat with knee-high black leather boots, she reached one gloved hand to steady herself on the handrail while she used the other to restrain the mass of red curls from the tug of the cold winds.

If any part of him had hoped the magnetic effect she had on him would dissipate once he saw her in person, the hope evaporated now. In the eight years he'd spent building his business, it hadn't been difficult for Desmond to keep relationships simple and straightforward. He'd invested everything he had in building the casino business from nothing. He'd devoted little time to women, and then only in the most cursory way. But right now, even with the wind chill hovering at freezing, he felt sparks just looking at Nicole Cruz.

As if called by his thoughts, she glanced toward the hangar suddenly, her gaze finding him. It was damned fanciful of him to think she might feel the same pull between them, so he straightened and headed toward the tarmac to meet her.

He was halfway to the metal stairs when it occurred to him there was no one else with Nicole. The pilot was already on the pavement, exchanging a few words with the guy from the ground crew while the two of them looked over the aircraft. Nicole's bag was on the small carpet at the base of the fold-down steps.

Bag. Singular.

Suspicion stirred as his gaze darted back to hers, but he held himself in check while he greeted her.

"Welcome, Nicole." He extended a hand when he halted a few feet from her. "Thank you for making the trip."

His fingers closed around the leather of her gloved palm, and he had a brief impression of her warmth. She was tall for a woman, her brown eyes nearly level with his in her heeled boots.

"Thank you for having me. I'm as eager as you are to find answers about my nephew," she assured him before she pulled back, her tone cool as they sized one another up under the harsh glare of the outdoor lights. Her face appeared free of cosmetics, yet her full lips were a rich berry color that drew his attention as she spoke.

For a moment, his attention snagged on her word choice. But of course, he wouldn't be *having* her. She was here in the interests of her ward, and Desmond was here to protect the men who were like brothers to him. It wouldn't be possible to explore an attraction to her, even if it was distracting as hell.

A red curl escaped her grasp and wavered along her cheek. Behind her, the worker from the ground crew closed the cabin door while another woman jogged to-

ward the runway and pulled on a headset, lights under
one arm to direct air traffic.

"Speaking of your nephew." Desmond glanced from
Nicole to the jet and then back again, wondering what
kind of game she was playing. "Where is Matthew?"

They all wanted to meet the boy, whom their former
mentor, Alonzo Salazar, had secretly supported. Once
they met Matthew, maybe they would recognize the connection. See something familiar in the boy's features or
manner that they couldn't pick up through a mere photo.

Her pointed chin jutted at the question.

"Back in boarding school." She reached for the handle of her rolling canvas bag as if that handful of words
could end the discussion—the same one they'd had over
the phone when he'd first arranged for her to bring the
boy to Montana.

Annoyance flared. Desmond took the suitcase for
her, his hand brushing hers as the sound of an approaching aircraft hummed on the breeze.

"We had an agreement," he reminded her tightly, un-
accustomed to his directives not being followed. At his
casino, he ran a smooth, efficient business because his
plans were executed to the letter. Even at Mesa Falls,
where he shared control with his partners, there was
still discussion, compromise and agreement.

Not open defiance.

Her full lips compressed into a flat line before she
spoke. "As I recall, we had a *dis*agreement since I
wasn't keen on being followed by your private detective. I told you Matthew didn't do well with change,
and that he needed to return to a known environment
where he thrives. You insisted I bring him against my
better judgment."

The wind kicked up around them. The pilot for Desmond's jet returned to the cockpit as if to park the aircraft for the night.

"Those were the terms," Desmond reminded Nicole.

"Your terms, not mine." Her brown eyes flashed with a fire that didn't come through her cool words, revealing a passion that might have intrigued him if she hadn't just upended all his plans. "Now, I'm here and I'm going to find answers with you or without you. So what will it be, Desmond? Do you want me to return to Mesa Falls with you or not?"

A few minutes later, Nicole sat in the passenger seat of Desmond Pierce's shiny black luxury SUV, her suitcase stowed in the back as he drove west toward the Bitterroot mountain range and Mesa Falls Ranch.

It was clear from the long silence following his terse request that she accompany him, Desmond was not pleased with her refusal to dance to his tune.

Too. Bad.

She focused on the scenery outside the window as they drove closer to the jagged peaks, the open fields dotted with the occasional barn or equipment shed. She was done caring what the privileged men of Mesa Falls thought about her, so Desmond could brood all he wished. Her sole concern was finding her nephew's father and holding him financially accountable for contributing to his son's upbringing. Even though his education was taken care of by Salazar's book profits, it was an arrangement she wasn't completely comfortable with. Mattie had a unique set of skills and needs that were well met at the private school where he'd boarded the last few years before Nicole's sister, Lana, had died suddenly. The hurt of Lana's passing still caught Nicole off guard sometimes, stopping her short in the middle of the day, the pain of it so sharp she felt like she couldn't breathe.

But remembering Mattie helped. Especially when she knew that her sister's son would naturally grieve even more for Lana than she did. The fact that Lana had died without revealing anything of Mattie's father—other than a vague reference to the child being taken care of thanks to Alonzo Salazar's tell-all book—complicated Nicole's life exponentially. She hadn't minded taking time away from her freelance graphic design job to search for answers, but the weeks had stretched to months and her savings dwindled. She didn't have the luxury of turning down Desmond Pierce's offer of making the travel arrangements for her return to Montana.

But she couldn't ignore her nephew's needs in favor of the man currently in the driver's seat. Turning her attention back to him, Nicole let her gaze wander over Desmond while he drove. Even angry with her, he remained ridiculously attractive. Thoughts of their morning phone call—waking up to his face while she was still in bed—had never been far from her mind today.

And Desmond wasn't just pleasing to the eye with his stormy gray eyes, dark hair and shadowed jaw that called a woman's fingers to test the texture of the bristles there. There was more to it than a strong build and fine physique evident even under the winter layers of his black wool jacket with a taupe-colored fisherman's sweater underneath. It was something intangible about the way he looked at her, the way he spoke, the way he moved that just flipped a switch inside her.

A strange phenomenon she'd never experienced before. In the past, the few men who'd been in her life had been there for practicality's sake—someone fixed her up with a friend because it was easier to group date. But the sexy, charged encounters that other women seemed to have just didn't happen for her.

Although one look at Desmond—one moment to feel the draw between them—gave her some clue about what she'd been missing. It seemed wholly unfair that the universe put this compelling man in her path right *now* when she needed to focus on finding her nephew's father. Barely containing her frustrated sigh, Nicole couldn't stand another moment of the heavy silence in the luxury SUV. The wealth of supple leather and sleek engineering in the vehicle did little to put her at ease, the bespoke interior reminding her how much power and influence this man wielded.

"I'm not sure we're going to find the answers we seek about Matthew's dad if we aren't speaking," she observed, unbuttoning her long coat now that she was out of the damp cold.

Or maybe she just needed to cool down the heat of her thoughts.

Desmond's fingers flexed on the steering wheel as the sun dipped out of sight behind the snowcapped mountains, leaving the sky painted with streaks of purple tinged with gold.

"We'll come up with a new plan." His glance slid sideways. "We have no choice."

The undertone of blame nettled.

"I hope you're not expecting me to feel guilty about doing what's best for Matthew." She'd expected better from Desmond based on the two phone calls she'd had with him. He'd eased her concerns about returning to

Montana, and—she'd thought—done what he could to make the trip easier. "I won't apologize for taking care of him to the best of my ability. I owe my sister that much."

She was horrified to hear the crack in her voice as the last words left her mouth. She would not show weakness now. Except thoughts of never seeing Lana again still had the power to take her legs right out from under her.

Blinking fast, she glanced out the window again as the darkness deepened. Near the road, a tractor tilled the ground with the help of headlights.

If Desmond heard the emotions in her voice, he didn't acknowledge them. But he continued, more gently, "What's Matthew like?"

"Brilliant," she said without hesitation, grateful for the conversational about-face. "The more time I spend with him, the more I admire my sister for recognizing his unique abilities early on and finding a program to help him thrive. He's great in math, with an uncanny memory for facts. He also draws really well, which has given us some common ground, since I work in graphic design."

She'd been fascinated by her nephew's detailed ink sketches of skyscrapers and cityscapes he drew while in Prince Edward Island. The last-minute trip had been an attempt to keep him out of the spotlight in case the news of how he'd benefited from the Salazar book became public, but Desmond had assured her that information—for now—remained private.

He steered off the county route and onto a private road, the movement hitching at his coat sleeve enough to expose a sleek silver Patek Philippe watch that cost more than she made in a year.

"How are you adjusting to life as the guardian of a thirteen-year-old boy?" he asked with surprising insight. Caring, even.

"Honestly?" She thought about how much her life had changed in the months since her sister died. Her world had been flipped on its ear. "It's been a little overwhelming."

"I think any parent of a thirteen-year-old would agree it's a lot of work." He gave a nod to the operator of a tractor with a snowplow attachment traveling in the opposite direction.

"It's not because of Mattie, though," she assured him, unwilling to give a false impression of her smart sweetheart of a nephew. "He's great. I just worry I'm not doing things the right way. I'll wake up at night in a panic that I messed up his health insurance or somehow compromised the educational services he receives any time I go into the school's website to file a form."

Desmond's phone chimed through the dashboard Bluetooth, but he hit a button to silence the screen, giving her his undivided attention.

"From what I hear, that's effective parenting. If you're worried whether or not you're doing a good job, you probably are."

For a moment, she thought his tone sounded almost wistful. But one glance over at his inscrutable expression told her she must be imagining it. Everything about Desmond Pierce suggested he'd been born to wealth and privilege, a background underscored by his attendance at the exclusive Dowdon School on the West Coast. All of the Mesa Falls owners had attended the expensive private institution that educated so many of America's elite.

"I hope that's true." She kept an eye on the road ahead for her first glimpse of the ranch after weeks away from Montana. "Has there been any progress from your private investigator about who was responsible for terminating me during my brief time working here?"

A muscle flicked in Desmond's jaw, a brief sign of displeasure despite his impassive visage.

"Yes. And I can assure you it wasn't any of my partners. But I'd like to save the debriefing until after you're settled." He glanced her way, his expression thoughtful. "I realize trust won't come easily for either of us, but I want answers about your nephew as much as you do."

The sincerity in his voice was hard to miss. From their phone calls arranging this meeting, she'd had a glimpse of how much Desmond trusted his business partners. She understood he wanted to clear their names of all scandal having to do with the book their mentor had written that profited off real people's misfortunes. But she didn't share his faith in the men of Mesa Falls. Someone powerful had made sure she lost her job here.

And maybe there was a reason Lana hadn't identified the father of her child. Maybe he wasn't a good person.

"That's fine," she agreed as the impressive main lodge came into view. Built in the style of the National Parks lodges, the split-log structure combined woodsy appeal with elegance, the landscape lighting drawing attention to deep second-story balconies and huge glass windows overlooking the Bitterroot River. "But keep in mind I'm not some kind of diva guest who needs to unpack twelve suitcases' worth of clothes for every occasion. I'll be ready to go in an hour at most."

Desmond was silent for a moment as he pulled the SUV around the horseshoe driveway, stopping under a sheltered portico in front of the lodge. A liveried attendant approached the vehicle, but Desmond halted him with a gesture.

"Would you like to have an early dinner?" Desmond turned toward her, his thigh shifting against the leather seat now that the vehicle was parked.

His gray eyes met hers, the invitation she saw in them tickling her insides in a way that felt all wrong for a man she needed to be wary around. If any one of the Mesa Falls partners turned out to be Mattie's father—Desmond included—they would have cause to take the boy away from her. Certainly any one of them would have the financial ability to hire the best attorneys to make that happen. Her stomach knotted.

"I had something on the plane." It wasn't technically a lie, because she'd eaten the protein bar she'd packed from home. She had questions she wanted answered about her sister, and the sooner she got started on the quest, the sooner she could leave Montana for good. "I can meet with any of your partners who are free this evening—"

"Me. I'm free this evening." He looked at her with a singular focus, like she was the only thing he had on his agenda for the rest of the week. Or—a wicked part of her brain amended—like she was the only item on his personal menu. "I'll meet you in the lobby in an hour, and we'll get started."

Her pulse kicked up in answer, as if he'd suggested something more intimate than a business meeting. Her reactions were all off around him, distracting her from something important. She needed to put her nephew first no matter how confusing the sensual undercurrent between her and her host.

"Good." She gave a nod of confirmation, hating that

her voice had sounded breathless. Hungry. And *not* just because she'd only eaten a protein bar. Grinding her teeth against the surge of unfamiliar feelings, Nicole shoved them to the back of her mind. "See you then."

She must have missed a sign between Desmond and the valet, because no sooner were the words out of her mouth than the passenger side door was opened by an attendant.

"Welcome to Mesa Falls, miss," the young man said with a smile while another plucked her suitcase from the back. "I hope you enjoy your stay."

Off-balance but unwilling to show it, Nicole wrapped her coat tighter around her waist and turned to step outside.

But not before Desmond's parting words to her stroked along her senses.

"I'm looking forward to it, Nicole."

Two

Thoughts full of Nicole Cruz, Desmond walked into the state-of-the-art stables near the paddock, the building that housed the ranch offices. While not as outwardly showy as his private office at his casino resort in Tahoe, the Mesa Falls executive suite complemented the place.

The stables downstairs were immaculately kept, for one thing, with each horse's name on a stall. Only the best of their stock was kept here, prized studs available for a fee. He paused in front of a heavy stall door to stroke the nose of a racing champion quarter horse, Sundancer, his personal favorite. The chestnut tossed his proud head and whinnied when Desmond headed for the stairs to the upper story.

The commitment to horses was an important mission of a ranch run in memory of Zach Eldridge, a schoolmate of the owners who'd cliff-jumped to his death on a horseback riding trip fourteen years ago. The friends who'd been with Zach that weekend had bought the ranch together as a way to keep his memory alive, although they'd never agreed on the exact circumstances of his death. The conditions had been all wrong for the jump. Had Zach known he wouldn't survive and jumped to end his life? The question haunted them still. Zach had been the closest friend Desmond ever had, even though their friendship had been far too brief.

It was always tough to be in Mesa Falls because of the memories it evoked of Zach, even though his dead friend had never visited Montana. Just being in a place that Zach's friends purchased to honor him messed with Desmond's head. And now, chances were good that Matthew Cruz could be Zach's son, which meant Desmond needed to find a way to get comfortable with talking about Zach, as Nicole would obviously have a lot of questions. Starting with—how could they prove Zach was the father?

Desmond huffed out a frustrated breath as he reached the top of the staircase. Since he needed to pick up Nicole again in an hour, there was no point making the longer trip to his house on the ranch property when the executive suite had been built close to the main lodge.

He shoved open the exterior door, giving a nod to the administrator in the seat out front as he passed him, grateful the assistant appeared busy with a phone call, so Desmond didn't have to make small talk. He unlocked the private office in back and allowed the door to close behind him before sinking into the high-backed leather chair behind the glass-topped stainless-steel desk. He swiveled to look out the windows at the mountains and expelled a long breath.

Nicole had completely disregarded his request to bring her nephew to the ranch. What's more, she made no apology for doing what she thought was best for Matthew.

I just worry I'm not doing things the right way.

Her words about parenting echoed in his mind, reminding him that she was her ward's advocate first and foremost, no matter what Desmond wanted. It inconvenienced him. But at the same time, the part of him that had been emotionally abandoned by his own parents cheered for her fierce dedication to the boy. What child wouldn't want her on his side?

The thought wreaked havoc with his plan to interrogate her about her sister's past, and it sure as hell didn't sit well with his fear that Zach would turn out to be Matthew's father. The idea of his best friend's son growing up without a father thrust another knife of guilt into a conscience already weighed down with ways he'd failed Zach.

Underneath those concerns lurked a whole lot of undeniable physical attraction. Too often he'd found his thoughts drifting to the video call that had given him a glimpse of the too-sheer pink camisole. Meeting her in person had done nothing to dim that memory or the damnable interest that went with it.

The chime of the intercom halted the feature film of tantalizing images replaying through his head.

He cursed the interruption even as he knew he should welcome it, then pressed the button to answer. "Yes?"

"Miles Rivera to see you," the assistant intoned through the speaker.

Miles had returned from the West Coast already? His friend and fellow partner in the ranch must have something important on his mind if he'd left Los Angeles where he was supposed to be reuniting with his social media star sweetheart, Chiara Campagna.

"Send him in," Desmond returned, getting to his feet as the office door opened to admit Miles Rivera.

The older of the two Rivera brothers who'd attended school with him, Miles was a levelheaded rancher in contrast to his wilder, risk-taking sibling, Weston.

Desmond came around to the front of the desk to shake hands with his friend.

"Good to see you, Miles." He gestured to one of the leather armchairs near a window overlooking the paddock. "Do you have time to take a seat?"

"Definitely," he answered in his distinctive, slightly raspy voice. Miles unbuttoned his dark blue jacket before he sat, his clothing game always top-notch. "Chiara and I flew back this morning after deciding to spend a couple of weeks in Mesa Falls to reconnect. She enjoyed the privacy of life in Montana."

His smile was unmistakable. And the obvious happiness on his face was something Desmond hadn't seen in the serious rancher for a long time.

"I'm glad things worked out for you two," Desmond observed, knowing how desperate Miles had been to see her and put things right between them.

"I'm grateful as hell for the second chance. But I was curious to hear your initial thoughts on our guest while Chiara is having a meeting this morning. Do you think Nicole is here to make trouble?"

Defensiveness spiked as Desmond took the seat by his prep school buddy, but that made no sense when they all had every reason to be on guard around Matthew Cruz's guardian.

"Hard to say. We didn't speak for long on the drive from the airport, but I'm seeing her again shortly. She's eager for answers."

"Aren't we all?" Miles asked dryly, reaching toward the windowsill to flip a decorative hourglass full of dark sand. At one time, they'd used the device as a silent timer for group meetings when they were setting up the ranch business. "Did you see our alma mater is cashing in on Alonzo Salazar's name now that our former teacher has been unmasked as the author of *Hollywood Newlyweds*?"

"What's this?" He'd been too busy with the logistics of getting Nicole and Matthew to Montana to notice much else.

"The Dowdon School is hosting their fiftieth anniversary party this year as a fundraiser—"

"I remember. We're all attending." Desmond had RSVP'd a week ago.

"—and they've started running social media teasers about famous alumni, including a pitch about Salazar's book. Something like, 'At Dowdon, you'll be in the know.'" Miles quoted the ad copy with a heavy dose of mockery.

Desmond scrubbed a hand over his head. "How could they think that's a good idea? That book ruined lives."

"Some media relations expert probably convinced them there's no such thing as bad press." Miles sat forward in his seat. "But I spoke with a rep at the school today to let them know my thoughts on that, and when I did, I also talked them into renting out our old dorm rooms for us that weekend."

Desmond's gut dropped as memories slammed him.

"You can't seriously want to stay there?" They were small, for one thing, especially since most of them would be attending with significant others. But for another, the whole trip was going to remind him of Zach.

The small room he'd once shared with him most of all.

"I get it." Miles leaned forward in his chair to clap a consoling hand on Desmond's shoulder. "I do. But this gala might be a chance to really close the doors on that time. For good. Besides, we don't have to sleep there. I just figured we could have a pre-party toast on-site before we head to the gala."

"Right. Okay." He nodded, recognizing it was probably a good plan even if it stirred old ghosts for him personally.

"Good. Glad you're on board." Miles rose to his feet again, a rare smile pulling one corner of his mouth. "Well, I told Chiara I'd meet her, so I'd better be on my way. Chiara is organizing a dinner for Nicole and Matthew, by the way, so we can meet the boy."

Desmond walked with him to the door. "About that—"

"I don't envy you entertaining a thirteen-year-old." Miles mused as he withdrew his cell phone from his jacket pocket. "Weston and I were hellions at that age."

Irritation stabbed through him again. "Nicole didn't bring the boy with her."

Miles stopped short, his phone forgotten. "But that was part of the deal. Seeing him in person might let us see a familiar gesture or some other small detail that we might miss in a photo."

The defensiveness he'd felt about Nicole earlier in the conversation redoubled. And what was that about?

He'd had the same problem with her decision that Miles did now. But he couldn't deny her reasoning had gotten to him.

"She's protecting him." He recalled her expression when she'd told him *I'm not some kind of diva guest...* "She's not what I expected."

Frowning, Miles narrowed his gaze. "Let's just hope she keeps away from the media. I don't think we want any more attention on Alonzo Salazar or that damned book of his."

Desmond agreed. News that the profits from their mentor's book supported a fatherless child would be sensation enough. But if the father proved to be Zach— a man whose death had been kept quiet for years—the outcry would be significant. Who would support the green initiatives of the ranch if the owners had been part of the reason that a child with special needs had grown up without knowing about his father?

"That won't happen on my watch." No matter how much Nicole infiltrated his thoughts, Desmond would protect Mesa Falls and the legacy they'd built for Zach. "I'll ask Nicole about a dinner tomorrow if you still want to meet with her."

After agreeing to message him in the morning, Miles left, and at the same time Desmond's phone buzzed with a notification.

Couldn't sit still in the lobby. Meet at the dartboard in great room instead.

Desmond didn't need to check the identity of the texter. Nicole hadn't been kidding that she hadn't required much time to settle into her room—only forty-five minutes had passed since they'd parted ways.

Pocketing his phone, he locked up behind him and headed to meet her.

Closing one eye, Nicole focused on the bull's-eye while an old country classic played on the sound system in the lodge's great room. The tile floor under her feet was softened with colorful Aztec rugs in the conversation areas of the room, the reds and burnt oranges repeated in the throw pillows and framed prints on the natural log walls. A small bar held top-shelf liquors under the watchful eye of a stuffed American bison standing near the pool table. Bar stools were padded in black-and-white cowhide.

A couple of older women sat at a nearby table, their conversation punctuated with occasional laughter. Other than the two of them and a twentysomething male bartender engrossed in his phone, Nicole had the room to herself. The whole gaming area was empty except for her. The pool table was untouched, the balls racked in the center of the green felt. A classic Skee-Ball arcade game waited for her to try next.

For now, in front of the dartboard, Nicole lined up her shot in an attempt to burn off nervous energy. She spun the tungsten barrel a few times in her fingers, getting used to the dimpled grip. She preferred razor cuts or crosshatching, but the darts were high quality, unlike the sets she'd come across in most pubs that were brass with warping or split tips. Flexing her wrist, she fired.

One. Two. Three.

A low whistle sounded behind her, alerting her to a newcomer.

Turning, she spotted Desmond's gray gaze focused on the board where her darts had notched in a tight group.

"Three triple twenties." He arched a brow before his attention veered toward her. "Impressive."

She doubted she had many skills that would impress this cosmopolitan man, but her father had taught her his favorite game well. "Do you play?"

"No." He edged around the pool table until he leaned a shoulder against the Skee-Ball game, where he could observe her more closely. "As the owner of a casino, I've learned to avoid games people bet on."

"Wise of you, I'm sure." She could only imagine how many people lost hefty sums under this man's watch. "But darts isn't a game of chance. The outcome rewards skill."

"Poker does, too. Sometimes those games are almost more dangerous, because players can have false ideas about their skill level." His gaze lifted to the board again. "Although there's no denying you've got a good throw."

"We can play just for fun then." She reached for the green darts in a game box on a low table nearby, then passed three to him, settling them in his hand.

The look in his eyes gave her pause, his pupils dilated so only a ring of pale silver remained on the outside. Her finger remained on the heel of his palm before she yanked it back.

"What?" she asked, suddenly too aware of him. Of herself.

Her heart skipped a beat and then sped too quickly. Her skin heated.

"I'm tempted to play with you, Nicole." He lowered

his head to speak more softly. "But I think we should talk first."

She swallowed, her mouth dry. Her thoughts scrambled. Was it possible he experienced the attraction to the same degree she did? Could he be struggling hard against it, too?

"Right. That's why I'm here." She'd taken up the game because she felt antsy and anxious to begin her quest for answers. But now? She felt even more antsy and anxious, for a whole other host of reasons. Warmth crawled over her skin.

"We can speak in my office," he offered, returning the darts to the metal game box with the others. "Or find a quiet table in the back."

The idea of being alone with him sizzled through her already overheated senses. She couldn't afford to let this heady awareness sidetrack her.

"Let's go watch the ice-skaters." She blurted the first outdoor alternative that occurred to her. Having worked at the ranch, she knew the terrain well, and right now, cold air and more space would be welcome. "That is, it should be a nice night by the pond. I saw a bonfire burning out the window earlier."

"Did you bring a jacket?" Glancing around, he spotted the coat she'd worn earlier and retrieved it from where she'd thrown it over the back of a chair. "The temperature has dropped since I picked you up at the airport. Are you sure you want to go out?"

Seeing his broad hands splayed on her coat spurred more thoughts about his touch, which was all the incentive she needed. "I'd love some fresh air."

She reached to take the garment, but he shifted behind her to lay it gently on her shoulders. A shiver stole through her, and she hoped he didn't notice.

"What about you?" Stepping away from him quickly, she took in his black dress shirt, dark jeans and boots.

"I left it with Simon up front." He referenced one of her former colleagues in guest services. "I'll grab it on our way out."

Minutes later, they circled around the building on a stone path, through a courtyard behind the lodge and toward the skating pond. Drifts of snow still circled the pond, but the ice had been cleared along with the pathways, the property impeccably groomed by the grounds staff.

"Are you warm enough?" Desmond asked as they reached a wooden bench close enough to see the ice but isolated enough for a private conversation.

He gestured for her to sit.

"I'm good," she answered honestly, grateful for the chilly night air cooling her cheeks. Even the added layers of winter coats between their bodies was welcome. She took a seat on the bench and enjoyed the sounds of the skate blades on the ice mingling with laughter and the low hum of conversation from around the bonfire on the opposite side of the small pond.

"How does it feel to be back?" He seated himself beside her, not too close, but then again, having him within five feet of her stirred her insides. "I hope there's no awkwardness for you."

His thoughtful concern caught her off guard. Her gaze skittered away from him to focus on the skaters. "Not really. I wasn't employed here long enough to make friends, so I don't think anyone spent time wondering what happened to me when I was terminated."

She followed the progress of a young father holding a little girl's hand as she wobbled on her skates. She was probably four or five years old, mittens hanging from strings from her coat sleeves while she clutched her dad's hand in both of hers, giggling as he towed her along on her skates.

When Desmond was silent for a long moment, she turned to him again and found him studying her. He'd stretched his arm along the back of the bench behind her while she'd been absorbed in the skating, and she swore she could feel the warmth of his hand on her back even though he didn't touch her.

"You were here for almost a month," he said slowly. "I'm sure people noticed your absence."

"I'm a bit of a loner," she found herself saying, realizing too late she was disclosing something personal. Something he didn't need to know about her. She straightened more, putting distance between his hand and her back. "You mentioned earlier that you had learned more about who'd fired me?"

"Our private investigator looked into it. Your supervisor turned in his notice the next day, and he wasn't easy to track down, but apparently he'd been given orders from Vivian Fraser."

"I don't recognize that name."

"She was Alec Jacobsen's assistant until last week, when she was arrested." She knew Alex Jacobsen was one of his partners, a game designer. "At the time, your supervisor assumed the order to fire you came from Alec."

His words about an arrest shocked her. A chill went through her at the thought of someone criminal so close to her. Or worse—close to Mattie.

"Why was she arrested?" Unthinking, she reached toward Desmond, her hand landing on his knee. "Could Matthew be in danger?"

"No." Desmond's hand covered hers. Steady. Calming. "She's still behind bars. And her arrest was for harassing Chiara Campagna—"

"The social media star." Puzzling over the details now that her panic about her nephew had eased, she would have freed her fingers, but Desmond's palm still covered them. "I did notice she posted a couple of photos from Mesa Falls recently."

"Yes." He nodded, but the word was clipped, and she had the feeling there was more to that story. "Vivian apparently has feelings for Alec, and she thought she was protecting his privacy by threatening Chiara if she continued to post about Mesa Falls."

She tipped her head back to peer up at the stars, struggling to pull the pieces together. What was she missing? Sliding her fingers free of Desmond's, she folded them in her lap, still feeling his touch where it had been moments before. Every whorl of his fingertips left an impression that hummed along her skin.

"Why do you think she had me fired? Do you think she saw me as a threat, as well?" Recalling her time spent here, trying to find out more about Alonzo Salazar and the identity of Matthew's father, Nicole remembered there was only one person who knew her real goal. "Only April Stephens, the financial investigator who looked into Salazar's book, knew what I was doing."

"But April shared your motives with Weston Rivera, who revealed it to the other owners." His breath huffed a mist of white between them before it cleared, the night air feeling suddenly too cold.

Although maybe the loss of Desmond's touch had more to do with the chill.

"So all of you knew what I was doing here. And you think Vivian found out because she worked closely with Alec?" She had her work cut out for her here with too many questions that still needed answers in order to offer her nephew security. Stability. He was a defenseless kid who needed her.

"That's the theory." Desmond's gray gaze missed nothing as it wandered over her. "We should go in soon. You'll catch a chill."

His other palm slid from the back of the bench to rest between her shoulder blades. The contact should have just warmed her, perhaps. But even through her coat, the touch reminded her of the fierce attraction that lingered between them.

Or, for her, at least.

Did he feel it?

"I still have so many questions, but I'm out of my depth with all of this," she admitted, referring to the intrigue that hung heavy over the ranch even though it aptly applied to the magnetic pull she felt toward the man beside her. "Now I feel like I need to speak to Chiara Campagna, if that's possible."

"She's organizing a dinner with the other partners, so we can all talk then." His hand rubbed the center of her back gently. "Let's go in, Nicole. You must be exhausted after the flight last night and another one today."

"And I woke up early—" She cut herself off, remembering the nature of the call that awoke her.

Seeing Desmond on her phone. Feeling her senses wake up along with the rest of her. What possessed her to bring that up?

She could tell he was remembering that moment, as well. His gaze darkened. But he rose to his feet and tugged her after him. "Since that was my fault, I feel all the more compelled to send you inside. You can get some sleep, and I'll text you tomorrow with details about the dinner so you can meet Chiara and the other partners."

She nodded mutely, not trusting her wayward mouth not to betray her in more ways.

Walking beside Desmond, Nicole returned to the lodge at his side, her thoughts still on his dictate that she get some sleep. She'd awoken in bed this morning to the sight of this man, albeit on her screen. And she knew without question she'd return to bed tonight with the image of him on the backs of her eyelids.

Three

Late the next morning, Desmond had the ranch's rifle range all to himself. The mountain meadow had a covered stand to protect guests from inclement weather where they could practice shooting reactive targets up to four hundred yards away. But for Desmond, shooting wasn't about getting out of the elements. Instead, he lay prone on a short rise off to one side of the covered stand, where a ranch employee waited to take his weapon when he finished.

His steel targets were just over a thousand yards away, the sport made more challenging by the crosswind coming off the mountain. He'd been lying here for almost an hour, getting a feel for the steady wind versus the gusts, timing his shots when the latter went still.

He'd hoped to clear his head after a restless night

without much sleep, his thoughts too full of Nicole Cruz. So far it wasn't working. He still wanted her with a hunger he'd never felt for any woman, and telling himself she was off-limits wasn't making a dent in that need. He needed to put his friendship with Zach—his loyalty to his friends and partners—ahead of his fascination with Nicole.

Indulging in his hunger for her would only cloud his vision where she was concerned, and it was crucial that he remain clear-eyed and focused to wade through the mystery of Matthew's paternity. Maybe it was a futile hope that lying in the snow would chill him out. But Desmond didn't get out to a range often since he'd purchased the casino, so he indulged the urge now to redirect his thoughts.

With the gusts quieted for a moment, he focused on his breathing, his finger bared on the trigger. Inhale. Exhale.

Inhale. Exhale.

An empty-lung shooter, he was ready to fire when he finished the exhale, eye on the target through his scope. But an old, unwanted voice sounded in his brain as he gently squeezed off the shot.

Aim small, miss small.

Gunfire sounding, Desmond cursed himself for giving his father's voice any bandwidth in his head.

"Nice one," the tech from the ranch's gun club called over to him from the stand. "You're just a hairsbreadth from dead center."

Which was a miss according to the man who'd dragged Desmond out hunting when he'd been far too young to handle a weapon. Securing the rifle now, he tugged off his hearing protection and levered to his feet.

As he walked down the hill to return the Winchester to the tech, he saw another figure inside the covered wooden stand.

Gage Striker, one of Desmond's partners, stood off to one side. A New Zealander with a devil-may-care way about him that flew in the face of his uptight family's political ambitions for him, Gage was a former investment banker who'd turned to angel investing, giving him more free time after years of working 24-7. Gage had recently reunited with Elena Rollins, the woman he'd nearly married six years ago until Gage's father had interfered with their relationship.

"Gage." Desmond greeted him with a nod before turning over his weapon to the waiting tech. "Are you waiting for the range? The crosswind is trouble, but it comes and goes."

"No." Gage waved away the offer of the rifle. "Waiting to speak to you, if you have a few minutes." He gestured toward the ATV waiting nearby.

"I'm surprised you knew where to find me." Desmond packed his hearing protection in the accessories bag before he joined Gage in walking toward the ATV. The snow was well packed here, the shooting range a popular guest attraction year-round.

"When you weren't at home this morning, I took a chance you'd be out here." Dropping into the driver's seat, Gage turned the key in the ignition, thankfully not remarking on Desmond's tendency to shoot when he was stressed.

It made no sense, really, since the dad he'd grown up resenting—often physically fearing—had been the one to teach him. But as time went by, his skills had surpassed his father's. And there was a comfort in being better with a firearm than your enemy. His dad had died of a heart attack nearly a decade ago, but the ugly legacy he'd left behind still resurfaced sometimes.

Desmond slid into the passenger seat, the frustration of the sleepless night still heavy on his shoulders. He didn't feel any need to share what being around Nicole was doing to him personally. There were enough more obvious reasons they were all tense this week.

"When did you get in?" Desmond withdrew his glove from his coat pocket and returned it to his shooting hand. "Is Elena with you?"

"Yes. We flew in this morning. She's been upset ever since she heard about Chiara being targeted by Alec's assistant." Gage put the ATV in gear and headed in the direction of Desmond's house. "I wanted her to stay away until we got to the bottom of this mess, but with Nicole and Matthew arriving, she booked the next flight out for us."

Gage and Elena had been in Los Angeles, where Elena still kept an apartment, but Gage resided in Silicon Valley, where they were planning to live full-time. Elena had been a fashion and lifestyle social media influencer, on a smaller scale than Chiara Campagna, but Chiara convinced her to expand her fashion design talents.

"So you're just in time for tonight's dinner with Nicole Cruz," Desmond observed, unable to leave her out of the conversation for long when she dominated his thoughts.

"Yes. Miles texted us this morning about that." Gage picked up speed as they reached a smoother road along a field they would use for grazing in the spring. As part of the ranch's green initiatives, they rotated grazing areas frequently. "But I wanted to get your thoughts on the situation before we all meet."

"On what?" Desmond grabbed the roll bar to steady himself as Gage took a bump at high speed.

"On Matthew Cruz's father. You know Chiara has been adamant that she saw Zach kissing Nicole's sister, Lana Allen, a student teacher at Dowdon."

Desmond remembered Chiara from their school days, before she'd reinvented herself with a new name for social media. Back then, Kara Marsh had attended the girls' school down the road. She'd had a crush on Zach and had been devastated to see him kissing Miss Allen the week before his death. Had Nicole's sister really preyed on a teenager? If it was true, Zach had kept it a secret from his friends. Lana Allen might have been young at the time—just twenty years old to Zach's seventeen. But Zach had been a minor in the care of the school, so a relationship would have been criminal.

"I'm aware." Desmond's temples throbbed, the stress of wading through the past weighing heavy. Miles had told them about Chiara's revelation just days ago, but the news had been overshadowed by Vivian Fraser's arrest for stalking and hacking. "I haven't asked Nicole about it yet. I don't want to bias her toward Zach until we see what she knows first. She might have an entirely different angle on this."

Part of him still held out hope that Matthew wasn't Zach's son. That Alonzo Salazar, their old mentor, had been helping support the boy just because Lana Allen had been his student teacher and not because Alonzo had been a friend or mentor to the child's father.

"But what's your gut telling you?" Gage scrubbed

a hand along his jaw, squinting through a light haze of snow that whirled through the open cab of the ATV when the treads kicked up loose powder. "Why would Zach come out as gay to us if he wasn't?"

"Damned if I know." Desmond had turned over the puzzle plenty of times and came up empty. "He could have been bisexual but didn't realize it that summer when he told us."

"But why come out at all if he wasn't certain?" Gage shook his head, dark eyebrows furrowed as he frowned. "Zach seemed fearless to me in a lot of ways, but even for a guy who seems like he has it all together, that's a bold step. Who does that if they aren't sure?"

An uncomfortable thought occurred to him, not for the first time. "You don't think he did it to help hide an affair with a teacher?"

"Absolutely not." Gage's voice was certain. Adamant. "He wasn't deliberately deceitful."

The knot in Desmond's chest eased a fraction, Gage's faith in their friend reassuring him. He'd echoed Desmond's own long-held opinion that Zach was the best of them. They'd always looked up to him.

"And yet he kept the relationship with Lana a secret. But if Zach wasn't Matthew's father, and we know none of us are, either, who else would Alonzo Salazar have been covering for to financially support Matthew Cruz?" He asked the question aloud, but of course Gage wouldn't have any answers, either.

Riding the rest of the way in silence, Desmond hoped they'd learn more once he introduced Nicole to his friends.

And if some part of him felt defensive of her being

put in the hot seat by the Mesa Falls partners, Desmond would just have to squelch it, along with all the other tangled feelings he had for Nicole.

Standing in front of Desmond's massive home on the Mesa Falls property, Nicole wondered how one person could possibly need this much space. The three-story stone-and-cedar-shingle structure perched on the edge of a small pond, with only a few wandering elk nearby for company. She'd ridden a snowmobile over from the main lodge, eager to continue her quest for answers today even though he'd texted her details about a meeting with his partners later tonight.

Did he honestly think she was going to sit idly all day when Mattie's future rested on her locating his father?

Frustrated, she pressed the button for the doorbell again, peering in through the leaded glass in the front door. She could hear the resonant sound of the chimes inside, although the place was so large she wondered if it could be heard in the farthest rooms. She pulled out her phone to text him that she was outside while she listened for signs of life within the house. But before she could open up the contact information on her screen, she heard a distant hum of a motor from somewhere behind her instead.

Stepping out from under the arched entryway, she stayed on the shoveled stone path to keep her boots out of the packed snow. The engine noise grew until she spotted a two-seater ATV heading toward her through the woods behind the pond. Pocketing her phone again, she wandered onto the back patio, where heavy outdoor furniture sat in a ring around a built-in fire pit. As the ATV neared, she spied two men in the front seat.

One of whom was definitely Desmond.

Her skin flushed despite the cold, awareness and anticipation combining to remind her that she needed to guard herself around him at all times. The heated draw was as distracting as it was compelling. Last night, as they sat outside watching the ice-skaters near the lodge, she'd been tantalized by the feel of his hand on hers. When was the last time she'd had skin-on-skin contact with any man?

The vehicle slowed near the patio, the driver parking the vehicle close to the shoveled cobblestones. A Plexiglas windscreen shielded them in front, but the low side doors had no windows, allowing her to see Desmond clearly as he unlatched the passenger side and stepped out near her.

"Nicole." His gray eyes sizzled over her with words unspoken, his attention as stirring as any touch. "I didn't know you were looking for me."

"I should have messaged you." She hadn't because she'd feared he might be avoiding her until the larger meeting with his friends.

"Nicole, this is Gage Striker." Desmond stopped beside her, gesturing toward the driver of the vehicle. "He's one of my partners you'll be seeing more of at dinner."

"Nice to meet you." She smiled politely, her manner businesslike. And although the dark-haired man with a square jaw and powerful shoulders was technically as handsome as Desmond, she found it easy to maintain her distance.

"You, too, love." He used the endearment the way some people said "friend" or "ma'am," although his New Zealand accent lent the word a different sort of

charm. "Thank you for making the trip to Montana."
He gave her a nod. "See you soon."

Then he pulled away, the engine humming louder
for a moment before quieting as the ATV headed up
the driveway toward the main lodge.

Leaving her alone with Desmond on the patio of his
rustic mansion.

"Would you like to come inside?" Desmond's voice
held an intimate note as he delivered the simple question.

Or was she hearing a subtext he didn't intend?

Her heart sped faster. She looked more carefully at
him now, taking in details she hadn't noticed before.
The crusted ice on the placket of his field jacket. His
red cheeks.

"If you don't mind," she said carefully. "But if I'm
interrupting your plans—"

"I have no plans other than warming up." His gloved
hand brushed the small of her back through her long
coat, guiding her toward a back entrance. "Let's go inside."

Her belly tightened as she moved in that direction,
hoping she hadn't overestimated her ability to remain
immune to this man now that she was accompanying
him into his house alone. Although she was curious
about what he'd been doing to leave ice down the front
of his jacket, she didn't want to take things to a more
personal level. Instead, she focused on the house as he
reached around her to disarm the alarm and open the
back door.

"This is a beautiful home." She stepped onto a three-
season porch with a stone floor and firewood neatly
stacked along one wall. Colorful wool blankets draped

over the arm of a sofa that looked out on the snowy backyard.

"I can't take much credit for it." He reached around her to open another door into the main house. "I told a builder what I wanted in a vacation residence when we first bought the ranch and haven't spent much time here since."

She followed him into a French country kitchen with cream-colored distressed wood cabinets and a white oak floor with wide planks. A wrought iron chandelier hung over an island that dominated the room. Everything was absurdly neat, with no personal items left on countertops or photos on the wall.

He waved her through to a smaller living area that was more like a den at the back of the house. A beige rolled-arm couch sat close to a hearth built into a stone wall. A real wood fire burned in the grate behind a wrought iron screen, though the warmth came from mostly embers now. Bookshelves lined one wall while another looked out over the frozen pond and snowy yard.

"If you give me your coat, I can get you something hot to drink while you make yourself comfortable." He moved behind her to take the long, fawn-colored garment, his hands on either side of her shoulders but not yet touching.

The heat of him radiated into her all the same.

"You don't need to go to any trouble on my account," she protested, taking in the intimacy of the small room.

Why hadn't she asked him to meet her at the lodge, where there were more people around? Less temptation to look her fill at the man near her.

"It's not just for you." He lifted her coat from her

shoulders and eased it down her arms. "I've been out at the rifle range this morning and I'll need something to thaw out."

For a moment she caught a hint of his scent as he stood behind her—sandalwood and musk. But before she could take a deeper breath to be sure, he moved toward the fireplace to lift a poker and stir the fire to life.

He added another log from a basket off to one side, then laid a second at an angle to the first. The dry edge of one caught fire almost immediately.

"In that case, thank you." Nicole lowered herself to sit on the couch, leaving him three-quarters of the space for when he returned.

She didn't ask him about the shooting hobby, even though she was curious about that, too. She hadn't come to Montana to make idle chitchat with Desmond Pierce, no matter how much he intrigued her. Withdrawing her phone as he left the room with her coat, Nicole pulled up her checklist of questions she wanted answered and things she needed to accomplish today.

In the kitchen, she heard him rummaging through cabinets and turning a burner on the stove. One of the items on her list was to call Matthew to make sure he'd settled back into his routine after their trip, but she didn't know how much time she had before Desmond returned.

When it seemed quiet in the kitchen, she rose from the sofa to glance at his bookshelves until he returned. Because while she didn't want to ask him personal questions directly, she couldn't deny it would be helpful to learn more about him in order to help her decide if her sister, Lana, had ever pursued a relationship with him.

It seemed impossible that her uptight step sibling

who always did the right thing could have had an affair with a student her first year as a teaching assistant. Frankly, the idea flew in the face of every belief she'd ever had about high-achieving Lana.

But who else could Alonzo Salazar have been covering for when he'd arranged to send that financial support to Matthew? Her gaze skimmed the titles on the shelves—business books, guides to interior design for consumer spaces, photo collections of famous casinos. No matter that Desmond said he hadn't spent much time here, those looked like books he would have chosen. Her fingertip followed the movement of her eyes as she came to the end of a shelf and spotted a row of leather-bound volumes beneath it that looked older, the titles in faded gold leaf. A few early American playwrights, some histories of Montana, a biography of a regional artist.

Her index finger came to rest on a copy of the Kama Sutra, and her mouth went dry. Not that it mattered one way or another that he possessed a copy of the world's oldest guide to pleasure.

Of course it didn't. But that didn't stop her cheeks from flaming when he stepped into the den with a stoneware mug in each hand.

"Find anything interesting?"

Four

Well, damn.

Desmond stilled where he stood near the couch, watching the interesting play of color over Nicole's lovely features. Pink flushed her cheeks. Her breath quickened between parted lips. He could see the rapid rise and fall of her breasts through the fitted, ivory-colored sweater she wore with dark gray jeans. As he watched, her teeth sank into the fullness of her lower lip, holding it fast. And he couldn't seem to drag his gaze away from that spot, certain he felt a phantom bite on his own skin.

Apparently he hadn't needed to bother preparing hot cocoa. This woman fired up his insides just being in the same room with him.

"I was admiring your book collection," she murmured finally, long after he'd forgotten what he'd asked.

Thankfully, the words broke whatever spell her hectic color had aroused in him, forcing him to get his mind off her delectable mouth. And hell, he had no business thinking about her that way when he had a job to do as intermediary with her for the other ranch owners. He couldn't put off talking to her about the DNA test results any longer.

"I've forgotten what volumes I have here," he admitted, setting down the two stoneware mugs on a marble tray resting on the coffee table. "I read most of them during the summer we spent hashing out the ranch mission. Other than that visit, I haven't been in Mesa Falls in years."

She moved around the opposite end of the sofa from where he stood, taking a seat in the far corner. "I haven't had enough time for reading since my sister's death. My life changed so dramatically overnight." With one hand, she slid a sofa pillow onto her lap, her fingers flexing in the burgundy-colored velvet. She kept her phone held tight in the other. "I'm only just starting to get my feet underneath me again."

He couldn't help but feel a pang of empathy for her as he focused on her hands. Her fingernails were unpainted, and gold filigree bands threaded around two fingers on each hand. Chips of colored gemstones were woven into a few of them.

"I'm sorry for what you've been through." He dropped onto the sofa cushion at the other end of the couch, not wanting to crowd her. Needing distance for his own peace of mind, too. He slid the marble tray closer to her so she could reach her drink more easily. "I never lost a blood-related sibling, but the death of someone I thought of as a brother left me walking around in a fog of grief for the better part of a year."

Longer, really, since he'd felt responsible for Zach's death. All his friends did in some way. They'd failed Zach when he needed them most, because whether or not he'd intended to jump to his death, he'd definitely been upset that weekend. They'd taken the trip to try to be supportive of whatever he'd been going through. Zach hadn't wanted to discuss it, but he'd wanted to leave campus, and they'd all gone with him.

The guilt was heavy. But Desmond wouldn't keep failing him now. If there was any chance Matthew Cruz was Zach's son, Nicole needed to know about him. He'd hoped to wait for that discussion until tonight, to gauge his conversations with her in case she had other ideas for whom her sister had been seeing nine months before Matthew's birth. But with Nicole sitting in his den beside him, Desmond couldn't wait any longer.

She reached for her mug, staring at him curiously.

"Lana wasn't my sister by blood, either," she confided. Surprising him. His private investigator had only just begun to search for answers about Lana Allen. They hadn't known the connection to Nicole and Matthew until days ago, when Chiara Campagna had picked out Lana Allen in the background of a yearbook photo from Dowdon School. "Before I was born, my father married her mother to protect Lana and her mom from Lana's abusive dad."

Thoughts of Zach faded as this new information came to light. Desmond had more in common with Nicole than he ever would have suspected—the death of a sibling figure, for one thing. Domestic violence for another.

He went cold at the possibility of anyone hurting Nicole.

Or, hell, Matthew.

The idea of someone like Desmond's dad getting anywhere near this woman and the vulnerable kid she guarded, who could be Zach's son, had him shooting to his feet.

"Is he still in the picture? The abuser?" Desmond's voice hardened. He heard it but couldn't help it as he walked woodenly to the fireplace and tossed more logs on the fire. Even though he'd already done that when they first came in the room.

The twitchy need to move was too strong to ignore.

"No." Nicole set her mug back down. "God, no. Lana never saw him again. And I kept an eye out at her funeral just in case her dad could have somehow heard about her passing, but there was no one."

"You're sure?" He ground his teeth, hating the way his own past with his father could still freeze him from the inside out.

He used one log to move the end of another one already in the fireplace, sending sparks onto the stone hearth. The scent of burning applewood intensified.

"Positive. My father was deep in his own grief at the memorial service, but if Lana's father had been in attendance, Dad would have recognized the guy." She scooched forward on the couch, her auburn hair spilling over one shoulder as she moved. "Why?"

He had no intention of bringing up his own past with his father. Sebastian Pierce had moved on long ago, leaving Desmond's mother once he'd taken as much of her estate as he could get his hands on. If only the guy had been just a thief and not a violent thug. Desmond had more than made up for her financial losses, but he couldn't give her back the emotional security and sense of self his father had stolen. With an effort, he tamped down the old anger to refocus their conversation.

"I'm just thinking of Matthew's safety." Rising again, Desmond paced around the den, pausing in front of a small, leather-topped wooden desk. He opened the center drawer to retrieve an envelope. "And in regard to your nephew, I've heard back about the paternity tests." Withdrawing the envelope, he laid it on the marble tray between their mugs. "We already had the results from Alonzo Salazar's heirs, and there is no genetic tie between Salazar and Matthew, either."

"I never suspected Mr. Salazar. Lana looked up to him, but he was much older than her." Nicole lifted her drink, pursing her lips to blow gently across the hot surface.

His mouth went dry as he imagined the cooling stream of air over his heated skin. For a moment, he simply stared at her, wondering what was happening to him that this woman could make him lose perspective so fast.

When she raised her warm-chocolate eyes to his, he realized he'd been quiet too long, lost in thoughts of her. Steeling himself, he forced his brain back to the painful task to come.

"We're in agreement there. None of my partners thought Alonzo would have violated a professional code of conduct that way." Desmond would forever be grateful to the only teacher at Dowdon to have an inkling of what they'd been through after Zach's death. "But I have the other paternity test results, as well. There were no genetic matches between Matthew and any of the Mesa Falls partners, either."

Confusion clouded her gaze before her focus went to the documents he'd placed before her.

"You've already heard back?" Setting the mug down, she thumbed through the papers briefly, then huffed out a breath as she set them on the couch. "What am I even doing here if none of you are Matthew's father? I'm back to square one in my search."

"Not exactly." He braced himself for the pain of what had to come next—talking about Zach, whose death had rewritten his whole life and everything he knew about himself. "The friend I mentioned earlier—the one I said wasn't related by blood, but he was like a brother to me?" At her nod, he continued. "Zach Eldridge went to Dowdon with us. He died in a cliff-jumping accident fourteen years ago, but we've heard recently that he might have had a relationship with Lana."

For a long moment, Nicole stared at him blankly. "Fourteen years ago?"

"He died the autumn before Matthew's birth." Desmond knew the boy's birth date from the private investigator's files. It was seven months after Zach's death.

Blinking fast, Nicole shifted aside the sofa pillow. "Do you have a photo of him? Of Zach?" She rose to her feet, still appearing a bit dazed as she hugged herself with her arms. "Was this friend your same age?"

Leaning a shoulder against the stone fireplace surround, Desmond withdrew his phone to search for an image while the flames in the hearth popped, the logs shifting.

"I have a photo somewhere. He was in the same grade as me, although he was a year older." Desmond had never spoken about his friend to anyone outside the group he'd attended school with. "Maturity-wise, however, he was light-years older than all of us."

"It just seems entirely out of character for my perfectionist sister to have an affair with a student." She twisted one of the gold rings around her pointer finger, an agitated gesture as she came to a stop in front of him. "No matter how mature your friend was, it's tough to imagine Lana being tempted into a deeply unethical relationship that could have resulted in prison time. I couldn't get past that part whenever I thought about one of the Mesa Falls owners as being Matthew's father either. It doesn't seem like something Lana would have done."

"I understand. A relationship like that is upsetting to consider. But it could explain why my friend was so upset that last weekend before he died." Desmond continued scrolling, wishing he had better answers for her. Answers that wouldn't bring Nicole more pain in a year that had already been beyond difficult for her.

"I'm just surprised I haven't even heard of him before now. Zach Eldridge," she mused aloud, testing out the name.

"He was in the foster system, and his death was problematic for both the state and the school. News of it was kept to a bare minimum, and never in connection with Dowdon."

Zach had taught Desmond how to fight. A lesson that had meant the difference between merely surviving his home life and getting rid of his bastard father for good. The only sad part of the day Sebastian Pierce packed up his bags forever was that Desmond hadn't been able to share it with Zach.

"Thank you for helping me," Nicole said suddenly,

her hand falling lightly on his forearm. "Especially now that you and all the other Mesa Falls owners can't be Mattie's father. It's kind of you to continue to help."

Her touch affected him like a lightning strike. But damned if her deep brown gaze wasn't just as compelling. Maybe even more so.

"If my mentor risked his name and reputation to write a book that would support Matthew's upbringing, then the boy is important to me. To all of us at Mesa Falls. Period. I just wish Alonzo was still alive so we could ask him what he knew."

He passed over his phone with an image of Zach standing next to a painting he'd done at a school art show. "Do you recognize him?"

Nicole took the device with unsteady hands.

Part of her unease came from this latest development in her search for Matthew's father. But a bigger share was the awareness that lit through her just from standing beside Desmond in the cozy room that smelled pleasantly of wood smoke. Touching him hadn't been wise since her fingertips still hummed from the contact.

Did he feel any portion of this electricity? Maybe if she had more experience with men, she would have a better answer to that. But seeing the way her sister's plans for her future had evaporated once she'd gotten pregnant had had a dramatic impact on Nicole at an impressionable age. She'd avoided boys altogether, gathering none of the experience most girls had by the time they went to college. Even then, Nicole had focused on her studies. Afterward, her few dating choices had been purely practical, lacking any of the charged sensation she felt around the man beside her.

Angling Desmond's phone screen to see the photo better, she felt her breath catch at the sight of a young man she did indeed recognize. Brown eyes full of laughter stared back at her from an angular face with dark hair that swept over thick, straight eyebrows. He stood on a grassy hilltop flanked by a younger version of Desmond Pierce, whose gray eyes were as chilly and forbidding as his friend's were warm and inviting. The contrast made her all the more curious about Desmond, even as she wondered how his friend figured into her sister's life.

"To think he's only a few years older than Matthew is now," Nicole murmured aloud, her brain full of questions about Lana's past and the secrets she'd kept. "I don't see a resemblance between them though, do you?"

"Nicole." Desmond's voice was close to her. The lone word spoken like a demand. "You *do* recognize him, don't you?"

She was too rattled to think through potential consequences, too intrigued to be cautious. Besides, Desmond could apparently read her well, so she didn't bother holding back.

"I saw them together the summer before school started," she admitted, her gaze veering between the two faces in the photo. "It didn't occur to me he might be a student. I though he was a local."

"Zach went to an art program that summer." The words sounded pulled from him as if by an effort, and she recognized that even now, talking about his friend was painful. "He was on campus then. Where did you see him?"

"He walked her home once." In her mind's eye, she could still see Lana smiling up at the tall, broad-shouldered young man. "We lived off-campus even though my father did gardening work for Dowdon. When the weather was nice, Lana liked taking walks into the nearby village."

At least, she assumed that's where Lana had been coming from on the day Nicole recalled. She would have paid better attention if she'd ever guessed her sister's life and the company she kept would be of so much importance now that Nicole had guardianship of Lana's only child.

"Did they seem…close?" Desmond asked, studying her face as if the clues he sought might be written there.

"Maybe?" She bit her lip, wishing she could recall more than a vague impression of her sister flirting with the guy. "I was still young, so I might not have understood the nuances of their body language."

"And that was the only time you saw Zach?" Desmond pressed, forcing her to explain herself.

He stood close enough to touch. Close enough that if she breathed deeply she could catch a hint of his sandalwood scent.

"That was the only time I'd seen them *together*," she insisted, wanting justice done. "But I saw Zach alone at an art show near the end of summer."

His eyes flicked to hers, stirring the uneasy interest again, the one that made her insides ache and her skin feel twitchy.

"What does your gut tell you, Nicole? Do you think your sister had an affair with my friend?"

Her stomach knotted. That actually would account for a lot of strange things that had happened that year. Lana had quit her college program without finishing her student teaching. Then she'd moved away suddenly, taking work in a library in Oregon. Once Nicole had learned about her sister's pregnancy, she'd assumed that was why, although it hadn't really accounted for not getting her teaching degree when she'd been so close to finishing. But if she'd had an illicit affair?

It made her ill to think about it. And she wasn't ready to share that with Desmond. Plus, as much as she wanted answers, she also feared what she might find out about the other side of Matthew's family. What if another legal relation—someone with an actual blood tie to the boy—wanted to take Mattie away from her?

"I don't know. Can we get a DNA sample from one of Zach's relatives?"

"He doesn't have any that we know about," Desmond told her flatly, his eyes fixed on her. "That's one reason he was in the foster system. He lived on the streets for three months after his father died, but then child services picked him up. He attended Dowdon on a scholarship."

"How sad for him," she murmured, more to herself than Desmond. She paced away from him, thinking out loud, her finger running idly over one of the rows of books on a nearby shelf. "Although it makes sense that Alonzo Salazar would pitch in to help Lana's child if he knew the father of her baby was dead and there were no relatives who could help my sister support him."

"Perhaps." Desmond's noncommittal answer made her look up sharply to peer at him over her shoulder.

"You don't agree?" She halted at the end of the bookshelf, her fingers pausing to rest on a leather volume.

"I just wonder how Salazar knew your sister's circumstances in the first place." Desmond followed her across the den, stopping beside her. "She left school suddenly and we never heard any more about her."

His nearness made her heart race faster. She glanced down and away from him, her gaze falling on—of all things—that too-intriguing Kama Sutra book she'd noticed earlier. She wrapped her arms around herself, needing more barriers between her and the man who affected her so strongly.

"Lana argued with my dad and moved out over Thanksgiving break. Then, my father packed us up and moved us to a new town after that." At just four-teen years old, Nicole had been furious at the time—at her sister as much as her dad. Little did she know how difficult the situation had been for both of them, too. "I never understood why, but I thought it had something to do with my sister's refusal to name the child's father."

Nicole's parents had already been divorced by then, but the move had made it difficult to see her mother. Not that her astronomer mom had ever made great ef-forts to see her, since she was attached to her work more than her family.

"Lana must have left school the same time Zach died. No wonder we didn't hear anything about her preg-nancy," Desmond mused aloud, his gray eyes wander-ing over her, missing nothing. "That must have been a difficult time for you."

The empathy in his gaze seemed to tug her toward him. Blinking, she told herself it was an illusion. She didn't have any reason to trust Desmond. And she sure wasn't trusting her own instincts right now when her every atom was pulling her toward the man in front of her. She wanted to kiss him, she realized with total clar-ity and more than a little surprise.

She wanted to fist her fingers in his shirtfront and drag him the rest of the way to her before rising up on her toes and brushing her lips over his for a long, thorough taste.

"Desmond." His name escaped her on a sigh so needy-sounding she wished she could call it back. Appalled at herself, she covered her mouth with her fingers for a moment while his eyes darkened. Her hand fell away from her lips to try and steer the conversation away from the awkward moment. "That is—I could use some fresh air."

Oh, that was smooth, she chastised herself. Her heart pounded harder, and she imagined her face growing redder with each beat.

"That's probably a good idea," he agreed in a reasonable tone even as he reached for her. "But I need to do something first."

When his fingers landed on her shoulders, she knew she wasn't alone in feeling the electric connection between them. He must feel it, too, or he wouldn't look at her this way right now. Like he was a starving man, and she was a gourmet meal he needed to devour. Yesterday.

So she didn't question what he needed to do, because whatever it was, she wanted him to do it. Immediately.

Preferably with his hands, his mouth and his delectable hard body, too.

But then his lips crashed down on hers and she couldn't think at all. She could only sink into the most sinfully hot kiss she'd ever known.

Strong arms enveloped her, pressing her close. Her nerve endings flamed to red-hot life, set afire by all that taut masculine strength. The scent of his aftershave teased her nostrils while his lips coaxed hers wide, his tongue sweeping over hers until she swore she could feel that same sensual caress in her most intimate places. She shivered with the thought, her nipples puckering into tight points.

He backed her up a step, guiding her toward a wall that steadied her when her knees felt weak. Her head tipped back as she offered her neck for another kiss. He licked his way lower, the heady feel of his mouth at her throat calling a whimper from her.

She wrapped her arms around his neck, all sense of caution lost when he edged back a few inches from her, his eyes dark with desire. For a moment, they breathed each other in from that close distance as the world slowly returned.

Desmond's eyelids fell shut for a moment. When they flicked open again, there was a coolness in their depths.

"Fresh air might not be enough to quench the fire." He levered away from her but took one of her hands in his as he led her toward the door. "We'd better keep an eye out for a snowbank."

Five

Desmond didn't have a plan other than trying to get himself under control again. Something that wouldn't happen if he remained in close quarters with Nicole another minute.

That kiss.

He hadn't wanted it to ever end. Even now, as he retraced their steps from when they entered the house to retrieve their coats, he felt the residual flames her touch had incited. Heat roared through him while the need to taste her again was an insistent ache. Knowing he didn't dare help her into her long overcoat for fear of peeling all her clothes off instead, Desmond passed her the garment before punching his fists through the sleeves of his own. Then, on second thought, he returned to the kitchen, grabbing an insulated picnic hamper from the pantry and bringing it to the Sub-Zero, where he transferred a package with the day's catering delivery into the basket.

"Would you like a hand?" Nicole offered as she pulled her outerwear tighter around her, the belt accenting her narrow waist.

"No, thanks." His gaze skipped over her, his eyes lingering on curves that even layers of wool and cashmere didn't hide. "I just thought I'd bring something to eat."

If he was feeding one hunger, he couldn't very well act on the other, more insistent one.

"Where are we going?" she asked, absently twining the ends of her hair into a braid that started at her shoulder.

"I'd love to show you around the ranch on horseback," he offered, suggesting the first thing that came to mind that would keep them out of the house.

"Sounds wonderful. I love to ride." She trailed her fingers over the lapel of her long overcoat. "I'm not dressed for it, though."

His gaze followed the motion of her hands, his brain mentally replacing her palms with his. Hell, he could practically feel her just imagining it. He ground his teeth together and charged toward the back door.

"There are extra jackets in the tack room," he said with a growl in his voice, recognizing his surly manners and powerless to soften them.

He held the door for her, though, arming the alarm system behind them as they left the house and started toward the stable. The structure was small compared to the horse barns near the lodge or the even bigger, utilitarian building situated on the portion of Mesa Falls that served as the operations base for the working ranch.

But the three stalls inside a cedar-shingle building were more than enough for Desmond's needs. He led

Nicole into the stable, the scent of fresh hay and horse mingling with the fragrant cedar of the walls.

"What beautiful animals." Nicole stopped at the stall door of a pretty buckskin mare, and stroked her nose. "What are their names?"

"That's Spirit, and the chestnut is Sundancer. These are two of my favorites." He paused by the stall to greet the animal. "A ranch hand brought them over from the main lodge's stables last night. I've only been on-site at Mesa Falls for three days myself, so I'm still getting settled." It hadn't helped that he'd been preoccupied as hell ever since arriving.

He'd been intrigued by Nicole after one phone call. Then, after the accidental video chat while she'd been in bed, Desmond's fascination with her had grown exponentially. Spending time with her in person now— alone—was killing his resolve to keep his distance.

"I'm sure the transition between life at the casino and the ranch is considerable." She cooed at the horse and tipped her forehead to the mare's. "But I can help prep if you show me the tack room."

Desmond set the insulated picnic hamper on a shelf by the door and walked to the back of the stable. "You don't need to do that."

"I insist." She surprised him by following him toward the pegboard where the bridles were lined up on metal hooks. "My father raised me to care for animals that served me."

He passed her a lined canvas jacket for riding, and she eased out of her more formal cashmere and wool coat. While his instincts as a gentleman barked at him to assist her, he still didn't trust himself not to kiss her again so soon after the scorching clinch in the den. He'd memorized the exquisite feel of her pressed against him, and he burned to recreate that moment, only with less clothes between them.

Preferably none.

He busied himself with the bridles, pulling two down from the hooks while he tried to forget the swell of her breasts, the rapid tattoo of her heartbeat and the swift intake of her breath when he'd swept his tongue into her mouth that first time.

"Your dad sounds like a good man." He cursed the harsh note in his voice as he passed her the bridles and carried the saddles himself. "You said he was a gardener?"

He stopped outside the stalls, hefting the saddles onto the racks near the cross-tie points in the aisle. Nicole laid one of the bridles near the rack and kept the other one in hand as he led Spirit out of her stall.

"Yes. He was head gardener at Dowdon for five years." Nicole helped him secure the animal in the cross ties, then cooed to the mare while she slid the bridle over her head. "I wasn't excited to move there when he took the job, since my parents had just divorced, and my mom made it clear she wasn't seeking any visitation rights. But I came to like the town."

"Wow. That had to have been rough. How old were you?" He ran a brush over the mare's back, curious about her.

"Nine. Mom is a renowned astronomer." She hesitated.

At her pause, he stopped brushing the horse to see her face. She looked out one of the open windows, her teeth nibbling at her lower lip in a gesture that made his throat go dry.

When she continued, she turned her dark eyes on him, and he set down the brush to lay a saddle blanket over the mare.

"I'm proud of her. She leads her own research team studying solar magnetics. But it wasn't always easy to take second place behind the sun." She reached over to smooth the blanket while he retrieved the tooled leather saddle. "I've vowed to make sure Matthew knows he comes first with me. Always."

He couldn't help but respect the conviction in her voice. His own mother hadn't been able to put him first, either, because Sebastian Pierce had demanded her full attention at all times. What would it have been like to grow up with a parent who advocated for him?

"Matthew is lucky to have you in his life." Desmond bent to tighten the cinches, grateful for something to keep his hands busy when he wanted them on Nicole. "There aren't many people who could have devoted as much time to finding answers about his parentage as you have."

"Thank you. But it's getting to be *too* much time." She helped him unfasten the cross ties now that Spirit was ready to ride. "I guess I'm fortunate to freelance my graphic design skills so I can take the extra weeks away from the job, but if I want to pay Matthew's next tuition bill, I'll need to return to work soon."

He brooded on that while he led Sundancer from his stall to saddle him. He didn't want to offend her by intruding on her finances, but since they affected a child who could be Zach's son, he couldn't keep silent.

"What about the legacy from Salazar's book? I thought the nominee service that forwarded profits had instructions to continue payments after his death?"

Securing the horse, Desmond repeated the procedure with Sundancer while Nicole held Spirit's reins near the barn door.

"It does." She spoke stiffly. Unwillingly? "But I can't in good conscience continue to let Matthew accept the income from a book that ripped apart a family and profited on a scandal that caused real people harm."

He understood her reasoning but her scruples weren't going to give the family depicted in *Hollywood Newlyweds* back their lives before the scandal. He'd have to convince her to continue taking the funds Alonzo had worked hard to ensure could support the boy. An argument he'd save for the next time he needed distance from those too-compelling dark eyes, or the siren's call of her full lips.

For now, he adjusted the saddle and sufficed to say, "If Matthew is Zach's son, he's entitled to a portion of Mesa Falls. This whole place was built as a way to remember Zach, so it's only natural we'd share it with his son. That would ensure Matthew's financial future."

He didn't need to check with his partners about that. They would insist upon it as much as he would. They'd rewrite the deed into sevenths instead of sixths to include Zach's heir.

"That's a big *if* we may never be able to prove." Nicole stared at him with challenge in her eyes, her chin tilted up. "And no matter what we learn about his parentage, I'm not going to relinquish my spot as his primary guardian no matter the financial incentive. It's probably best we're clear on that from the start."

Her voice vibrated with emotion he hadn't expected. But before he could assure her that wasn't his intent, she was leading Spirit from the barn, her head high and her back ramrod straight.

Damn.

He'd wanted to cool things off between them. He hadn't meant to send her into deep freeze.

Steeling himself for riding beside her for the afternoon, he told himself it was better this way. Safer for all parties if he kept Nicole at arm's length. But the part of him that remembered how she tasted sure as hell mourned the loss.

Nicole fumed for the first twenty minutes of the ride, aggravated by the idea of the wealthy and powerful ranch partners involving themselves in Matthew's life. Yet, as she eyed the Bitterroot River from a high vantage point above the valley, she admitted the fresh, pine-scented air had helped ease some of her indignation over the next hour. Seated on Spirit's back with the calls of woodpeckers and kestrels in the trees above, she soaked in the natural beauty of western Montana, still dusted with snow, thinking how much Matthew would enjoy this place.

Ahead of her, Desmond reined in his mount, forcing her to slow Spirit's trot to a walk. Her host had spoken little during the tour of the ranch, but she hadn't required a guide to observe the appeal of the picturesque vistas.

"Are you hungry yet?" he asked, breaking a long silence.

Her stomach growled in a reply she was surprised he couldn't hear even a few yards ahead of her.

"I wouldn't mind something to eat." She glanced around the trees for a comfortable place to rest. "Should we stop?"

"There's a tree house up ahead if you're game to try it out." He nodded toward the north in the direction they were already moving.

"A tree house?" She couldn't hide her skepticism as she peered around again, wondering if she'd missed a residence. She remembered all of the owners had homes on the Mesa Falls land, though none of them had been built close to the others. "Way out here?"

"Yes." He shifted his weight in the saddle, cueing the sleek chestnut he rode to pick up the pace again. "We're almost there."

By the time he halted again, she'd given up keeping an eye out for a structure. Now, she looked up as she slowed her horse.

They stood surrounded by trees, the heavy limbs branching in all directions making a thick network overhead even without leaves. Yet ahead of her, she spied the underside of a two-story structure perched between four maples, a cedar staircase climbing through the trunks and then forming a walkway that circled the coolest tree house she'd ever seen. On closer inspection she could tell the lower level was an open-air deck with a table and chairs. Above that, a snug house of cedar with black-painted shutters looked like something out of a fairy tale. A few different rooflines gave the structure visual interest, with a wide peak over the hobbit-size front door, a dormer on one side and a connected mini-building that looked like a gatehouse tucked into the V of heavy tree branches to the west.

"Wow." She breathed the word reverently, charmed in spite of her determination to keep Desmond at arm's length. It was hard to hang on to her anger with him when it felt like she'd just entered Wonderland. "Is this some kind of retreat for ranch guests?"

"No." Swinging a leg over Sundancer's back, Desmond dropped to the ground. "The builder who designed my house talked me into using the leftover materials on this. He gave me a deal because he wanted to test out a new blueprint."

"It looks like something Hansel and Gretel would find in the forest." Following his lead, she slid off Spirit and secured the horse next to Desmond's.

"I'm hoping no witches have taken up residence since the last time I was here." He unclipped the insulated bag from his saddle and tucked it under one arm before waving her toward the tree house. "But let me know if you want me to go in first and clear the building, just in case."

She laughed until it occurred to her maybe bears could be up there. Wrapping her arms around herself, she scanned the place again, looking for signs of movement around the open deck on the lower level.

"That's not such a bad idea." She hurried to keep up with him as they crossed the soft bed of pine needles, the snow cover thin beneath the trees. "Don't you have a lot of wild animals in Montana? My father might have raised me with an appreciation of the natural world, but I'm still more of a city girl at heart."

"Mesa Falls has worked hard to bring back more of the animal population with our conservation efforts, so we're proud of the fact that there are more wild animals here than ten years ago." He waited for her at the base of the cedar stairs, the wind ruffling his dark hair. With the high color in his cheeks from the outdoor air, he looked at home here. More relaxed.

And very appealing.

Her heart thrummed faster as she reached his side to peer up into his gray eyes. "Don't wild animals bother the cattle?"

A grin pulled at his lips. "The elk and antelope can peacefully coexist with ranch animals. But I'll go make sure there are no wolves waiting for you up here."

Her gaze tracked his progress, lingering on the way denim hugged his thighs as he climbed. Her pulse fluttered at the thought of being alone with him again, even as she reminded herself that she should be on guard around him. All the reminding in the world wasn't easing the magnetic draw of the man.

When they reached the lower level with the open deck, she saw the small table and chairs that would be perfect for an outdoor meal. Yet Desmond didn't pause there. Rounding a corner, he continued up the next flight of stairs toward the main building. The scents of cedar and pine permeated the air until they reached the front door, where he entered a code into a security panel.

"You can't possibly have electricity out here," she exclaimed, glancing around from her higher vantage point to see if there were other buildings close by. But even up here, she could only see more trees.

"I assure you, I do." Opening the front door, he stood back to admit her. "It cost a small fortune to run the underground cable out there, but this way if we ever want to rent out the space to guests, we'll have the option."

She stepped into a miniature living room, complete with hardwood floor and a small wood stove built against a river-stone hearth. A low leather sofa sat before it, with an antique steamer chest for a cocktail table. Behind the living area, a small kitchen with a two-burner cooktop and wet bar area was partially surrounded by a countertop with three wooden stools.

A heavy chandelier hung over it all, drawing her attention up to the high ceiling, where a ladder led to a loft bed that looked out the dormer window she'd seen from outside.

But on the main floor, to one side, she saw the hall that must lead to the second building built to resemble a gatehouse. Through the open door, she could see a larger bedroom with what looked like a queen-size bed, and a connected bath area.

Her attention returned to the bed, heat streaking through her. Momentarily robbing her of her voice.

Thankfully, Desmond continued to speak as he closed the door behind him. "We'd need to convert the wood stove to a gas model if we let guests stay here. But for now, I prefer a real wood fire." He lowered the picnic hamper to the counter in the kitchen and strode the few steps to the cast iron unit, where he tossed in a few logs and some kindling from a nearby basket.

Shaking herself out of her inappropriate thoughts about testing the bed, Nicole's cheeks heated as she darted toward the food he'd brought.

"Guests would love to stay here. Especially kids. There's something so fanciful about the design." Peeling off the lined canvas jacket she'd borrowed from Desmond, she pulled things out of the hamper in a hurry, needing to redirect her brain. A variety of sandwiches were individually wrapped and neatly labeled. There was also a fruit plate and a large bottle of sparkling water. She found glassware in a cabinet under the counter, then poured water for both of them. "Matthew would think this was the coolest thing ever."

Desmond was quiet for a moment while he struck a match to light a twisted mound of kindling.

Then she recalled their exchange back at his house had been about Matthew—about whether or not they'd be able to prove the boy's relationship to Zach Eldridge. Would she ever bring Matthew here if he was related to Desmond's friend, knowing what a strong allegiance Desmond felt for his long-ago roommate? Or would she refuse to bring Matthew precisely because the Mesa Falls partners might use their wealth and influence to interfere in her guardianship? She was only just beginning to know Desmond. And she didn't know his friends at all.

Lost in a tangle of worries, she hadn't heard Desmond approach until he suddenly covered her hand with his. The warmth of that simple gesture called her from the swirl of questions she couldn't answer. It seemed like all she'd done was worry since her sister's death. For this one moment, with Desmond's hand on hers, she couldn't help but feel a comfort that—right now, at least—she wasn't alone.

"Nicole?" He stood close to her in the small kitchen, his big body taking up all the room.

Or maybe just all her thoughts.

His grip tightened ever so slightly on the back of her hand, the touch reassuring and inciting at the same time. With just that one simple contact, she remembered the way he'd kissed her back at his house. Like he couldn't get enough of her.

How ironic they'd ridden all this way to escape the

intimacy, only to dive right back into it at the slightest touch. Clearing her throat, she tried to make an answer.

"I'm—" *Drowning in desire.* She couldn't tell him that, though. She waited for her brain to start working again, to think about anything else besides memories of his mouth on hers.

His smoke-colored eyes darkened as he seemed to read her thoughts. His nostrils flared, his chest rising and falling harder, as if he'd been running.

"I assure you, I am, too," he muttered under his breath, skimming a hand along her cheek to cup her face and turn it up to his. He tunneled his fingers into her hair, lifting it from her back and twisting the length around his hand. "Whatever you're feeling right now, I'm so right there with you."

Her scalp tingled from his touch. Her skin was suddenly too tight. A wicked heat curled through her belly, pooling deep inside her. She pulled in a sharp breath that tasted like wood smoke and Desmond. She remembered all too well the flavor of his kiss. Her gaze dipped to his mouth, longing thick in her veins.

"How did you know what I was thinking?" she asked, her fingers trailing up the front of the fitted olive-green Henley he wore, her touch dipping and rising along a roller coaster of hard-muscled ridges until she splayed her palm on his broad, warm chest.

"I didn't." His free hand curved around her waist, his fingers skimming her back while his thumb rode the waistband of her jeans just below the hem of her sweater. It circled the spot idly. "I just felt the temperature spike in the room when you looked at me."

Her throat was too dry to answer. She was out of her depth with him. She only knew she needed his kiss.

But he didn't close the rest of the slight distance between them, even though the heat kept rising. Confusion clouded her thoughts.

"Desmond." Her hand fisted in his shirt. Restless. Needy. "Please."

He tipped his forehead to hers, his skin even hotter than hers.

"Please what, Nicole," he urged her, lowering his lips to her ear to speak directly into it. "Just tell me what you want. I need the words."

The huff of his breath on her sensitized skin sent a shiver trembling through her. She canted toward him, her breasts brushing the solid wall of his chest in a way that sent pleasure streaking through her.

"Kiss me," she demanded, unable to think of anything else. "Kiss me again like you can't get enough."

Six

Nicole suspected she'd lost her mind along with her tenuous control, hardly recognizing the sultry command in her voice.

But she couldn't regret it. Not when Desmond edged back to look at her and she caught the moment that his gray eyes turned molten silver before lowering to fix on her mouth. One hand cupped the curve of her hip, the other settling on the back of her head to pull her to him. Then she sank into him.

His lips molded to hers, teasing and tasting. Exploring hers like new, uncharted terrain. Sensation fluttered in her belly, her fingers twisting in the fabric of his cotton shirt as if she could pull him any closer. Then he nipped her lower lip, sending pleasure arrowing through her while she gasped at the feel of his teeth. He licked the spot, soothing the sweet sting before his tongue slid inside her.

And she was lost.

She disappeared in that kiss, her mouth the center of a deep longing she hadn't known existed until he took his place there, tilting her head to perfect the angle of their joining. Making her melt. A moan escaped her, a soft, needy whimper she couldn't have hidden if she'd tried. Her knees went limp, her body trembling with shivers of anticipation. Want.

Luckily, his arm banded around her waist then or she might have slid to the floor. She couldn't have held herself up, not with this tumultuous hunger cartwheeling around inside her.

Desmond's hold tightened, sealing her hips to his, acquainting her with how much he wanted her. A lot.

A whole lot.

She wound her arms around him then, not just to anchor herself, but to ensure his lips remained where she needed them. Although, as heat seared through the rest of her body, there were other parts clamoring for that talented mouth, too. She craved that kiss everywhere, her brain too fevered to consider anything but how good it would feel. She'd been in survival mode so long. Grieving. Hurting.

She needed this hot forgetting. This burning away of everything else but addictive pleasure. His tongue stroked hers, sucking, demanding more. And she gave. Meeting his thrusts, dueling. When a low groan rumbled through his wide, hard chest, her nipples beaded to tight, aching points.

He broke the kiss abruptly, but his hands remained on her. The warm huff of his breath tickled her wet lips as he stared down into her eyes.

"If we keep this up, it's not going to end at just kissing." His voice, passion-roughened and deep, vibrated his chest and hers. "Tell me now if you're not okay with that, Nicole."

That he checked in with her was a credit to him. Swallowing hard, she couldn't find it in herself to put the brakes on an escape she needed. Desperately.

"I'm…very okay with that." She gave a jerky nod. Not because she was uncertain. Only because any movement that didn't involve fanning the flames between them felt awkward. Unnatural. "Just please, don't stop."

Later, maybe she would regret letting the depth of her need show in that hungry plea. But she couldn't possibly regret accepting the gift of his touch, just this once, when she needed to lose herself.

This. Woman.

Desmond's breath whooshed out of his lungs like a wind tunnel, taking any reservation along with it. Nicole might not *want* to desire him—he'd seen her hesitation in her fast retreat after their kiss earlier—but there was no arguing that she felt the same incendiary attraction that was burning him up from the inside now.

He would have backed off at the slightest hesitation. But her request was clear. Definite. And he had no intention of denying her when he wanted her every bit as much and more.

"Nothing would give me more pleasure than fulfilling that request." Instead of untangling her arms from around his neck—he liked them right there—he bent to lift her, hauling her body higher against his.

Gripping the backs of her thighs, he wrapped her legs around his waist to carry her to the nearest bed.

Her hum of approval pleased him almost as much as

the warmth of her body where it met his. Every step he took sent mind-numbing friction between them until it took all his restraint not to back her against the nearest wall and take what they both wanted. Instead, his fingers flexed, cupping her hips to hold her steady as he turned sideways to enter the bedroom.

Don't stop.

Her dictate circled in his head, his very own sensual mantra. He had no intention of stopping until her beautiful body came apart in his arms. Until she gasped and clung to him, giving him everything.

Securing her with one arm, he dragged her creamy-colored sweater up and off her with his other. The sight of her full breasts wrapped in ivory lace would have tempted a saint, which he most definitely was not. He tugged down one strap and then the other, gaze fixed on the swell of her flesh above the cups.

He used his free hand to trail a finger down the soft valley between her breasts. "I've been seeing this spot on the backs of my eyelids every time I close my eyes. Even when I blink." He lifted his eyes to see her watching him intently, her breathing as shallow and erratic as his. "Ever since you picked up your phone for that video call, all sleep-tousled and sexy as hell, the need to see you that way again has been a fever in me."

Gently, he lowered her to the bed, cradling her back as she hit the pillowy white duvet, red hair spilling out to either side. A fantasy come to life.

"You have an advantage over me, then." Unlinking her fingers from behind his neck, she skimmed both palms down his chest and then slid cool fingers beneath the hem of his shirt. "You've seen more of me than I have of you."

Satisfaction vibrated through him that she wanted more, even as her light touch sent a blistering wave of heat over his skin. Both stunned and grateful she'd said yes to this, he wouldn't question his good fortune. He reached behind him to tug his shirt up and off, grinding his teeth against the surge of need that made him want to sink into her now. But he forced himself to take his time. If this one encounter was all he ever got with Nicole, he would make it memorable.

But he hadn't counted on her lifting up to sit on the bed in front of him while he knelt between her thighs. And he sure hadn't counted on her tongue darting out to lick a path down his naked chest. Because both those things distracted him from his plans for her.

"Damn." He breathed the word on a long exhale, hardly daring to move while she worked the fastening on his jeans and lowered the zipper.

It took every shred of his disintegrating control to move her hand away from him before she stroked him through the cotton of his boxers. Especially with her lips still gliding damp kisses just below his hip. But he captured her fingers and somehow managed to lever himself off the bed.

"Don't move," he warned her, laying a kiss on her sexy auburn waves. "I need to find protection for us."

Charging into the small bath area off the bedroom, he hoped like hell there were condoms in there. He'd had a housekeeping service refresh the tree house before his visit, and he knew there were fresh towels and sheets. But he couldn't recall what he would have ordered for personal supplies. His eyes landed on a package. Seizing the box, he scanned for an expiration date, hoping against hope.

And...*yes*. Still good.

Packet in hand, he returned to the bed, weaving around an actual limb of the maple tree that grew up through the room. Then, catching sight of Nicole, he almost swallowed his tongue.

Her back to him, she stood by the bed, her hips in midshimmy to ease off the gray denim jeans she wore. An ivory-colored lace thong graced the curve of her hip, the fabric covering little and firing the need to have her under him. Over him. All around him.

"Let me." He set the condom on the bed and took pleasure in dragging the denim down her thighs.

She steadied herself on his shoulders, the silken fall of her hair brushing his back when he leaned down. On his way back up, he kissed the skin just inside her hip, inhaling the fragrance of coconut soap or maybe something she used on her skin. She smelled delicious, and damned if he didn't want to eat her all up.

But she pushed him back onto the mattress and he let himself fall, mesmerized by the sight of her taking control over him.

"It's been a long time for me," she murmured in his ear, her breasts grazing his chest as she reached for the condom on the bed near him. "I need...this. You."

"Then I should help," he reasoned aloud, wrapping her in his arms and reversing their positions. "For expedience's sake. I'm not sure I can keep it together if you're the one to put that condom on me. It's been a while for me, too."

Just the thought of her hands on him that way was enough to send a tremor through his muscles. He stripped off the rest of his clothes, mindful of her avid gaze, and rolled on the condom without delay. He left her panties in place while he joined her on the bed, though, dragging a knuckle down the center of them, gratified to find her every bit as ready as he was.

Still, he couldn't forget what she'd said about it being a long time since she'd been with anyone. He would make certain this felt good for her. Better than good. The need to imprint himself on her memory shouldn't have been so imperative, yet he couldn't deny it.

"Desmond." She gripped his wrist, steering him, her breathing faster. Edgy.

"Trust me," he said into her ear, slipping his fingers beneath the lace and watching her expression in the gilded touch of sun streaming through a high window. "I know exactly where I'm going."

She let go of him then. Both with her fingers and with the rest of her body. Relaxing a fraction, she bit her lower lip, her eyelids fluttering as he found the touches she liked most. He kissed her cheek, and her lips parted on a breathy moan. She was so unbelievably sexy.

Levering up on his elbow, he freed the clasp on the front of her lace bra, and the fabric fell away from her full breasts. He drew on one rosy nipple, suckling her, and her back arched off the bed. He switched to the other breast and slid his finger inside her. Her muscles spasmed hard around him while she cried out. Stroking, he drew it out for as long as he could, relishing every sweet shudder of her body. When she finally settled, he drew the lace thong down her legs and off.

Then he settled between her thighs.

Her dark eyes met his, her cheeks still flushed and her lips glistening. He couldn't resist kissing her as he edged his way inside her.

She felt incredible.

So amazing he fought the urge to sink into her over

and over again. He didn't want to rush her while she was still adjusting. He breathed through the need. Waiting.

"You okay?" He stroked a hand through her hair, let his thumb play over the fullness of her mouth.

"Good." She nodded, moving her hips as if to test the fit. "Really good."

Her sexy swivel was nearly his undoing. With pleasure, he returned the favor, working his hips. Taking what she offered. She was generous. Uninhibited. Passionate.

And he wondered if he could ever get enough.

The thought pulled him up short for a moment, but he shoved it away from him fast, needing to focus on Nicole. On her needs. Her wants. Her gorgeous body.

He rolled her on top of him, watching her, learning what she liked and how she liked it. But too soon, he felt his own release, too strong to hold back anymore. Reaching between them, he teased a touch over her. Once. Twice.

She stilled the third time, her body arching hard against him before she came with a soft, sweet cry. He let himself follow her, his shout drowning out hers until he was pretty sure he forgot his own name for a little while.

His breath rushed out in harsh pants, everything in him drained. Rolling to his side, he skimmed a hand through her hair.

Replete for the moment, he held her in his arms. He pulled the duvet over them to keep her warm, hoping what they'd just done didn't sabotage the working relationship they needed to have if they were going to find out the truth about her nephew.

About Zach.

At the thought, the temperature in the room dropped a few more degrees. A pit opened in his stomach. If

Zach proved to be the father of Nicole's nephew, Desmond would want to maintain some kind of relationship with her in order to ensure the boy had everything he needed. What if he'd just impaired his chances of doing so by acting on the attraction? He stilled, the first shadow of guilt creeping over him. He couldn't afford to alienate Nicole. But hell, he couldn't afford to let her think this thing between them was more than—

"Don't go there," Nicole said quietly, stirring beside him. "Whatever you're thinking right now...don't. Don't worry about it."

He realized she'd been watching him. And damn it, he was usually better at concealing his thoughts. Regret for whatever she'd seen reflected in his face made him want to fix it. He cleared his throat and tried to pull his thoughts together.

"I was only thinking we should—"

She covered his lips with her fingers.

"We should eat." She sat up, releasing his mouth to clutch the duvet to her chest as she went. "Shouldn't we?"

Clearly, she didn't want to have a discussion about what had just happened.

He wished they'd met under any other circumstances so that they could not think about the consequences and simply enjoy each other over and over through the night. But he steeled himself, knowing that wasn't an option.

"Or we could discuss the monumental shift that just happened when we need to work together this week," he reminded her dryly. He switched on a small lamp near the bed, the low-wattage bulb still making him blink. "It's bound to change the dynamics between us."

She closed her eyes for a moment. When she re-opened them, she met his gaze head-on. "Food first. Awkward conversation second. I'm too hungry to tackle uncomfortable subjects."

Was it wrong to table the discussion? But he understood about distracting hungers all too well. Or maybe he was ready for any excuse to delay talking about the inevitable—about why this attraction between them could never go any further.

She hurried to pull on her clothes again, and knowing she probably was battling possible regrets, he tried not to enjoy the view.

Tried.

When she was done, he pushed himself out of bed, guessing by her hasty retreat that he wasn't going to talk her into spending the night with him. Repeating what had just happened a few more times before dawn broke. Which was as it should be, no matter how much he wished otherwise.

He understood her distress. He couldn't deny having some of his own based on the difficult quest they needed to undertake together. As long as they both understood whatever was happening between them was temporary, they'd be fine. Because regretting what had just happened was impossible when he was already craving the chance to be with her again.

Nicole guessed the food was good, but she barely tasted anything in the aftermath of what had just happened in that bed. The incredible sex had been a revelation. The aftermath? She'd never forget the dark clouds that had filled Desmond's eyes afterward. She didn't know what he'd been thinking, exactly, but it had obviously been some form of "I've made a huge mistake" based on the furrow that had deepened between his eyes. The haunted expression in his gaze.

But for now, she could regroup while they ate.

Thankfully, Desmond had served them both, unwrapping dishes so she could expend her mental energies on pulling her thoughts back together. They sat side by side at counter stools in front of the narrow bar separating the tree house's living area from the small kitchen. Desmond, in deference to her wish to delay the inevitable discussion of what had just happened, made small talk about the ranch and its eco-friendly mission.

Nicole, in the meantime, absently stacked apple slices on her plate while wondering how to recover her footing in this relationship. She'd never experienced anything like what she and Desmond had shared. The intimate encounters that she'd had in the past had either been awkward or mildly enjoyable. There hadn't been anything close to urgent need, insatiable passion or a chemistry so potent it stole her breath. That she should feel all those things with Desmond, a man she had no reason to trust and every reason to be wary of, was unaccountable.

The situation made zero practical sense. She'd never thought of herself as the kind of woman who could just…combust like that. She could only attribute it to the stress she'd been under these last months since her sister's death. Her own grief had shaken her to her core. But her father had been—remained—inconsolable, and Matthew had needed a parent. So there hadn't been time to deal with her grief—she'd just had to push through.

Could that suppressed stress account for her over-the-top reaction to Desmond? Still too aware of him beside her, she considered the possibility while staring out a window at the graceful limbs of the maple trees that braced the cabin in the sky.

"Desmond." She interrupted his polite observations about the wildlife resurgence around Mesa Falls, needing to get the worst of the awkward conversation over. "I know that what happened today can't happen again." She congratulated herself for how steady her voice sounded despite the anxiety on the inside. "You don't have to worry that I'll have the wrong impression."

"It's not that I don't want it to happen again. Hell, if it was up to me, we'd—" His gray gaze roamed over her in a way that turned up the heat all over again. But he seemed to call back whatever he was going to say with an effort, shuttering the hunger in his eyes. "I just didn't want to give you the wrong idea about what it meant."

The hurt of that particular phrasing was sharp. And it pierced her far deeper than it should have. But she nodded, hoping he hadn't seen her flinch.

"I won't misunderstand," she assured him. Then, with an effort, she steered the conversation away from that land mine of them sleeping together. "Can I ask you a question about something unrelated?"

Hoping she appeared unaffected, she picked up a knife to spread a mild goat cheese onto a baguette slice. If she wanted any hope of redirecting her thoughts from their combustible chemistry and the emotional fallout of the aftermath, she needed to think of something besides how his touch had elicited the hottest moments of her life.

"Of course." He watched her, his gaze as sharp as ever.

"Earlier, when we were in the barn with the horses, you mentioned that Mesa Falls was built as a way to remember your friend Zach." At the time, she'd been too indignant at the prospect of the Mesa Falls partners flexing their financial weight to increase their say over Matthew's life to really look beyond the surface of the comment.

"What of it?" Desmond pushed back from the counter in his chair, his green Henley still lightly wrinkled where she'd fisted the fabric to draw him closer.

The memory of how he'd made her feel warmed her skin all over, although the realization that it couldn't happen again cooled her off again.

"Why Mesa Falls?" she asked in a rush, needing to return to her real reason for being here—unraveling the mystery of Matthew's father. "Did Zach like Montana? I'm just wondering why you chose this place when you all went to school in California."

Desmond refilled his water glass from the bottle before he answered.

"Two reasons. First, Zach liked Thoreau's book about life in the woods, and he talked about doing something like that. Getting a remote cabin and living away from everyone for a while." The words were so halting that she wondered if it was still hard for him to talk about his friend. "And also because he loved horses. The last trip we all took together, we were on horseback."

Nicole tried to remember what he'd told her about his friend's death. When Desmond mentioned Zach the first time, she'd been preoccupied with the potential connection to Mattie. "He died in a cliff-jumping accident?"

A quick flash of emotion darted through his eyes before it was gone again. This time she didn't question if talking about his friend hurt, because clearly it did. But then, she knew she'd never get over the hole left in her since Lana's passing.

"Zach died during that last horseback riding trip.

He jumped into a river from a well-known local spot. But it had rained the night before, and the water level was too high." Desmond stared without seeing, lost in a memory. "He'd been upset that weekend, but we didn't know why. He had a rough past, so we all assumed it had something to do with that."

An awful thought occurred to her. "You don't think he could have been upset because—"

"Because he'd just found out Lana was pregnant?" Desmond shook his head, not in denial so much as despair. "Believe me, I've been weighing that possibility myself. No doubt it would be upsetting news for any teenager, especially if it meant an illicit relationship with a teacher was going to come to light."

Her appetite fled, and she shoved aside her plate. "It can't have happened like that. If Zach jumped to his death right after Lana informed him of the pregnancy, she would have been devastated. She never would have been able to keep the news to herself—"

"She wouldn't have known." Desmond sounded so sure of that point. "I didn't remember when she'd left teaching, but you said it was over Thanksgiving Break. That was the same time Zach died. And Dowdon kept the news of his death out of the papers for weeks. Even then, it was only a death notice with no reference to the school."

"She moved to Oregon. She probably wouldn't have seen it anyhow." Her belly knotted at the thought of her sister's affair. She'd always assumed Lana's boyfriend had rejected her, but if Zach was Matthew's father, the circumstances had been so much different than she'd imagined. It would make sense that Lana never admitted what had happened. "I'm surprised she wouldn't have tried getting in touch with him after Matthew was born. Or maybe she did…"

She trailed off, trying to recreate what could have happened. Feeling like she'd never known Lana at all. How would Matthew feel to learn something like this about his mother—that she'd had an affair with a student? "We're only just guessing that Zach knew about the pregnancy. She also could have broken things off with him without telling him about the baby, to protect them both from scandal. A breakup could also account for why he was upset that weekend." His jaw flexed as he began to wrap up the leftover food and clear the dishes they'd used.

She couldn't deny that sounded plausible. "Possibly. Maybe finding out she was pregnant made her come to her senses about what she was doing. She had to know that kind of relationship was wholly inappropriate. Not to mention illegal."

"If it even happened," he reminded her, tucking the food back into the insulated bag. "That's another big *if*, since we still can't be sure Zach is Mattie's father."

The frustration of the unanswered questions was evident in his voice. For the first time, Nicole began to see why Desmond needed to uncover the truth about Matthew's father, too. Clearly, Lana's pregnancy had significant implications for someone he'd cared about.

"Maybe meeting with your friends in a couple of hours will help." She found herself wanting to reassure him even though she had a lot of worries of her own.

She told herself that was just natural human empathy, but as they packed for the trip back to the ranch, she couldn't help but wonder if her need to comfort Desmond was part of the emotional fallout of getting close to him today.

"I hope so." His words were brusque, and something about his tone told her the subject was closed as he hefted the bag on his shoulder and passed her her jacket. "But before we go to dinner, I just want you to know that *I've* never believed Zach jumped to end his life."

Sliding her arms into the outerwear, Nicole followed him from the tree house. Any relief that she might have felt over avoiding an awkward conversation about where they stood since sleeping together was mitigated by the troubling new information about Zach Eldridge and her sister.

She'd almost reached the door when a small framed photo near the exit caught her eye. She hadn't noticed it on their way in.

"Desmond?" The image stopped her in her tracks. She reached up to trace the wavy line of a horse's mane behind protective glass.

Ahead of her, he stepped back into the tree house, sealing off the blast of cold air from outside.

"What's this?" Wary excitement teased the back of her brain, even though she wasn't sure what it meant. "Where did you get this?"

"It's one of Zach's sketches." He stood shoulder to shoulder with her, his nearness stirring her. "If it looks familiar, it might be because Alec Jacobsen, one of our partners, uses a stylized version in a popular video game he designed—"

He stopped himself, probably because she was already shaking her head.

"I have almost this same exact sketch at home." She'd never played a video game in her life, so she hadn't seen it there. "It belonged to my sister."

Seven

"You look like you could use a drink, mate," Gage Striker observed as he refilled Desmond's tumbler.

A drink? Desmond seriously doubted chugging the whole decanter of their host's best bourbon would take the edge off this evening. He'd brought Nicole to Miles Rivera's house for dinner with a few of his partners and their significant others. In theory, it should have been less tense than the last few meetings of the Mesa Falls partners since it was more of a social occasion. There had been less media focus on the ranch in the weeks since Vivian Stephens's arrest, plus the public was content with the explanation about Alonzo Salazar's book profits going toward humanitarian efforts.

Tonight, no one was looking over their shoulders, so they could relax. Jonah Norlander was back in Tahoe with his wife and daughter. Alec Jacobsen was globe-trotting to promote one of his new games. But the rest of them were here. Dinner had been pleasant enough while they'd been making small talk. Gage's fiancée, Elena Rollins, had made a visible effort to put Nicole at ease, comparing notes with her about some of the more remote areas of Southern California they'd both visited.

Desmond had been intrigued to learn more about the redheaded bombshell who'd rocked his world only a few hours before, but he'd been forced to quit eavesdropping at that point to respond to something one of his partners had asked. Now, the group had relocated to the billiards room downstairs. The younger of the Rivera brothers—Weston—had challenged Miles to a round of eight-ball. Desmond sat at the sleek mahogany bar behind the game table while the four women made themselves comfortable on the leather sectional that wrapped the opposite corner of the room.

From his vantage point at the bar, Desmond could see Nicole peering at something Chiara Campagna showed her on her phone. A red wave slid forward over Nicole's shoulder as she leaned forward, her simple emerald-colored sheath dress hugging her curves the way he wanted to. Lost in thought about the dress and—damn—the curves, it took him a minute to register Gage's snicker from the bar stool near him.

"I'll take that as a 'Yes, I'll have a double.'" Accordingly, his hulking New Zealander friend splashed more bourbon into Desmond's tumbler before returning the decanter to the tray on the bar. "Care to explain why you can't tear your eyes away from our guest long enough to form coherent sentences?"

Desmond's response was a string of very coherent expletives that only increased Gage's amusement. Miles turned up the volume on the surround-sound speakers playing country music while Weston took the opening break and called his first shot.

Gage tucked a boot heel around the footrest of his bar stool as he straightened in his seat. "Hey, I'm only pointing out what's obvious to all your friends. Something's going on between you and Nicole Cruz, and it's more than just the mystery of her sister's son. The weird vibe was there from the moment you two entered the house before dinner." Gage lowered his voice as he raised his glass in front of his lips like a shield. "And when I say weird vibe, I mean the attraction is evident, so don't bother to deny it."

An attraction he'd stupidly shut down too fast by letting Nicole glimpse his doubts. He regretted that his need to define the relationship—to make it clear she couldn't expect more from him—had prevented them from enjoying each other again since that first time.

"Should I blame your engagement for this sudden intuitiveness? Or have you always been this full of sensitivity?" Desmond unbuttoned his suit jacket as he leaned an elbow on the bar, their seats swiveled to watch the pool game. Weston was on a run, calling his third shot. "And when I say *sensitivity*, I mean you're full of—"

"Skip the protests," Gage cut him off. The ice cubes clinked in his glass as he shook it lightly. "You know as well as I do you lose objectivity that way. I just finished walking that fine line myself, and I can tell you I'm glad to have come out on the other side of it."

Desmond couldn't question his friend's insight, not after what he'd been through. Gage and Elena had been estranged after a bitter separation six years prior, due to Gage's father's interference. When Elena had come to Mesa Falls for a scoop on the notoriously reclusive owners about the Hollywood tell-all book linked to their ranch, she'd not only been looking for a way to pay her bills. She'd also been ready to throw Gage under the bus because of their unhappy past. But the mutual attraction had undermined the efforts, leading them to renew their former engagement.

The whole scenario had been over-the-top. And lightning didn't strike twice in the same place. Although, looking around the room, where financial investigator April Stephens's eyes tracked Weston as he played pool, and social media influencer Chiara Campagna sent a cheeky wink to Miles, Desmond amended that thought. Some Bermuda triangle kind of electrical storm must be hitting the Montana ranch to make three of his closest friends lose their heads over women in the last few months.

But he'd be damned if he'd follow their example.

"I'm not losing objectivity," Desmond countered, tossing back half of his bourbon in the hope it would give him enough patience for this conversation. "If things seem strained between Nicole and me, it's because we spend our time together talking about the past. About Zach."

Which was partially true. Her revelation about one of Zach's pictures belonging to her sister had circled around Desmond's head every bit as often as memories of being with Nicole. She'd taken a photo of the framed sketch in the tree house and planned to share it with the group, starting with Chiara, who knew the most about Zach's art. In fact, seeing the way Nicole pulled her phone from her narrow leather clutch, he guessed she was about to do just that.

Gage clapped a hand down on his shoulder. A brief,

tangible commiseration. "No doubt, the memories can be rough. I'm hoping maybe, once we get through this mess and have more answers about the past, we can put the bad parts behind us for good. Focus only on what Zach gave us."

Desmond lifted his bourbon glass in silent toast to that idea.

"I hope." He took one more sip and then set the tumbler aside, needing to be clearheaded to get through this evening. After the dinner party, he'd be driving Nicole back to the main lodge. Just the two of them. And he couldn't afford to make any more decisions based on the chemistry between them. "There was a time we thought Mesa Falls was going to do that—put the past to rest so we could focus on the good memories we all have of Zach."

"Alonzo Salazar's book being linked to Matthew Cruz made that impossible," Gage reminded him. "What remains to be seen is whether or not Matthew is Zach's son."

"And if he is, what role do we play as Zach's friends?" Nicole hadn't wanted to hear about the possibility of Matthew being deeded a portion of the ranch, but he knew his friends would insist on it.

Hell, *he'd* insist on it.

But he couldn't help a competing desire for Nicole's happiness, too. And it bugged him to think that she would be upset about him and his partners being more involved in Matthew's life. Just because he had no desire to be a parent himself didn't mean he'd jeopardize Matthew's future. Far from it.

He watched as Chiara took Nicole's phone from her, clearly engrossed in whatever Nicole showed her. The other women leaned closer to peer at the screen over Chiara's shoulder.

Nicole looked on, a tiny furrow between her auburn brows that made him want to kiss the spot to ease whatever worry put it there. And where the hell were thoughts like that coming from? He had thought—hoped—maybe acting on the heat between them would excise the tension between them. But if anything, taking her to bed had only added fuel to the fire, forcing him to acknowledge his fascination with her wasn't going away anytime soon. No matter that he'd made it clear things could never move beyond the physical.

He wanted her with a hunger—a fierceness—that backhanded him. The thought was interrupted when Chiara rose to her feet, Nicole's phone still in her hand.

"Gentlemen." Chiara stepped up to the billiards table, her floor-length gold gown making her look like she'd just stepped out of her own Instagram. But although she was one of the most photographed women in the world, her looks didn't compare to the redhead in emerald still seated on the love seat. At least, not in Desmond's eyes.

Miles put down his cue stick as she neared him. "What is it?"

"You all need to see this," Chiara announced before glancing back to where Nicole sat. "Right, Nicole? It's okay to share?"

Nicole nodded, but that small worry line was still etched in her brow. Desmond fought the urge to cross the room and sit beside her. Tuck her under his arm. It didn't matter that he'd made it clear their relationship had to be temporary.

He slipped off the bar stool, needing to see whatever Chiara had indicated. Gage followed him, and soon all eight of them crowded around the pool table as Chiara laid Nicole's phone next to her own. Nicole remained on the opposite side of the table from him, though her gaze landed on his once before flitting away again.

On the green baize–covered surface, Nicole's screen was lit, displaying the image of Zach's framed drawing in the tree house.

"When Nicole recognized one of Zach's sketches in Desmond's tree house earlier," Chiara began, "she had her father photograph a similar one that had been in her sister's possession." Chiara swiped a finger over Nicole's phone screen, revealing a second image almost identical to the first, except there were more background details and shading around the central image of the horse. "I think we can all agree the artist must be the same, especially put in context of the time they were drawn. Nicole knows Lana framed the drawing to hang in her son's bedroom, so she had it in her possession before Matthew's birth."

There was a murmur through the group.

Desmond's gaze darted to Nicole's face, wondering if he'd see any hint of guilt for not sharing the information with him first. Impatience simmered along with irritation that she'd kept quiet.

Chiara hit the home key on her own phone, bringing the next screen to life with an image of the box for Alec Jacobsen's most popular video game—*Hooves of Thunder*. The game box featured the main equine character prominently, and no doubt there was a resemblance between Zach's drawing and the now-iconic figure.

"We knew about that, though," Miles reminded his girlfriend, slipping an arm around Chiara's waist. He spoke gently, but somehow the tone brooked no argument. "And Alec gives Zach credit in the game."

"Right," Chiara acknowledged. "Posthumous credit for one character." She tapped Nicole's screen to brighten it once again and then swiped to change the image. A fox, a boar and a rooster appeared in quick succession, each one taking up a page in a sketchbook. "What about all these?"

Desmond sucked in a breath even before she tapped the second screen and swiped through those same characters as they appeared in screenshots from the popular video game. The resemblance was marked. Obvious.

Weston swore under his breath. Gage leaned closer to the table, blocking Desmond's view.

Instead, he looked to Nicole to gauge her expression, wondering if she'd made those connections. But her dark eyes were shuttered, leaving him to keep on wondering.

"What's the source of the sketchbook images?" Desmond asked, his attention still on Nicole.

She seemed to become aware of being everyone's focus, and she folded her arms around herself. Her chin lifted as she answered him. "I found a sketchbook in Lana's things when I cleared out her apartment. I boxed it up along with a few other important items because I recognized the style from the framed image she'd hung in Mattie's nursery."

Miles reached for Nicole's phone, stretching one of the images and scanning the borders of the paper. "None of the drawings are signed?"

Nicole's dark gaze shifted toward Miles. "No. My dad made a special trip to my house to photograph these things, and I asked him if he'd ship them all here tomorrow so you can examine them for yourselves."

The tension in the room was palpable, and not just because of the awkwardness between him and Nicole. Meaningful looks passed between all of the couples. A new uneasiness crept through Desmond.

He shared it with the group because it had to be on everyone's mind. "We're going to have to discuss what it means for us—for Mesa Falls—if Matthew Cruz is Zach's heir."

That didn't mean he wanted to have that discussion now, in front of Nicole. But they needed to acknowledge the likelihood. Prepare for it. Alec and Jonah would need to be roped in for a conference call since they weren't on-site.

Miles replaced the phone on the table. Nicole recaptured the device, squeezing the cover in a tight grip.

When she spoke, her tone was knife's-edge sharp. "Will you discuss what it means if your friend stole Zach's intellectual property? Or are you going to sweep that under the rug the way you've conspired to cover up Zach's whole existence?"

No doubt the accusation insulted every man in the room. But to Desmond, it sure felt heaped on him.

"That's not fair," he began, but she didn't seem interested in the explanation, because she swept up her leather clutch from the arm of the sofa and walked out of the room.

A few minutes later, Nicole stood alone in the front foyer of Miles Rivera's huge house on the ranch property, staring out the floor-to-ceiling windows onto the horseshoe-shaped driveway illuminated solely by landscape lights. She heard someone coming up the stairs from the billiards room and tensed.

She wasn't ready to talk to Desmond.

But the light tap of high heels on the tile floor made her turn around.

Chiara Campagna strode toward her, so beautiful she looked like her own personal filter followed her around at all times. With her perfect skin, rosebud lips and sheet of long, dark hair, she had fairy-tale princess beauty. Add in the flawless fit of her gold gown, the tasteful—and no doubt hugely expensive—accessories like the red-bottom shoes, sapphire cocktail ring and a bag by one of France's most coveted designers, and it was easy to see why the woman turned heads everywhere she went. And why her Instagram following rivaled the biggest celebrities in the world. Nicole couldn't help feeling underdressed by comparison.

Even so, Chiara and all of the other women at the small dinner party had welcomed her warmly. Chiara in particular had shown real interest in Matthew, asking about his childhood and his school program, demonstrating an earnest desire to know more about the boy. By contrast, her kindness had brought into stark relief how little Desmond had wanted to know about Nicole's nephew. The realization had been the first of two unhappy epiphanies over the course of the evening.

The way Desmond and his friends had hidden their dead friend's life and achievements rather than celebrate them put into perspective why it had been so damned hard to learn more about Matthew's connection to Mesa Falls. It was beginning to become clear to her now, however. Who could doubt Zach Eldridge had fathered her sister's son?

As Chiara drew nearer, Nicole refocused her thoughts.

"I hope I didn't offend you with my remarks," Nicole offered with an apologetic smile. "You've been nothing but kind to me."

Chiara took Nicole's hand and squeezed it briefly before letting go. "On the contrary, you asked the same kind of hard questions I've been putting forward to Miles for weeks."

Perhaps she didn't conceal her surprise very well, because Chiara continued.

"Trust me, I want answers as much as you do about Zach." A flash of pain streaked through the woman's eyes before she blinked, and the hurt was gone again. "And I think Miles and his partners—Desmond included—all want that, too. But they're torn and confused about what their next move should be."

"Then why have they conspired to hide Zach's life from the world?" Nicole had never seen a reference to him, making her question how the group would welcome his son. "If Mesa Falls is really their way of honoring Zach, where is the plaque in the lobby? Why no mention of him in the mission statement? They say they care, but it's like he never existed."

Chiara leaned a shoulder on the pane of glass overlooking the front yard, her golden gown reflecting the glow from a wrought iron chandelier in the foyer. "I think not talking about him is a habit long engrained. At the time, Gage Striker's politically ambitious father intervened with the school administration to keep the news of the death out of the local papers, and Dowdon was only too happy to oblige. And since none of Zach's friends had professional grief counseling as teens, they did a patch job on the trauma and somehow limped along with it, paying homage to Zach with the ranch."

Nicole mulled that over, wanting to believe things could be easily resolved. She knew how difficult Lana's loss had been for her. What might it have been like if something had happened to her when she'd been a teenager? She remembered Desmond's words when he'd first told her about it.

The death of someone I thought of as a brother left me walking around in a fog of grief for the better part of a year.

"What do you think they'll do now? They can't possibly deny that one of their own has been profiting off Zach's talents." Nicole had been stunned to see the images Chiara pulled up on her phone from Alec Jacobsen's popular video game. The similarity to the drawings in the sketchbook were obvious.

Chiara's dark eyebrows furrowed. "What's the earliest date you remember seeing that sketchbook in your sister's possession?"

"The year Matthew was born. I saw it in one of Lana's drawers when I was babysitting Mattie." She'd made the trip to Oregon for a visit, and to help watch her nephew while her sister worked.

"Good. That means no one can suggest the sketches were drawn after Alec's game came out. Whoever drew those images—and I know for a fact it was Zach—was a huge contributor to the success of the video game series." Shadows flitted through the other woman's eyes. "But it might take some time for Desmond—for all of them—to come to terms with the idea that one of their own is a traitor."

"I just hope the news doesn't distract them from figuring out if Zachary Eldridge is Matthew's father. It seems significant to me that my sister hung one of his drawings in her baby's nursery, almost as if she wanted a connection to the boy's father there. Finding out the truth about Mattie's dad is my only reason for being here."

The sound of footsteps preceded a man's voice behind her.

"Nicole, are you ready to leave?"

Desmond stood just a few feet away. Close enough that he must have overheard at least some of their conversation. She'd been so engrossed, she hadn't heard his approach. His steely eyes were cool now. His expression remote.

No hint of earlier intimacies lingered.

Which was just as well, right? He'd wasted no time making sure she didn't "get the wrong idea" about what had happened between them.

She needed to focus on tracking down Mattie's father, not indulge in a hot affair. So it didn't matter what Desmond thought of her now. Although she couldn't deny a sense of loss at the memory of his arms wrapped around her just hours ago. His kiss. His touch.

She blinked past the desire.

"Very ready," she assured him, matching his coolness. "Let me just say my good-nights and we can go."

Turning from him, she reminded herself it was for the best they break things off now rather than run the risk of someone getting hurt later. But knowing what was best for her didn't make it any easier to distance herself from the most compelling man she'd ever met.

Eight

Desmond stared at the computer screen in his study, poring over the details of Zach's drawings from the sketchbook that Nicole said she'd found in her sister's things.

Desmond hadn't wanted to wait until the actual book arrived. He'd asked her to send him digital copies of the photo images after the dinner party at Miles's house. It had been the extent of their conversation on the ride home, since neither of them had been in the mood to talk.

Finding out the truth is the only reason I'm here, she'd told Chiara, referring to her search for Matthew's father. The simple statement shouldn't have been any surprise to him. He'd known as much. But considering what had transpired between the two of them—the desperate can't-get-enough-of-each-other sex—maybe

Desmond had hoped that he'd ranked somewhere in her reasons to be in Montana.

Apparently not.

While he shoved that thought aside with the weariness of a man who'd done the same thing a hundred times, a knock sounded on his study door.

"Come in," he answered, never glancing up from the screen.

"Mr. Pierce?" A woman with his cleaning service opened the door a sliver. "A Miss Cruz is in the front room for you."

His stomach dropped like he'd just buckled into an amusement park ride. But he simply powered off the screen and stood.

"Thank you." He dismissed her with a nod. "I'll be right with her."

He told himself that whatever Nicole wanted didn't have a damned thing to do with him. No doubt she had more questions for him about Zach's past or the drawings, or some other connection between her nephew and Mesa Falls. But knowing as much didn't stop a jolt of hunger for more.

Much, much more.

As he closed the study door behind him, he wanted to believe that the need for her was purely physical. Their connection had been unlike anything he'd ever experienced before, the memories of it so hot and all-encompassing that thinking about her could drag him right back to that afternoon, enticing him to relive every minute of it over and over again. And something about that overwhelming sensual immersion made him fear what he felt for Nicole went beyond the physical. Her protectiveness for Matthew made her a force to be reckoned with, a job she'd undertaken even though she wasn't Lana's—or Matthew's—blood relation.

Desmond admired the hell out of that kind of loyalty, especially after growing up in the kind of household he had. Nicole's commitment to Matthew humbled him.

Nearing the formal living room at the front of the house, Desmond braced himself for the inevitable effect of seeing her. He'd thought his first glimpse of Nicole in her sleep camisole had been the reason for his fascination. But he now realized she could have been wearing layers of sweats and he still would have been every bit as captivated.

"Nicole." He spoke the name like he was releasing a breath, all the pent-up need for her appeased—in part, at least—by seeing her again.

Today, she wore a pale blue sweater with a gray wrap skirt, the hem printed with the image of an iris bloom. Her long auburn hair hung in loose waves around her shoulders, the ends spiraling in ringlets he wanted to coil around his fingers. Had she gone to extra effort for him, he wondered? The idea was appealing, but he dismissed it, recalling her words.

Finding out the truth is the only reason I'm here.

He'd do well to focus on that.

"I hope I didn't disturb you," she began, turning from the view of Trapper Peak and the Bitterroot Mountains. "I received the sketchbook by special delivery today. I thought it might help to see the physical object, since my father didn't photograph all of it."

She pointed toward a flat package he hadn't noticed propped against a table near the front door.

There was something detached in her manner today, the same reserve that had been there since they'd left

Miles's house the night before. He should be grateful for it.

Instead, he could only think about how much he'd rather have her hands on him. Peeling off his shirt. Her fingernails pressing into his shoulders as he did something that pleased her. Yeah, he hated the distance between them.

"You didn't disturb me." He took another step toward her, as if pulled there by invisible force. "I was looking at the photo images of the sketches, so if anything, the arrival of the original makes the work easier."

The cover of the book hadn't been photographed, for instance. He wondered if there were clues to the owner's identity on the inside cover or on the back.

"What are you looking for in the drawings?" she asked, sounding a little breathless.

Because he was closer to her? He hoped so.

"I'm not entirely certain," he admitted, wishing he had more concrete answers. "But finding something new of Zach's—something I didn't know existed before—is like hearing his voice again."

Her dark eyes tracked his. The fact that she looked up at him now made him realize he'd somehow moved closer still.

"I know what you mean." She nodded, the red curls dancing around her shoulders with the movement. "I spent a long time going through Lana's belongings after her death. Touching things she'd touched. Discovering little treasures that I knew must have been important to her based on where I found them. A note in a jewelry box drawer. A dried corsage from a long-ago dance."

A vulnerable look passed through her eyes, and he couldn't resist the urge to touch her. He stroked a hand over the silky length of her hair, sifting his fingers through the soft curls.

"I can't imagine how tough this year has been for you." He admired her grit for taking on all that she had. Loss of her sister aside, there would have been a lot of practical matters to take care of in securing legal guardianship of her nephew. "It couldn't have been easy to become a parent overnight."

For a moment, she stood very still. Not moving nearer, but not moving away, either. He fought the need to bend his lips to her hair and kiss the top of her head. To pull her against him fully and offer her the comfort of his arms around her.

But then she stepped back and out of his reach. She returned to the window overlooking the mountains.

"It was awful." Her voice revealed the power of her emotions or he might have been more troubled by her need for space. She hugged her arms around her waist. "My father was devastated. He's still inconsolable about losing Lana. So I didn't have any help from him in comforting Matthew." She glanced back at him over her shoulder. "And Matthew processed his grief a little differently from how you might expect a boy his age would."

Desmond shook his head. "If I learned one thing from Zach's death, it's that people—all of us—process grief uniquely. Alonzo Salazar was good about finding us all outlets to deal with it."

"How did you deal with it?" she asked, surprising him.

He debated how much to say. He'd never been comfortable revealing that part of his life, but if he ever wanted the chance to be close to this woman again, he couldn't keep pulling away. He'd been the one to put the distance between them that he already regretted.

"Good works." He crossed the living area to stand near her at the window. "I put every second of my free time into helping at a local shelter that benefited battered women and kids. I needed to build something positive. It was my way of honoring a cause that was important to Zach."

Her dark eyes were perceptive.

"I remember how concerned you were when I mentioned Lana's father was abusive," she remarked softly. "Did Zach come from a violent home?"

"We both did." It was an admission he'd never made to a woman before. Only his friends knew about his past. "Zach was the first person to recognize what my home life was like. He—"

The memory of that bond—of finding someone who understood, someone he didn't have to explain to—the relief and gratitude he'd felt were beyond explanation to anyone who hadn't lived that particular hell. "He helped me get through it. To fight back."

She slid her fingers through his, a touch so welcome he couldn't help but squeeze her palm tight at the wordless support. The understanding all the more valuable because it wasn't tinged with pity.

Dragging in a long breath, he continued. "Anyway, I put all my grief into volunteering at the center. Sorting donated clothes, refereeing games for the little kids, cleaning the place. Whatever they needed. I organized a class fundraiser through Dowdon that helped the center purchase a new building."

"You were far more productive during your mourning than I've been during mine. Some days I feel like

I'm barely hanging on." She stared down at their interlaced fingers. "When I let myself think about the fact that I'll never talk to her again, it hurts so much it's almost hard to breathe."

With his free arm, he pulled her against him, pinning their locked hands between their bodies. For a long moment, he simply held her, wishing he could take away some of the pain. Knowing there was no way to fast-forward through the steps of grieving a loss like that. He couldn't tell her that the loss got any easier, because in his experience, it didn't. You just got better at finding ways to deal with the pain of missing someone.

She stirred against him and he released her, sensing she might need to collect herself. She ran a hand through her hair, her long skirt swishing around her calves where high leather boots hugged her legs.

"I should show you the original sketchbook my father shipped to me," she murmured, half to herself, as she paced near the narrow package leaning against a table. "Chiara seems positive this book belonged to Zach. She didn't remember seeing him with this one in particular, but she pointed out a few doodles on the cover that he liked to make on all his books."

"Has she already seen the original?" Desmond moved to help Nicole lift the kraft paper–covered book onto the coffee table. He held the paper while she tugged the book free.

She dropped into the closest love seat, and he sat beside her. His knee grazed hers, the contact enough to send his thoughts hurtling back to the tree house, where he'd gotten intimately acquainted with every square inch of her. Their gazes collided, and he would bet from the way hers darted from his that she was remembering the same thing.

"No. But last night she texted me photos of some ink drawings she made from memory. Then, when this arrived today, I sent her a picture of the cover." Nicole withdrew her phone from her leather handbag and turned the screen toward him. "These were her images."

Desmond took the device from her, carefully reviewing the ink sketches along with Chiara's note about the designs Zach liked to doodle while he was thinking. They were simple, repetitive patterns that were shaped into bigger designs. Feathers and scales, flower petals and leaves.

"Would you agree he drew that kind of thing?" Nicole asked, glancing at the phone.

The scent of her hair tempted him to lean closer, to bury his face in the softness of all that red silk.

"It looks sort of familiar, but I wouldn't be able to say for certain. Chiara would know, though. They attended an art camp together that summer, and from what I gather, she paid close attention to his work."

"She told me she had a huge crush on him." Nicole smiled. "I'm sure she hoarded every scrap of information about him that was available to her fifteen-year-old self." She slid the sketchbook toward him. "Now take a look at this."

Desmond set down the phone on the coffee table and took up the softbound book held shut with an elastic band. Artwork covered the formerly brown cover. A partial lion's face covered half, the elaborate mane consisting of all the variations of doodles Chiara had anticipated—feathers, scales, petals, leaves. Each section of the mane was a little different, so that even though there might be four sets of feathers, each of them was decorated a different way, with broken lines or dots, squiggles or solid shading.

He traced the bisected lion's face with his finger, lost in thought. He remembered Zach drawing all the time. Between classes, during classes, even at night in their dorms when the rest of them were shoving, wrestling or otherwise hanging from the rafters. Hell, Zach had drawn while doing homework, one hand on his pencil, the other cueing up a video lecture. Desmond would have lost those memories without this reminder right in front of him. A tangible voice from the past that Nicole had given him.

She leaned closer, her hair spilling partially onto his shoulder as she looked at the book with him.

"The similarities can't just be coincidence," she observed quietly before peering into his face. "Can they?"

He knew she wanted him to confirm her suspicions. Give her some kind of proof that his dead friend was the father of her nephew. But as much as he wanted to help her solve the mystery, he couldn't be positive.

"I wish I had answers for you, Nicole. But we're trying to reconstruct the past with a patchwork of guesses. We've lost all of the people with the power to confirm or deny our suppositions."

She frowned, edging back to consider him. "You don't think this is your friend's sketchbook?"

"Actually, I do." The memories of Zach drawing returned to his brain. Clear. Crisp. Like they'd just been back at Dowdon the day before. "Not just because Chiara recalled the things he drew. But because of the sketches inside. The similarity to the horse in the tree house. The similarity to the images Alec used."

There were too many things that tied Zach to the book, including when it came into Lana Allen's possession.

"Then why did you hesitate?" She retrieved her phone, returning it to her purse.

Inserting space between them.

He knew he needed to let her go. They weren't going to end up in each other's arms again anytime soon, no matter how much he wanted that. Wanted her. But he couldn't help wishing he could rewind things, and... hell. He didn't know. He couldn't give her the answers she needed.

"Because even though I think this book belonged to Zach, it still doesn't seem like enough proof that Zach is Matthew's father. And bottom line, that's what you want to know."

She went very still. Then, stiffly, began to slide the sketchbook back into the packaging.

"Let me," he offered, taking over the task.

He tucked the corners of the paper cover around the book and then stood it on end beside the love seat.

"Has anyone reached out to Alec Jacobsen to ask him about the images he used in his game?" As she rose to her feet, her skirt brushed his leg briefly.

The need to pull her back to him was so strong that he jammed his hands in the front pockets of his pants as he stood.

"We've tried." He hated to be the one to deliver the news, but she had a right to know. "He was supposed to be watching over things at the casino for me this week, but he hasn't been seen on-site since last night."

"What?" Tension radiated from her stiff shoulders. Her fists clenched at her sides. "Meaning he took off as soon as one of your friends tipped him off that we know he stole more of Zach's artwork than he gave him credit for."

She whirled away from him, skirt flaring.

"No." He hastened to place himself between her and the door. "There's no way that happened. I'm positive."

"Oh, really?" She halted just inches from him. Close enough to touch. "Last night was Miles's dinner party. Last night eight of us stood around a billiard table and saw evidence that suggests Alec Jacobsen is a thief. The timing is damning." Her breathing was hard. Fast.

He wished it was because they were almost touching. But anger sizzled off her words.

"No one tipped him off," he repeated, staring directly into her furious brown eyes.

"How do you know?" Her gaze narrowed.

She didn't back down.

And it was a good thing he'd kept his hands in his pockets, because the need to touch her still rode him.

"Because I employed the same private investigator that followed you to Prince Edward Island to keep an eye on Alec for us."

Did she trust him enough to believe him?

The misplaced awareness she felt for Desmond was short-circuiting her brain, making her unsure what to think. Falling into bed with him had shaken all her prior convictions like so many puzzle pieces, scattering them in every direction until she couldn't put them together anymore.

Recognizing the effect was all the stronger the closer she stood to him, she edged back a step. She needed a breath that wasn't tinged by the sandalwood scent of his aftershave.

"If you're having him watched, why don't you know where he is?" She crossed her arms. As if she could create a barrier between herself and the desire for the man standing between her and the exit.

Not that she wanted to leave now.

"I never said I didn't know where he is." His hands were still fisted in his pockets, his shoulders looking every bit as tense as hers felt right now. "I said no one has seen him at the casino, which he's supposed to be managing for me."

She arched an eyebrow. Waiting.

"He's in New York," Desmond continued. "I still hope he's got a damned good reason to be there, but his movements make me think he could be planning to leave the country." His gray eyes scanned her, and he gestured toward the living room. "Will you sit back down, and we can discuss it?"

She wasn't sure she trusted herself to be that close to him again. The memories of their time together were never far from her mind. Seeing his hands move over the sketchbook earlier had brought her right back to those hot moments when his palms had wandered all over her naked body. Even now, she had to suppress a shiver.

"I'm fine here, thank you." She sounded terse. She couldn't help it. "What makes you think he's leaving the country?"

"The PI reported that Alec updated his passport. Also that he has an appointment with his financial adviser this afternoon."

"Why did you have him followed? Is it because you believe—like I do—that your friend profited from Zach's work without giving him any real credit?" She'd researched the game thoroughly before falling asleep last night. She'd even bought a copy to give to Matthew. "I read the credits on the box, by the way. Zach's name isn't there."

"I had him followed because I'm not entirely convinced Vivian Fraser would have acted alone to threaten Chiara, the way Alec's assistant claimed." He sounded troubled about that. "And for what it's worth, Alec acknowledged Zach's influence on his video game in a well-publicized video—"

"Anonymously. I saw the video." She couldn't help but feel indignant. She'd only just learned about Zach Eldridge, the young man who'd died too soon, but she felt defensive of him. "And I noticed how Alec protected himself from having to share any earnings with Zach's potential heir by never mentioning Zach's name."

Desmond watched her, the muscle in his jaw flexing. She hadn't made up her mind that Matthew was Zach's son, but she couldn't deny the evidence in favor of Zach as the father was strong. She knew for a fact that Lana and Zach had spent time together before she'd started working as a student teacher at his school. The fact that Lana had kept his artwork was telling, as was Zach's mentor offering anonymous support for the boy after Zach's death. Add to that the realization that Lana had left town distraught, at the same time Zach had gone on that horseback riding trip, also extremely upset, which strongly hinted at a falling-out between them.

When Desmond finally spoke, his words were slow. Deliberate. "I promise you, if Matthew is Zach's son, I will move heaven and earth to be sure he's well provided for."

Everything in Desmond's voice and his manner echoed his sincerity. But the commitment brought her back to another fear that had never gone away since she'd set foot in Montana. Would the powerful men of Mesa Falls use their influence to somehow supplant her in Matthew's life?

"Thank you." She appreciated his promise, the first and only time anyone had offered her tangible help in her sudden role as a parent. "I'm grateful for that. Just as long as you agree to recognize my rights as his acting parent."

The small smile he gave her was a sad one. "Of course. After my childhood, I have no aspirations to fatherhood, believe me."

They spoke a little longer about the next steps in potentially proving Matthew was Zach's child. Nicole would contact the California Department of Social Services to request information about Zach's relatives in order to obtain a DNA sample that would legally prove paternity. Desmond agreed to retain a lawyer to help her with a claim since Alec's gaming empire was worth a fortune, an expense Desmond insisted on bearing since Zach was his friend. But by the time she left his house to show the sketchbook to Chiara, the only thing on her mind was Desmond's assurance that he would never be a father.

It shouldn't be any of her business.

Yet telling herself that didn't ease the hurt she felt for him and the painful past he'd admitted. She'd be willing to bet he didn't share that part of himself easily. Or often.

Having him trust her with that part of himself made her feel closer, more connected to him. Although knowing that he wanted no part of family life put him farther out of her reach than ever.

Nine

Nicole met Chiara and Elena at Gage's house on the Mesa Falls property.

The women gathered around a table in Elena's studio, a workspace in progress that Gage had helped design for her new career in fashion design. Dark hardwood floors and neutral walls scaled up to the cathedral ceilings, broken only by tall windows and a huge skylight to increase the natural light. Architectural salvage pieces— old doors and window frames of various sizes—stood against one wall waiting to be incorporated into the room. The only finished section was a reading nook with a faux-fur chaise lounge surrounded by built-in bookshelves.

While Elena and Chiara flipped through the sketchbook, Nicole admired the aesthetic of the work space, along with the obvious care and thought that went behind it. Her home office amounted to a corner of her living room where she'd stationed a consignment-shop table to hold her laptop and her drawing supplies for when she wanted to create by hand. How much more productive might she be with this kind of inspiration and room to work? She was busy imagining where she'd place an easel to paint when Chiara's voice interrupted her thoughts.

"There's not a single doubt in my mind that this is Zach's sketchbook," the social media star announced after she'd been reviewing the book for about ten minutes. Her long dark hair pooled on the table as she bent over the pages. "And every one of Alec's trademarked game characters is in here—years before his game came out. So if you prove that Zach is Matthew's father, you'll also have legal grounds for suing Alec for stealing intellectual property from Zach's heir. If you end up needing me to testify that this is Zach's work, I will do so gladly."

That all sounded so far in the future given that she hadn't even confirmed Zach was her nephew's father yet. But she was touched that Chiara was willing to go on record about the creator of the sketches. Desmond would be hiring an attorney for her paternity claim, and Nicole had already contacted Social Services in between her stop at Desmond's place and Gage's.

"I appreciate that." Nicole joined them at the table where a stylized sketch of an owl in flight filled the page. "Do you mind sharing what makes you so certain that this is Zach's work?"

In the pocket of her skirt her phone vibrated, but she ignored it to focus on whatever Chiara had discovered.

"His name on the cover, for one thing." Chiara

flipped to the front of the sketchbook, her black-and-white-striped nail art a contrast with the simple brown cover.

"But there's no handwriting anywhere." Frowning, Nicole scanned the few doodles around the bottom edge, searching for hidden letters.

"See these dots and dashes?" Chiara ran her index finger along the top edge of a geometric border drawn in shaded triangles.

"Morse code," Elena announced, spinning the book so she had a better angle on the pattern of dots and dashes. "My father taught it to me when we were camping in the desert, only we used a flashlight to communicate with it—pulsing the light on and off."

"Seriously?" Nicole wondered if she could have missed it in other drawings. The possibility made her want to review all the other sketches more carefully. "How did you know Zach used that?"

Her phone vibrated again, and she squeezed it to shut off notifications for now.

"He liked the idea of incorporating letters and symbols into graphic patterns." Chiara sketched a squiggle on a piece of notebook paper nearby while she spoke. "He showed me some things he wrote with Chinese characters and Sanskrit the summer we took an art class together. And once, he used Morse code in the scales of a snake he painted. Sort of like this." She twisted her sketch toward Nicole so she could see the lines on the snake's back were actually a series of dots and dashes.

While Nicole's gaze went from the note paper to the sketchbook, Elena brought up the Morse code alphabet on her phone.

"Look at this." Elena held it above the cover of

Zach's collected sketches. "Here's the Z. Two dashes and two dots."

Excitement knotted up with apprehension at the chance of confirming the identity of Matthew's father. The notebook didn't prove it, of course, but it was one more piece of evidence that underscored the importance of Lana's relationship with Zach. She'd kept his drawings all her life, and carefully framed one of them to hang in Matthew's nursery. The picture remained in the boy's room even now. Proving for certain who fathered her nephew would be a huge worry relieved. And while Nicole regretted that Matthew would never have the chance to get to know his dad, at least his father wouldn't be a giant question mark in the boy's mind. Zach's friends all mourned him deeply. That said a lot about his character.

After everything Desmond had confided about his friend, Nicole couldn't imagine Zach had been consumed by despair when he'd jumped into the river that day. His death was an accident. Desmond believed that. And she trusted his instincts.

About that, at least. She wasn't so sure about his instincts where she was concerned. Seeing him just now had stirred up the attraction and—if she was being honest—feelings, too. She closed her eyes briefly to block out those thoughts and focus on why she was here. Finding answers about her nephew so she could return home.

"Mattie will enjoy the puzzle of the Morse code," Nicole remarked aloud, recalling the way his mind worked. "He'll think that's very cool when I show him the sketchbook." Then, another thought occurred to her as she addressed Chiara. "Did Zach ever mention being on the spectrum?"

"Not to me. And if Miles or any of his friends had thought so, I'm sure they would have mentioned it once they knew about your nephew." Chiara straightened from the table and stretched her arms over her head as if to work out a kink in her back from bending. "But if you can prove paternity, the Department of Social Services will have to share any medical records relevant to Matthew's health. They might be able to tell you if Zach was ever tested."

"At least I know they shared one trait in common." Nicole withdrew her phone to check her messages. "Matthew is artistic, too. He loves to draw."

Glancing down at her device, she saw the calls had been from Desmond.

"Does he really?" Chiara asked, her gaze as warm and inviting as her tone. "I hope we get to meet him one day. Whatever happens with the paternity case, Nicole, he already feels like Zach's family to me."

The kindness in the sentiment tugged at her, distracting her from whatever reason Desmond had phoned her. She wanted more of a sense of family for Matthew. He'd grown up without a father, and now his mother was gone, too. His grandfather—who'd always been close to him—was still reeling from losing his daughter. How nice would it be to introduce Matthew to someone like Chiara, who'd known the man who was, in all likelihood, his father. To hear stories about his father from someone who'd known him. Like Chiara.

Also like Desmond, a troublemaking portion of her brain insisted on reminding her. But just because Matthew would like Desmond didn't mean she should introduce them. Desmond had made it clear he wasn't interested in children. And even if he might be interested in a boy who wasn't his child, that didn't make him a good bet for being around a teen who needed stable, consistent figures in his life.

But before Nicole could tell Chiara how much her kindness meant to her, a sharp rap sounded on the door to Elena's workspace.

"Elena?" Gage stood in the open door, his knock apparently more of a courtesy than a formality as he stepped just over the threshold. "Sorry to interrupt, love, but I thought you should know I just heard from Desmond." The New Zealander's gaze shifted to Nicole. "He tried to reach you first, Nicole. He wanted you to know he received a message from Vivian Fraser's attorney."

Chiara drew in a sharp breath. "That's Alec's assistant," she reminded Nicole. "The one who hacked my social media and tried to silence me in my search for answers about Zach."

Nicole recalled all too well why Desmond had Alec followed. He didn't believe Vivian acted alone. "What did she want?"

Gage walked deeper into the room, looping an arm around Elena's shoulders as he spoke. "Vivian claims she has new information about both Alec and Zach, but she won't talk to police unless Matthew Cruz's guardian is present."

Uneasy, Nicole went still, unsure what her next move should be. Could the woman know the relationship between Zach and Matthew when no one else had? Or had Alec known all along and purposely kept it hidden to deny Matthew his rights and potential inheritance as

Zach's heir? "Maybe Vivian isn't pleased her former lover is leaving the country without her. Perhaps she's ready to share more about his scheme to deny Matthew the legacy and inheritance that should have belonged to his father."

Chiara asked, "Is Vivian still being held in Tahoe?"

"Yes." Gage tucked Elena even closer as he spoke, a swirl of dark tattoos around his wrist visible as his shirtsleeve rode higher on his arm. "Nicole, Desmond said he already called our pilot. If you want to meet with Vivian, Desmond dispatched a car to pick you up here and take you to the airport."

His words broke through her uncertainty, reminding her of her only objective in Montana—to find Matthew's father. If that meant leaving Mesa Falls, she would. With or without Desmond. And since Desmond had made no mention of joining her, she couldn't imagine that he would. Which made sense since it was her quest, not his.

Although she couldn't deny a spike of envy for the obvious support a couple like Gage and Elena were able to give to one another. Seeing the comfort they took just from touching triggered a whole host of memories and emotions for what she'd shared with Desmond.

It hadn't been the same, of course. Desmond had made it clear that their time together had been an isolated incident. Something they didn't carry back into their day-to-day lives. In theory, she appreciated that. But since then, she couldn't deny she'd thought of him often. Wondered about the possibility of being with him that way again.

Realizing the others stood around her, no doubt waiting for her reaction, Nicole scooped up the sketchbook.

"I need to find out what she knows," she murmured, tucking the book under her arm. "Thank you for everything. Your welcome and support mean a lot to me."

Elena stepped forward to wrap her in a quick hug. "Good luck, Nicole. Let us know if we can help."

Touched, Nicole hugged her back, letting Elena's lavender fragrance and good wishes surround her. "Thank you."

No sooner had Elena stepped back than Chiara followed suit, hugging Nicole. "You'll be back here soon with Matthew, I hope," Chiara reminded her. "Or I'll come to you if that's easier. I can't wait to meet him."

Nicole thanked her, too, and let Gage accompany her to his front door. Outside, a car was already waiting for her, a uniformed driver standing in the driveway near the rear of the sleek black SUV with heavily tinted windows.

She would text Desmond once she was inside to let him know she'd received his message and would gladly accept his offer of the flight to Tahoe. Although maybe a little part of her was hurt that he was so efficiently facilitating her speedy exit from Mesa Falls. Was he so eager for her to be out of his life? A tender part of her heart resented that he didn't want the complications of a child. What use would she have ever had for a man without room for Mattie in his heart?

Indignant, she greeted the driver with a nod as he opened the rear door of the SUV while a cold wind whipped off the nearby mountains.

She stepped up into the warm interior, the scent of expensive leather tickling her nose as she took her seat and withdrew her phone to text Desmond. The door shut behind her at the same time the front partition window lowered with an electronic hum.

Glancing up at the sound, she realized two things simultaneously. First, that the driver was still outside the vehicle swiping snow from the hood.

Second, that Desmond sat in the passenger seat. The sight of him seemed to flip an invisible switch inside her, lighting up all her nerve endings.

He held his phone in one hand as he pivoted to look at her over one broad shoulder.

"I'm finishing up some business before the flight and didn't want to bother you if you had your own calls to make. Do you want to stop at the main lodge before we take off?" He must have told his caller to hold, as he directed all his attention to Nicole while he waited for her to answer.

She suppressed a shiver of awareness, resenting the tangible physical reaction she felt around him. Especially when her focus should be on this new development in her quest to find Mattie's father. But there was no denying Desmond's attentiveness—from arranging the flight to anticipating her desire to leave as soon as possible—stirred her as much as the thought that he planned to join her.

"Yes, please. I'd appreciate a stop at the lodge for my things." She cleared her throat to try and banish the smoky sound of her voice before she continued, "I take it you're…going to fly to Tahoe with me?"

"I have every intention of hearing what Vivian has to say. I want answers as much as you do, Nicole." His gray eyes turned the molten silver shade she remembered from their time together. "Assuming you don't mind if I join you?"

She opened her lips to speak, but her mouth had gone dry at the idea of them spending more time together. Alone. She settled for a nod.

No doubt Desmond read her thoughts, because there was an answering heat in his gaze. But thankfully, their driver returned to put the SUV in gear and start their trip, allowing Nicole to hide her suddenly warm cheeks as she ducked to look at her phone.

Desmond gave Nicole space on the flight to Tahoe.

He'd purposely taken a seat on the opposite side of the aisle from her in the private jet. Although they were facing one another, they each had their own worktable to spread out their things during the flight. He'd sensed her confusion—and, yes, her reaction to him—in the car ride on the way to the airport. He didn't want to press her if she was feeling unsure about their time together. Hell, she wasn't alone in the confusion or the attraction.

Ever since the heat had overtaken them in the tree house, Desmond had questioned himself about letting things spiral out of control. But he was also very aware of her every time they were in the same room. And trying to ignore their chemistry was an exercise in futility. If anything, the distance he'd attempted to put between them had only intensified the draw. Or maybe it was intensified because now he knew what it was like to be with her.

In the seat opposite him, Nicole powered off her tablet and tucked it into its neoprene sleeve. When they'd stopped at the main lodge before the flight, she'd changed into a simple black knit dress with boots and a pale beige tweed blazer for travel. The rich color of her hair seemed all the more vibrant against the neutral colors.

"How much longer until we land?" she asked, running a finger under her gold watchband to adjust the position on her wrist.

He glanced at his phone before leaning back in his seat. "Less than thirty minutes."

"Do you have any guesses what Vivian could want?" She switched from fiddling with her watch to flipping the oval pendant she wore around her neck on a long gold chain. "Or why she's suddenly decided to reveal more than when she was first arrested?"

He fought the urge to reach across the table and cover her restless fingers. But then, maybe he was just looking for an excuse to touch her again.

"I reached out to her attorney to let him know that Alec was on the move, possibly to leave the country." It still galled him to think that a man he trusted—one of his closest friends—could have been working against their interests all this time. "I suggested he relay the information to his client in case she knew more about Alec's activities than what she'd admitted when she was first arrested."

Nicole's fingers paused in their twirling of the pendant.

"That was clever of you." A gleam of respect lit her dark brown gaze. "How well do you know her?"

"Not well at all. Which, in retrospect, I see must have been by design on Alec's part. Vivian attended Brookfield, the girls' school closest to Dowdon. He's known her that long, and yet he always kept her apart from us."

"So she wasn't just his employee. They were friends?"

"Yes. And lovers at times, apparently." Some of that

had been covered in the news articles he'd forwarded to Nicole about Vivian's arrest. "Did you have the chance to read the press I sent you?"

"I did. Thank you." She tucked a red wave behind one ear and glanced out the window before lowering the shade a few inches to block the setting sun. "Just wondering your take on their relationship versus what the news outlets had to say."

"Alec has been focused on building a gaming empire. Personal relationships haven't been a priority for as long as I've known him." For him, either. Even when life had been less complicated.

"It sounds like you have that much in common with him." Her gaze slid briefly to his before darting away again.

He studied her for a long moment, not sure how to respond. He folded down the table in front of him so he could switch seats to the one beside her. Heat flared in her eyes when he looked at her again.

Even though, damn it, that's not why he'd closed the distance between them. Was it?

"I may not have wanted personal relationships to be a priority in the past, but I'm rethinking that now." He let her mull that over while he did, too. Because the realization surprised him also, but that didn't make it any less true. He hadn't been able to stop thinking about her. And not just because of their heated connection. He wanted to help her. To know more about her. "Recently, I've started to remember what my mentor told me long ago about all work and no play."

His fingers lifted, as if by their own volition, and sifted into the cinnamon strands that framed her face.

He combed through the tendrils slowly, watching them glide over his skin.

The only sound besides the rumble of the jet engine was Nicole's swift intake of breath.

A wash of color crept up her cheeks, flooding over the smattering of freckles. The need to kiss everywhere that flush landed was a sudden overwhelming need.

"I can't afford to play, Desmond." Her words were softly spoken, with little volume behind them, but they still delivered a gut punch to his midsection. "I'm the head of a family now. I need to make smart decisions."

"I have no doubt that you will. You've already championed your nephew to ensure his future is secure, and I admire that." His thumb traced her cheekbone, smoothing along impossibly soft skin. He would let her go in another moment. Once he was sure she really wanted to walk away. "But we still have a brief window of time together before our responsibilities claim us again. Would it be so wrong to indulge something we want? Something solely for ourselves?"

She closed her eyes for a moment, and he thought he'd lost any chance. Without opening them, she said, "When we land, we'll go see Vivian. Find out what she knows. And then I'll go resume my life while you resume yours." Her lashes fluttered open again, her look fixing him. "I thought that's what you wanted. You were adamant that I didn't get the wrong idea about what happened between us."

He'd had plenty of opportunities to curse those words he'd spoken. But the fact that he hadn't been able to organize his thoughts after being with her only underscored how much she'd gotten under his skin.

"I wanted to be honest with you. Then and now. I

know I don't have anything to offer beyond tonight, but I won't pretend I don't still want you." So. Much. She was ever present in his thoughts. In his memories. In fevered dreams. "Visiting hours at the jail will be over when we land," he continued, hoping he wasn't deceiving himself that there could still be one more night to be with her. "We won't be able to meet with Vivian, the police and her attorney until the morning."

Her indecision was clear as she nibbled her lower lip, worrying it between her teeth.

When, at last, her gaze dipped to his mouth, he knew he'd won. Still, he wanted to hear her say it.

"Will you spend tonight with me, Nicole?" Not for anything could he have kept the growl out of his voice. "Let me touch you. Taste you. Make you feel good."

The rapid rise and fall of her breasts called to his hands. But still he waited for the words.

"I'd like that," she said finally, hovering closer until her long waves brushed his shoulder. Her dark eyes smoldered with new fire when she peered up at him again. "Yes. Please."

Ten

Her whole body hummed with anticipation as the car service deposited them in front of Desmond's modern stone-and-wood estate overlooking Lake Tahoe.

Nicole's gaze latched on his square shoulders as he unlocked the tall double doors at the entrance, the sight of him anchoring her. Somehow, knowing that she wasn't alone in this heady attraction, that he'd thought about their time together so much that he wanted another night with her, soothed the wound she'd felt to her feminine pride at the way things ended the first time. Dragging in a breath of cool mountain air, she noted the remote feel of the property before she followed him inside, the trees close on every side except for the back, where deep terraces provided patios for enjoying the waterfront. Desmond had pointed out the casino he owned on their way through town, less than a mile from his house.

Now, she stood to one side of the open-concept living and dining area, leaving room for the driver to bring things inside while Desmond flipped switches to turn on lights and close blinds. All around her, the banks of windows were soundlessly shuttered, folding them in privacy. Pendant lamps blinked on over a long island wrapped in gray quartz near the dining room, followed by a lamp in a downstairs suite she could see into thanks to the open door. A white brick fireplace taking up a whole wall in the bedroom brightened with the leap of gas flames before Desmond set aside the home remote.

He thanked the driver and sent the man on his way. Desmond closed the door behind him, then rearmed the alarm before toeing off his leather dress shoes on the front mat.

And somehow the sight of sock-clad feet on the hardwood floor as he neared Nicole made what they were about to do the most real to her. There was something intimate about that small, private act of removing his shoes. Making himself comfortable to be with her.

"Nicole." He strode toward her, shrugging off his jacket and flipping it onto one of two low barrel chairs in the living room. "Don't be nervous." He stopped just short of her, relieving her of the leather bag she still clutched by the shoulder strap. He set it on the chair near his jacket. "It's not too late to change your mind."

His hands slid around her upper arms, where too many layers—her blazer and the sleeves of her dress—prevented her from feeling the texture of his palms as he touched her.

"I'm not nervous anymore." Her heart thumped faster, everything inside her accelerating like she'd just put her foot on the gas. Her breath. The hot rush of blood in her veins. The leap of nerve endings.

"Were you before?" His focus lasered in on her as he lowered his hands from her. Instead, he flicked open the buttons on his shirtsleeves then folded back the cuffs. "Is everything okay?"

His thoughtfulness of her feelings shouldn't make her feel even more fluttery inside than his touch. But she couldn't deny she appreciated the way he checked in with her.

She told herself not to get attached to this. To the way he made her feel. But she had no way of knowing if she would take her own advice.

"I might have been a little nervous that nothing could top the way you made me feel last time," she admitted in a rush before she could stop herself. She laid her hand on his chest, feeling his heart thump steadily through the starched cotton of his white shirt. "I wondered if maybe I embellished it in my head because it was the first I'd been with someone in…a long while."

She'd come up with a million and one reasons to account for why she'd let herself go so completely with him. The months of overwhelming responsibilities, the grief of losing her sister, the fear of not providing everything Matthew needed. No doubt she'd been battling through a rough time in her life. And maybe that accounted for why being with Desmond had been so incredible. It had been a release valve for all that.

"I'm sorry that you worried for even a minute." His hands flexed gently around her arms. Up to her shoulders. His thumbs brushed her collarbone before they dipped inside her jacket, spreading the lapels wider to give him access to her neck. His lips fastened on a spot just below her ear, his tongue flicking lightly before he spoke against her damp flesh. "I promise you the first time wasn't a fluke."

Her knees wobbled a little, and she gripped the fabric of his shirt, steadying herself in the rush of pleasure warming her skin. Not just where he kissed, either. Liquid heat flooded her senses.

"I believe you." She shivered as he pushed her jacket down and off her shoulders.

"Good." He kissed a path along her jaw, ending at the corner of her lips. He nipped the lower one before he drew on it. When he broke the contact, he tucked a finger under her chin and tipped her face up to his. "Tonight's going to be so much better."

She felt the truth of the promise in the electric current running through her. She might not trust him with her heart or her feelings, but she absolutely trusted him with her pleasure. And after the way she'd shouldered so much on her own these last months, it was a heady gift to be able to hand that off to this sexy, capable man staring at her like she was the most appealing woman he'd ever laid eyes on.

"You set the bar high." Dragging her fingers lightly down his chest, she sketched the ridges of his abs. "I have a lot of good memories from last time."

He let go of her chin and plucked her hand from where she'd veered close to his belt. He took his time threading his fingers through hers, interlocking them.

"Multiply that by all the extra hours we have before the sun rises, and you'll see why it's easy to be confident you're going to be thoroughly…" He leaned close again to speak into her ear, the huff of his breath a teasing stroke. "Pleasured."

Oh.

The math of hours and pleasures was almost as enticing as the feel of his body close to hers as he led her toward the bedroom with the fireplace. She tried to focus on that and not the way he'd deliberately put her at ease, making sure she was comfortable. Because if she thought too much about him beyond the delicious release he could give her, she risked getting lost in feelings she wasn't ready for.

Feelings he refuses to share, a cruel voice in her head whispered.

But she refused to let that rob her of this night with him. She deserved it. Hell, after what she'd been through this year, she *needed* it.

In the bedroom, he let go of her hand to shut the door, and she gathered up her hair before presenting him her back.

"Unzip me?" she asked over her shoulder, little tremors of eagerness racing through her.

She liked the way his eyes blazed with an internal heat. And she definitely liked that he allowed his attention to travel the length of her body.

A moment later, he closed the distance between them. He wrapped one strong arm around her, drawing her against him so his hips notched against the back of hers. She gasped at the feel of him, his need for her deliciously evident as he tugged down the long zipper of her black knit dress.

He let the fabric fall away as it parted, his breath tickling against bare skin while he shoved the material down and over her hips until it fell at her feet. She let go of her hair to stroke his forearm where it was wrapped around her waist. She glimpsed them together in a whitewashed cheval mirror, their bodies lit by the orange flames from the fireplace, her hair tousled and unruly. But while she was halfway to naked save for her simple black undergarments and boots, Desmond remained fully clothed. White dress shirt folded back at the forearms, he still wore dark wool gabardine pants that teased the backs of her thighs.

"Keep looking," he breathed into her ear, his gray gaze meeting hers in the glass. His fingers trailed down her hip to trace the elastic of her panties. "And you'll see how much you like me touching you."

Powerless to look away, she watched. A riot of sensation rocked her as his touch descended lower, sliding under the waistband of her underwear. When his other arm banded around her, higher on her rib cage, he cupped her breasts through the sheer fabric of her bra, teasing the tips to tight, hard points.

Trapped against him in the best possible way, she panted with the sensual onslaught, her eyes sliding closed to lose herself to the skilled, seductive plucking of his fingers.

"No." His sharp command was a whisper in her ear, the word damp on her skin. "Keep watching." His voice had a jagged edge over his rough breathing, as if he was as affected by the touch as her. "It's the hottest, sexiest thing I've ever seen. I haven't been able to stop thinking about what you look like when you come apart for me."

Tension coiled tighter between her thighs. She hauled her eyes open again, mesmerized by the sight but too caught up in the slick pressure of his fingers right where she needed him most.

"Please." She didn't know if she wanted him to take her to the precipice faster or slower. Wasn't sure if she wanted the sweet thrill in her body to find an outlet or to remain in this breathless, perfect anticipation forever. "It feels so—"

She broke off, the build of tension arching her back. Robbing her ability to speak. Slamming her eyes closed.

"That's it." He praised her with hoarse satisfaction as his fingers plunged inside her. "That's what I've been dreaming about every night."

Her release shattered her, rocking her body and turning her knees to liquid. She would have fallen if not for being pinned to him, his hands never ceasing their carnal work, calling forth every last spasm from her shuddering form. When at last he slowed to a stop, he turned her in his arms before carrying her boneless form to the bed, pausing only to peel off her boots. She wanted to protest, to give him the same incredible fulfillment he'd just provided for her, but her words died in her throat as she slivered her eyes open to see him undressing.

He'd never been in such a hurry to be naked.

Desmond tore off his shirt with a muttered oath, needing to be inside the tousled siren who twisted in his bed covers, reaching toward him with hungry hands. His control had started slipping about the time she'd asked him to unzip her. By now the tattered remnants of it had barely enough strength to remind him to find a condom before giving up the ghost.

Later, he'd wonder how she wielded this kind of power over him. At this moment, he could only scavenge the wherewithal to locate the necessary protection and sheathe himself while she shimmied out of the sheer black underthings that had made him forget his own name. Then again, seeing her naked was even more potent, her red hair trailing over her shoulders to frame the perfect curves of her breasts. He kneed one slender thigh wider, making room for himself where he most wanted to be.

Levering over her, he was poised to sink inside her when she cupped his jaw.

"This is the part I've been dreaming about," she whispered, echoing his words back to him. "You. Filling me."

His need unleashed. He sank inside her fully, driven by her words. Her thighs clamped around his waist like a vise, her hips lifted to him. For him. Over and over again, he took what she offered and gave her more. All of him.

She moaned and whimpered, urged him on with a train of hungry demands in his ear. He lost himself in her, straining closer to the pleasure that he'd only ever find with her.

The thought blindsided him. Slowed his thrusts for one protracted moment while his heart hammered in his chest, blood rushing in his ears. Her passion-fogged eyes met his, her bee-stung lips full and damp from his kisses and bites. Seeing her that way, knowing she was every bit as lost as him, was the tether that kept him in the moment. The realization that made him need to deliver on every sensual promise. To give her everything she wanted.

He lowered his mouth to her breast, drawing hard on the pebbled peak. Her hips bucked against him, arching closer. Angling. Sensing what she needed, he reached between them to touch the place certain to send her flying. He circled the tender flesh while he thrust faster, harder, pushing them both higher.

When her back arched this time, tension curving her spine, he was ready. The soft pulls of her feminine flesh squeezed him, and he let himself go with her. On and on her body worked his, one shudder calling forth another until they were both spent and damp. Sated and replete.

For now, at least.

Desmond knew that just lying beside her would incite his hunger again, all too soon. So for now, he wrapped her close to him, holding her without questioning the need that seemed to have written itself in his soul.

He breathed through the idea, telling himself it was over-the-top and nonsensical to think so. Knowing better all the while. He respected the way she championed her nephew, the way she protected him and put her whole life on hold to make sure she got the answers she needed about the boy.

But the torment of his thoughts eased as Nicole nestled sweetly against him, her silky hair a warm blanket on the side of his chest where she lay under one arm. He wasn't going to question the rise of unexpected feelings where she was concerned. Not when he could breathe in the apple scent of her shampoo and stroke the smooth curve of her hip.

He admired her strength. Was grateful for the way she loved and advocated for a boy that Desmond should have been protecting all this time. He'd always felt indebted to Zach for giving him the courage to stand up to his father, and yet he'd let him down by failing to look out for his heir. And yes, he felt sure in his gut that Matthew was Zach's kid. He would do whatever it took to help the boy from here on out. And Nicole, too, as his guardian.

She won't welcome your help.

He remembered how defensive she'd been about preserving her rôle in Matthew's life, warning him she wouldn't give up her guardianship "no matter the financial incentive." Not that he would contest it, of course. But if she was that prickly about accepting help, it would make his path forward uncomfortable.

He kissed Nicole's damp forehead and vowed to uphold the promise he'd made to give her this night of pleasure. That much, at least, he could provide.

And, he hoped, whatever they shared tonight would soften her for the moment when she realized Desmond would need a place in Matthew's life if the boy was truly Zach's son. As the long-lost heir of Desmond's best friend, Nicole's nephew would become his highest priority. That was an obligation Desmond would never relinquish.

Not even if it put him at odds with the woman in his arms.

Eleven

Nerves stretched taut the next morning, Nicole sat beside Desmond in the interview room at the correctional facility in Nevada City. They'd been subject to security screening after the hour-long drive from Desmond's house, but apparently the meeting place was more secure for the group than at the local lockup in Truckee.

She sipped the tea a kind corrections officer had brought for her while they waited at a conference table. The room was sparsely institutional, with cream-colored walls and a mirror that they'd been informed was a viewing panel, even though they'd been assured no one watched on the other side. The meeting would be recorded, however, since Vivian Fraser had promised information about Alec the police would find helpful, according to her attorney.

Did she plan to throw her former lover under the bus

for the crimes she'd committed? Even Desmond had questioned whether Vivian would have acted alone to threaten Chiara and hack the influencer's social media accounts. Or did Vivian plan to accuse Alec of some other crime?

The tea was barely warm, but the orange pekoe flavor provided a welcome distraction from the tension that had been growing between her and Desmond ever since breakfast. Their morning had been awkwardly polite and cool after the night had stripped her defenses bare. She'd followed the scent of pancakes to the kitchen and been ready to wrap her arms around his waist. Rub her cheek against his broad back. Absorb his strength and warmth the way she had all night long. Except then he'd turned around and greeted her with a formal good morning that left her reeling.

Her appetite had vanished, and the nervous knot in her stomach had started twisting and never stopped. Luckily, she'd been able to spend their car ride texting with a counselor from Matthew's school and making arrangements for a parent conference next week. Nothing urgent, the administrator had insisted. Just to check in after the tumultuous personal year Matthew had experienced. The exchange had helped her put the day in perspective, reminding her of her priorities. Nothing was more important than making sure Matthew was well adjusted and had whatever help he needed to cope with the changes in his life. As much as she wanted to find her nephew's father, that task came second to his emotional health.

She wouldn't let the hole in her chest with Desmond's name on it keep her from returning to San Jose and the life she had there. Desmond had backed off after their time together. Again. And that spoke volumes about how he viewed her. She'd gone into the evening thinking she was going to focus on the physical. But even though he'd delivered every ounce of pleasure she could have ever imagined, Nicole had discovered a wellspring of tender new emotions underneath the physical connection.

After the way he'd flipped the switch on that this morning—retreating once more—she now understood that she wouldn't be able to share that kind of encounter ever again. Physical pleasure didn't exist without deeper emotion behind it. At least, not for her. She'd only been fooling herself to think otherwise.

The door to the interview room swung wide a moment later by a trim, uniformed female officer leading the way for a petite brunette in a prison jumpsuit two sizes too large for her. Behind her, a burly older man in an olive-green suit strode in carrying a briefcase. A second officer brought up the rear, a middle-aged guy with thinning blond hair that had been carefully combed.

While the officer shared names and explained the interview was being recorded, Nicole studied Vivian in the seat across from her. In the stories about Alec's assistant online, she'd been a redhead, but now there was no hint of the color or her former curls. But even with no makeup and the orange jumpsuit, Vivian remained a lovely woman. She possessed delicate features and graceful movements, although her eyes were shrewdly assessing when they landed on Nicole.

The officer leading the meeting, Lieutenant Bragg, opened the floor to Vivian, who glanced briefly at her attorney before beginning to speak. Unfortunately, Nicole missed her opening words because Desmond's hand crept over to hers underneath the table. The warmth of his palm covered the back of hers where it rested in her lap, and she felt another piece of her heart slide into his keeping, even though he'd made it clear he didn't want any such thing.

"The long and short of it," Vivian was saying when Nicole was able to dial back into her words, "is that Alec promised to bail me out if I'd take the fall for him for hacking Chiara Campagna's social media. I knew it might take him a couple of days to make that happen, but now that it's been weeks, I know he has no intention of following through on that promise."

The male officer interrupted her, leaning forward so that his tie clip clunked against the conference table. "Are you suggesting Alec Jacobsen hacked into Ms. Campagna's accounts and threatened her?"

The lawyer began to bluster about immunity and protecting Vivian's rights, but the prisoner resumed speaking. It worked to quiet the others since she had the microphone.

"I have kept Alec's secrets for fourteen years because I—" She stopped herself. Made a wry, angry face that twisted her features. "That is, I *used to* love him. But I won't protect him any longer, and I'm done keeping his secrets. Alec stole Zach's art and ideas for his video game. He knew about Zach's child and needed to prevent Zach's heir from claiming intellectual property theft."

Nicole didn't realize she'd gasped until all eyes swiveled toward her. Desmond shifted his chair closer to hers in order to drape a protective arm around her shoulders. The weight and the warmth of him helped her steady her breathing. She clasped a hand around the gold pendant she wore that had belonged to her sister, the one containing Matthew's photo as a baby.

Zach Eldridge was Matthew's father.

"How do you know for certain?" Nicole managed finally, questioning the woman directly. "About Zach's child?"

At this, Vivian turned to her attorney, but the older man nodded.

The prisoner's eyes met hers. "Alec hacked Zach's email and read all the exchanges between Zach and Lana. The notes made it clear they were having an affair and that Lana broke up with Zach when she found out she was pregnant." She shrugged as she shifted in her seat. "Maybe she grew a conscience? Or maybe she realized it would be uncool to raise a kid with a student. I don't remember her exact reasoning."

"You saw the emails?" Nicole asked, wondering if this woman's testimony would be enough to prove that Zach was Matthew's father. Then again, maybe she would say anything, considering she was under arrest and seeking a deal.

"I read some of them," Vivian admitted, her dark hair falling forward as she leaned over the microphone on the table. "Alec liked showing them to me to prove he was recovered from his crush on Lana. Alec and Zach were both fascinated with her, and all three of them hung out a lot the summer before she started working at the school." The woman's eyes flicked to Desmond as she explained, "At first, Zach and Lana were just friends, because Zach thought he was gay. But then she started seeing Zach alone, and things heated up between them before school started. It sounded like Lana tried to put an end to it once she began student teaching at Dowdon."

At least she'd had some scruples about that, Nicole thought with a sliver of relief. It had upset her to think Lana would have approached a student in her care, no matter how close their ages, but if the friendship had begun earlier, it was at least a little more understandable. Nicole wondered how her sister had met the boys that summer, but it had been a small town. They could have crossed paths most anywhere.

Before she could ask any questions, Vivian continued.

"Anyway, Alec turned sort of bitter about it because he was honoring Lana's wishes to stay away and Zach still met up with her. Alec started keeping tabs on them so obsessively, I figured he still liked her. Plus Alec started keeping notes on Zach's idea for a video game, always prodding Zach to think through all the different levels of the game and what should happen for the battles." Her expression grew more animated, eyes widening. "Zach's ideas were brilliant."

Nicole felt Desmond tense beside her. His grip tightened on hers.

"Are you saying the whole game was Zach's idea?" Desmond asked in a tone that might sound composed to someone who didn't know him. But Nicole heard the anger underneath.

She felt a cold, indignant rage of her own growing. A sickness, even, at the idea of how people could quietly hurt those they professed to care about.

"Pretty much." Vivian shrugged. "Although before you get any worse ideas about Alec, he was as devastated as anyone when Zach died. Their friendship might have been in a weird place, but Alec admired his genius. He immortalized it with the game."

There was something so wrong in that statement, so out-of-touch with human emotions and what real friendship meant, that Nicole felt ill. How could Zach's so-called friend have kept his "brilliant" mind a secret all those years, soaking up the adulation of fans and game critics for work that hadn't been his own? Worse, how could he have purposely cheated an innocent child out of learning about his father?

The room wobbled a little. She *really* didn't feel well.

"Will you excuse me?" she murmured, relinquishing Desmond's hand in a sudden need for air as the room closed in on her. Her vision narrowed to pinpricks of images in front of her while her heart raced. "I'm so sorry." Standing, she lurched for the door while chairs scraped back around the table to follow her. Or maybe help her. "Please. Finish without me. I just need—"

Her remaining vision blurred a bit as she pushed through the door and into the hall.

A strong arm gripped her. Steadying her.

"I've got you."

She didn't need to look to know Desmond was beside her. His voice anchored her. His scent, so achingly familiar by now, felt more comforting than it should. Especially since, now that she had the answers she needed about Matthew, she would have no reason to see Desmond again.

That wasn't the reason for her panic. But it didn't help.

"I'll just splash some cold water on my face, and be out before you know it." She needed a time-out. From Vivian. From the hurt she felt for her sister, her nephew.

For herself.

Her stomach knotted tighter. Glancing up, she saw the door to the ladies' room nearby and threw herself toward it. Out of his grasp. "I'm fine. I'll be fine." Maybe if she said it enough times, she could make it true. "I just need a minute."

"Are you sure you're okay?" Desmond asked Nicole on the car ride to his home two hours later.

He regretted not hiring a car service for the trip so he could have given her his undivided attention, but that morning he'd been so amped up after their night together that he thought driving his own Range Rover would give him a way to stay busy. Now, when he kept turning anxious eyes to Nicole to scan her pale face, he hated that she wasn't his sole focus.

He hadn't trusted her not to faint and hit her head in the bathroom by herself, and he'd had every intention of remaining by her side. But a woman who worked at the security checkpoint at the correctional facility had intervened, insisting she would make sure Nicole was safe.

He'd waited outside the bathroom for fifteen minutes, until Nicole had opened the door long enough to ask him to please finish the interview without her. She couldn't look at Vivian Fraser again after the things the woman had admitted.

Thankfully, Vivian hadn't protested the absence, since the woman had conveyed the main point she'd wanted Nicole to hear. Matthew was Zach's son. She'd promised digital access to some of the emails that would prove it, as she'd kept an old hard drive in a safe-deposit box to protect herself in case Alec didn't bail her out as he'd promised. Desmond had related everything he could remember to Nicole for the first half of their trip home, but she'd gone silent afterward.

"I'm fine." She'd said that more than once back at the jail, but he had yet to believe it. Her head tipped against the passenger side window, her eyes sliding closed. "Just tired after the emotional upheaval. I don't know if I really had a panic attack like Heidi—the woman who sat with me in the women's room—believed, but it was scary. I suddenly felt like I couldn't breathe even though all I was doing was breathing."

Guilt for what she'd been through—not just today, but for all the weeks she'd worked to uncover the truth about her nephew's father—was a ten-ton weight on his shoulders. He hadn't seen the truth that had been right in front of him for years because of misplaced loyalty that Alec Jacobsen had never deserved.

Hearing how Alec had worked to undermine Zach, and later Matthew, had detonated inside him, decimating his old beliefs and trust. The damage to the Mesa Falls partnership—which would require legal intervention to buy out Alec's share—was the least of Desmond's concerns. He hated that Zach's heir had gone thirteen years without knowing the people who'd loved Zach.

"I'm so damned sorry I didn't recognize that Alec was a lying, dangerous bastard. Even sorrier that I stood in your way while you were trying to find out the truth for yourself." Grip tightening on the steering wheel, he took the access road that led to his home. "Vivian admitted she was the one who got you fired when you were working at the ranch after the holidays, by the way. Alec knew you were asking questions and interceded."

Another fact their private investigator hadn't turned

up. But then, Alec had seen to it that the supervisor who'd fired Nicole was let go—and paid well to take an extended overseas vacation—the next day. One more failure that was on Desmond's shoulders.

"I'm just glad to go home," Nicole admitted, her attention still focused out the window. "My questions served their purpose to get things moving. Alec started making mistakes, which is how we finally learned the truth." She turned to him as the Range Rover climbed the incline toward his property. "Don't you think it's strange that Alonzo Salazar knew about Matthew and never told you?"

"I'm guessing Lana never revealed the father's name. If she never told you, why would she tell the teacher who oversaw her? Alonzo probably just wanted to help her with the child since he knew she was raising Matthew alone." Desmond remembered so many ways his old mentor had guided him through the worst year of his life, helping a devastated kid find his way. "He was good like that."

"It was a kindness I can never repay, since Matthew has thrived at his school." She twisted the gold pendant that hung from the chain around her neck. "With any luck, I can borrow against a future settlement of Matthew's claim the game *Hooves of Thunder* was stolen from his father. Even if he only wins a small share of the proceeds, it will certainly cover his tuition."

Desmond had never been so grateful to reach his house before, because he needed to put the vehicle in Park to turn and address what she'd just said. Something that had raked over his every last nerve.

"Nicole." He switched off the ignition for good measure, buying himself a few extra moments to make sure he approached this conversation the right way. "You don't need to borrow a cent. As Zach's heir, Matthew now owns a share of Mesa Falls, effective as soon as I contact a lawyer to draw up the paperwork. The ranch has operated at a profit for years."

She tensed in the passenger seat, her hands sliding into her lap, fingers twisting together.

"Zach was never an owner of the ranch. We're not interested in charity, just what Matthew is legally entitled to." Her words, softly spoken, cut straight through him.

On a day of hurt and anger, that her refusal of his help sliced him deeper than anything else was a testament to how much she'd come to mean to him. He had to swallow past the ball of pain in his chest.

"Everything we worked for in Montana was because of Zach. Because we couldn't save him. Because we loved him, respected him and hated that the last days he spent with us—time that we were *supposed* to be helping him forget about his problems—ended with his death." The wound had never healed. Desmond had just built his life around the hole in him, but it would always be there. "He saved me, Nicole. Caring for his son is not charity. It's a debt."

Something like understanding, or maybe just a temporary need to appease him, lit her dark eyes. She returned to twisting her fingers, locking them together at one angle and then another.

"I understand why you feel that way," she said quietly, her whole slim body still. "But you've already offered to retain a lawyer to help Matthew with his claim. That's more than enough. I didn't travel to Montana so you'd rewrite your whole business. I just wanted to know the truth about Matthew's father. And now that I do, we can go back to our lives."

The hits kept coming. He shouldn't be surprised.

He'd retreated from her just this morning because he didn't want to give her the wrong impression, but now he wondered if that hadn't been an act of self-preservation as much as anything. He'd known all along she might not accept his help where her nephew was concerned.

"You're in that much of a hurry to leave?" He studied her face, regretting that they had to have this conversation now when she'd admitted she was tired. When they'd both had hellish days.

"I think it would be wisest. Last night made it difficult for me to remember what we are to each other on a day-to-day basis." A flash of hurt might have streaked over her expression, but it was gone again before he could be sure. "There's no sense pretending that spending time together will lead anywhere."

Damn it, he hadn't meant to hurt her.

Just thinking that he might have only added to the weight of guilt threatening to drown him. He would do anything to fix that. He owed her everything for stepping in to care for Matthew.

A boy he hadn't even met.

The wrongs he'd done kept adding up as it occurred to him that he needed to meet Zach's son. But first, he had to keep Nicole here long enough to figure out the best way to make that happen.

"Spending time together could help us iron out the problems we're discussing right now." He started to reach for her. "Matthew's guardianship—"

"Is not up for debate," she said sharply, pulling back. "I've been clear about that from the beginning."

Hell.

He wished he could bring her inside so they could talk over dinner, but he feared as soon as she left the vehicle, she'd start packing. It was his fault for putting this wall between them again. He shouldn't have been so adamant about managing expectations in their relationship, but he'd been afraid of hurting her.

Unfortunately, he'd done just that anyway.

"I understand." He reached for her hands again, covering them with his. When she didn't pull away, he stroked the back of one, reminding himself he wasn't going to have another chance with her. He needed to find a way to maintain a dialogue with her and protect Zach's son at the same time. He owed it to Zach. To Nicole, for turning her whole life upside down to step into her sister's shoes and be a mother to Matthew. "I'd never question your right as a parent."

A fraction of the tension seemed to ease from her. Her hands stilled.

"Thank you." She let out a long breath. "It's a lot of responsibility. I'm just trying to do my best with him. He's such a great kid. He deserves to be happy and secure. Loved."

Hearing her speak helped Desmond see that he wanted the same thing. Matthew's happiness and security had become the most important thing in his world today. And considering that the responsibility weighed heavily on Nicole—no matter how much she loved the boy—made Desmond realize he wanted to offer a more concrete kind of help.

There had to be a way he could ensure the boy's future…

The answer hit him hard. Legally, there was a way to make sure Matthew had every financial advantage and future protection. A way to ease the burden on Nicole so she could spend her time being a guardian instead of worrying about paying tuition or facilitating her nephew's legal recognition as Zach's heir. But would Nicole ever consent to it? Desmond recalled with unease how she'd refused to accept his offers of financial help. He didn't want to be at odds with her, but he was out of time to figure out how to best appeal to her.

"I agree with you." The more he thought about his idea, the more he liked it. The more it seemed like the simplest solution. "Matthew should be happy and secure. And he has the right to know more about his father while maintaining the same attachment to you that he's always had."

One auburn eyebrow lifted. Curious.

His heart pounded in anticipation of sharing his plan. He hoped she would at least hear him out because his intentions were good. Desmond had never considered taking on such a big role in a child's life before, but this was Zach Eldridge's kid they were talking about. A boy who'd been overlooked for far too long by the people who loved Zach.

"What do you mean?"

He dug deep to offer her words he'd never thought he'd say to anyone.

"Marry me, Nicole."

Twelve

"Excuse me?"

Shifting on the leather bucket seat in the front of Desmond's Range Rover, Nicole needed that last thing he'd said repeated. She had zoned out during the panic attack back at the jail, so she guessed she could be having a recurrence of whatever had happened then.

Because Desmond couldn't have possibly proposed.

"You'd maintain complete say over raising Matthew, of course," he continued, speaking in a rush, as if he had a lot to say. "But legally, a marriage would give Matthew immediate financial security along with my name. We could spend part of the year at the ranch so he could get to know—"

"Are you suggesting a marriage between...*us*?" She didn't want to presume when she still felt disconnected and confused. Her whole life had changed—again—

after today's visit to the jail, and she hadn't come close to wrapping her head around what it meant.

"Yes. Between you and me." He seemed to slow himself down with an effort. "I think it would be beneficial for all of us. Matthew especially."

Her heart fell. There'd been no misunderstanding after all. No feelings. No connection.

Realizing his hand still rested on hers, she tugged her fingers free. She couldn't afford to indulge in the feel of his touch—something that had offered such comfort a moment ago—when he was making a mockery of their whole relationship by suggesting this bloodless arrangement that would apparently benefit Matthew.

She wanted to yell. To screech, *How dare you?* right into his oh-so-composed, far-too-handsome face illuminated by the dash lights. But doing that would let him see how much this coldhearted contract hurt.

"I thought you had no aspirations to fatherhood." She remembered his exact phrasing, because it had punctured a hole in the stupid balloon of hopes that she'd somehow allowed to expand too far, too fast. "I don't think Matthew deserves a figurehead father who isn't really interested in filling the role."

She saw the remark make a direct hit, but it gave her zero satisfaction considering Desmond looked genuinely distraught at the thought. On some level at least, he cared enough to not want to inflict hurt.

"You're right," he told her quickly, recovering. The muscle in his jaw flexed. "He deserves better than that. Better than me. But I'm here. I'm just trying to figure out how to cover a lot of concerns, and I'm not doing that effectively by strategizing in a hurry."

The hollow in her chest echoed with the empty proposal, already withdrawn. Or as good as. Clearly, he understood why it wasn't a workable idea. But it still hurt that he would have suggested something guaranteed to break her heart by reminding her of all that Desmond wasn't interested in pursuing with her.

Love. Happiness. Family.

They may not have known each other long, but she already understood him well enough to know she couldn't settle for a fraction of the affection he was capable of giving. No matter how incendiary their lovemaking had been. He had far more to give than what he'd offered to her. And she wouldn't sign on to a relationship that made it easy for someone she cared about to walk away from her again. Her mother's defection had shown her how much that could level her.

"There's no need to rush only to have regrets later," she assured him, needing to end this conversation and put distance between them before he saw how much his suggestion had rattled her. How much it tweaked the foolish feelings she'd developed for him. "We can communicate long-distance and arrange a time for you to meet Matthew. Maybe one day, when he's a little older, he can visit Montana and meet all of his father's friends."

She wanted that for Mattie. He deserved to see for himself how much his father had been loved and respected by the Mesa Falls owners, Alec notwithstanding.

"One day? Nicole, I'm serious about wanting to meet him sooner than that." His gray eyes were sincere. Hurt, even? "I'd like to spend some time getting to know him."

Her fingers gripped the leather upholstery to keep

from reaching across the car for him. She couldn't bear to look into those gray depths and see feelings that he hadn't shared with her before. Feelings that—she reminded herself—were about her nephew. Not her.

Still, she wouldn't hold her misplaced love for Desmond against him. And yes, she knew it was love because it hurt so much to think about walking away from him. But she needed to do just that, sooner rather than later, to save herself an even deeper heartache sure to come from letting herself see an answering feeling in him that wasn't there.

"Of course you can see him." She conceded the point, wanting Matthew to know Desmond even if she couldn't be a part of his life anymore. "I will make sure that happens. Maybe at his school, where he's most comfortable."

Matthew was even more comfortable at home, with her, but no matter how much she loved her sister's son, she wouldn't be able to bear memories of Desmond in her house with them. Just imagining it for a moment threatened to make her throw her arms around his neck and ask him to reconsider his refusal to be a father.

His refusal to let her close to him.

Desmond started to speak, perhaps just to thank her, but the tears burning the backs of her eyelids were too hot. Too imminent.

For the second time that day, she had to excuse herself.

"I'm sorry, Desmond. I can't finish this right now." Levering open the passenger door of his SUV, she blinked away the worst of the coming flood. "I need to pack my things. It would be best if I return home now."

Thirteen

"It's strange being back here," Weston Rivera observed from the top bunk of a double dorm room at Dowdon School shortly before the anniversary gala fundraiser was due to begin.

Seated next to a window overlooking the grounds of their former boarding school, Desmond sipped his bourbon and tried not to ruin everyone else's evening with his sour mood. It was strange enough for him being *anywhere* without Nicole, but she'd returned to San Jose a week and a half ago, and he hadn't been able to stop thinking about her since. He missed her so much more than he would have ever expected.

Desmond glanced from Weston's tuxedo-clad legs hanging over the edge of the bunk to where Miles finished the knot in his bow tie at a mirror mounted over a study desk. Then his gaze continued to Gage doing pull-ups on the door frame between the en suite bath and the rest of the room, the New Zealander's breath whooshing out each time his chin reached the top of the door. He hadn't even put a shirt on yet.

Jonah Norlander was dressed and ready for the gala, the new father finishing up a video call with his wife and baby daughter on the far side of the room, rounding out the five friends who had flown in to support their alma mater and show the press their unity in condemning Alec Jacobsen. The story had leaked about the stolen game, and Alec's fall from grace had been swift and well publicized. Fortunately, the public seemed to feel almost as deceived and outraged as the Mesa Falls partners, so the backlash had landed squarely on Alec's shoulders. Business remained good at Mesa Falls and the partners were researching the best way to buy out Alec's share.

Questions about Zach had followed, with reporters racing to uncover the most facts first. Public opinion about Alonzo Salazar had shifted to the favorable when it was revealed his tell-all book had been an attempt to provide financial support for Zach's fatherless child. The gaming community was leading the way in championing Alonzo since interest in Zach's brief life—and his heir—was rabid now that his original drawings has been released. Nicole had issued a statement requesting privacy for her family, and it seemed to have been respected. Desmond had phoned Matthew's school to inquire if they wanted private security to help keep the boy and his classmates safe, but they'd assured him that they had all the necessary measures in place.

Making Desmond unnecessary there, too. Just like he'd been with Nicole. The empty space inside him yawned wider. Had it only been ten days since he'd seen her? It felt like ten years, every day dragging on forever. He'd been useless at the casino the week before, unable to think about anything but her.

"Damn right it's strange being back here," Gage announced as he finished the pull-ups and jumped to the floor. "The whole place shrank since we were kids." He toed the bottom bunk where he used to sleep. "I don't think I'd even fit in that thing now."

"If you ask me," Miles added, finishing his bow tie and turning away from the mirror, "it's good to be here tonight with people I know are my real friends. No more knives in our backs."

Weston leaped to the floor with a thud and scooped up the champagne bottle out of the ice bucket that someone from the school had delivered earlier as a thank-you for their donation. "I was going to say I'd drink to that, but I think it calls for something more potent. Gage, where are you hiding that bourbon?"

Desmond lifted the bottle from the arm of his chair and told himself to get with the program for his friends' sake. He might not have a knife in his back anymore thanks to Alec's arrest on the charge of harassing and hacking Chiara Campagna, but the hole in Desmond's chest still gaped thanks to Nicole. A sure sign she'd affected him far more deeply than he'd allowed himself to believe at first.

"Right here." Desmond passed the bottle to Wes. "I've already helped myself."

Jonah ambled over to join them as glasses were procured from the catering cart that had delivered the champagne. While his friends laughed, poured and passed the bottle, Desmond tried to dial in on the evening, even though he didn't feel much like celebrating when he hadn't heard a word from Nicole in ten days. He'd tried to give her space after he'd screwed up with that ill-advised marriage proposal. Even in his cluelessness, he'd read the misstep in her lovely features right away.

He'd hurt her, and that killed him.

And it hit him in a flash why he missed her so much, why he was at such loose ends. He understood why that pained him so much, because it turned out he'd fallen for her in spite of all his best precautions to make sure that didn't happen. The feeling made him want to surge to his feet and find her, fundraiser be damned.

He started to rise from the chair, then hesitated. Looking back on that final conversation with her, he couldn't help but wonder why it had hurt *her*, too? Was there even the smallest chance she'd developed feelings like the ones that had taken his legs out from under him?

Even if by some incredible coincidence she had, that didn't alleviate his biggest concern. *I don't think Matthew deserves a figurehead father who isn't really interested in the role.* Nicole had never been so right about anything. How could he be a father to Matthew—even if Nicole cared enough for Desmond to reconsider—when he didn't have the slightest idea how to be a father? He'd had the worst role model on the planet.

His heart grew heavier than ever. Love was supposed to make things better, wasn't it? Apparently not.

"Desmond, you're missing the toast, man." Miles's distinctive voice rasped the words as he leveled a glance at him. The others all had their glasses poured and lifted for a toast. "Get your glass over here now, then put yourself out of your misery and call Nicole afterward."

Straightening his jacket, Desmond joined the circle

in the middle of the floor where they used to have epic Friday night wrestling matches.

"Clairvoyant now?" Desmond asked as he raised his drink.

Miles shook his head and—fortunately for him—didn't crack a smile. "More like I had that same expression on my face when Chiara left my ass to go back to Los Angeles a few weeks ago, and it wasn't a good look then, either."

Desmond recalled all too well. And somehow the guy had won her back, but Miles didn't understand everything that kept Desmond from being the right man for Nicole. With an effort, he shoved that aside long enough to focus on his friends.

"You're right." Desmond looked around the circle, meeting the eyes of each man there. "Tonight is about remembering Zach and how many good times we had. He left a hell of a legacy for a guy whose time was too short, and it's on us to celebrate what he gave us."

No one spoke, and he knew every person there was remembering how Zach had touched their lives. For Desmond, it had meant getting free of his abusive father. And his mom getting free, too.

"To Zach," Miles echoed a moment later, lifting his glass.

"And Salazar," Wes added, raising his. "No way we would have weathered the aftermath to stand here and drink to Zach tonight without him."

"Best father I ever had," Gage quipped, since his elitist old man had always made it clear how much Gage disappointed him. "I'll drink to that."

Jonah stepped in last with his glass, simply saying, "Always."

Shorthand for a whole hell of a lot since they'd made that toast around a long-ago campfire.

Desmond drank deep, finishing his bourbon, musing over the toasts while Gage cranked up a Bluetooth speaker to blast "The Boys Are Back in Town" while they filed out of the dorm room to join the anniversary gala in the main reception hall. Something about Gage's words—*Best father I ever had*—circled around Desmond's brain.

Alonzo had been like a dad in a lot of ways, making sure all of them got through the shock and grief of losing their friend. Because of Alonzo Salazar, Desmond was a successful man today. And, thanks to that success, he'd been able to contribute a lot to the shelters he'd worked with. Didn't that mean Desmond actually had a damned good role model for fatherhood after all?

The possibility cracked open a whole new world for him.

He just hoped Nicole would agree.

Because as soon as the formal part of the Dowdon School event finished—once Desmond put in his appearance to support Mesa Falls and his friends—he was getting in a car and driving north to San Jose. He wasn't going to let another day go by without seeing the woman he loved and missed and needed more than air.

Pencil scratching softly over her sketch pad, Nicole sat cross-legged on her bed to flesh out some ideas for a local agricultural client who needed graphics for their farm's website. Her bedside clock said it was 11:00 p.m., long after her evening call with Matthew from his boarding school, but sometimes she worked best at this hour.

Or maybe she'd just decided to work since it was the night of the Dowdon School anniversary gala and she needed to prevent herself from watching the Twitter feed showing photos of the guests.

She pressed harder, determined at least not to refresh the page on her laptop the way she might have already done a few times like a pathetic, heartbroken fool. Why did Desmond have to look so handsome in a tuxedo? The man looked like he'd been born wearing Hugo Boss, the custom fit tailored exactly to his mouthwatering physique. A body she'd never get to see again.

One she'd never hold again, or take comfort from—

The doorbell chimed, halting her pencil along with thoughts that weren't helping her emotional recovery from the man she couldn't have. Who would be ringing the bell at this hour? She'd thought the reporters had all dispersed days ago.

Sliding from the bed, she slipped a long, comfy cardigan over her soft camisole and pajama pants, comfort wear for her broken heart. She padded toward the door in the dark, not wanting whoever was outside to see her looking through the peephole…

Desmond.

She clapped a hand over her mouth, but maybe she'd already emitted a sound, because his deep voice resonated through the door.

"Nicole?" A muffled sound against the door. Like maybe he'd touched it or leaned against it. "I'm sorry it's late. I saw your lights were on, and I really need to talk to you."

Her heart started a frantic rhythm, as if it could leap through the door to get to the man on the other side. But her heart was not in charge tonight, damn it. She squeezed her eyes closed and told herself it would be wrong not to answer the door because she was afraid of…everything. Of somehow revealing what she felt for him. Of losing her self-respect if she flung herself against him.

He was still wearing the tuxedo from the gala. Glancing down at her camisole—the same one she'd been wearing when she'd picked up that video call the first time she'd seen him—she yanked the sides of her sweater closer together before releasing her hair from a lopsided ponytail. Then, cursing herself for caring, she was tempted to put it back up again, but she ended up tugging open the door instead.

He went still on her front step, his gray eyes fixing on her face.

She wasn't sure how long they stood there, locked in silent perusal. But belatedly remembering her manners, she scuttled back a step to make room for him to enter.

"Did you want to come in?" She found the hair tie in her sweater pocket and played with it, stretching it between her fingers. "It's cool out there."

"You're right. Thank you." Appearing to give himself a shake, he stepped over the threshold of her house, effectively ruining her living room for her forever since she'd never be able to see the spot without him in it.

He seemed larger than life here, his shoulders and height more suited to a Montana ranch than her simple bungalow. She didn't invite him any deeper into the house at first, but then, realizing she was being churlish, she waved him toward the kitchen. He silently followed.

"Can I get you anything to drink?" She switched the burner on under the teakettle, then realized she still carried her sketch pad.

She slid it onto the round table just big enough for two.

"No. Thank you. Don't go to any trouble on my account when I've interrupted your evening." He glanced down at the spiral-bound paper. "Is this your work?"

Pulling a mug from the cupboard to give her something to do, she felt her throat go dry at the sight of his strong hands smoothing over the border of the paper. A visceral memory of his palms stroking her nearly made her shiver.

Having him here in her kitchen was too much. The space was too small, and he was such a presence. She could smell a hint of his aftershave if she got close enough.

"It is." She shifted her attention to the drawings she'd made of wildflower varieties. "I'm doing design work for a local flower farm. I've been enjoying the job since plants were one of the first things I ever drew, back when my father was gardening at your school."

She had happy memories there, growing closer to her dad in the months after her mother had left. She'd had a good conversation with her dad a few days ago, the first she could remember him talking about Lana for any length of time since her death. Her father had wanted to know everything Nicole had learned about Matthew's dad, and she considered that a good sign for his grieving.

"They're so lifelike," Desmond said as he studied the images. "You're obviously very talented."

"Thank you." She scooped a blend of chamomile and lavender tea into a strainer basket inside her mug, thinking there was a lot they didn't know about each other. He'd never seen her work. She'd never set foot in his casino resort, where he spent his primary professional time. But there was no reason for them to learn more about one another when they weren't part of each other's lives. "Please. Have a seat. Tell me why you're here."

His hand fisted and he tapped the counter lightly with his knuckles before he moved to the café-style table and took a seat while Nicole poured her tea.

"I've missed you, Nicole."

The words surprised her so much she nearly sloshed the hot water over the side of the cup as she settled it on the table. Biting the inside of her cheek against the emotions he stirred inside her, she met his eyes across the table.

"That surprises me when you were very clear about the boundaries of our relationship. Or do you mean you miss the physical aspect? Which isn't really the same as missing *me*." She hadn't realized how much hurt she'd harbored about that—about his ability to pull away from her the morning after their incredible night together at his house.

"I miss *you*." His focus zeroed in on her, as if he'd thought about it a great deal. "It was stupid of me to try and dictate how our relationship should move forward instead of just enjoying the privilege of getting to know you. Getting close to you."

The warmth in his gaze was too much, and she wasn't ready for it when she didn't understand what he wanted or why he was really here. She took her time lifting the herbs from the tea and settling the metal strainer in a finger bowl she kept on the table for that purpose.

When she finished, she could only lift the cup to her lips and wait for him to continue. Her throat was dry at the possibility that he'd missed her. She'd missed him so much. Not just his touch, either, but his voice, his thoughts, his concern for her that had felt genuine in spite of everything. He'd tried to sit with her in a jailhouse ladies' room when she hadn't felt well. If that wasn't thoughtful, she didn't know the meaning of the word.

"But that wasn't the worst thing I did." He dragged his chair closer to hers. Right next to hers. "I can't tell you how many times I've regretted my unwise proposal. Not that I didn't want to be in your world every day and take care of you and Matthew forever, because I did. What I regret is that I let you think for a minute I only asked you so that I could provide legal benefits that I would have found a way to provide anyhow."

Blinking through the maze of words, she set her mug down, the scents of lavender and chamomile not strong enough to mask the sandalwood aftershave that strengthened in the steam from her cup.

"I'm sure I did not misunderstand you when you asked," she said carefully, wondering if he could have really meant the part about wanting to be in her world every day. That had sounded decidedly good.

More romantic than practical. More caring than dutiful.

"You didn't misunderstand." He reached to shift the mug farther away, then took both her hands in his, his warmth enveloping her. "I was the one who didn't comprehend anything. I was the one telling myself that I could keep you with me if I trotted out some lame arrangement that would provide you a material benefit instead of just admitting—to myself and to you—that I love you."

Fourteen

Nicole searched Desmond's face, knowing now she must have dreamed it all.

Of course she was dreaming. She must have fallen asleep drawing and somehow conjured the most hopeful longings of her heart to have the man she craved show up in her kitchen—wearing a tuxedo, no less—and saying words she secretly yearned to hear.

Desmond Pierce was a business tycoon who circulated in a totally different world from the one she inhabited, where her sole financial splurge was good tea. Glancing down at his hand clasping hers, a part of the dream she wanted to be real almost as much as the words he'd just spoken to her, Nicole swallowed hard and forced herself to blink. To wake up from imaginings that were all the more cruel for how impossible they were in reality.

"Nicole?" That sexy, deep voice of his tripped over

her skin like a caress. His free hand slid under her hair to wrap around the back of her neck, cradle her head. "Say something, sweetheart. Did you hear what I said? Do you think there is any chance, in time, you might return those feelings?"

The sensation of his fingers in her hair couldn't possibly have been fabricated by her tired imaginings. The effect on her body was sweetly wicked, stirring things only this man had ever made her feel.

"Please tell me I'm not dreaming." She took his hand, the one that still held hers, and brought it to her cheek, needing reassurance that her heart hadn't tricked her. "Did you really just say—"

"I. Love. You." Gray eyes bored into hers with an intensity she couldn't mistake. A heat and tenderness that were so much better than any pale fantasy. "Just give me a chance to be in your life and I'll show you how much."

Her heart surged with happiness, emotions thick in her throat. If only she could be trust what she was feeling. She needed to understand.

"I have feelings for you." She'd known that she loved him that last night they'd spent together. That's why the cool morning after had hurt so much. "But you said you couldn't—that you'd never be a father."

Cold reality sliced back into her chest.

"I couldn't have been more wrong about that." He lowered his hands to stroke over her shoulders. Her arms. "I thought I had the worst possible father—I did, actually. But I thought I'd never have anything to offer a child after what I went through, and I didn't want to taint someone with that."

He hadn't told her much about his youth, but the torture in his voice communicated a world of pain. She was grateful for the glimpse inside him, even if he shut it down quickly.

"I'm sorry. Every child deserves to be safe and loved." She slid her hand beneath his jacket to stroke his chest through the tuxedo shirt. "But you have so much more to offer a family than the legacy of the monster who raised you."

"I know that now." He covered her hand with his, then lifted it to his lips to kiss the back. Then he flipped it to kiss the palm. "While I was at the gala tonight with my partners, feeling like my world had ended because you were gone, someone raised a toast to Alonzo. And we got talking about what he did for us. How much he taught us. It was like someone flipped a switch and lit up a neon sign to remind me I could look outside my gene pool for inspiration. That I had a damned good father figure and that I could be one, too."

The last of her reservations dissolved at the certainty in his voice, relief and joy for herself second only to her happiness for him. She was so glad he'd seen the same thing in himself that she'd long known about him. He was a strong, honorable man with a huge, generous heart.

That he wanted to share it with her, and with Matthew, humbled her.

"I know you're going to love him and he's going to love you. You'll find your way together. I can't wait for you two to meet." She trailed her fingers over his lips, happy tears pricking her eyes. "And nothing would make me happier than to have you in my life. You're already in my heart."

He swept her off her seat and into his lap before she'd

even seen him moving. Settled on his broad, splayed thighs, she wrapped her arms around his neck as his lips met hers.

He kissed her breathless, his heart beating a fast, erratic rhythm where her breasts pressed against his chest. That simple sign of emotion, of how much this moment meant to him, sent an added thrill through her.

When he edged back, his forehead tipped close, his sandalwood scent bringing back sensual memories.

"I've wanted to kiss you every second since I walked through that door." His lips trailed along her temple, then down her cheekbone. "I can't believe you're wearing the camisole that has haunted my every daydream since you picked up that video call."

Pleasure curled through her as it sank home that this incredible man loved her. That she had his heart as much as he had hers. That they would build a future together with Mattie.

"It seems fortuitous that you arrived at bedtime." The need to be with him, to wrap herself around him and feel how very real their future could be together, was a sudden imperative. "And as much as I really like you in a tuxedo, you're probably overdressed."

She felt his body react to that, and everything feminine inside her fluttered. He was already peeling away the cardigan from her shoulders.

"You like the tux?" His palm slipped under the strap of her camisole, skimming it aside. His voice was low and full of promise. "You'd be surprised how good I can make you feel while still wearing it."

Her mouth went dry. The fringe benefits from loving this man were going to be incredible. A sudden heat wave made her squirm in his lap, a move that had him bolting out of the chair with her in his arms.

"Your clothes have to go, however," he growled in her ear as he carried her through the living room to her bedroom. "That's a given."

He stole her breath as he settled her on her bed, his palms already tugging her pajama pants down her hips. His words continued to huff against her ear, a seduction that only heightened the way he touched her. "I might have you unfasten my cuffs, though. I'm going to need my hands for this."

A lightning bolt of sensation darted right though her, her only response a breathy moan as he kissed his way down her body. "I promise you, when I'm done, you'll be sure it's no dream."

And he was as good as his word, because he absolutely made her a believer.

Epilogue

Six months later

Squinting into the sunlight streaming through the tall pine trees along the edge of Gage's yard during a summer barbecue, Desmond tried to catch sight of Matthew on horseback with Marcus Salazar. Contentment rolled through him in waves. Life was good for him and Nicole and Matthew. And having his friends here for vacation only added to the fullness of his life.

Gage and Elena had decided to spend the summer at Mesa Falls after their honeymoon and ended up talking all the other owners and their significant others into doing the same. For the last two weeks, even Alonzo Salazar's sons had joined them, Marcus and Devon both accepting Weston's idea that they make it an annual trip with their families.

Now, Gage was in his element, grilling steaks near his pool while everyone else watched Jonah's baby daughter, Katja, take a few wobbly steps. The kid was adorable, and seeing Jonah as a dad gave Desmond more hope for his own parenting skills. Matthew had given him some confidence by making it easy on him the first time he'd met him, effectively interviewing Desmond for hours about his life, his job, his intentions toward Nicole, and all that had been before Matthew asked a single question about his biological father. The meeting had been scarier than the toughest job interview of his life, but he must have done okay, because Matthew had shaken his hand and welcomed him to the family before walking away to play video games.

Desmond couldn't love the kid more. Not just because he was Zach's son, but because he was an amazing individual, uniquely special in his own way.

He'd been even more grateful earlier in the summer when Matthew had agreed to Desmond's proposal—laid out in businesslike terms, because Matthew preferred to have all the facts—to adopt him once he married Nicole. But the thoughtful genius with dark eyes who shared more in common with Zach the more Desmond got to know him, had only further cemented their excellent bond that day by suggesting they make that date as soon as possible.

Nicole had married him in front of a judge two days later, making one of Desmond's biggest dreams come true. He'd been able to give Matthew his name and all the legal standing that brought with it right afterward, fulfilling a debt to his dead friend that had only added to the deepest sense of peace he'd ever known.

Although not being able to see Matthew through the trees right now was unsettling that peace a little. Marcus Salazar was an excellent rider, and he'd formed a tie with Matthew over their mutual interest in horses, so Desmond had figured it was okay to let them ride together. But they'd been gone half an hour.

"He's fine. You should come join us by the pool." Nicole's voice beside him soothed his worry almost as much as the warm press of her body, her thin summer dress printed with pretty flowers making his hands itch to peel it off her.

He'd never get used to the way she could ease him and stir him up at the same time. He hugged her closer, grateful for the feel of her curves and still not believing he got to call her his wife.

"In a minute." He kissed the top of her head while he kept his eyes trained on the trees. "How did you know what I was thinking?"

She laughed, a light, musical sound that sent a little more of his worry packing. "You mean how do I know you're the most adorable father of any fourteen-year-old ever? Only because I get to enjoy watching it every day we're here. I never want this summer to end. Seeing Matthew happy has brought me so much joy."

"You think he's okay?" Logic told Desmond he didn't need to worry while his son was with Marcus. But figuring out how to parent with a kid half-grown wasn't easy. Nicole, however, was a natural.

He turned his attention to her, trusting her.

"Remember his first two-hour interview when he met you?" she reminded him, threading her fingers through his as they walked toward the pool deck. "I'll bet he has a lot of questions for Marcus, too."

"He's an incredible kid." Desmond stopped short before they reached the others, letting himself take in the sight of all his friends gathered in one place.

Weston and his fiancée, April, were in the pool, Weston hanging off the side of her float while she sipped a margarita and fed him grapes. Gage was playing air guitar to the rock song that filtered through his outdoor speakers, while Elena, Astrid and Chiara danced in the grass.

Miles and Jonah had just started a game of horseshoes. Devon Salazar and his wife, Regina, took over watching Jonah's daughter. They were seated on either side of her baby blanket while Marcus's wife, Lily, supervised from a chaise lounge. Lily was very pregnant and Regina only a little less so. The Salazar brothers seemed to have healed their old rift, their wives obviously fast friends.

"He is an incredible kid," Nicole mused from beside him. "And he's got a fairly incredible life."

Desmond pulled her fully into the circle of his arms so he could see her lovely face. He leaned in to kiss her when she spoke again.

"The only thing he's missing is a sibling," she said in his ear.

A year ago the idea would have sent him running. Now? It felt so right he only wanted her all to himself to get started.

"Be careful what you say to me in public, wife." He couldn't resist lifting her in his arms. "I might give you exactly what you ask for."

Her flushed face was the best possible answer. But he put her back on her feet before he forgot all about the barbecue.

"Tonight," he warned her, as he headed for the cooler. He'd need something cold to get through the next few hours.

After that, he had every intention of making more of their dreams come true.

* * * * *

COMING SOON!

We really hope you enjoyed reading this book.
If you're looking for more romance, be sure to
head to the shops when new books are
available on

Thursday 4th February

LET'S TALK
Romance

For exclusive extracts, competitions
and special offers, find us online:

- facebook.com/millsandboon
- @MillsandBoon
- @MillsandBoonUK

Get in touch on 01413 063232

For all the latest titles coming soon, visit
millsandboon.co.uk/nextmonth

MILLS & BOON

THE HEART OF ROMANCE

A ROMANCE FOR EVERY KIND OF READER

MODERN

Prepare to be swept off your feet by sophisticated, sexy and seductive heroes, in some of the world's most glamourous and romantic locations, where power and passion collide.
8 stories per month.

HISTORICAL

Escape with historical heroes from time gone by. Whether your passion is for wicked Regency Rakes, muscled Vikings or rugged Highlanders, awaken the romance of the past.
6 stories per month.

MEDICAL

Set your pulse racing with dedicated, delectable doctors in the high-pressure world of medicine, where emotions run high and passion, comfort and love are the best medicine.
6 stories per month.

True Love

Celebrate true love with tender stories of heartfelt romance, from the rush of falling in love to the joy a new baby can bring, and a focus on the emotional heart of a relationship.
8 stories per month.

Desire

Indulge in secrets and scandal, intense drama and plenty of sizzl hot action with powerful and passionate heroes who have it all: wealth, status, good looks…everything but the right woman.
6 stories per month.

HEROES

Experience all the excitement of a gripping thriller, with an inten romance at its heart. Resourceful, true-to-life women and strong fearless men face danger and desire - a killer combination!
8 stories per month.

DARE

Sensual love stories featuring smart, sassy heroines you'd want as best friend, and compelling intense heroes who are worthy of the
4 stories per month.

To see which titles are coming soon, please visit

millsandboon.co.uk/nextmonth

JOIN US ON SOCIAL MEDIA!

Stay up to date with our latest releases, author news and gossip, special offers and discounts, and all the behind-the-scenes action from Mills & Boon...

 millsandboon

 millsandboonuk

 millsandboon

It might just be true love...

MILLS & BOON

HISTORICAL

Awaken the romance of the past

Escape with historical heroes from time gone by. Whether your passion is for wicked Regency Rakes, muscled Viking warriors or rugged Highlanders, indulge your fantasies and awaken the romance of the past.

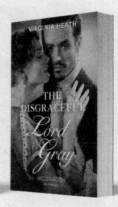

MILLS & BOON

HEROES

At Your Service

Experience all the excitement of a
gripping thriller, with an intense romance
at its heart. Resourceful, true-to-life
women and strong, fearless men face
danger and desire - a killer combination!